In the Shadow of a Wish

By Maci Aurora

A Fareview Fairytale

Maci Aurora Books

In the Shadow of a Wish, book 1
In the Shadow of a Hoax, book 2
In the Shadow of a Dream, book 3
In the Shadow of the Truth, the Novellas, Book 4
In the Shadow of an Obsession, Book 5

The Accidental Seraph, Carran Hollow book 1

The Secrets of Roan Island written with Thea Masen

Coming Soon

Book 2 in the Carran Hollow Series

Book 2 In Roan Island Series written with Thea Masen

CL Walters Books

Swimming Sideways
The Ugly Truth
The Bones of Who We Are
The Messy Truth About Love
The Stories Stars Tell
In the Echo of this Ghost Town
When the Echo Answers
The Letters She Left Behind
The Ring Academy: The Trials of Imogene Sol

Coming Soon

The Ring Academy: The Cipher of Tolo

In the Shadow of a Wish

A Fareview Fairytale

Book 1

By Maci Aurora

Mixed Plate Press
Honolulu, Hawaii
www.mixedplatepress.com

In the Shadow of a Wish
Fareview Fairytale Book 1
©2022 Maci Aurora w/ Mixed Plate Press
Honolulu, Hawaii

cover art: Sara Oliver Designs

ISBN: 978-1-7350702-9-2 (eBook)
ISBN: 979-8-9850325-0-5 (paperback)

About this book: *In the Shadow of a Wish* was inspired by the Grimm's Fairy Tale, "The Golden Key". It contains explicit sexual situations and is intended for mature audiences (18+).

The first wish is dedicated to the doers; thank you for keeping the dreams in forward motion. Auri is for you.

My husband is a doer. Thank you for keeping me in forward motion. I love you.

Author's Note

In the Shadow of a Wish is a reimagined fairytale, but even fairytales travel down dark roads and battle scary monsters. This story—while a romance—does focus on that happily-ever-after, but that doesn't preclude the protagonists from facing some very real and possibly disturbing obstacles. I felt it was important to share what could possibly be triggering for those who wish to know. *If you don't, please stop reading here and begin the story.*

Auri Fareview and her sisters live in a land dominated by men, where women are subjugated to them. What Auri wants more than anything is freedom and agency for herself and her sisters. There are several instances when this agency is stolen from her. She is attacked by a character named Crossbie (this assault is not graphic, but it is intense) and her first and third wish-obligations also steal agency from her, which creates tense and uncomfortable situations (also neither graphic or glorified). I have done my utmost to care for Auri (and my readers) and hope both scenes are presented with that caution in mind.

Thank you so much for being willing to take a chance on a new author. I hope you love this story as much as I enjoyed writing it, and I hope all of your wishes for love come true.

Once upon a time . . .

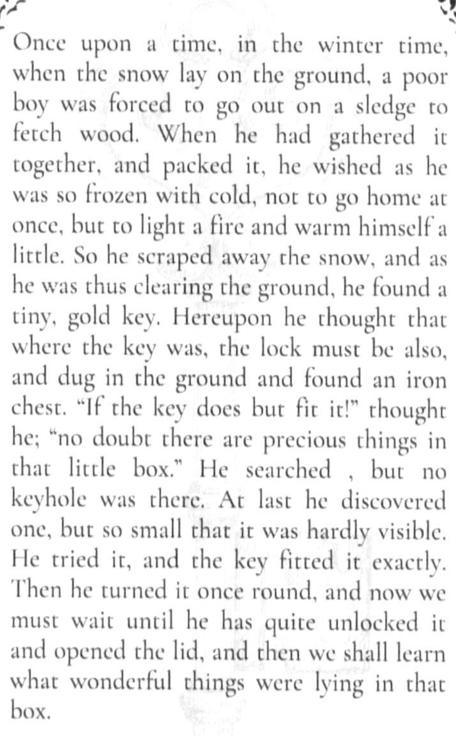

Once upon a time, in the winter time, when the snow lay on the ground, a poor boy was forced to go out on a sledge to fetch wood. When he had gathered it together, and packed it, he wished as he was so frozen with cold, not to go home at once, but to light a fire and warm himself a little. So he scraped away the snow, and as he was thus clearing the ground, he found a tiny, gold key. Hereupon he thought that where the key was, the lock must be also, and dug in the ground and found an iron chest. "If the key does but fit it!" thought he; "no doubt there are precious things in that little box." He searched , but no keyhole was there. At last he discovered one, but so small that it was hardly visible. He tried it, and the key fitted it exactly. Then he turned it once round, and now we must wait until he has quite unlocked it and opened the lid, and then we shall learn what wonderful things were lying in that box.

The Golden Key

A Grimm's Fairytale

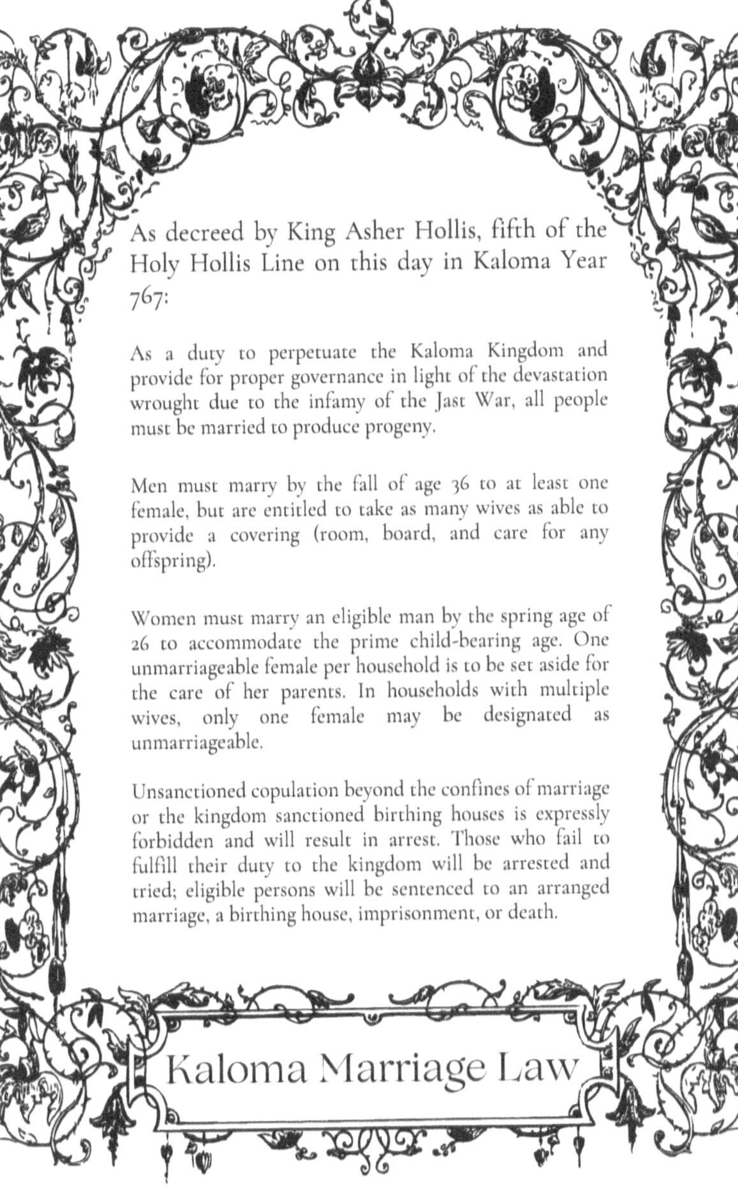

As decreed by King Asher Hollis, fifth of the Holy Hollis Line on this day in Kaloma Year 767:

As a duty to perpetuate the Kaloma Kingdom and provide for proper governance in light of the devastation wrought due to the infamy of the Jast War, all people must be married to produce progeny.

Men must marry by the fall of age 36 to at least one female, but are entitled to take as many wives as able to provide a covering (room, board, and care for any offspring).

Women must marry an eligible man by the spring age of 26 to accommodate the prime child-bearing age. One unmarriageable female per household is to be set aside for the care of her parents. In households with multiple wives, only one female may be designated as unmarriageable.

Unsanctioned copulation beyond the confines of marriage or the kingdom sanctioned birthing houses is expressly forbidden and will result in arrest. Those who fail to fulfill their duty to the kingdom will be arrested and tried; eligible persons will be sentenced to an arranged marriage, a birthing house, imprisonment, or death.

urielle Fareview, fourth daughter of Tomas and Scarlett Fareview, stood in the marriage market booth next to her sisters, waiting for the prospective husbands she wasn't sure would ever arrive. She leaned over the balustrade separating them from the aisle and noted the nearly empty corridor. Instead of feeling upset about the lack of eligible marriage partners in attendance, relief fluttered through her like a refreshing summer breeze.

The building was quiet but for the sparse and sporadic conversations between traders echoing in the cavernous space between the wood planked floor and the roughhewn beams crisscrossing the space above. The rustic, round chandeliers shining with lit candles, hanging at even intervals from one end of the building to the other, were the primary source of light, though the mullioned windows offered additional light.

Auri and her sisters were currently the only women in the marriage market waiting to be looked over by eligible men. It was usually the case. Aside from booths selling wares, food, rations, and supplies to hunters and fur-trappers, there weren't many in Sevens who were looking for wives. Those who lived in their village were already married, widowed, or weren't yet looking to comply with the law. The young trappers and hunters would come by their booth to flirt, which was a fun way to pass the time, but those young men didn't have the same impending deadline concerning their duty to the Marriage Law. They had ten additional years before needing to take a wife and could buy permits to attend the birthing houses if they wanted.

Auri turned from the corridor back into their dark booth, the flame waving under the glass chimney. Brinna, her older sister by a year, was pushing a needle strung with blue thread through the taut fabric stretched between wooden embroidery hoops. She squinted in the lowlight, but it didn't seem to bother her. She insisted she'd rather keep her mind busy than be idle dreaming up the worst.

Tarley, on the other hand, hated embroidery and everything else for that matter. She folded the months old, Kaloma bulletin she'd been reading and set it in her lap. "Can you see what the weather is like?"

"I don't think it's snowing. Poppa and Mattias should be on time," Auri said, wishing this thrice-weekly endeavor was over.

Tarley, her older sister by two years and in danger of being collected that coming spring, frowned. Tart Tarley might not have wanted to marry, but the impending deadline was a horrific reality offering equally horrifying consequences if she didn't. She sighed. "If I could hide away in the woods and avoid this ridiculous law, I would, but I'd never survive the blasted snow." She leaned forward and looked up and down the corridor, her bun bobbing like an egg in a puffy nest as tendrils brushed her neck. Tarley sat back down fiddling with the ribbon on her wrist.

She was probably comforted by the ribbon tied there, as Auri often was. She'd seen Brinna do the same thing, and Jessamine, their oldest sister, as well. They all found comfort in the simple gift their mother had given them before any of them could remember. Auri now knew it was because their mother had tied it on when they were babies; when she was seven, she'd watched her mother gift one to Mattias, their younger brother.

"There's an idea," Auri said. "What if we found a cave?" She leaned forward to try and catch Tarley's eye. Discussing ways around the law had become a standard practice to pass the time. They'd considered dressing as men and becoming hunters. They'd imagined seeking out a Whitling witch to invisibility spell them, which brought about gales of laughter at all the things they could do while invisible.

"Too bad the kingdom sends out hunters," Brinna replied, offering the flaw. This was always a part of the game. For example, finding a witch was impossible; magic didn't exist.

"But if we found it when the snow thaws, stashed away inside before the first snow, then we could avoid being tracked," Auri said, hoping to make Tarley feel better.

"Bears," was all her older sister said, then with a puff of her cheeks, blew out a puff of air. A tendril of hair fluttered around her face. It was clear she wasn't getting the enjoyment from their schemes as she usually did. Of course, of the three of them, she was at immediate risk. Auri had the horrible impression her usually unflappable sister was on the verge of crying and wasn't sure how to handle it. Tarley fluffed her burgundy skirt—the finest she owned—which Auri thought was more of an exercise in spending energy to keep her emotions corralled than concern over her appearance.

Auri wished she could take away her sister's immediate concerns, but even more wished she could change the circumstances for them all.

"Maybe we could escape to Jast," Brinna whispered so no one else would hear. Bringing up Jast in such a way could be construed as treason—not that there was anyone there to hear them. After the war, there was no love for the kingdom north of Sevens that had decimated Kaloma, though it had been long before any of them had been born. All that separated Kaloma from Jast was the Whitling Woods and the treacherous peaks of the Jast Mountains.

"No collection there," Brinna added. At twenty-five, she was in danger of collection too if she couldn't find a match in the next year.

"No Marriage Law either," Auri said.

She was right behind her sisters, having turned twenty-four, and though she had a little more time than Tarley or Brinna, in a provincial village of Sevens, it wasn't likely. They would all face the collector's wagons that rolled through the village each spring filled with unmarried men and women and surrounded by armed guards carting them to Kaloma's capitol city. In New Taras, they would face a forced marriage arrangement to a stranger's household, placement in the King's or some High lord's harem, assignment to a birthing house in the kingdom, or death.

Tarley snorted. "Escape to the kingdom who forced the king to sign the Kaloma Marriage Laws in the first place?" Her tone was biting. Auri figured Tarley would probably choose death if given the option. "Brilliant, Brinna. Seriously. Who knows what kind of terror awaits women in the kingdom that decimated ours over a slight? Your imagination will get you into trouble one day." She took a breath. "Besides, I hear those mountain passes are treacherous."

"I don't know that he *had* to sign that law," Auri

observed, smoothing her green skirt, then twisting her red ribbon around her wrist. She'd read about the pressure put on the king to sign the law when she'd explored the old bulletins stacked in the loft of the barn. Neither of her sisters responded to her observation. It didn't matter now, anyway.

"Fareview girls!" A crackly voice grabbed their attention.

Auri leaned to look past her sisters at Mr. Cobble, who traded leathers and dried goods a few booths down. He smoothed the five gray hairs he had over his speckled, bald head and smacked his gums with a mostly toothless grin. "There're some fellows wandering this way. And since you all are the right prettiest girls inside these woods, I reckon they'll stop."

Auri didn't have the heart to tell him that besides the Fareview sisters, the only other unmarried girls in their village (other than the women at the birthing house) were the two Pennington girls who were ten and twelve, and the Jenza twins, who were still toddling about. Any other eligible maiden traveled outside of Sevens to attend the larger marketplaces for better prospects, but Auri's family didn't have that kind of income.

Mr. Cobble's intentions were kind, however, so she held her tongue. His one and only wife had died some years prior. They'd never had children, and he'd taken a fatherly liking to their mother, who provided him with her homemade tinctures, that helped with his joints, along with baked goods and jams she sold on non-marriage market days.

"Maybe I should just offer to marry Mr. Cobble," Tarley had remarked late one night in their bedroom as they prepared to sleep. "He's a single man—old as the tree at the center of Sevens, but kind—and it would get me off the market to avoid collection. I could help him."

Jessamine had smiled in that normally subdued way she did, while Brinna and Auri had collapsed into a fit of laughter.

"Mr. Cobble wouldn't allow it," Jessamine had said while brushing her long dark hair. "He's too honorable a man."

"You think there are honorable men," Tarley had remarked her eyebrows high over her gray eyes, as she barked a laugh. "He would do it because he's a man like all the rest, and I'm being serious," Tarley said. "I'd rather do that than face collection."

"You'd lie with Mr. Cobble?" Brinna had scrunched her nose and glanced at Auri.

While they were all aware of the mechanics of what happened between a man and a woman to get children, they weren't exactly sure of the specifics. It was against the law to know beyond the confines of marriage or birthing houses, anyway.

"He's too old," Tarley had stated.

Jessamine had smiled and chuckled. "Momma has a tincture for that. She makes it all the time."

Brinna had giggled.

Auri had frowned, unsure why one would need a tincture. "Tarley. You're going to want children one day. Besides, that's the point of the law in the first place, and Mr. Cobble probably isn't eligible anymore."

"I don't know that I will. Would you want to bring a daughter into this world? To face this?"

They had all grown serious, understanding her reasoning. She had a point.

Now, the old man used his head to indicate there were men moving down the aisle at the market toward them. Their boot falls echoed in the large building like the sound of an ax hitting a tree trunk as they walked across the wooden floor. When one of them stopped at Mr. Cobble's booth, the old man pointed in their direction.

The men—three of them—approached the booth. Auri's stomach clenched with dread at the realization that there was one for each of them. One man was tall and wiry. His light hair was thin and sparse on the top of his head. He had kind eyes, however, though that didn't always reveal truths.

Old Mrs. Flimm on the other side of the river had married a man with kind eyes, but he'd been violent with drink and had met a violent end in the woods with a bear. Or so it was said. The explanation didn't save Mrs. Flimm, who'd been accused of being a witch who cast spells on the bear to get rid of her husband. She'd been weighed down with rocks and thrown in the river to keep her spirit from casting more spells.

Another of the men was dressed rather elaborately

for someone in Sevens. Auri figured he was a lord flaunting his status. He was rotund, which hinted at his wealth, and older, which meant he wasn't looking for a first wife. She didn't like his look—a little too eager— and it made her wary.

The third man was handsome-ish if a little unkempt—his red beard, his hair, his haphazard homespun attire. He reminded her of a skittish animal, and his eyes were disconcerting, jumping between her and her sisters as if they were horse flesh. She had the impression he wanted to inspect their teeth and feel the width of their bones.

While the romantic idea that one of these three strangers might prove to be a love match darted through her mind like a hummingbird, Auri was a realist. Love matches like their parents were hard enough to come by. Most likely, these men were desperate. Sevens wasn't a marketplace that enticed noble men, so those that came through, if not desperate, were hard-boiled and practical, or worse, depraved. Unfortunately, the latter were more common in a remote marketplace like Sevens where they could get away with it. Women in a small marketplace were desperate to avoid collection, desperate to avoid a birthing house or a harem. Like Tarley. They couldn't afford to be choosy. It was easier to gamble with what could be seen rather than what couldn't.

Tarley sighed heavily again. "Gods, I hate this," she muttered.

It made Auri sad for all of them. She looked down at the table and fought the tears climbing up the back of her eyes, clogging her throat.

Brinna reached over and grasped Auri's hand, and Auri ran a thumb over the ribbon tied around her sister's wrist, then met her sister's watchful gaze.

Brinna's smile seemed to say: *It's okay. We've got each other.*

Auri wanted to reply, *but for how long?* Instead, she returned Brinna's smile, lifted her chin, and drew strength from the feel of her sister's hand in her own. But it couldn't alleviate the discomfiture and unease regarding the marriage market. She was practical enough to know that three men didn't just drop into Sevens every marriage market day. She'd been forced into being at the marketplace too long and knew better. Giving these men time was the right course, even if every part of her was screaming that she needed to run.

"Good day, maidens," the ostentatious man said. He offered a bow then straightened, tugging on the bright purple jacket stitched with golden thread. He smiled, his gaze starting with Tarley and lingering as he said, "I'm Midlord Buteress." He had a strange mole on his chin with a bunch of stubby hairs growing from its center that Auri couldn't stop watching. It was horribly distracting. "My companions are Lowlord Gromley."

The tall, thin man with the easy eyes inclined his head but didn't smile, scanning them each in turn before his gaze stuck to Brinna.

"And this is Mr. Crossbie, a farmer." The skittish man grinned, showing his stained teeth, but the smile didn't reach his eyes, and so looked more like a grimace. His eyes were a color like the sky on a hot summer day. When his intense gaze met Auri's, she looked away.

Tarley cleared her throat. "I'm Tarley Fareview. These are my sisters, Brinna and Aurielle."

"It is a pleasure to make your acquaintance," the pompous one said.

A silence stepped between them and stretched its arms, the span of awkwardness stretching with each passing moment. Auri watched the men exchange glances, either unsure themselves, or unsure what protocol dictated, for it appeared they weren't familiar with one another.

Gromley stepped forward. "Miss Fareview," he said to Brinna and smoothed a hand over his drab, brown jacket, seeming to check to make sure all the clasps were closed properly. Auri's gaze caught on his hands as they moved over his clothing, thin, soft, and supple. So different from their father's wide hands, course and calloused from work.

"I'm looking for a first wife. I have a modest manor several days travel from Sevens to the southeast. It makes a healthy living, and my deadline is approaching. I'm thirty-four. Perhaps, you would consent to consider my suit? I need a wife to help me with running the home. And—" He paused, his skin pinking as his lips puckered at whatever he'd been about to say.

"Offspring," Crossbie finished, his eyes darting from Gromley to Auri. His gaze ran from her face across the bodice of her dress to the hem and back up. "We're all here for that."

Mr. Crossbie was very off-putting, Auri decided. She didn't like him or his manner.

While Gromley appeared a good sort, his pragmatic approach wouldn't appeal to her dreamy sister. Of course, Brinna was wise enough to recognize a safe option, but Auri figured she might hold out a bit longer for the love match they all wanted. Having parents who adored one another made it difficult to accept anything less.

Before Brinna could respond to Gromley, however, Buteress interrupted, stepping up to the railing. "I should think that perhaps my expansive estate could provide for you and your fair sisters. One and all."

Gromley and Crossbie looked nonplussed by Buteress's insertion, their heads snapping in his direction, their brows furrowed.

Buteress continued, "It's to the south, near Fulstrom."

His gaze swept over each of them, taking in not only their faces, but skimming the bodices of their gowns. His eyes lingered on Auri, and lifting his gaze to hers, he smiled with yellowed teeth. Auri wanted to rush home, lock the door, and bathe. The fact he was looking for another wife and had just offered for all three of them sent disgust rolling through her body.

This man was probably the deviant sort. He could have gone to the Fulstrom market but had probably over shopped his welcome and was now forced to the outer kingdom markets.

She shuddered.

"Now, come man," Crossbie said, his voice as sharp as his gaze. "We agreed this would be done civilly. Three of us. Three of them. One for each." His gaze jumped back to Auri. "I'm nearing the arrest mark," he told Auri. "I need a woman, and I need her with a child. I don't want the older one." His head tilted in Tarley's direction. "I need a younger one." He pierced Auri with that disturbing gaze before looking at the men next to him. "You have children, Buteress, and you have two years, Gromley. I'm in a hurry, here."

Auri's face opened with shock at the man's bluntness. Perhaps his pragmatism would have spoken to her normally practical nature, but there was a difference between being a realist and just being rude. She was right in her assessment that she was nothing more than horse flesh to this man.

Tarley cleared her throat, pressed her lips together, and narrowed her eyes, a tell of her impatience. If there was a queen in Sevens, then frosty Tarley would take the office, that is, if women were allowed to do so.

"Let us be clear, gentlemen, we are sitting here in compliance with the law. Nothing more." She looked down her nose at each of them, and Auri loved her sister's spirit despite the circumstances.

Auri wanted to be more like Tarley: brave and bold.

She often found that she imagined she could be brave, but then wilted when faced with something she was afraid of, like these men.

"We haven't deigned to agree to any one of your suits, nor are we obligated to, so perhaps you should be on your best behavior rather than your worst," Tarley concluded.

Buteress's gaze jumped from Auri to Tarley and assessed her in a new way. His smile indicated he liked something he saw in her. "Ah. Miss Fareview." A lecherous glow lit his pudgy face. "I'm delighted by your spirit." He interlaced his leather-gloved hands in front of his heart and bent slightly at the waist. "But you are nearing collection, are you not? Perhaps you would consent to my suit."

Auri watched Tarley blink slowly, but nothing else gave away the disgust she knew her sister felt at the prospect of marrying this man. Auri could see the wheels spinning in Tarley's head. She was twenty-six. Did she take the gamble to be collected and possibly assigned to a birthing house, or consent to marriage with such a man? Knowing her sister, she'd stand up, walk over to Cobble's booth, and tell him they were about to marry, hightail it out into the woods to hide there, or run herself through with a weapon from Mr. Dennig's table.

"Do you have a wife, Midlord Buteress?" Tarley asked.

His smile deepened. "I do, Miss Fareview. I am acquiring a fourth." He said this with pride, as if it was in his favor because he had the economic means to support all of them, which would be the only way he'd be allowed to marry repeatedly. He looked well fed, which revealed he had enough to provide, but Auri knew that didn't mean he did. She'd overheard stories told between trappers and traders of things they'd seen and heard.

Tarley tensed. Auri could sense her sister's disgust as clear as if it were stewing in the bottom of her own gut. It was as she thought: a deviant. This man was a collector—not the same as the spring collector, but a collector of women. And he had the means to do it legally in Kaloma. There were rumors about these kinds of men and how they treated their wives. The dark things they did to them behind closed doors, and sometimes even to their children.

Auri shivered.

The clanking sound of the marketplace bell rang out, signaling the close of the day—and of the horrid ordeal. Auri leaned to scan the corridor for her father and brother, who should be along shortly to escort them home. Though Sevens didn't get dark—it hadn't since Auri's childhood—it was far safer to have an escort. One couldn't predict what sorts of unsavory characters or dangers were lurking in the woods.

"Perhaps I could call upon you next market day?" Gromley asked Brinna. "Will you be here then?"

"I don't have much of a choice, now do I, Mr. Gromley," Brinna replied.

"Lowlord."

Brinna glanced at Auri, who squeezed her sister's hand with frustrated understanding.

Brinna turned back to the stoic man, who to Auri, now just seemed austere and unfeeling. "Forgive me, Lowlord Gromley, for my mistake."

His face turned hard and grim, and his eyes flitted from Brinna to Auri as if trying to measure their complacency. His already thin lips tightened and puckered before he said, "I don't like mistakes, Miss Fareview. I want propriety in my wife and offspring. They will need to know their place, and I would discipline them when necessary." He slapped his leather gloves against his thigh.

Brinna squeezed Auri's hand harder.

"Daughters." Their father's voice interrupted with a congenial shout as he entered the building. It was his usual greeting on market days. Usually there weren't any suitors.

Auri turned her head to watch Tomas Fareview stride up the wooden walkway with their brother a pace behind him, their steps loud and even. Safety seemed to settle into the space with their arrival, and Auri relaxed—slightly.

Both were large men, imposing, even if their personalities weren't. Her father's brown beard was full, his dark coat covering a dark homespun shirt, stretched across a broad back built from years chopping wood, woodworking, and farming their small patch of land. He had a dark hat on his head and a walking stick in his hand that he didn't need, but always carried when he wasn't holding an ax.

Mattias, the youngest Fareview at eighteen, still had many years before he had to worry about this endeavor. He resembled their father, with his build and his brown hair, though his eyes were lighter like their mother's. Mattias would have had a beard if he could grow one, but as it was, it looked rather patchy. The sisters teased him incessantly for it. He, too, had on his dark winter coat, with his hands shoved into his pants' pockets, and his hat pulled low over hair that needed a trim.

"Are you ready?" their father asked, then paused.

Auri watched her father's warm hazel gaze jump between his daughters to the strangers outside the booth. His smile faded, eyes narrowing as the sugar glaze inside of them hardened—a Tarley-look if Auri had ever seen one.

Mattias was also frowning. He pulled his hands from his pockets and took his hat off his head.

Their brother had once expressed his desire to go to second school in New Taras to study law and repeal the Marriage Law for his sisters. As sweet as the sentiment was, Tarley had pointed out, "While the thought is noble, brother, it's not like it will do much good for us by then."

Buteress's greedy gaze swept over Mattias, and Auri shuddered.

"Mr. Fareview? You have lovely daughters," Buteress simpered. "And a son? He looks strong and like a good worker." He licked his lips.

Auri wanted to jump over the table and stand in front of her brother. There were rumors about these kinds of men, too. Those who would pay the poor for their boys and girls for servitude to their land—only that wasn't what became of those children. Using children in such a way was against the law, of course, but Kaloma officials did an excellent job of looking the other way when enough coin was involved.

Mattias tightened his grip on his hat, and his knuckles turned white. "Come on, sisters." Instead of speaking to the older man as rules of propriety required, Mattias ignored him. "Let's get home."

"Now, wait a moment," Crossbie said, stepping closer to the rail. "I need a wife. I'm going to have one of these women. I want this one," he said and like a striking snake, he snatched Auri's wrist before she saw what was happening, yanking her toward him.

Her hip slammed against the handrail; it creaked and wobbled, threatening to topple. "Unhand me!" she snapped, wrenching her arm from his grasp and scurrying backward away from him.

Mattias—stars bless him—placed himself between Crossbie and Auri on Crossbie's side of the rail. Crossbie had her brother by several stones, even if Mattias had height and youth on his side.

"Try and touch my sister again, you prick," Mattias said, his voice low and dangerous.

Tomas stepped between Mattias and Crossbie. "It doesn't work that way, and if it did, I wouldn't allow you to take my daughter," her father said. He was seething, his jaw tight as he spoke. The diplomacy he usually employed in situations that involved bartering was now nonexistent.

"It does. Law says so. I get the wife of my choice," Crossbie said.

"As long as she accepts your suit," Gromley added. He was very in tune with rules and regulations.

"Why wouldn't she?" Crossbie peered around Tomas and Mattias to look at Auri. "She's unlikely to find a better prospect up here in the boonies."

She had the horrible feeling he would toss her over his shoulder, run, and rut her like the bull she'd seen with the cows if he could. The thought reminded her of a story her mother had shared with them once after a home visit in the outer region. As they had waited for the delivery of a babe, the women told the story of a poor girl who had been found attacked and left for dead in the river. The victim had been returned to her family, but then forced to marry her attacker.

Her father lifted his walking stick, so it rested on his shoulder. "The law provides for a woman's choice."

That wasn't exactly true, but it didn't seem prudent to correct her father. Auri rubbed Crossbie's touch from her wrist and checked the ribbon, surprised to find it still there.

Mr. Cobble shuffled over from his booth.

Auri liked that the old man cared enough to see what was happening but didn't think he'd be very effective help if it came to it. She glanced at Brinna, whose eyes were the size of cream saucers, then at

Tarley, who was frowning. Tarley glanced at Auri, at her rubbing her wrist, and shook her head in disgust.

Two of the other men they knew in the marketplace wandered over as well, standing to the side should her father and brother need assistance.

Midlord Buteress, recognizing the odds had shifted, offered a nod of his head, and reached out to block Crossbie from stepping any closer. "Please, accept my apologies for Mr. Crossbie. He's not familiar with the marketplace, given this is his first attendance. I shall endeavor to help him with his approach for tomorrow's visit."

"See that you do," her father said, his affability still a winter's day. "The market is closed." He lifted his chin toward the exit. "See yourselves out."

Two of the three men—the lords—bowed, but Crossbie stabbed Auri with one more stare before turning and walking away.

When the sound of their footfalls on the wooden walkway had disappeared altogether, Auri shuddered another breath of relief.

Her father turned to look at them, his face drawn and bleak as he ran a hand over his face. "Gods." He looked up and glanced at the other men, nodding with gratitude for their support. "I'd hoped for more time," he muttered, more to himself than anyone else.

Auri didn't understand her father's strange comment, but then, he was prone to random thoughts at strange times. Perhaps he was referring to Tarley's coming deadline?

"We'll see you folks out," one of the men from the marketplace said, interrupting Auri's curiosity. "Make sure there isn't anything unsavory beyond the doors of the marketplace."

"I'd appreciate that." Their father paused and took a deep breath. "Come. Let's get you safely to the cottage."

Led by their father and guarded from behind by their brother, Auri and her sisters started from the market house flanked by the village men.

"That was rather dramatic," Brinna said as they moved down the walkway. "I can't wait to tell Mother and Jess."

"They aren't home. Mrs. Grenden's baby is coming," Mattias said.

"Pray for sons." They chorused the common blessing upon learning of a pregnancy or a birthing.

Her father glanced around. "Let's get home before the sun falls. Don't need to be traveling in the woods without the sun."

"It won't get dark," Brinna said. "We should see anyone coming."

"There are clouds," Father said. "Storm coming. It will be dim enough in the woods to hide in the shadows. We won't be safe until we get to the cottage."

Once they were settled in the wagon, they started toward home. The trees thickened the further they traveled from the village, the bushes, brambles, and trunks outlining the snowy roadway. When they were beyond the village, their father said, "None of you will go to the market tomorrow."

"What will we do?" Tarley asked.

"We'll stay close to home. Work about the cottage."

"Not that. About the marketplace. The men. The collection." Tarley worked the ribbon around her wrist.

"Isn't there anything we can do?" Mattias asked.

"Got a magic spell that can whisk you all from Kaloma?" their father asked. He snapped the line to get the horse moving a little faster. "We'll figure something out. Mama and I always do." He looked over his shoulder at them, then refocused on the rutted road ahead. The wagon lurched over a divot but rolled onward. "I promise."

But what could be done? Auri looked up at the dark, gray sky, wishing she could change things, though she held no illusions that that such magic existed to change their circumstances.

"Auri?" Her father's voice drew her from her wishes.

"Yes, Father?"

"You'll be in the woods collecting tomorrow. Jessamine and Mother will be with the Grendens a while, I think. Mattias and I will be in the woods with you, cutting."

"Yes, sir," she said. Maybe she was supposed to hate that he'd given her a tedious chore, but rather than being a drudgery—like sitting in the marriage marketplace—foraging for winter herbs felt like being granted a wish. Freedom.

The next day, Auri tucked one hand into the pocket of her coat, and pulled on the cart's rope with the other, listening to the slice of the sled's runners through the snow. As she high stepped through the fresh fall, her wool skirt dragged, collecting snow, and she groaned with frustration, yanking the fabric, wishing she could don pants like her father and brother. Despite the cold seeping into her clothing and boots, she was warm with the exertion of walking and grateful to be anywhere else other than the marketplace where she and her sisters were stuffed like jarred fruits waiting for some suitor to come along and select one of them from the shelf.

A flash of sunlight on the fresh white powder caught her eye. It was beautiful, as if the sun dropped dollops of golden syrup on the trail making the snow sparkle a moment before fading. She didn't ponder the fact that sky was overcast, and the snow wasn't melting under the heat as it should. Content, she hummed as she continued through the forest.

A noise—something subtly different from the slice of the sled runners through the packed snow—captured her attention. She stopped and looked about the woods. It was quiet. No animal sounds. No tree-falling from her father and brother, who she knew were also out in the woods. The thwack-thwack of their axes in a syncopated rhythm resounded in the distance. The stark white of the new snow against the black, leafless branches of deciduous trees mixed with the evergreens obscured her view of what might be out there.

She squinted at the shadows, imagining she saw a play of golden sparkles in the dark recess. But when she blinked, it was gone. Nothing new caught her eye. Nothing moved but snow slipping from a low hanging branch, causing it to snap back into place. Her imagination. She continued forward, unable to go home yet with so few supplies, and blamed the unnerving shivers that danced up her spine on the incident with Crossbie and Brinna's stories.

Brinna loved to tell stories about the Whitling Woods. Roaming monsters hungry for flesh, wizards and witches trapping people's souls in flora and fauna or using them for sinister spells, crazed men on the run from the government, pirates, thieves, and sometimes saviors bent on saving the women of Kaloma. But that was all they were: stories.

Auri suppressed a smile at her sister Brinna's insistence that magic had once led her to a meadow "...full of kindling and cleared of snow as if it were spring. Touched by magic," Brinna had whispered to Auri in the dark.

"Why didn't you bring any proof home?"

"I blinked, and it vanished," Brinna had said, her whisper just a touch louder in her exuberance. They'd been squished together in the bed they shared, in the room they shared with Jessamine and Tarley, where no one could have a thought without the other one knowing.

"Oh hush," Tarley had said from the dark. "Don't be daft. Magic isn't likely to touch the lot of us, just like love. Neither of which will ever find us in this gods-forsaken hovel."

"Be nice, Tarley." Jessamine's sweet voice contrasted with Tarley's acerbic one. "It's okay to dream, Brinna."

"Easy for you to say, Jess. You don't have to marry at all," Tarley had replied. Their oldest sister Jessamine had chosen to be their family's one unmarried female and would care for their parents. Tarley's bitterness was at their circumstances rather than Jessamine's decision.

"We should go to Sparrow City," Auri had offered.

"Or Fulstrom."

"With what coin?" Tarley had asked. "And in the middle of winter? Beggars can't be choosers, now can they?"

Leave it to Tarley to offer a heavy dose of reality. Auri understood Tarley's pessimism, even if she longed for optimism. And she knew she couldn't let herself get caught up in her imagination like Brinna might. Allowing herself a place to dream and imagine, wish and hope was too painful when their only options for a future were the likes of Crossbie or Gromley or Buteress. With Jessamine, Tarley, Brinna, Auri, and Mattias all still unmarried and at home with their parents, there were a lot of mouths to feed and very little income to do it. It left little room for dreaming.

With a sigh, she continued forward, enjoying another dollop of sunshine in the snow, then another, as if she were following woodland fairies. There couldn't be any harm in imagining here, for now.

The wind had blown the snow into drifts ahead, clearing her a path that was so much easier to traverse. With a tug on the sled, she pulled it down the path through another copse of trees, then stopped short and stared.

A giant bank of snow blocked the path forward. It rose like a fortress, though there was a narrow space that allowed passage. At the moment, the space seemed illuminated by sparkling golden light.

Everything about it said, "This way!"

An awareness wrapped around the back of her

neck and drifted down her spine, but it wasn't foreboding exactly, rather something less tangible that made her feel foolish. Brinna's stories were getting into her head. Anything to take her mind off the perils of what happened the day before at the marketplace.

With a glance up through the brittle bones of the trees trying to poke holes in the thick, gray clouds, Auri knew it would snow. The air was heavier and reminded her that the brisk cold would become life threatening. She'd have to return home soon, but a glance back at her wagon told her it was a little too empty yet.

She surveyed the snowbank. Perhaps it wasn't so surprising the snow would have drifted into such a structure. *I can go a little farther.* She started forward. Maybe the wood sprites had more in mind for her today.

She slid through the narrow opening of the snowbank, pulling the sled behind her, then halted in mouth-open awe. Despite being the dead of the winter, she stood in an awakening meadow with golden sunlight dappling the surface of the forest floor. Grass and early blooms mixed with kindling, herbs, and spring fruits to collect, all scattered with clumps of melting snow littered the glen. Evergreens, deciduous trees with spring blooms, thin reedy saplings, and the fat trunks of hearty oaks, their boughs bearing the first suggestion of green life surrounded the meadow. Every so often, the branches swayed, revealing the wall of snow beyond the shadows. It was as if she'd walked into a private room in the woods. Brinna's magical meadow.

Auri laughed aloud with surprise and delight, deciding that Brinna's imagination was more astute than they gave her credit for. Even if Auri didn't believe in magic, it was hard to refute it while standing there. She blinked, wondering if it would disappear like Brinna's story, but when she opened her eyes, she was still standing in the springtime glade.

Leaving the sled, she collected twigs, fallen branches, and anything else that would be useful for the family's winter work. There were herbs and supplies for the medicines to be made in her mother's kitchen. And springtime ones at that! Wild carrots! Wild strawberries! It was a treasure trove. She began to hum again, pleased she could contribute to her family's business, and before long felt the heat of her exertion.

Removing her coat, she laid it on a large slab of basalt taking residence in an outcropping of rocks near the narrow entrance, then stashed her sled near it, still in the snow. With a glance up, she noticed the clouds had broken, revealing a patch of icy-blue sky hovering over her. Curiouser and curiouser. She leaned down to inspect some plants growing near the base of the boulder, and something on the ground glinted in the sun, catching her gaze. Tilting her head, she bent to search for the glittering object, and after moving some detritus of a forgotten winter, she uncovered a gleaming, golden key.

She gasped and picked it up. A pleasant pulse of energy surged through her hand, the gilded object warm to the touch. Strange. The blade, the length of her thumb, led to an opulent bow curled and inlaid with what looked to be five jewels while at the opposite end rounded with two equidistant prongs. In addition to its ornate design, its weight had her guessing it was made of solid gold. It had to be worth a fortune!

"Where do you belong and what are you doing here?" She turned and looked at the ground as if there might be a treasure chest or a trap door nearby to change her fortunes. Then she scoffed at her silliness, studying the key once again.

"Do you always talk to yourself?"

Auri twirled at the voice, hiding the treasure in a tight fist behind her back.

Standing at the edge of the forest's shade was a stranger. His face was obscured in the shadows that seemed to undulate around him, but she could see he was tall. He wasn't wide like her father, but shaped with a hint at his strength, somehow, dressed to match the shadows as if he wore the darkness, which she found disconcerting.

Her heartbeat was frenetic. She lifted her chin to appear braver than she felt, channeling Tarley, afraid her voice might fail her. "Were you following me?"

He chuckled and took slow steps toward her, leaving the shadows of the trees behind. "No. I have only just entered the meadow, and there you were, talking to air." He waved a hand, and the darkness pulsed with his movement as if it were stitched to him. The shadows were following him.

That couldn't be.

She shook her head of the thought and focused on the tangible. His clothing—unlike the garments she'd seen on the menfolk in her village—adhered to him. A shirt, not a tunic, with buttons—actual buttons!—open at his neck so she could see the hollow at his throat. A dark wool coat that stopped at his thighs, covered in black trousers not homespun but tailored. They fit his frame so she could see the strength of his thighs, the length of which disappeared into polished black boots that hugged his calves. No hat. No gloves. He must have been rich, from the city with a carriage nearby to be dressed so. Maybe even the royal city, New Taras.

And he was standing in the shadows that rippled around him.

Impossible.

She looked up to find the sun, to understand what was happening with the shadows, and realized the meadow had darkened. The slice of blue sky was gone, replaced by twilight dark with thick clouds once more. No. Shadows.

When she looked at the stranger, the shadows still billowing around him as he moved across the meadow, a snowflake landed on her cheek and melted. Her heartbeat was frantic. She turned and picked up her coat, knowing she needed to leave the meadow.

Her grip tightened around the key, the prongs digging into her palm. She knew this trinket could provide her family a tidy sum even without a treasure chest, and this well-dressed man didn't need it, obviously. They could go to Sparrow City or Fulstrom for a proper marketplace and a proper match. They could have what seemed a better choice.

"In a hurry?" the stranger asked.

Instead of answering, she asked him her own questions as she shrugged into her coat. "What are you doing here? Where are you coming from? Where are you going?" She glanced over her shoulder for another opening in the wall of snow but couldn't locate one.

He stopped and tilted his head. "That's a lot of questions all at once."

He was so much closer, and now she could see his features. Her breath caught. He was beautiful, objectively, and though she had limited experience to compare his beauty to, she knew it to be a fact. His hair was raven black and curled around his face, shaped and gentled with day-old shadow. His eyes were dark and framed under thick, dark brows. His nose was perfect and straight. She wasn't sure she'd ever seen such a perfect iteration of a nose before. It led to a proportional mouth with lips that gentled his angular jaw.

She had to look away, reminding herself to draw a breath as her body betrayed her. Being drawn to his exterior when she knew nothing about his interior was misguided and dangerous. Her mind told her she should be afraid of a stranger, with her racing heart and tense muscles, ready to dart away like a frightened hare. She understood fear, and Crossbie's face flashed through her thoughts, but this wasn't fear. Not exactly.

Her body wanted to step closer and inspect this man like they did to the women at the marketplace.

When he didn't answer any of her questions, she supplied one. "The marketplace?"

He took another slow step toward her. "No. I'm not sure why I'd go there." He looked her up and down, inspecting her, then glance around her at her wagon. "Is that where you're going to?" He continued across the clearing, in no hurry, his steps assured.

She shook her head and swallowed again, hoping it would calm the mutinous nerves. His question was an honest one. She could have been—should have been—at the marketplace. At twenty-four, it was a good assumption to make. But it was clear he wasn't from Sevens. This gave her pause as she considered her experience at the market the day before with Buteress, Gromley, and Crossbie. What was a stranger like him doing here, in the Whitling Woods?

"It isn't my day for the market," she stammered. "I'm collecting kindling and winter herbs." She glanced at her pile near the boulder, then hurried to put them in her sled.

"That's what you sell at the market?" His gaze followed hers to the pile, then returned to her. He looked at her skirt again, which made her feel self-conscious about her threadbare clothing, the patches on her skirt and coat announcing her peasantry.

"Sell?" She shook her head. "I wasn't talking about the normal market, but we sell my mother's jams and medicinal tinctures."

He tilted his dark head and continued his walk toward her. "There's another kind of market?"

"The marriage market."

He stopped moving for a moment, his shadows billowing like sheets hung out to dry, and his confused look startled her. The impossibility of those shadows struck Auri again, along with his confusion.

"Marriage market?" he asked.

She looked from his shadows to his face and struggled to maintain her gaze. "You don't–" she stopped, even more confounded. Everyone in Kaloma knew of the marriage law. "Where are you from?" She stepped back. "Jast?"

If he was from Jast, he might have nefarious intentions, or perhaps he was a marauder, which put her in danger of kidnapping. Except he didn't look like she might imagine a marauder, and one this far in the northern woods and without quick passage to the sea? It didn't make sense in the whole series of events thus far, but she couldn't make sense of this man. Even if he was attending the marketplace, what was he doing so deep in the forest?

He shook his head. "I'm not from around here." He continued toward her.

Auri realized how close he was now, the darkness reaching toward her, surging around her ankles. "So I realized." She lifted her feet as the darkness wrapped around her; it wasn't any different than fog, wisps of it moving with her movements.

"What is this marriage market?"

"It's where women go to find prospective husbands. It's the law." She stopped stomping at the shadows and looked at him.

His brows shifted over his dark eyes with an incredulous look. "That's barbaric." Now before her, he stopped and looked her up and down again. "I bet you've snagged yourself a husband." He grinned, but it wasn't filled with humor. Something heavier and darker.

He was so close. Auri took quick, frightened-hare steps backward and got caught between him and the rocks. *Snagged?* The metal of the key grew even hotter against her skin.

She shook her head. "No. My sisters have to… not snagged… they're trapped. I don't want–" But she stopped and clamped her mouth shut. "Are you a collector?" She'd never known one to come through before spring, but her mind wanted to cling to something that made sense.

"Collector of what?" he asked and moved even closer. "What don't you want?"

She lost her fight with the boulder and thumped hard against it, having to sit down because her knees gave. Looking up, she realized the man was close enough she could see his dark eyes glittering.

And suddenly her fear made her angry.

She thought of Crossbie the day before and how afraid she'd been, of his hand grabbing ahold of her and yanking her to him. Of how powerless she'd felt. The powerlessness and trepidation she felt about this stranger now, though not a Crossbie, made her furious.

She rose, gripped the key harder, and stepped toward him like she was the Queen of Kaloma, or Queen Tarley. She wouldn't be cowed. "You are being rude. You frighten me, make accusations, then stalk me across the meadow."

"Frighten and stalk? What am I, a wolf?"

She made an irritated noise. "What do you want from me?"

He crossed his arms over his chest, and her traitorous mind noticed the way the fabric of his coat stretched around his arms and shoulders. "I was just interested in learning a bit more." He waved a hand about. "Of being here. A new place."

"Learning what?"

"About you. We will be together for a while."

She resisted the urge to shrink away but couldn't exactly dart past him since he was blocking her path. "You're an enforcer? I'm twenty-four. I still have two years! I don't have to go anywhere with you."

"You speak in riddles. An enforcer? Of what? Two years until what?"

It made her even angrier. "The law!" she snapped, clinging to what she knew.

Auri snatched the lead for the sled and moved around the man. She realized too late she should have taken a wider path around him. As she passed, his hand reached out and grabbed her arm.

A bright heat flashed through her like the fireworks she'd once seen in Sparrow City to commemorate the birth of the new princess, burning through the fabric of her clothing to her skin. And whereas Crossbie grasping her felt invasive and repulsive, this touch didn't. This touch seemed to hold a promise, though of what she couldn't say.

When she looked from his hand on her arm to his face and saw perplexity carved upon his brow, she wondered if he too had felt the effervescent heat. Though her heart was pounding, she understood the heartbeat wasn't afraid. It was anxious for something. This touch felt dangerous, though in a different way from Crossbie's. Something else entirely.

This close she could see the glittering in each of his dark eyes, gemstone colors with striations in his irises. Otherworldly eyes. Brinna's stories resounded in her mind. She wanted to dismiss them, but now it was harder to do so. She glanced around the meadow touched by spring and back to his eyes.

"Magic?" she asked. "You're a wizard? A witch?" She hated how timid she sounded.

He smiled then, a smile that made her think of a predator. It wasn't unkind, but chills raced across her skin nevertheless. "Not a wizard or a witch. I am the night. I am every dream you've ever had, and I carry answering nightmares for good measure."

"Let me go." It came out like a whisper.

He smiled. "You have touched what is mine."

She couldn't stop looking at his mouth. This smile awoke something else deep inside of her, flooding her with heat.

She tore her gaze away from his smiling mouth and wrenched her arm from his grasp. "I don't have anything of yours. I don't even know your name."

"Oh, but you do."

Auri had the impression that he moved closer, even though neither of them had moved. It was as if the darkness emanating from him was wrapping around her, drawing her closer.

"You're a stranger. What could I possibly have that is yours?" she asked with as much disdain as she could muster. "Look at me. I have nothing. I'm in the forest collecting twigs and weeds so my family won't freeze to death." She looked the length of him.

"You don't understand," he said, his voice no longer easy and companionable but not exactly threatening. Bitter perhaps?

"I don't."

His eyebrows shifted, as if offering her the opportunity to challenge his claim, and he looked down at her coat pocket where she gripped the golden trinket. "The key," he said.

She had picked up the key. As she searched his face, the shadows moving around and between them, his touch and now the darkness holding her captive, she noted the colored striations of his dark eyes. They reminded her of the gemstones on the key. "What? How can that be?" she asked, feeling foolish for even thinking it. And still, she voiced her question. "You're the key?"

He scoffed with very little amusement and shook

his head. Then he leveled that gemstone gaze on her and said, "No. I'm the god the key trapped."

Set the trap
Bait the trick
Entice the fly
With honey thick

Hold it down
Pluck its wings
Make it feeble
It's power to glean.

Touch one jail
Touch two play
Three wishes with
Prices to pay.

Make wishes thrice
Pay three times.
Loathe the wishkeeper
Trapped inside.

Choose a vice
        Pure and worthy
Cast it blood
        An oath sacrifice
Candles and fire
        To open the door
Pernicious flood
        To pay the price

"With this blood
I call forth here
Imbue the vice
With malice adhere

Ensnare entrap
Entreat Imbibe
The price of blood
Locked up inside."

Freedom gained
Or prison renewed?
A single choice
The End imbued.

Heed the spell
The cost is great
Blood oath to swear
Blood price to fate.

Completion:
One begins
Seven to call
A feast to End.

End the spell.
One to start,
Seven to complete
No magic to restart–

–Open doors
Realities transcend
Freedom and Power
A Feast to End.

The Spell

The Key Keeper's 1st Wish . . .

Stars, he had a terrible headache starting behind his eyes. He was confident he looked like death warmed over. If he were well and truly dead, however, it would mean being reunited with his older sister in her realm of the dead and out of this hell of an enchantment. A boon. That wasn't the case, of course. His pounding headache, disheveled appearance, and day-old shadow was because he'd imbibed too much scotch and was wallowing in the pain of a hangover. Within the spell, and because he was a god, he could conjure whatever he wanted, smooth away the consequences of excess, avoid the pain and perils of the body, but it made his imprisonment and isolation worse. The hangover reminded him he was still alive, and still sane. Whatever it took to keep his shit together, he supposed.

At the moment, he was struggling to string together thoughts, which meant he might have to negate the hangover's effects sooner rather than later. The new key keeper—who was rather pretty—was talking about marriage laws, or some such nonsense. What the fuck? One moment he was brooding with a bottle of scotch in front of his fireplace and the next, he was standing in a meadow watching a peasant woman look around as if she'd lost something. He knew, however. This was the seventh time, so of course he knew. She was the new key keeper, and the key was, predictably, in her hand.

How long had it been since the last key keeper, he wondered? At least ten years for him, give or take, though his twin brother Luc would insist it had only been one. There were rules to the spell, and that was one of them. Time functioned differently. He'd lived for a century within the confines of the spell while Luc claimed only ten had passed beyond it.

Spells were fixed, and it was impossible to deviate from the rules. He'd tried, but like anyone else, god or otherwise, he was beholden to the pattern set forth by the spell's language. It didn't matter how much he ranted or raged. It didn't matter how much he pleaded or fought. It didn't matter how much he manipulated or cajoled. The spell was fixed.

A key keeper as the wish maker.

Three wishes were granted.

Three consequences were paid.

And a sacrifice was offered for his freedom. Unless the key keeper chose the sacrifice at the end of their allotment—and not a single one had—he would remain imprisoned by the spell placed upon him.

Hence his continued entrapment.

Fucking Luc.

Nix blinked to reorient himself and shook his head to alleviate the pain of his hangover. It melted away as if it had never existed at all.

"You're the key?" the key keeper asked.

The new key keeper was lovely, though Nix wouldn't allow himself to continue to consider that fact. The braid of her dark hair hidden under a knitted, green cap and draped over the shoulder of her ivory homespun tunic, the gray woolen coat haphazardly donned, the vibrance of her angry-sky eyes, the lucidity of her skin-tinged pink by the winter air, and the way her generous mouth frowned at him were things he wouldn't allow himself to ponder.

"No. I'm the god the key trapped," he replied. There wasn't any reason not to be forthcoming. He couldn't lie to her anyway—a rule of the spell—but equivocation and omission weren't off limits. He'd already tried that to procure the outcome he wanted.

She had a job to do. He had a role to play. No matter the circumstances or the way it played out, there were factors involved he couldn't control, like the fact this rotten predicament always ended the same: the key keeper with their wishes and Nix left behind, still imprisoned by the spell. He didn't have any hope this one would be different. In the end, humans and gods were all the same: greedy, self-centered asses. Gender hadn't changed this fact, and he was sure this key keeper wouldn't be any different despite her beauty.

Though, Nix noted, that spark he'd felt when he'd touched her still burned his hand. That was different, but he refused to ponder that either. Whatever might be the same or different, they both had to play by the rules of the spell moving forward.

"I guess I should be thanking you," he told her and offered a placating smile as he released her arm. Swiping his hands over his thighs, he returned them to the pockets of the coat he'd conjured upon entering the glade. He couldn't feel the cold, but it was certainly easier for her if he looked the part. He also knew he was more likely to get what he needed from her—which was her out of his hair so he could go back to drinking himself into a stupor and conjuring sex fantasies—by being accommodating. Especially because the moment she made her first wish, she would hate him. She'd rush to be rid of him.

That was a pattern too, though maybe not a rule.

She lost her footing in her rush to move around him, and he reached out to steady her. Ebullient warmth shot through his hands, straight up his elbows to his shoulders and danced down his spine once more, leaving pleasant tingles in its wake. She yanked herself from his grasp, her eyes flashing like lightning in a storm.

A bad sign, Nix thought. *Perhaps when she learns about the treasure offered with the key, she'll be more inclined to be friendly.*

But did he need her to be friendly?

The question stopped him and clogged his breath for a beat.

He didn't.

He refused to examine why he'd initially wanted it.

"You're trying to tell me that you were inside this key?" She held it up.

The gold glowed with the spells enchantment even though Nix had taken most of the light from the meadow. His darkness moved around him, spreading out into the expanse of the glen as he commanded it to drift toward its edges. It was time to get things moving.

"I understand your incredulity." He started with the deference he provided all the prior six keepers. Each of those wish makers had undergone the same pattern of emotions. First came incredulity. They doubted him and the truth of their circumstances. Next was the bewilderment that such an occurrence was even a possibility. This led to their curiosity about the situation and the details of the bargain. Finally, the key keeper would invariably accept the position in which they found themselves and make their first wish.

He allowed himself just a moment to look at her. She studied the key before her gray eyes flicked to him. Awareness buzzed at the base of his spine, and he looked away.

"I speak the truth," he told her. "It is the only thing I'm allowed to speak."

"Then why would you need to be locked up in a key?"

He shrugged, not inclined to tell her any more than he needed to for the moment. Telling the truth and having a conversation were two distinct endeavors. He didn't have to talk. He didn't want to get to know her. He didn't want to consider her beyond her role, and he didn't think she should want to know him either. She'd make her wishes and be gone.

"I'm going home." She started across the space.

"It won't allow you to leave."

She stopped at his words, turning to stare at him.

Her jaw set, that ire on her pretty face again that he found amusing. Mortals were so quick to feel things.

"Here, then." She held out the key to him.

This was a first. He'd never once had a key keeper offer to hand the trinket back to him. But he didn't take it; he couldn't. He might be able to see the golden key, but only a key keeper could touch it. He could feel the sensation of her touching the ornate key. He looked from the key to her face.

"I'm giving it back," she said, shaking it slightly in front of him as if that might entice him.

"I can't." He slipped his hands into the pockets of his coat. He wished he could. Wished he could wish himself from the spell, but he wasn't the wish maker. And while she would endure the temporary discomfort of the consequences of the wishes she made, she would ultimately return to her life. He wouldn't. The inevitability left an awful taste on his palate—sour and metallic. He thought about conjuring a drink to wash it away, but now wasn't the time.

"But I can't leave with it?"

He shook his head.

Her eyes narrowed. "Then you've lied."

"I didn't."

"You said I had to give it back to leave."

"I didn't. I said, 'you have something that is mine,' and 'it won't allow you to leave'. I never said anything about you returning it to me. First lesson of the spell: words matter. You found the key. You won't be able to leave. You're tied to me, and I to you until you have fulfilled the bargain of the spell."

"Bargain? What bargain?"

"As the key keeper, you will be granted three wishes, but each wish will exact a price from you for making it."

"What? Why can't you–"

"I'm trapped by the enchantment. I can grant wishes through the spell's power but am equally bound by them and the consequences they bring. You are the wish maker."

"Let me get this straight. I have three wishes and have to pay three penalties for the wishes I make. Then I can leave?" Her hands were on her hips, and she was leaning toward him, slightly. Nix could feel the heat of her frustration. When he didn't answer, her hands flew out to her sides. "This is ridiculous," she said and dropped the key at his feet, turned, and stomped away, fixing the fit of her gray coat as she went.

This was very new.

He conjured snow to fall in the meadow, as he looked down at the ground where she'd dropped the key. It wasn't there. When he looked up, she was looking for the entrance that must have brought her here. He wasn't sure how she'd found it, considering the entire space was enclosed in a tall snowbank, but it had been ages since the last key keeper, so he wasn't going to question it either. He watched her pick up a stick while attempting to dig through the snow to escape. But as soon as she made a divot, it refilled with fresh snow.

He slid his hands into the pockets of his jacket. "That won't work."

"I'm getting out of here," she said, continuing her efforts at escape.

Nix found this curious. She'd been told she had three wishes. All the key keepers at this point had found that prospect enticing, but this one had dropped the key, stormed away, and was trying to find a way out. Different.

"Check your pocket," he said.

She turned from the wall and looked at him, breathing heavily. He didn't like that his mind immediately imagined her straddling him, riding his cock. He blinked to clear the vision and his skin heated, embarrassed by the direction of his thoughts, which was even more disconcerting. Gods didn't get embarrassed. Where the fuck had that come from?

She glared as if she could read his mind. "What for?"

"Just humor me." The sooner he got her through these stupid wishes, the sooner he could return to existing in his alcohol-induced stupor, at least until the next key keeper arrived.

With an exasperated and incredulous roll of her eyes, which Nix found amusing, she slid a hand into her pocket. He felt her skin caress the metal as she took ahold of the key. and chills danced across his skin. When she withdrew her hand, key in her grasp, she looked up at him, eyes wide. "What–?"

"You are the key keeper. It will not let you go."

"I don't want it!" she yelled and threw the key at him.

A flash of golden light flared between her and the godman across the glen, and the key disappeared. Just when she thought it was gone, the weight returned to her pocket. Auri fished inside her coat again, only to find the key. She wrapped her hand around the warm metal and pulled it out once more.

It won't let you leave.

She looked up at him. "I'm trapped here?"

"Until you make your wishes."

Auri wrapped her arms around herself and looked up at the sky, which was even darker now that snow had begun to fall in earnest. She shivered and looked down at her booted feet, scuffed with wear and worn with use, then closed her eyes. "This isn't happening. This isn't happening." She muttered the chant as if it too were magical and would override everything else to send her home.

Then, because it didn't make sense to fight against what was, she sighed and made a deal with herself to accept whatever fate was offering, even if it was magical. Too many things had happened in the last hour to make a very good argument for magic's existence. By the time Auri opened her eyes and looked around, still in the meadow with an enigmatic stranger watching her, she bowed her head, resigned.

"What about my family?" she asked. "They will worry. I don't want them to worry."

"Key keeper," the man said. "This is temporary for you. You will return to your family, and what you gain from the spell could be a fortuitous favor rather than a trial. You could wish for wealth, long life, or the deepest love. You are limited only by your heart's desires."

She raised her head to meet his dark gaze. Deepest love? Had it only been the day before that she'd longed for love matches for herself and her sisters. If all this were real, could that be something she wished for? "Have others made those sorts of wishes?"

He walked away from her to the opposite side of the glen. "Yes, among other things." As he walked, he left sparkling gold dust in his wake, like stars in the night sky.

"But what about my family? Will they know I've gone? Will they think I've run away?"

He turned and headed back in her direction. "I don't have those answers for you."

As he approached, she realized the meadow was changing around them. The trees were disappearing in the golden swath of light that seemed to eat them with its fire. Left behind was opulence Auri had never known. Deep blue walls were marked at intervals with glowing sconces, reflecting flickering with light on an ivory coffered ceiling, painted with colorful reliefs she wanted to study. Artwork in gilded frames stacked along walls and ornate furnishings that spoke of leisure and time filled the space: two chairs, an ottoman, a love seat. A dark plush carpet, elegant with golden whorls and swirls in contrasting colors rolled out over the stone floor. A fire flickered in the massive hearth.

She moved out of the man's way so he could continue with the transformation, but he stopped in front of her while the changing meadow continued without him. The sparkling light of the magic passed around them, enclosing them both in its golden embrace. Auri chased the transformation with her eyes, turning her head to watch the magic do its work until the meadow was well and truly gone, and they were standing inside the dazzling room.

She turned to the man. "Who are you?"

"Perhaps the more accurate question, and more relevant to you, is what," he said. "If you need a name, I am Nixus, but you may call me Nix."

I'm the god the key trapped.

Auri leaned away from him and bumped into a high-backed chair behind her. "As in, the god, Nixus?"

This couldn't be. She knew the stories and worshipers of the gods: Lucian and Nixus, Myna and Janor, Saphra and Lexa—light and dark, revelry and contemplation, life and death—along with a plethora of other deities and their legends.

"The god of night?"

"I have been called that, yes."

"If you're a god, then you can use your power to let me go home."

"I wish it worked that way."

"Why doesn't it?"

He nodded at her, his eyes dropping to her hand. "The key. The spell on it."

"This key?" She held it up and threw it across the room.

It smacked into the frame of a bed and fell to the floor with a thud. Auri straightened when she realized she was standing in a bedroom, and that bed was one of the most magnificent things she'd ever laid eyes on in her life—besides the man near her, who she refused to look at just then.

The bed was enormous, stretched out against one of the walls, hung with dark velvet curtains with gilt edging and tassels. Her entire family could have laid side by side on that masterpiece. Having shared a room with her three sisters her whole life, the idea of sleeping in something like that seemed like a dream.

"Have I died?" she asked.

"Why? What? No. I told you the truth."

She believed him, sort of, she supposed, as much as her brain would allow her to believe anything that had happened in however long since she'd touched the key. She was losing track of time.

"Why would you think that?"

"The bed."

"The bed." He offered the words slowly, with a tone of skepticism.

She glanced at Nix, and upon realizing what she'd said, and where she was, she closed her mouth as heat raced over her skin. Suddenly at odds with her upbringing and her baser nature, she realized she'd been staring at a bed.

With a man.

She was in a bedroom. Alone. With a very beautiful man she found intriguing.

She was supposed to maintain her composure. Having been tempted so easily by the illusion of comfort was shameful. Tarley would never! Auri's heart sputtered to a stop, suddenly afraid, though not necessarily of Nix.

Of all that being alone with him here implied.

"Why are we standing in a bedroom?" Her heart compacted into its smallest form, worried. Her experience with men, despite her initial belief that she wasn't afraid of this one, led her to shrink away from him anyway.

He shrugged. "Are you afraid I'm going to try to get you into it?"

"It's against the law."

"What law? Laws don't apply to gods or enchantments." He removed his coat and laid it over the back of one of the wingback chairs.

Right, she was talking to a god. "It's just that laws apply to me. I'm a woman. A mortal. I'm not supposed to…" But her words died away, and she swallowed. Then she raised her chin to grasp onto the bravery she wasn't sure she felt, channeling Tarley. "I'm not–"

But her bravery melted away. She wasn't exactly sure what to say in the current circumstances. "I don't… I mean–" And finally, she said, "I could get arrested and sentenced to a birthing house—or to death—for being alone with you. Just for the implied loss of my virtue."

He smiled and laughed quietly at that. "Loss of virtue." He laughed harder, then as if it were a joke, shaking his head.

Oh goodness. His smile reached into her chest and tugged on her insides. Like all of him, his grin was beautiful in a way that was enticing, and perhaps that was what he was supposed to be. Tempting.

She frowned. "You think that's funny?"

He shook his head. "I'm not sure loss is the right description." He glanced at her. "Rather, the better perspective is what is gained."

He let that comment linger, his eyes jumping up to meet hers, and Auri felt the weight of his words, her heart unfurling in her chest as if it too wanted to grab ahold of that kind of promise. She hadn't thought of it that way before.

"If done right, that is." His grin deepened, drawing a dimple out in his cheek, and his eyes jumped from her to his hands. "Don't think it escaped my notice that you are a woman." He unbuttoned his shirt at the wrists. "You are safe from me. My bedroom wasn't a ruse to trick you. On my virtue." He chuckled.

Her cheeks heated watching his display, hearing his words that did more to her than she liked. It was alluring to watch him undress. She could imagine him unbuttoning those buttons on the front of his shirt as she watched him pull his sleeves up to reveal his forearms. "Do you have virtue?"

He smiled, and she liked the way the edges of his eyes crinkled with it, lighting his whole face. "Not much." He finished tugging on his sleeves. "What is your name?"

"Auri," she said. "Aurielle."

"Aurielle." His gaze flicked over her once more. "Auri. It suits you. Now, why can't you be alone with a man? Or specifically, me?"

"The Marriage Law forbids it."

"Right." He shook his head. "The mortal realm and their barbaric stupidity." He crossed his arms over his chest.

She noticed the way his shirt stretched across his shoulders. She noticed the shallow hollow at the base of his neck, with a glimpse of hair visible just below.

"You have nothing to fear here."

Her gaze slid from the bare skin to his face.

His dark eyes seemed to be cataloguing everything she did, and she wondered if he could read her mind.

"Laws want to keep you in cages," he added. "Like this spell cages me." He quirked an eyebrow at her. "Women in cages are dangerous."

"Like you?" she asked.

Nix grinned at her again, and she had the impression he was enjoying himself. Then, as if he'd remembered something, the grin faded, and he looked away and straightened.

She'd noticed he hadn't replied. "I thought you said I have nothing to fear."

When his eyes met hers again, the gems in his eyes glittered brightly. They carried a weight she could guess at.

Though procreation was against Kaloma law to engage in pleasure activities outside of the marriage bed except by permit in the birthing houses, she'd once read (and reread, if she were being honest) a kissing scene in a book that made her heart quicken and run away with the thrill of her imagination. After that, she'd had kissing dreams or woken with her hand between her legs, needing something though not understanding what.

So, she understood the reaction of her breath quickening, her heart racing, her stomach tightening, and her spine tingling, the very reactions moving through her body at that very moment. She tried not to put too much emphasis on her physical response to this beautiful man. He was a god, after all. It probably wasn't an anomaly.

"Yes. Well–" he took a deep breath, as if to reset himself– "you don't. But there are terms of the bargain we need to discuss. Let me show you to your quarters and provide you some time to take care of your personal needs. I will see to some food."

"Gods eat?" It seemed such a mundane thing.

"Love to," Nix replied.

He led her to the door of his room, and she followed him into a hallway. It stretched in both directions, so far that she couldn't see either end. Wall sconces flickered at even intervals, revealing doors upon doors.

"What is this?" she asked.

"The labyrinth."

She looked at him. "You mean, we could be lost?"

"No. Never fear being lost, only found."

It was a strange thing to say, the idea of being afraid to be found. "How do you know?"

"You only need to say my name, and I will be there." He turned down another hallway, and it moved of its own accord, racing past them as they walked.

Disoriented, Auri reached out to grab ahold of a wall, but couldn't and grabbed Nix's shoulder instead. It was sturdy under her hand, warm with his lifeforce. Heat raced along her arm, down her spine, pooling low in her belly.

He turned his head, his walk slowing to a stop, and looked at her hand on his shoulder.

"I'm… sorry." She pulled her hand away and curled her fingers into a fist. "It made me dizzy."

The hallway came to a standstill, and Nix turned toward her and tilted his head. "My apologies." He opened a door, then stepped aside to let her into the room.

The wall opposite the door was lined with windows, glowing dark with a starry night. At one end of the space was a closed door, along with a centered fireplace and a gilt mirror hanging over it, tilted slightly so that Auri could see the whole of the room. A love seat in dark green damask with light green roses faced the flickering fire and was framed by two emerald velvet chairs with gold painted armrests facing each other. At the other end of the room was a large bed set upon a dais like the first, but instead of an ornate headboard, this one was framed with four large posts, the dark wood carved with roses. An emerald velvet canopy offered added weight and warmth, rose gold tassels tying it in place to the posts.

Auri swallowed. "This is mine?"

"While you are here, yes. That door is to your bathing room." He nodded at the closed door near the fireplace. "Inside is a wardrobe where you'll find clothing."

"But–"

He raised a hand. "Magic is the easiest explanation. You will have everything you need."

She didn't understand how, but with sliding hallways, transforming meadows, magic keys, and an enigmatic god, it was probably best not to ask. "Thank you," she said instead and turned to offer him a grateful smile.

But he was gone.

Auri walked to the row of windows and discovered a view of a nighttime countryside, which seemed strange considering they'd been standing in the middle of a forest. Then she explored the room, testing the bed, standing by the massive fireplace to revel in the warmth. Eventually, she opened the door and walked into the bathing room, the likes of which she could never have imagined.

The tub, made of white and gray marble, was set into the floor, and there were knobs made of gold to turn that released the water. Instead of a chamber pot, there was a commode with a lever and chain. And the wardrobe wasn't a piece of furniture, but a room with all manner of clothing from evening and dinner dresses, colorful day dresses, shifts for sleeping, underthings—and also things her brother would be allowed to wear: trousers, shirts (with buttons!), jackets, vests, and knitted sweaters. The wardrobe was not only full, but it was also more than she could use in a lifetime.

Nix had said there was nothing to fear here.

Auri stepped from the bathing room and looked at the door where she'd last seen the god. She put her hand in the pocket of her wool skirt, still damp and discolored at the hem from the snow she'd been traipsing through, and found the key stashed there once again. Though the god had said he couldn't lie, she was sure that was a falsehood. She knew, without a doubt, there was much to fear here.

Nixus

Nix stepped from Auri's quarters into a room he'd conjured to resemble his father's study. Not that Nix needed one. He had nothing of substance to occupy his time. No need to control the night. No estate to manage. No business to attend to. No projects to serve others. Nothing to fix or repair. He was useless and idle. Being an idle and useless god was perhaps a volatile combination. What was the point, after all, of him? When one was trapped by a spell for a century and there was no work to be done but to wait for key keepers and their wishes?

With a frustrated sigh, he stalked across the room to a demilune black marble table pressed against the wall where there were several decanters of spirits to drink his misery away. He unstopped one with a frustrated yank and dropped the stopper onto the tabletop, where it cracked, then immediately repaired itself. He filled a glass with a healthy pour and knocked it back, emptying the glass. As he turned away, the snifter refilled with a thought.

Useless.

The room was extravagant. Filled with things he'd found pleasing as an adolescent god who worshiped his father. Floor-to-ceiling windows lined one wall. He could change the view at will. Now, it was a night sky speckled with diamond stars and awash with the gasses of distant galaxies, a rainbow of color. This was his favorite, but he enjoyed an ocean view at night, the country vista of Elcadia with a bright moon washing the landscape in its white light, or even the mystery of a forest's deep shadows at twilight. When he was morose, the view was just the black shadow of nothing to remind him where he was: nowhere, stuck inside a spell.

The wall perpendicular to the windows contained floor to ceiling bookshelves. They were ornately built with a crown of gilt carvings of gods and goddesses in varied repose showcasing their responsibilities. An attached ladder slid along the bookcase for access to the books housed within the shelves. They were favorites he'd read over his many years. He glanced at the metallic etching on their spines, but couldn't focus on any one title, his thoughts swirling with the new key keeper.

He pictured her standing in the meadow, her beguiling face turned up to look at him. Her gaze had felt like a caress. She'd liked what she saw, and the thought brought a pinch to his heart.

He didn't want to think about her and moved to the center of the room to sit at his desk, a rarity since he usually chose to sit in a chair near the fireplace.

The desk was a monstrous thing, with ornate, gilded scrollwork on the legs and drawers that contained whatever he decided he needed when one was opened. Nix knew it was a bit much, but it reminded him of his father's desk he remembered as a boy, and Ur had always been ostentatious.

Nix could picture his father sitting behind his desk, book in one hand, the other unconsciously moving back and forth over his coffee cup handle. Then, because Nix and Lucian had usually been playing in the room and the play had turned into a fight, his father would look out from behind his book and say, "Boys. Settle."

He missed his family.

Why was he thinking about his family? Traversing that mind trail never ended in a good place, which was why he didn't. He pictured the key keeper standing in the meadow, her head bowed, and when she'd looked up, her gray eyes had been bright with tears.

But she had surprised him. She hadn't begged to leave; she hadn't bargained for herself. Instead, she'd asked about her family, resigned that she was a part of the enchantment.

Nix stood. He couldn't keep the key keeper from his thoughts, and he didn't want to think about her.

He walked to the fireplace recessed into the wall, one of the many in the manor. He conjured fireplaces in every room. Something about the movement and heat of the fire made it feel more like home, or what he remembered home to be, whether he had been in the Elcadia townhouse or the country manor. His parents, despite their flaws, had filled their children's universe with love.

This manor and everything he conjured it to be, how it moved and flowed, the maze it often became, represented Nix's working mind. Most of the rooms, he knew, were replicas of his youth with his family. The labyrinth and his conjuring were the only power afforded him here.

He could summon Luc and Poe—the spell's casters—but he didn't very often. Gods were fickle and suffered from flights of fancy, as Luc exemplified so well. It wasn't worth waiting for them to appear, to hear of their exploits beyond the confines of the spell, and Nix was still furious they had stolen his life from him. Beyond those uses of his power, he was as beholden to the power of the spell as the key keeper trapped with him.

Another key keeper.

The seventh.

Nix sipped the drink and watched the fire undulate in the firebox. It crackled, and he smiled unconsciously thinking about the new key keeper's eyes—the fire inside of them—but then frowned at the direction of his thoughts. As they'd stood in his room, her eyes wide with… not fear exactly, but something else, talking about being alone together, his thoughts dove right into the idea of kissing her. Of how she might taste on his tongue.

Stupid. Idiotic. Dumb move on his part. He knew better.

He took another sip of his drink, then sat in a chair facing the fire, contemplating the key keeper, his ridiculous reaction to her, and why it was foolish to allow himself room to ponder her.

The first key keeper—Flora—had been a mortal, and he'd believed he wanted to tie himself to her for eternity. He'd met her during his travels and been taken with her. Honestly, he'd been taken with her pretty face, willingness to fuck, and her tits. What else could a young god want? Or so he'd believed. Of course, he told his twin—who couldn't stand to see Nix happy—and Luc dropped the news he'd already fucked her. Luc insisted she was only after the god gift of immortality. Luc had claimed she'd tried to lure him into gifting it to her first, and when Luc had spurned her attempts, she'd dumped him like a bag of rocks thrown into a river. Nix refused to listen to his brother, too angry and stubborn to hear his twin's warning and led more by pride that his brother had been with the woman he thought he loved.

Nix shook his head, embarrassed by his idiocy, and took another sip.

They fought, like they always did. A turn of fists and insults, and they parted ways, Luc to control the day and Nix the night. They didn't need to be together, but Luc had decided he need to teach Nix a lesson. To demonstrate the truth of Flora's true character, he had concocted the idea to cast the spell where Nix was now trapped.

What Nix hated the most was that Luc had been right about Flora. She'd made her wishes and left Nix stuck, more loyal to her greedy desire for wealth, immortality, and youth than his love for her. But Luc had been wrong about the spell; he hadn't been able to break it with a drop of his blood as could be done with most blood-oath spells. Whatever he'd cast with their cousin Poe, goddess of chaos, was more powerful than either of them had been aware.

So here Nix remained. Useless and idle. Waiting for each key keeper to arrive and make their wishes.

Over the years, five more key keepers had found the key and called him forth. All five had made their wishes, paid the price, and left him to rot inside the spell. Not one had been willing to offer their sacrifice for Nix and his freedom.

It wasn't a surprise.

The spell was designed to make the key keeper loathe him. He'd grant the wish, then make them pay for it, often with horrific consequences. Wish for a lifetime of wealth, live what felt like a lifetime as a pauper. Wish for the greatest love of your life and experience the anguish of loss. When each key keeper had made their final wish and paid the final price, the spell would present them with a final test: choose the final sacrifice to end the spell for Nix or be free of the spell. Nix's freedom was their final choice, and considering it was he who seemed to be the origin of their painful consequences, why would any of them choose to sacrifice for him?

None of them had.

He sipped again, then leaned his head back, closing his eyes. Auri surfaced like a vision in his mind. He opened his eyes, shaking his head at the memory of her pretty face.

She would do the same.

Nix didn't want to consider there was something different about her. Even if everything she'd done so far was different. He didn't want the hope that accompanied every key keeper when they first arrived. The resignation they would fail always hit before their wishes were even complete. Mortals were predictable creatures: greed, love, youth, and life were the usual themes of their wishes. Even though Nix knew this to be true, hope sat there in the back of his chest anyway, offering him a glimmer of diamond starlight even as he reminded himself not to allow it.

He took another sip of his drink and rolled his neck, working the tension out of his shoulders as he pictured Auri standing in the meadow the moment she'd spoken aloud to the key. Her smile at an inanimate object, as if she thought herself a fool for doing it to begin with. The gentle, smoky refrain of her laugh. She was tall and shapely, her head bent as she studied the key.

When she'd turned her head to look at him, her beguiling face—beautiful to be sure, but he was a god; he could conjure beautiful women—rather, her beauty had been linked to something else he couldn't identify. A glow that seemed to shine inside of her, as if something was at work to keep it hidden, and though it didn't appear to be magic—not that he could sense— he'd caught an essence revealed like puffs of stardust when she moved, or when she spoke, or in the ire at him in the swirl of her dark silver eyes becoming a cosmos for just a moment when she looked at him.

Her throwing the key at him and yelling, "I don't want it!" had pushed him off balance.

No other key keeper had ever denied the wishes, not that they could. Every one of them had been immediately tempted by the idea of making wishes to fulfill their desires. This key keeper, however, even as she stood in the meadow in clothing he could see was patched and threadbare, in boots that had seen many winters and were ready to give out, scavenging for scraps for her family, had tried to return it. The promise of three wishes with the power to change her circumstance hadn't tempted her.

It had been the opulence of his bedroom that had captured her attention. She'd stood there in awe. He could see the interplay between what she thought she should feel and what she did so clearly written on her face. She didn't hide her feelings, but allowed them to be seen, free and clear.

Her first wish will be about wealth, he decided, taking another sip of his drink. It made the most sense.

He thought about her standing there staring at the bedroom, then the bed, and he'd been afforded a view of her profile. He'd watched the blush move across her skin, and she'd looked away as if to remind herself where they stood. A woman. A man, in all the ways that mattered. When he'd caught her staring at him with curiosity rather than anger, a sweet heat had lit the base of his spine, just like the moment he'd touched her in the glade.

He took another sip.

Then took a deep breath to clear his mind of all the thoughts pent up inside of him. He wasn't supposed to be thinking about the key keeper. He wasn't supposed to think of her at all. He had a role to play. He needed her to make her wishes and get the fuck out of the spell to leave him to his misery. This was the way it was to be.

He didn't need to be thinking about her, about the way she looked at him, about the way his body responded to her candor. He didn't need hope.

Nix stood and turned, the study now a dining room. He'd promised the key keeper dinner. The dining table was fit for a large dinner party—and stretched across the massive space. He never used this space, for who would he dine with but a conjuring or a key keeper, and there hadn't been one for years. The table was too big, so he conjured a smaller size and watched it shrink into a more intimate setting. Maybe he should have left it. Now it looked tiny in the massive room, so he shrunk the room around it.

Refusing to consider why he'd changed it at all, he walked to the single window at the end of the room, the panes crisscrossing the dark night beyond. He could hear the conjured servants—figments his mind created—move about the room, preparing it for a dinner for two. Two place settings. Two wine glasses. The servants lit candles, casting golden light in the dim room.

"Would you like a glass of wine, my lord?" one of them asked.

Nix looked over his shoulder. "Please," he replied and allowed himself to be served, though he only had to think the wine glass into existence. Watching the conjured servants made him feel less alone.

He turned away from the window and sat at his place at the dining table to wait for the key keeper, considering what he'd told her—Auri (though he didn't want to spend time pondering her name)—*you have nothing to fear here.*

He couldn't lie, and hadn't when he'd told her that, only there was a falsehood embedded in the layers of the words. Words mattered. She had much to fear here, and though she was technically safe from him, there was nothing safe about being caught in this spell.

He sighed, resigned to what was coming.

He was going to have to tell her the truth about what she would face, and she would despise him for it. One more key keeper who hated him. One more to choose to leave. One more to leave him trapped by the spell for an eternity. He needed her to make those wishes and bring an end to the misery of her being there. He needed her gone. Then he could return to the normalcy of his idleness and uselessness alone.

Auri

Auri sat at a dining table to the right of Nix. Covered with beautiful white dishes swirling with golden accents, the table was as opulent as everything she'd discovered in the manor. A golden candelabra glowing with candles sat in the middle, illuminating their immediate surroundings but casting the rest in flickering shadows. Servants waited on the periphery like works of art hanging on the wall until Nix wagged a hand to indicate it was time. Then, they erupted into movement around them.

Auri watched as servants added gorgeous food to

her plate. Food that was so much more decadent than she had experienced in her life. Roasted meat glistening with luxurious fat, fresh bread and butter, a variety of fruits and cheeses, vegetables swirled with a rich yellow sauce and luxuriant whipped potatoes to catch it all.

Her stomach rumbled. It wasn't that she didn't eat at home, but the fare was sparse, simple, and often watery to extend the reach of meat and vegetables to a family of seven. Fresh fruit and vegetables were a summer luxury.

"It's safe to eat," Nix told her.

Her gaze lifted to meet his, and she noted his dark eyes measure her before flicking away to his own plate. She was struck again with how beautiful he was. *A god*, she reminded herself. *A trapped one.* But the reminder didn't take away the tingly feeling that moved through her body when she looked at him, a feeling she didn't trust. "Isn't there a rule about eating the food of the gods and being trapped forever?"

Nix smiled, though he didn't seem to want to, the movement tight on his face. He looked at her again, then concentrated on his eating utensils, taking one in each hand. "No. You're thinking of the fae." He pointed at her plate with a fork. "Eat."

She wasn't about to argue with that, her stomach rumbling at the aromas.

"No experience with the fae, then?"

"Just in books." She cut a bite of the meat.

"A reader, then."

"Voracious." Auri took her bite and moaned the

moment the flavor burst against her tongue.

"Voracious about many things it would seem," Nix said. "A woman who knows what she likes."

Auri looked up from her plate to find him watching her, and the look ran a pleasant chill up her spine to the base of her neck. "It's delicious. And yes, to some extent."

Nix waved a hand, and the servants disappeared, flaring with light, then collapsing into the dark with sparks of gold dust, leaving Auri alone with him. The room glowed with golden candlelight, the atmosphere intimate.

"Oh. They aren't real?" She looked from where the servants had disappeared to Nix. He took a bite, and her gaze caught on his mouth—the shape of his lips—as it closed around the bite, the sensuous sort of decadence of the movement. Her heart tripped around in her chest, deciding on a faster rhythm, and she forced herself to look away, focusing on the meal and the necessity of eating.

She grabbed her goblet and took a drink. Wine. Delicious.

"As real as anything else here. You could touch them and feel them as if they were, just like eating that food will keep you alive."

Auri watched her food, expecting it to disappear or do something that looked magical, but it remained. Just a plate with food.

After a few moments, Nix said, "We should probably discuss the terms of the bargain."

Auri set down her fork and knife and dabbed her mouth with her napkin. "I would like to know why you were trapped in the key."

He cleared his throat, set down his own utensils, and leaned back in his chair. "You're the first key keeper to ask me that."

"How many have there been?"

"You're the seventh."

"And none of them were curious?"

"Not beyond the wishes." He picked up his wine glass. "What is it you want to know?"

"Why were you trapped? Did you do something to deserve it? Are you evil, Nixus, god of night and darkness?"

He glanced at her over the rim of the golden goblet as he took a sip, but the edges of his dark eyes curled up with amusement. After he swallowed—and Auri realized she'd been staring at his throat—he said, "My brother hates me." With graceful movement, he returned to eating the meal.

"That's it? Sibling rivalry? I have four siblings and though we fight, I'm not sure any one of them hates me enough to trap me in, oh, let's say, a hole they dug in the ground to then bury me alive."

Nix smiled. "That's good to know, but your experience isn't reflective of all sibling relationships, yes?"

She nodded and took a bite, waiting. When he didn't speak—but continued watching her—she lifted her eyebrows.

He smiled then, a real one, as though he might be enjoying her company. The thought flooded her with warmth. "Luc—Lucian, my brother—and I are like two sides of the same coin."

"Day and night." The realization she was talking to a god about another god was very strange, but she grounded herself by reaching out and taking another drink of her wine. It was real. The food was real. Real enough. When she looked back at Nixus, whose dark hair shone in the candlelight, she knew if she reached out to touch those strands curling over his forehead to sweep them away, they would feel as silky as they looked. She picked up her eating utensils again to keep herself from doing it.

"Yes. We go together, but like light and dark, we don't. We have competing agendas." He stopped speaking and stared into his wine glass for a beat. "Luc insists he was trying to teach me a lesson. Being trapped here hadn't been his intention. Or so he claims."

"You were trapped–"

"Are trapped."

"Are trapped in a key–"

"To a key." Nix set down his cup. "Words matter here."

"You are trapped to a key because of sibling rivalry."

"In a sense, yes."

"That must be a story." Auri smiled and picked up the wine goblet again.

He leaned back and watched her sip her wine. "It was over a woman. I was a younger god, then."

Unnerved by his gaze, Auri set the goblet down. "Are gods ever young?"

He nodded. "Of course. We are born to our parents, age to our peak, and gain experience and wisdom. Then we fade, making room for our successor—or our progeny—to take our place." He paused and took another drink.

Auri wondered if he had children, or if he ever would having been trapped so, but couldn't bring herself to ask such a question.

He sniffed a breath as if righting himself and continued, "I was inexperienced then, I suppose. I had intended to make the mortal my equal in marriage, but Luc, who had also cast his attention upon her, didn't like losing to his brother. With the help of Poe—"

"The goddess of chaos?"

He tilted his head and regarded her. "You know the Elcadia tenets?"

"Religion?"

He hummed an affirmation. "Not what I would call it, but yes, if that fits."

"I know of it, but my family aren't faithful followers."

"You don't believe?"

"I don't disbelieve." She raised her eyebrows and her glass and enjoyed that she could make him smile. "I fear the fallibility of the faithful leaves much to be desired. Makes it difficult to reconcile my own understanding with what they espouse as absolute truth."

His eyes widened, his dark brows arching over his eyes, but he didn't comment.

"My mother, on the other hand, has firmly instilled in us that any possibility of altruistic deities is a fabrication, and if they exist, they wouldn't give two shits about mortal lives."

"Your family isn't opinionated then?" He laughed into his cup.

Auri chuckled with him and took another sip of her wine. "Sorry. You were saying?"

He moved a bite around on his plate as if to recall the spot his story had shifted. "Right. Poe, the goddess of chaos, and Luc. They set a trap. Poe spun for me a story of young lovers pining for one another and to find eternal love, one of them had to free the other. It was a romantic tale, of course, and as a young god who thought himself in love, I had romantic notions. Poe convinced me that to secure my intended's affections, I needed to offer her a grand gesture."

"This does sound romantic," Auri said, the wine easing her earlier tension. She took another bite and closed her eyes, savoring the flavor.

"I'm not sure I would call this romantic," he said, his tone captious as he looked about the room.

"Perhaps not in the aftermath." She offered him the concession.

Nix studied his wine glass, his finger swirling around the scroll work of the stem. He looked up at her and caught her eyes with his. "You're a romantic, then?"

She looked away from his measured smile and shrugged, slicing her meal into smaller bites. "Not particularly. That would be my sister, Brinna. They would say I'm practical, but I don't think that precludes me from enjoying the idea of romantic love."

Nix leaned forward, listening, and she glanced at him, having caught his movement from the corner of her eye. He tilted his head, as if waiting for her to continue, his dark gaze intense.

She needed to change the subject, so she looked back at her plate. "And the rest of your story?" When he didn't answer, she glanced up.

He looked around. "As you see."

"I mean how it happened."

He picked up his wine goblet. "Poe convinced me to lure my love to free me from a room where I would await with the intention of gifting her immortality. When she unlocked the door with the key, I would declare my intentions. A romantic gesture."

"But it was a trick."

He investigated his wine goblet, nodded, then drained it. He held out the goblet and a flagon of wine appeared, floating in midair, tipped, and filled the empty cup. Then it was gone.

Auri was beginning to find these magical moments of floating flagons, disappearing servants, clothing that fit, the swirl of gold dust, normal occurrences. While it was fantastical, it was frequent here, and she was enjoying it immensely. Brinna would have loved it. "What happened?"

"Besides me being a fool and trusting my brother and cousin?" He paused and swirled his wine.

"With the woman."

Nix shrugged. "The moment I stepped inside the room, and she touched the key, we were here—well—not here exactly, but…"

"I think I understand." Auri slipped a hand into the pocket of the decadent trousers she'd worn to dinner and touched the key.

Nix shifted in his seat and glanced down, as if looking for her hand in her pocket. "The spell on the key forced me from my corporeal form and tied me in my spirit form until the spell could be broken."

She released the key. "You look very corporeal to me."

His gaze jumped up to her face. "That's because you have the key."

She removed the trinket from her pocket and held it up between them, turning it back and forth in the low light. It gleamed, creating its own light. She set it on the table and ran a finger over the blade. "What if I hadn't found the key in the glade?"

"I would still be an entity here drinking myself into a stupor, waiting for the expected visitor." His eyes watched her finger on the metal of the key.

She paused at his admission, unsure if he heard it, the sadness of it, but didn't think he'd appreciate her empathy, so she skipped saying anything about it. "And there have been six others."

His eyes rose to meet hers. "There have. But as you can see." He opened his arms as though to exemplify he was still there.

Aware of the way he moved, Auri looked at the golden key once again. "So, I can't leave the key, and you can't either, which means we are stuck with one another." She looked at him at the same time his eyes shifted from watching her hand on the key. Their gazes locked, and energy buzzed through the muscles around her spine. Her skin tingled with awareness.

She looked away, attempting to make sense of the sensations and went for another sip of wine. The tingles weren't unfamiliar. She'd had a girlhood crush on a boy, Mikael, a farmer's son. She'd been fourteen then and felt the rush of attraction before. But this was different, as if all her body was involved in the response moving through her. She glanced at the food and wondered if it were laced with something to make her feel this way?

"So, the first key keeper–"

"Yes?"

"–didn't break the spell."

"She didn't." He took a sip of his wine and set down the cup. "Are you ready to hear about the bargain?"

She sniffed the food that was on her fork but figured she was being ridiculous. Why would a god need to drug her to make her feel things? He just needed to sit there and exude his godliness. He'd made servants disappear, for goodness' sake. "Is there no way for you to escape? You are a god."

He shook his head. "It's a blood spell made by gods, which means it's unbreakable unless broken by the blood of the gods who made it, or by the fulfillment of the spell bargain."

"Which is the bargain you've mentioned?"

He nodded. "The original premise of the spell was that my love was to unlock me and free me from the room where I'd awaited her to save me."

"Okay. So?"

"You are now locked in the proverbial room. With me."

Auri looked around. "This is the room."

He grinned into his cup. "Of a sort. I can transform it. I am a god, after all, as you so aptly stated. But in some ways, I am at your mercy just as you are at mine."

"How is that?"

"You must make three wishes."

"Like I wish to go home?"

His smile was amused. "That is a wish you could make, but remember, words matter. The wish will bring you here, because this is your home until the price of the bargain is fulfilled."

"Price?"

"Every wish you make will exact a price, or an obligation."

"I don't understand," Auri said. "Like if I wish for home, it keeps me here. Isn't that the price?"

He shook his head and looked down at his wine

again. "The price is the compulsion of the spell to exact a consequence against you. Therefore, the words of your wish matter. For every wish you make, the spell will punish you for it, and usually I'm at the heart of the punishment. My thoughts. My fears. My wishes. My desires."

"That seems—"

"Twisted?" He took a drink—a deep one—and she had the impression he wasn't as collected as he wanted to appear.

She tried to imagine being here, in this place, alone and waiting for someone to arrive to make wishes. Trapped. The thought was painful. It seemed so awful. Too much.

Auri narrowed her eyes. "How do I know you're telling me the truth?"

He appeared surprised but not discomfited by her question. "You know, you are the first to ever ask me this question, but I already told you. I can't lie."

"No. But you also said words matter, so depending how you use them, there might be falsehoods embedded in them. I think you did this earlier, telling me I hadn't anything to fear here."

He offered her a short smile. "That is an astute assessment, but after a hundred years imprisoned, I have more to gain by telling the truth than by remaining trapped. And you have nothing to fear from me, not intentionally, so that wasn't a lie."

Auri leaned an elbow on the table and studied him. "A hundred years? How old are you?"

"Old enough to have known better."

She missed the easy comradery they'd shared before talking about the spell but decided it was best to get it over with. "You said there is a final price. What is it?"

"After the three wishes and the three obligations, the spell creates a final test. The test has changed from key keeper to key keeper, but it always presents an option of releasing the key and returning to the keeper's present or choosing to sacrifice to release me, thereby ending the spell."

"You mean to tell me that you've been tied to the key for all of this time, and no key keeper has ever chosen to end the spell?"

He shook his head. "Obviously."

"Is it a one-of-us-will-die kind of sacrifice? Or the kind where I just have to give up eating meat for a set period of time?"

"Does it matter?" he asked.

"Well, yes. One is infinitely worse than the other. What's the alternative?"

"Being stuck forever."

"If that's so, where are the six others?"

He sighed and then drained his cup again. "The final price isn't for you, Auri. You are the one with the power. Once the three wishes are granted and the three obligations are paid, the final sacrifice must be chosen by you. For me. Either way, the key keeper is released, or so it would seem."

"Wishes intact?" she asked.

He shrugged.

"You're avoiding the question."

He grinned, but it wasn't born of happiness, staring at the flickering candles instead of her. "I don't know for sure, but it is probably safe to assume the final sacrifice would require a loss of some kind. The wishes already made, perhaps."

Auri watched him, his jaw tense as he kept his gaze on his goblet, the level of wine rising in his cup and hers, no flagon in sight this time. He wouldn't meet her gaze.

"It was my brother's final joke," he said and emptied the contents of the wine glass, set it on the table, and finally looked at her. "In order for me to be free, the key keeper would have to choose me, for me." He stood, his look weighted with disappointment. "The first key keeper didn't. No one ever has."

Then he walked from the room.

uri remained at the dining table for a time, contemplating what Nix had said, understanding that when it came to an end, she would have a choice. It seemed a strange irony that for once in her life she was going to have the power to choose for herself. Hadn't she just been lamenting her lack of choice as a woman? And here she was, trapped—which wasn't exactly her choice—but she would have the ability to decide her fate, as well as Nix's, after three wishes.

She stood, then reached out to steady herself using the tabletop. The wine had loosened her bones. When she found her equilibrium, she followed Nix through the door where he'd disappeared and stepped into a giant sitting room.

A coffered ceiling arched high above her head, crisscrossed with wooden beams and inlaid with a mosaic tile pattern of ivory, blue, red, and gold, along with a line of chandeliers glowing with candle insets hung at equidistant intervals. A massive stone fireplace dominated the room, with an intricate marble relief carved into the over mantle. There were plush rugs stretched over the expanse of stone floor and sitting areas with coordinated upholstered furnishings and tables. The opulence at every turn surprised her, and she wondered if she would ever get used to it.

Nix stood near the fireplace, his dark head bent as he stared into the fire, looking rather broody. Enticing, if she were being completely honest with herself. The thought was as unsettling as the wine making her feel tipsy. She steadied herself with a hand on the door frame and took a deep breath.

She was curious about him as a male, though he wasn't really an accurate portrait of a male. He was a god. The men she knew, besides her father and brother, paled in comparison. Though the men of Sevens probably weren't a very fair comparison. Besides her girlhood crush, she hadn't spent much time considering maleness. It was too dangerous and disgusting, as men like Crossbie and Buteress proved. At that moment, however, she allowed herself to be curious.

Perhaps because he was so beautiful.

"So…" she said as she started across the room, hoping she was walking normally.

At her voice, he turned his head, the black jacket pulling across his back as he moved, and his gaze swept the length of her. He looked away quickly, back at the fire.

Was it strange the loss of his gaze made her shiver?

"One hundred years, truly?" she asked, while wondering how it would feel to touch him. To run her hand along his shoulders and offer him comfort. To press herself against his back and feel his strength. Then she felt silly, for how could a mere mortal comfort a god? And one who had been trapped for a lifetime, at that.

"Here. Yes. Give or take," he said but didn't offer his gaze again.

She reached the sitting area nearest the fire and used a chair to steady herself. "When I was a girl, the night stopped." She wondered now if Nix being trapped in this spell was related, though she was still wrapping her mind around the fact that there were truly gods when she'd spent a lifetime not believing in them. But the timing didn't make any sense, she realized. That would have only been ten years ago, give or take.

He glanced at her over his shoulder. "I'm regretful that you have been dragged into this, Auri."

She looked for loopholes in his words but couldn't find any. "It is a double-edge sword, I think."

His dark gaze returned to her. "How so?"

"Well, besides the obvious, there do seem to be some perks." She smiled at him, moved around the chair, and sat, relishing the fact she didn't have to fuss with a skirt as she crossed her trouser covered legs, loving the freedom of wearing them. "Let's see. I haven't ever eaten like that, and I've always had to share a bed. I also don't think I've ever felt this warm in my life." She raised her legs, and they stuck out straight in front of her. "I've never had a pair of trousers. They're against the law for women. And wine." She put her feet back on the floor. "Wow. I really like the way it makes me feel."

He huffed a laugh and turned fully toward her. "You may not like the wine upon waking." He took a sip of his drink.

"You drink."

"I'm a god. It won't affect me unless I allow it."

"Do you? Allow it?"

He tilted his head. "Why would you ask that?"

"Something you said about drinking yourself into a stupor."

He frowned at his drink, then looked up at her but didn't comment.

"If you don't have to feel the effects and choose to—well… that sounds more like punishment than forgetting."

He made a humming noise, swallowing, and his eyes slid away from her to the fire. He took another sip. "Why are you drinking?"

"I like the way makes me feel… things." Auri

gasped and covered her mouth with her hands, her eyes wide with surprise that she'd allowed herself to say it. Loose tongue! She couldn't help but smile behind her fingers, not quite embarrassed—though she might be later.

He smiled at her, seemingly amused. "Things?"

Her innards boiled with heat, but in a pleasant way. She felt bold and brave, things she was usually at war with. *There is nothing to fear here.* She had already decided that wasn't true. There were things to fear here, just perhaps not the law, which made her wonder. If given the opportunity with no threat of prison or death, might she feel emboldened to seek experiences she otherwise wouldn't?

She allowed herself to look at Nix. Allowed herself to imagine her mouth on his and said, "Like kissing." Heat spread from her chest, up her neck, across her cheeks.

"A perk?" he asked with a single eyebrow crooked over his eye.

"Maybe? I haven't done it. I don't know if it would be a perk or a punishment."

He cleared his throat and stared at his drink again. "It can be both," he stated, as if they were talking about the weather.

The warmth from her chest rushed the other direction, grabbing ahold of her lungs and making it more difficult to breathe. When she didn't respond, Nix added, "In a good way."

"I think I might like a demonstration. Perhaps you

could summon me a kissing partner." She laughed at herself.

"I can do that."

People coalesced in front of the fireplace, a golden light starting at the floor and rising in front of her to form a man and woman between her and Nix. They were a beautiful display wrapped in rich fabric that hugged their forms. Each was attractive, with proportional faces, sensuous lips, and inviting tilts of their heads, but Auri found her gaze drawn to Nix and Nix alone.

He stepped between his conjuring. "I can conjure whatever you desire." His gaze met and held hers.

"Are you able to read my mind?"

Nix walked over and sat in a matching chair opposite her. "I can't, though I'm finding the longer I know you that I wish that I could."

She didn't stay with that admission and allow it to bloom for further study, instead looking back at the people. "So you summon kissing partners?"

"It isn't as satisfying as a kiss given freely." He waved a hand, and the people disappeared, the gold dust dropping to the floor and dissipating like steam from a pot.

"I like your perspective, Auri." He took a sip of his drink, no longer wine but a snifter of something amber. "Perks." He sort of snorted the word and chuffed a laugh.

Losing her nerve and flustered by the direction of the conversation, she changed the subject. "Are there rules for the wishes I'm to make?" she asked. "Would kissing be a wish?"

He stretched out his legs, crossing them at the ankle. "I have discovered some things about the wishes. Kissing could perhaps be a wish. Have you decided on your first one?"

She shook her head and folded her hands in her lap to keep from fiddling with the fabric of the armrest. "No. I haven't. I need more information. Tell me what you have discovered."

He tilted his head and regarded her for a moment as if perplexed, then made a noise that seemed to reset his thoughts. "You can't make a wish that doesn't directly benefit you."

"So wishing my sisters didn't have to stand up in the marketplace and could instead find a love match won't do?"

He smiled. "As kind as that would be, no."

"Okay. What else?"

"I already mentioned this one, words matter. So be very thoughtful about your words."

"And the obligations?"

"The same applies. It is important to remember that the obligation is a part of the wish. I'm not in control of how those play out since they are wish dependent."

Auri sighed and turned to look at the fire, trying to work out something about the arrangement that bothered her.

"Speak, Auri. What is it?"

Her eyes returned to his face, surprised. "You read me so well already? We've only just met."

"You are rather open with your thoughts, especially after wine." He smiled, one of those that met his eyes and offered her a peek at the dimple in his cheek.

She thought of her family but then frowned, worried she might never see them again. Three wishes. Three obligations. "Why would Luc—if he wanted to punish you so—create the obligations that benefit you?"

Nix looked away from her and focused on the amber liquid in his glass. "The obligations don't benefit me, and Luc didn't design the spell. He just cast it. The spell's design perpetuates itself. Who would ever willingly offer a sacrifice to the villain of their story when the villain exacts an obligation that requires a high price paid by them?"

Auri considered wishes and obligations and wondered about the reality of what would usually be considered frivolity. She figured it was human nature to have wants. She'd wished to save her sisters from the marriage market, to save them from the likes of horrible marriages like those that might be had with Crossbie. She'd wished to be in control of her own life, but what did that mean in action? Now she was being given the opportunity to test it—but at what cost?

"You said Luc could break the spell."

"He tried."

"Perhaps he could try again," she said. "My sisters

and I fight a lot. But we always find a way to reconcile."

"If only gods were so mortal." He offered a tight smile, obviously frustrated, though whether it was by her pushing him or the circumstances, she couldn't be sure without asking. "We are filled with our own hubris and prone to very long grudges, as you can see." He paused as though trying to find the humor but couldn't. "If you don't have a wish yet, is there anything I can offer you to pass the time?"

"Besides kissing?" She smiled.

His eyes met hers, but they weren't as amused as before. Now they seemed more intense, darker. "You only need to ask, and I will provide a demonstration."

She tightened her crossed legs, feeling a strange ache between them that needed relief. She cleared her throat. "Does it count as a wish—things to pass the time?"

"No. Consider it hospitality."

She couldn't get the image of kissing out of her mind. Of kissing Nix. She could imagine the feel of the scruff on his face against her palm, the way his lips might feel against hers, but these were things she could only imagine, never having experienced it before. She needed to stop thinking about kissing. Her body was doing strange things, like struggling to draw a meaningful breath. She blinked, attempting to reset herself, and asked, "Books?"

"Books? That I can do." He stood. "Follow me."

Auri trailed him from the room through a wide unmoving hallway, climbed a set of stairs, and moved down another hallway. The maze of the manor became clearer but not unraveled. It was ever changing. Eventually, they stopped outside a set of double doors, and Nix opened them.

When she walked into the room behind him, she drew in a sharp breath. "Oh!"

She walked deeper into the room, her eyes drawn up to a recessed ceiling glowing with hidden lights, like diamonds in a night sky, and traced its length to the floor to nearly ceiling windows across the expansive room, dark with a starry night. "Oh," she repeated, unable to find additional words to express what she was experiencing.

A double staircase, the entrance of each resting on opposite sides of the room, rose to a second story, drawing together to meet at a mezzanine which wrapped around the circumference of the room. Books upon books lined both stories, from floor to ceiling, accessible with moveable ladders on castors. She walked further into the room, running her hand along free-standing shelves that lined the first floor. Statues, sculptures, lamps, and globes were placed strategically along the surface.

Auri bent to look at one of the globes but didn't recognize anything marked on the map. She looked over her shoulder at Nix but didn't need to ask the question.

"There are many worlds in the cosmos," he explained.

She turned in a circle, eyes raised in awe to the

ceiling at the heart of the giant room and thought: *this is where a deity would reside, in a room filled with knowledge.*

When she looked back at Nix, he'd moved to the seating area outfitted with a table and chairs for study, a chaise, and a beautiful rug. He stood next to the table, a hip leaning against it, watching her. Behind him, a behemoth of a fireplace stretched across the wall, as artfully detailed as every other room in the manor behind him.

She took in the room again, making her way back to Nix. Every room she'd seen so far had been incredible, but this one, for some reason, felt more personal. "Do you enjoy reading?" she asked.

He nodded. "I do. Is this enough?"

"You know it is." She was unable to control her smile, feeling it stretch across her face. "For a hundred lifetimes! I've never seen anything like it." She held out her hands as if to offer him something. "See? Perks."

His dark gaze dipped to her mouth, then he turned back to the books. "I've discovered a lot of wonderful places here. Places to dream. Places to escape. Places to go on an adventure." He walked toward the closest set of stairs and turned to her, walking backward. "What kind of book would you like?"

Auri's heart slammed around in her chest, both because of the man, this beautiful room, and the glorious possibilities. When she'd been little, a man had visited Sevens and talked about the great library of New Taras. He'd told her father that it was so large the monks wouldn't be able to read through the collection in their lifetimes, combined. This was a little how this room made her feel. Overwhelmed but excited.

In Kaloma, women weren't encouraged to learn. Women were taught to be demure and silent. They were taught to smile, look pretty, and offer service to others. They married, bore children, and worked. The most famous Kaloma saying for women was "a silent woman is a wise woman." Women weren't encouraged to learn, or express their feelings, or to act upon their desires.

But Auri wasn't raised by Kaloma. She'd been raised by Scarlett and Tomas Fareview. Her parents had taught her to read, to think. They had raised their children to approach the world with clear eyes, to dream, and to know that no matter what, they had one another. And while Sevens wasn't the bastion of learning, her parents had taught her to use her voice and to know her mind.

You have nothing to fear here Nix had said, so she reached for bravery and smiled when she said, "A romance."

He turned his head as he started up the stairs, glancing at her over his shoulder, this time with an amused look that Auri realized she liked. His eyes softened around the edges, and his lips quirked upward a touch. "Not a romantic, huh? There's a whole section of romances."

Auri followed him across the second-floor platform, stopping just a moment to stare through the windows that ran parallel at the top of the stairs. The night sky was brilliant with unfamiliar constellations. As she walked past the bookshelves, she ran her fingers along the spines of the books, imagining what it would be like to read them all. Sevens didn't have a library, and books were a luxury. She had exactly four books at home, gifts from her parents over the years, and she'd reread them dozens of times. She'd read old news bulletins, advertisements, and anything else she'd been able to find with printed words.

When she finally caught up with Nix, he was waiting, leaning against the railing. She leaned over and looked at the first floor below, still in awe of this space. "You've brought me to my favorite room, so far." She straightened and shared a companionable smile, feeling comfortable with him for the first time, as if this room allowed her to see into his soul. "It feels like a gift."

He was smiling, as if the idea brought him pleasure, but just as quickly, it dropped off his face. "You must be tired," he said, straightening.

Disheartened by his mercurial mood, she said, "Yes. I guess it has been a stressful day. I am feeling tired now that you mention it."

"Reading can provide relief, among other things," he said, then stopped and indicated a wide array of books.

Auri wasn't exactly sure what he meant.

"Why don't you choose a book, then I'll escort you back to your quarters."

She nodded and looked around. There were so many books. Colorful spines with gilt titles, none of which she knew. "I don't know where to begin," she admitted.

"I could select one for you?"

She drew her folded hands to her heart. "Yes. Please."

Nix held up his hand, and a book appeared. The green cover was plain, and etched silver writing indicated the title. He offered it to her. "Since you're interested in kissing." He grinned, but the look in his eye was mischievous. "I liked this one."

"You've read it?"

"I have. A few times."

She took it, her fingers brushing his as she did, and read the title aloud. "The Romance of Lady Miriam." She glanced at Nix. "What did you choose for me?"

He offered his elbow. "A devilishly decadent book that might teach you about more than kissing." His grin deepened. "Maybe even offer a few grand gestures for someone who may or may not be a romantic."

Auri slipped her arm around his offered one, linking them. "More than kissing?" Heat moved through the fabric, dancing across her skin, and the place where her arm brushed against Nix's lit up with sparks of energy.

Without leaving their place on the second floor of the library, the room dissolved into a hallway. Nix walked her through it at an unhurried pace. "I think a lot can be learned between the covers of a book." He gave her a sidelong glance.

She thought about all the ways she'd read. Her

books, the papers, her father's almanac. "Yes. That is very true."

The walk through the manor's maze seemed extended with many twists and turns. They walked up stairs, down other sets, and around stone turret bends single file. There were doors upon doors, and though Auri had the impression that Nix could think them into the room, and she would be there, still they ambled arm in arm through the many hallways.

"What has it been like?" she asked him as they descended a wide staircase toward a hallway of paintings. Once they walked through, it was gallery of portraits.

"What has what been like?"

She stopped and looked at a portrait of an overweight man. He wore a golden crown on his head and held a golden goblet. A bowl of grapes rested near his elbow. "Being here."

He tensed. "This is my Uncle Revel."

"He looked like he enjoyed drinking."

He chuckled. "That he does. I don't think he allows himself to feel the effect."

"I might have guessed as much."

They continued through the room, stopping to talk about the family he'd displayed, all of them with funny stories.

"You didn't answer my question," Auri said as they walked through a doorway into another hallway.

"I would rather not ruin the moment."

She made a humming sound, but the answer told

her enough. She could imagine all the ways being here, despite the opulence, decadence, and beauty, wouldn't change the fact that he had been alone but for the company of conjurings, who seemed to offer no more than what was created for them, or key keepers, who'd left him alone.

When they stopped in front of a door, which she assumed was finally her room, Nix turned to her. "Thank you for a lovely evening, Auri Fareview." He lifted her hand to his lips and pressed a kiss to her skin.

Tingles wound their way up her arm, effervesced near her shoulder, and compelled her to step toward him, but Auri held her ground, unwilling to drop her guard with him completely.

He released her hand and stepped away. "It has been immensely pleasurable."

"Thank you. For the book." She waved it back and forth. "And the tour. And the dinner."

He smiled, his eyes caught on the book. Then his gaze returned to her face. "Remember, if you need anything, all you need to do is call my name. I'll be there." He dipped his head. "Good night."

Auri watched him disappear, the hallway dropping away with gold dust to reveal she was standing alone inside her bedroom without having had to move at all.

Nixus

Nixus Uraiahs didn't believe he was prone to whimsy. But as he leaned against the door of his bedroom, that's exactly what he knew the seventh key keeper had awakened in him. He didn't like it. Or need it. Or want it.

"Fuck," he said aloud as he pushed away from the door, tugged the jacket off his shoulders, and stalked across the room.

Unsettled. That was the best way to describe what he was feeling, he decided. The seventh key keeper had him unsettled.

He stopped in front of the fireplace in his

chambers and flung the jacket over a chair, then yanked at the shirt, pulling it from the waist of his black trousers. He plucked at the pearl buttons of his shirt, first the wrists, then at his neck, picturing Auri the moment she walked into the dining room.

His stomach clenched recalling it. She'd been dressed in wide, dark-as-night trousers and an ivory linen shirt tucked into the waistband that billowed around her torso and showcased her slim waist. In the right light, he'd seen the hint of her body's silhouette. She'd braided her brown hair; the thick plait had draped over her shoulder, the end resting on her breast, right where he imagined her nipple would be. Her smile had been easy even if her eyes still expressed skepticism, bordering on wonder, and her cheeks had warmed to a gentle rosy glow. He'd noticed a smattering of freckles across her cheeks, just a few, and found himself counting them. Seventeen.

When she'd walked through the door, he'd stood, surprised, and there wasn't a lot that surprised him. Of all the choices he knew to be in that wardrobe, she'd chosen something understated. She could have chosen a revealing dress to seduce, or perhaps a gown speckled with gems to demonstrate her love of wealth and entice with her beauty. Her choice of clothing and manner of presenting herself told him a story. Auri Fareview was comfortable in her own skin. She was practical. She was candid and approachable.

She was different.

A pulse of warmth had started then, right in the

center of his chest. And the longer they'd spoken, the more questions she'd asked—questions no key keeper had ever asked—the more intense the heat had become, pinching his heart and making him uncomfortable.

Then, despite having all the facts about the bargain, she hadn't made her first wish. They all made a wish the first day. Always. And it was always about their immediate needs in their current lives. Often, a wish about wealth. Like he'd thought hers would be. But she'd said, "I need more information."

Then her questions. Her observations. Those intuitive sharp points shot at him like arrows and hit him right in the center of his chest where he was already smarting. Why did he allow himself to feel the pain? Had he considered it before? No. How did he feel being alone? Who'd ever cared about his feelings? And the kicker: the library—his favorite room he'd conjured in the manor—being a gift.

Fuck.

Nix groaned and yanked his shirt from his arms, tossing it on the jacket. He knew he was wasting movement, but like allowing himself to feel hungover, it was satisfying to jerk it from his body. The movement expressed his annoyance at the way he responded to the key keeper. All these years, all the key keepers, with the first one being the exception, he'd kept his head.

Yes, Auri not making a wish had him unsettled. But the way she'd looked, the way she moved, walking across any room, her talk about kissing, that little smile accompanied by the blush, her questions and statements that flipped him upside down, those things had him frustrated. That realization seemed ridiculous. He could summon a conjuring to kiss, a conjuring to fuck, a conjuring to fulfill his every desire, except that wasn't satisfying. It hadn't been for a very long time.

He stopped moving, his hands on his hips and head tipped forward, chin to his chest, then took a deep breath.

He was frustrated and unsettled. Both.

Feeling this frustrated about a woman he'd just met seemed ludicrous, but it would be a lie to say he wasn't attracted to her. The more time he spent in her company, the more attracted he felt, and that was worrisome. The spell would use it against him.

Magic—the spell—didn't have its own consciousness. It was a set of words imbued with power that created the enchantment, but it fed from him as the wish granter. That was clear when he'd faced the first obligations with the first key keeper. Each of her wishes forced a consequence, at which he was at the heart. In the end, after her final wish, she'd achieved her desires, loathed him, and left.

The attraction to Auri couldn't be nurtured. She would make her wishes, and she too would leave. Hope was fragile, easily broken, and his hope had been smashed and drained of its substance long ago.

When the second key keeper had appeared, Nix had been determined to try and get out. He'd thought that if he could be accommodating, ingratiate himself as a friend with the key keeper—Penrowe had been his name—that forged bond might prove stronger. It hadn't. Penrowe had taken his wishes and left.

When the third key keeper had arrived—Ama—Nix had tried harder. This time he was compassionate and alluring, sweet and helpful. But the wishes were the same, the obligations painful, and he was always at the heart of that pain. Ama left him the same as the first two, and Nix understood there was nothing he could do to change the outcome of the spell. He would always be the villain.

Auri might be the seventh key keeper, and his heart might have been trying to tell him she was different, but the spell wasn't. As unique as she was, Nix couldn't let himself think that the outcome would change. It wouldn't, and he didn't want to cultivate any personal emotions that would offer the spell fodder to use to hurt either of them.

The next morning, Nix avoided her, which might have been cowardly, but the avoidance also seemed to be self-preservation for him, and in the long-term, for her too, he reasoned. He took breakfast in the yellow room but led her to the dining room for her own repast. As he sipped his coffee, he pictured Auri, brown hair spread out like moonbeams on a pillow, her body arched toward him, mouth open in ecstasy as he moved between her legs.

He set his coffee cup in the saucer with enough force the liquid sloshed over the lip of the cup.

He'd dreamt about her.

He couldn't remember ever having dreamt about a specific woman but considering the attraction he felt to her the night before, maybe it wasn't surprising. She was gorgeous, but it wasn't only that. There was the huskiness of her laugh that twisted his insides into knots, and a brightness in her smile that lit her eyes. Her curiosity and intelligence had his mind pinging with interest about how her thoughts moved. The way the library had made her defenses crumble. The way she talked of kissing, then immediately blushed intrigued him and made his body tight with anticipation.

After he'd eaten, he locked himself in the conjured office. He'd considered the library but wondered if she'd go there and refused to look and see. Instead, he conjured the boxing ring and a sparring partner. After time spent expending energy there, he returned to the office and tried reading, but his mind meandered from the book back to thoughts about her. He tried resetting his thoughts only to have them slip back to memories, curious wonderings, and the dream, back and forth until he slammed the book shut.

"Fuck."

He needed just a dose. As if he were potion addled. A single dose would satisfy his need. A moment couldn't hurt, and perhaps, he justified, she had her first wish. If he wanted her to get to wishing, then he needed to be around to grant them. Yes. It made sense in his mind, so he closed his eyes, seeking her with his senses, unable to contain the buzz of current that slipped through his body at the thought of just a moment with her.

He opened his eyes.

Auri was lounging in a chair in the room where they'd sat the night before talking about kissing. Rather than sitting properly, her legs were draped over an arm of the chair, one of which swung back and forth, a gentle rhythm of contentment. Her back was to the door. She was twisting a lock of her hair around her finger. He could see the edge of the book he'd given her in her lap, and though he couldn't see her face, he imagined she was smiling, not widely, but just enough it softened her features.

The fire fluttered in the fireplace beyond her, warming the room. The windows were dark. He gentled their starkness to a morning twilight, conjuring the Elcadian countryside. If he were to peer out the window, it would be a vista where grapes grew over trellises in rows on terraces cut into the hillside, and the mountains would rise in the distance like sentries guarding a treasure.

She noticed the change in light and looked up from her book.

"Hello," Nix said.

She jumped from her chair and spun, the book falling to the floor with a thud. A blush raced across her cheeks. She bent and scooped up the book, drawing it tightly against her chest. "Hello." She couldn't quite meet his gaze, but tried, then smoothed the front of her jade-colored dress. It wasn't fancy, just a normal, everyday sort of cotton dress with buttons from neckline to waist and a full skirt. The neck scooped, revealing the sharpness of her collarbone, and offering a lovely glimpse of her neck—tinted with her blush—but the rest he had to imagine.

And he did. She was tall and lithe, though more from necessity of the difficult life she'd hinted at, but her shape inspired his imagination as the fabric addressed her curves.

Nix smiled, recalling what she was probably reading, and wondered where in the story she might be. Miss Miriam's romantic adventures were quite an education. "Enjoying the story?"

She nodded, and the tint of the blush deepened. She drew the book away from her body and looked down at it. "I think perhaps you chose a book with far more than kissing."

He laughed, really laughed, delighted she wasn't coy or evasive, saying exactly what was on her mind. "I told you that last night."

She nodded with wide, sparkling silver eyes. "A real education." She grinned, waving the book, and he noticed she had a dimple in her left cheek, a fingertip from the corner of her mouth.

"I found myself needing to move and wondered if you might join me," he asked and felt immediately ridiculous. *Needing to move?* He'd already boxed that morning. *Needing to move, indeed.*

She set the book in the chair. "Yes! I was thinking

this morning how I'm never idle at home. It has been a treat, but I was beginning to feel a bit restless. Your timing is impeccable. Though I have a feeling it probably always is."

"A wish?" he asked, reminding himself he had a job to do—that wasn't standing there ogling her. But he watched her anyway, noticing her smile and that dimple, and impulsively thought about rubbing his thumb over that cute divot. His heart did an acrobatic move, and he resisted the impulse, embarrassed by it. What was wrong with him?

She shook her head. "No. I don't want to be frivolous with such an important endeavor."

For some reason, that brought him relief and he was able to take a deep breath, which made little sense. He needed the opposite. He offered her his arm, anyway, if only to be able to touch her. Just for a moment. "I could conjure you some work. What would you like to do?"

"A garden?"

He hummed, liking the image of her bent over in the dirt, and cleared his throat. "Why a garden?"

"I love being outdoors."

"I'm doubly sorry then."

She drew him closer with a squeeze of her arm. "No. I said it only because it's a truth. My mother is a healer of sorts. We spend an inordinate amount of time growing, harvesting, mixing, and brewing for her."

"A garden it is then."

The sitting room melted around them, revealing

the endless hallway lined with many doors in both directions.

He watched her glance over his shoulder in one direction, then turn and look in the other direction. "Oh my. This is daunting."

"I know exactly where we'll go. What kind of garden?" he asked.

"Flowers?"

The hallway rushed past them.

"I thought you wanted to move?" She grinned at him.

He liked that smile. He liked that little dimple, his eyes drawn to it. He licked his lower lip and scolded himself to keep himself together. *Just a moment with her. You checked on the wish.* He decided to take her to the garden and leave. It was the right thing to do.

"You're right. I did say that. But I think we'd rather walk in a garden than through the hallway." *No, fool!* It was an equivocation. He could have just opened any door. The hallway slowed to a stop. He hadn't needed to go through with all the hallway theatrics, but it had allowed him to look at her rather than walk. "How about you unlock it," he suggested. She didn't really need to, but for some reason, he wanted to please her, and somehow knew she enjoyed feeling useful.

He was right, because she smiled, and withdrew the key from her pocket.

He sensed the heat of her skin as she touched it, a strange sensation. His heart leapt in his chest, sputtering to life and warming. He swallowed as she inserted the key into the door, twisted the knob, and opened it.

Inside, he conjured his mother's rose garden at their country manor in the countryside of Elcadia at twilight. A dark green hedge maze dominated the core of the garden, at the center of which was a fountain. Pathways meandered around the fountain, with lit torches and trellises darkened with overgrown ivy and other creeping plants, some flowering with buds of white and pink. Rose bushes of every kind lined the walkway. Fireflies fluttered, blinking lights in the dim blue of the coming night.

"Oh!" she breathed.

He blinked, his dream surfacing in his mind. Her gasping for breath as he entered her.

She stepped into the mindscape he'd created. "It's so beautiful." She let go of his arm and walked into space.

He hated that he missed her touch but was glad for it, since his mind was misbehaving.

She took a deep breath and sighed.

He saw her sigh beneath him, her eyes closed, her lips plump and wet from his kiss, the way her skin glistened with the firelight of his mind.

"It smells so fragrant."

The taste and fragrance of her skin, imagined in his mind... Nix shook his head to clear it of the dream, his heart beating frantically, afraid the rest of his body might reveal the direction of his thoughts. He cleared his throat.

She turned to look at him over her shoulder. She looked so beautiful, the hint of a smile on her lips and her eyes sparkling with joy. "Are we really outside?"

Nix shook his head and turned to look at something else. "It's a conjuring. Like everything else." He wondered what he was doing. This had been a terrible idea, even as pleasant as it was being around her was.

"It's perfection," she said, turning in a circle, looking as if she belonged to the garden.

Nix considered conjuring a marble sculpture to replicate her, her head tilted up, her hands clasped in front of her. He'd put it somewhere inside the maze so he could remember— He stopped the thought, his throat growing tight.

She turned back to him. "You aren't ever able to go outside?"

He shook his head and followed her into the garden he'd created, going against his better judgement.

She waited for him, and when he reached her side, she started down one of the walkways. Her brows bunched together with whatever she was thinking, and he didn't have to wait for her question. "But what about when I found the key in the woods?"

"The moment you touched the key, you were inside the spell with me."

Their arms brushed as they walked, and fire raced across Nix's skin. She grasped her hands in front of her, and he stopped to smell a pink rose to provide himself some space while contemplating the pleasant tingle. Just a single touch, and he was struggling to catch his breath.

"I thought–" She paused and seemed to decide to change the direction of her own thoughts. "This seems so real."

"It is. As far as the spell goes." He reached out to touch the petals of the rose and thought of what her skin might feel like under his fingertips.

She leaned forward near him, dropped her nose into a fluffy pink queen's rose, and inhaled. "I love roses."

"Even the thorns?"

She grinned. "Even the thorns."

"And why is that?"

"If you think about it," she said, her face drawn into serious contemplation, "the thorns are for self-preservation. Protection. And I understand that, I think. They make me think of my older sister, Tarley, when I consider roses. She is beautiful, but definitely prickly." She smiled then, glancing at Nixus.

"She's got thorns?" Nix thought of his older sister, Lexa, but then dismissed the thought with a frown. He didn't think of them. Ever. And here he was, a few moments with this woman, and he was conjuring his mother's rose garden and thinking about his sister. What was he doing?

Auri smiled. "Lots of them."

"You love your family?"

"Fervently." She started walking again.

He knew he shouldn't but asked anyway, "Would you tell me about them?" He followed her, a few steps behind.

"What would you like to know?"

Everything, he thought, but didn't give it the substance of his voice. "Your parents?"

"Scarlett and Tomas Fareview."

"They must be amazing."

"Why would you say that."

Flustered, Nix turned to smell a flower. "Well…" He stretched the sound, trying to find a reason that didn't start with *because you're amazing*, which would sound like a lie, and ended up saying, "You are unique."

She grinned. "Unique. I like it. Yes. They are amazing. They met, fell in love, and settled in Sevens. That's the village where we live."

"You smile when you talk about them."

"Well, they are… my life," she said and continued walking. "I have three older sisters. Jessamine is the oldest, then Tarley and Brinna." She looked over her shoulder at him and smiled. It was a different kind of smile, unguarded. He could see it was because she was talking about her family. "Then me. And I have one brother, Mattias. He's the youngest."

"And how old is Mattias as the youngest?"

"Eighteen."

He considered the state of her skirt and boots when he'd met her. "And you all live together in Sevens?"

She nodded.

"How old is your oldest sister?"

"Jessamine? Twenty-seven."

"And no one has left?" Nix thought this strange.

She shook her head and continued walking. "It isn't because we are opposed to the idea, but with respect to marriage, none of us want anything less than what our parents have. Our parents adore one another. The other factor is that living in Sevens—and my parents' refusal to leave it—has made it difficult to meet anyone and to make a living to find the means to leave." She stopped under an archway where peach roses grew over to the other side, reaching out to touch one.

Nixus noticed a red ribbon tied around her wrist. It would have seemed an insignificant trifle, except it was wrapped with a swirl of golden magic. "What is this?" He reached out and touched the ribbon with a finger. The magic kissed his skin with a warm caress. Positive magic as opposed to the alternative, which heightened Nix's curiosity.

Auri looked surprised by his touch, her eyes jumping from where he'd touched her to his face. That blush he liked worked its own magic against her skin, and she grabbed ahold of her wrist. "This? A gift from my mother. Just a ribbon. She gave each of us one." She paused, then added, "We don't have a lot of extra, not with seven of us. It's just a ribbon–"

"It appears to be more than that–"

She tilted her head, and her brows bunched. "What do you mean?"

Nix could tell she didn't know it was spelled, and just by looking at it, he couldn't tell what it was for. As far as he knew, Auri's mother had taken it to a local witch who'd cast a protection spell for each of her children. He didn't remark on the magic and instead said, "It's obviously very important to you. That makes it a very special ribbon."

She smiled, looking away, and twisted the ribbon around her wrist. "Yes. You're right." She started back down the path.

"If living in Sevens is difficult, why have your parents not left?"

She stopped and took a quick breath, as if she'd never once considered the question or that it was an option to leave. Her eyes bounced from a rose to his. "I don't–" Her brow knitted together. "That's a good question," she admitted. "Means, I suppose."

He could see the question discomfited her and felt a slide of satisfaction at affecting her like she did him.

"What about your family?"

"That would take an eternity to explain."

"We seem to have that here."

"My parents are Ur and Aiah."

"And they are gods, too?"

He nodded as she flipped things back on him. "The cosmos and the seasons." He didn't like contemplating his family or the reality that he would never see them again.

She grinned, glancing over her shoulder at him. "Oh. Is that all?"

He laughed and realized he was having fun. But when she continued down the path, his smile faded. He was having fun, enjoying her, anticipating the rush of adrenaline of attraction, and that was why he'd stayed away to begin with. His heart picked up anxious speed, knowing that this camaraderie would end as soon as she made her first wish and had to face that first obligation.

She stopped at the opening in the hedge. "Is this a maze?"

Rather than answer, because he could see she was about to suggest they explore it, he took a step back.

"Is it like the maze you've made in the manor?" Even though he couldn't see her face, he could hear she was smiling by her tone.

He watched her step into the entrance. Longing to follow, he knew he couldn't. "This garden will do then?"

Auri stopped and turned. Nix could see her confusion at his change, but she nodded. "It doesn't need any work."

"I'll add some weeds for you," he said with a short grin and took another step away. Minor weeds sprouted along the flower bed for her to attend. "There are gloves and tools in a chest at the end of the pathway."

"Is something wrong?" she asked, turning toward him and stepping from the maze to follow.

He shook his head. A lie of omission, and he'd told her he wouldn't lie, so he added, "I just have a lot on my mind." Truth.

"You're leaving?"

"The garden. Yes. I can't leave the spell."

"But–"

Nix's heart raced with a mixture of trepidation and longing. He wanted to stay with her. He wanted to continue through this rose garden with her, learning more about her, but the more he learned the more he liked her. The more she shared, the more aware he became of his own interest. The spell would ruin it, ruin him. Getting to know Auri was a terrible idea. He could feel the danger in it, not only to her, but to himself. It had been a lie to think he could spend just a moment with her.

"There's a rose carved on the door," he told her, conjuring an engraving as he said it. He continued walking backward, away from her. "You can always find this room because of the rose on the door."

She stopped following him and folded her hands in front of her. Her eyes were steady on his retreating form, but before he turned to leave her, she said, "Stay."

He stopped, his breath catching. She knew he was running. Still, he said, "I can't."

"That's a lie."

"I won't."

She didn't move, didn't plead with him, didn't react in any way, as if she knew that is what he would say. But he sensed her hurt. Unfortunately, he alone knew why he needed to stay true to maintaining distance between them. This was too easy, and this would only bring them both pain.

So, as difficult as it was, Nix turned and walked away. He didn't look back.

As Auri buttoned her shirt several days later, she decided confusion was the first emotion she felt at Nix's hasty departure from the rose garden. That confusion hadn't abated. She hadn't been able to get the moment from her mind because of the stark contrast between their time together and Nix's shift. They'd been having a lovely time, or so she'd thought. They'd been talking with one another, and she'd gotten a slight glimpse at who Nix was beyond the spell. She hadn't understood why he'd suddenly rushed away. Her logical response was to ignore the confusion and accept it for what it was.

She reminded herself Nixus was a god, and a dark one at that. Any feelings she might develop were misguided and foolish. She didn't need to ponder emotions that weren't necessary to get her out of this predicament. It was making the wishes that would accomplish that, but she couldn't settle on any.

Auri smoothed the front of the shirt, the front of the trousers, and twisted to look at herself in the mirror. She could wish for beauty, she thought, but she didn't think she wasn't beautiful. She was content with how she looked, leaning forward a touch to study her reflection. She pressed her lips together and imagined Nix's, then blinked, sighing.

She considered wishing for wealth. It was the most immediate way to impact her situation of impending marriage suitors. And yet, something about it didn't feel quite right. There was something missing in that wish she needed to identify but hadn't yet.

Beyond that, wishes felt frivolous and selfish. Even wishing for wealth with its possibility to impact her family felt absurd. She was sure that she needed to approach wish making with wisdom, examining the want from all angles, especially considering the price she would have to pay for making it, but in the immediacy of being trapped there, of being around Nixus, Auri found she was struggling to think straight.

She straightened and sighed again at her reflection.

The second and more pressing emotion moving through her like a raging river was attraction. She did wonder if Nix thought she was attractive, sensing he did. He'd been isolated long enough to be attracted to anyone, but his conjurings were beautiful and real enough.

Initially, she'd blamed her curiosity and attraction to Nix on the book he'd given her. Lady Miriam's exploits in kissing made the skin of her chest hot, and the sensitive place between her legs ache. During her reading the night before, Lady Miriam and Sir Roderick, after much fussing after one another and kissing, had finally coupled. Auri's cheeks heated as she recalled the passage. She found herself imagining being with Nix when Lady Miriam was with Sir Rodrick in the story. Later in the book, after they'd discovered their love, Roderick had perished in battle, which made Auri cry.

Whether Nix had intentionally chosen Lady Miriam's story so she might replace the characters with her and Nix was a mystery, but she found she couldn't help it. Given her experiences beyond the spell, who else would she imagine? Crossbie? The thought made her shudder. The truth was, she'd been curious and attracted to Nix before he'd ever given her the book.

She ran her hands over her body, bringing them to rest over her breasts, feeling the swell of her own flesh, the tightening of her nipples through the shirt. She wondered what it would feel like to—but stopped the thought and sighed, dropping her hands to her sides, instead glancing around the room for the book. It rested on the nightstand next to the bed.

She sat, picked it up, and flipped it open to the next chapter, which she knew after skimming ahead was Lady Miriam meeting a new love. She closed the book and put it back on the nightstand. She didn't want to read. She knew—because her thoughts were so chaotic—she would spend time reading and rereading the same pages as her thoughts jumped to Nix.

After he'd left the garden, Auri had stayed and found the chest Nix had mentioned. She spent time in the rose garden that day and the next. Each day, Nixus appeared for dinner with her. He was polite and congenial, albeit reserved and distant. Each evening as he escorted her from dinner to her room, he would ask if she had her first wish, and she explained that she was still considering her options. He would nod, politely kiss the back of her hand, and take his leave.

And now, she stood in her room understanding the depressing monotony of what stretched ahead of her. Nix's distance made it more acute, which made her think of him, and what he'd lived through trapped inside this spell. She felt listless and empty.

She stood but found she didn't have it in her to go to the garden today. She didn't want to work in the flowers where her mind would wander to Nix and the short time they'd spent there together. She knew her thoughts would gather around him, and her curiosity to know more, regardless of what she was doing.

Auri stepped out of the room anyway, into that

infinitely long hallway that stretched endlessly in each direction, turned, and began walking. The first door she came to belonged to the library. She shut it, wanting more than the respite of the quiet space it provided, and moved on. The next door, marked with a rose etched in the wood, was the door to the garden. She sighed and continued walking, realizing how lonely she felt.

Alone wasn't terrible, but she was discovering lonely was. She remembered longing for time alone among her family. With seven of them in that tiny cottage, alone was a luxury. It was why she enjoyed foraging in the woods or weeding the garden in the Whitling Woods' short summer.

There was also joy in the companionship she shared with them. With her mother, who taught them the healing arts and bolstered their confidence in themselves with her love. With her father, who taught them how to use their bodies to defend themselves, how to wield an ax, and how to whittle even when they were terrible at it. Both her parents offered love, acceptance, joy, and advice. Her siblings, the same, all the while with teasing affection. She missed them.

While she didn't mind being alone here, she was beginning to understand how much she enjoyed Nix's companionship. His smile. The way he teased out her stories during dinner, or when he'd laugh at something she'd said, and she felt accomplished that she'd been able to offer him that slight enjoyment. When he'd share a sliver of his own memories beyond the spell, or that moment when he bent over her hand, his hand holding hers, the friction of his skin against hers, her heart would pitch to the side and her breath would hitch with the anticipation he might kiss her just a moment before he disappeared.

But he hadn't.

When he'd left her in the garden, she'd understood, on some level, he had thorns like Tarley. He'd spent a lifetime alone. Auri had been alone for a fraction of that time and felt listless with it, the need to fill that emptiness with something… new. He used his thorns to protect him from something, and she guessed it was his own need for companionship. If every key keeper left him, why would he ever want to get close?

She stopped walking, deciding that she didn't care if Nix had thorns. She was willing to face them if it would allow him the opportunity for companionship. And she needed him too, otherwise she wasn't going to be able to face this endeavor.

What had he told her that first night? *If you need anything, all you need to do is call my name. I'll be there.*

She didn't really need anything, but she wanted something. She wanted to ease the loneliness that was pressing in on her heart, to ease his loneliness. Testing his promise, she said out loud, "Nix?"

"Auri?"

She twirled in place to Nix standing an arm's length away. The candle sconces on the walls cast flickering light over his face. Her breath caught. Though she had spent time with him at dinner the night before, it felt an eternity since she'd seen him.

Her insides tilted and spun at the sight of him. He wasn't overly dressed, just those black pants that fit him perfectly and a black shirt not completely buttoned. His dark hair was damp, curling at the ends, in a way that made her want to reach out and feel the curl between her fingertips. His dark eyes squinted with concern. She noted the hollow at the base of his throat and how he swallowed, as if he were nervous somehow.

Her insides floated upward and made her smile, happiness unlike any she'd ever known in the whole of her life hitting her like a freak winter storm, and even if she was in a magical spell with a trapped god, the blizzard of feeling couldn't be contained.

It didn't matter anymore that she'd coaxed herself to understand feelings were foolish here. She couldn't deny them anymore.

"Are you alright?" he asked.

Auri attempted to stamp down the elation she felt. "Yes. I'm–" she cleared her throat of giddiness– "I was wondering if there might be something to do today? Together?" A vision of Lady Miriam and Sir Roderick surfaced in her mind, only it was her and Nix, his body pressed to hers. She blinked, clearing it away.

Nix swallowed again. His eyes widening with—she didn't recognize the look, but maybe it was hesitation.

"Unless you don't want to?"

He shook his head. "No. I would love nothing more," he said and lowered his eyes.

She had spent enough time with him to recognize that he wasn't being completely forthcoming. "You're not being honest," she said, unwilling to hide her assumption. Being stuck in a spell was hard enough as it was.

He looked up and took a step toward her. "I am." But he left something unsaid.

She narrowed her eyes and took a step toward him, the hallway constricting, shrinking around them, boxing them in. "But–"

He shook his head, and his eyes flicked down to her mouth, then retreated to her eyes.

Auri's heart turned in her chest like a fall leaf hanging onto a branch in a breeze. Was Nix thinking about kissing her? She looked at his lips, contemplating them, then met his eyes once again. "I didn't want to go to the garden or to the library today. I wanted something–" Her words died when she noticed his tongue wet his lips. Her breath became that swift river moving through her chest. "Different," she finally finished.

He hummed, and she noted that he stood so close that she could almost feel the reverberation of the sound in her own body. "Different," he repeated, the shape of his eyes changing as if he weren't exactly there, and he muttered something she couldn't discern.

"Excuse me? Butterflies?" she asked.

He shook his head and stepped away from her. "Butterflies?" He took a quick breath and ran a hand through his hair. It flopped back into place. "Right. I can do that."

The hallway dripped away, and they stood amidst a forest of tall and stocky trees, their trunks slick and leafy tops wide and expansive. In the flashes of blue light created by floating insects, she saw vines hanging from the branches. Though it was dark where they stood, those flashes of light, like stars, pulsed in the space illuminating thousands of butterflies fluttering around them.

Auri twirled. "Oh, Nix," she said, awed. "It's beautiful."

"Yes."

She glanced at him, but he was staring at her, and she felt her skin tighten with awareness and heat. As she turned and walked through the space, the flutter of butterfly wings like soft kisses against the skin of her face, she noticed it was impossibly warm. She unbuttoned a button on her shirt and pulled the fabric out, away from her skin, seeking relief.

"Is this different enough?" he asked, drawing her attention back to him.

Auri pulled the shirt back and forth so it fluttered like butterfly wings and could see Nix's eyes following her movement. "Yes. A bit hot, but yes."

Nix looked up as the first raindrop hit, followed by another, until the rain drummed the canopy above them. Water dripped through the leaves, then cascaded around them when the load became too heavy to carry. Auri watched the butterflies nestle in against the tree trunks and branches, folding their wings.

When the pulsing light disappeared, she looked for Nix in the shadows and found him a few paces away. Under the umbrella of the forest as the storm raged above them, there was a different kind of storm raging inside of her. He was soaked with water, as was she. It was just the two of them. A woman. A man. Her heart thrummed an enticing beat she wanted to dance to but wasn't exactly sure how.

"Cooler?"

"No." She moved toward him, suddenly needing to feel him, the concreteness of him. She might be drifting away into the fantasy of whatever was happening and burning up with it. When she reached him, she stopped herself from reaching out, nervous and unsure. "I felt lonely," she admitted, using words instead of actions, tilting her head up to meet his gaze.

Water dripped through his hair, ran over his skin, and he nodded, his dark eyes sparkling with golden light.

She shivered, not from the cold, but from his proximity, the effulgence of his gaze.

The forest effervesced around them until they were standing in a room that smelled of something clean and pleasant but earthy. The light was limited to burning candles placed sporadically through dark space. She could still hear water, as if still standing in the rainstorm, but she couldn't feel it. The cavernous room was stuffy with warmth.

Nix stood near her, close enough that if she reached out, she could grab ahold of him, but he stepped back and nearly disappeared in the dim light of the room.

"What is this?" She glanced around the cavern, though it wasn't a cave. Ornate white tiles were laid across the floor and up the walls to a dark rock ceiling, dripping with minerals. Like her bathing room, deep recesses in the floor were filled with steaming water.

"To warm you," he said and began to unbutton his shirt. "In Elcadia, bath houses are everywhere. My family's estate has one."

"What are you doing?"

"I'm getting in." He turned away and pulled the soaked shirt from his body.

The sight was mesmerizing. The magnificence of his form. Taut, the sinew that stretched from shoulder to waist rippled with power. Her eyes caught on one of his shoulders, the slope of it rounding over his arm. Her gaze followed the planes of his shoulder blade, the line of his spine, the curve of muscles arching over his hips. Feeling guilty, she twisted away to avert her eyes.

"You can join me in the water," he said. There was a slide of fabric, and she was certain he'd removed his pants.

Removing her clothing and getting into the water with him was such a bold thing to do. Auri took a deep breath. She'd never been bold or brave, not when it counted. She may have grown up around the Grimz River and knew how to swim, but she'd never gone into the water with a man before. And without clothes.

She reminded herself she wasn't in Kaloma. She

wasn't within the confines of the Marriage Laws, she was in the confines of an enchantment, trapped with Nix where the rules were dictated by the spell and the fantasy perpetuated by Nix's conjurings.

"You have nothing to fear from me, Auri," Nixus said from behind her, as if reading her thoughts.

She unbuttoned a button, followed by another and another until she was drawing the shirt from the waist of her trousers. She heard the water slosh behind her and imagined Nix getting into one of the pools. Shrugging out of her drenched shirt, she glanced over her shoulder at Nix, who was in the largest pool up to his waist, his back still to her. She hurriedly removed the rest of her clothing, feeling simultaneously weighted with fear and buoyant with euphoric delight.

"You know how to swim?" Nix asked.

She glanced at him, his back still to her. He'd sunk lower in the pool. "Yes. I do. Don't look," she said and turned toward him, naked as the day she was born. "I'm coming in."

She stepped into the water, walking down a set of mosaic tiled steps. It was warm, but not uncomfortably so, and there were bubbles somehow. She hurried into its depth, the water curling around her, caressing her skin, and dropped low so the water covered her intimate places. "In," she told him.

Nix turned but remained across the pool, where he stood in shadows. "How did you learn to swim?"

"My father taught us all. There's a river that runs through Sevens, and he didn't want any of us to drown.

You?" She unbound her wet hair from its braid.

"I don't remember. But I can imagine it was in a place like this. That my father would have brought me to the bathhouse with him and taught me that way."

"Do you often rewrite memories?" she asked.

"Distant ones, yes." His eyes skimmed her face and wound around in her hair.

She dipped lower in the water, wetting her hair before reemerging. "I think you are lonely," she said, grasping her hair to wring the excess water from it, and hoping what she'd said wasn't insulting.

He swallowed and moved across the expanse of the pool toward her. Her gaze dipped to the dark water, wanting to see him. But the golden flutter of the lit candles exposed nothing beyond their immediate vicinity. All she could see was the sheen of his golden skin above the water. He stopped a few arm's lengths away and found a place to perch near the wall.

"Because you are?" he asked, she assumed to turn it on her rather than commenting on the validity of her observation.

"I was missing companionship today. My family's. Yours."

His eyes darted from the dark water to her. "Mine?"

She moved a touch closer to him, the sound of the water somehow musical, pleasant. "Yes, Nix. Is that so surprising?"

He didn't respond immediately, his hands moving back and forth over the surface of the water. "Perhaps you are right. I have forgotten how to be a good host."

She noticed he'd ignored her question and wondered if he was surprised. "It might be difficult to maintain those skills when they aren't practiced," she teased. "How long has it been since the last key keeper?"

"I don't remember."

"When was the last time you interacted with a real person?"

"Before you? My brother and Poe are able to visit."

She tilted her head, surprised. "How?"

"I think it has something to do with the spell. They cast it, so it allows them entrance. It was a great shock the first time, and Lucian's been very careful since that first time. I tried to kill him." He shook his head. "I'm able to summon them, but I don't very often."

"But you do–" Auri gathered her hair together with her hands again.

He hesitated, watching her move, then nodded. "Sometimes."

Auri reached up, twisting her hair into a wet bun and holding it out of the water. She noticed Nix's dark eyes drop to the surface of the water, to her chest, and when she followed his gaze, she realized the tops of her breasts were above the surface, the shadow of her areola and nipple just visible. When she looked up at Nix, his eyes slid up her torso, as if caressing her skin, and he swallowed. When his gaze met hers, she recognized the want seeded in their depths.

Had she been beyond the confines of the spell,

maybe she would have grasped ahold of some semblance of modesty.

But she didn't. Instead, she held his gaze with her own, and she stood. Bold and brave. Her insides shook with trepidation, but she wanted... something. She took a step toward him.

Nix held his ground, his hands curled into fists on the surface of the water. "Auri," he said, but her name was filled with the sound of lamentation.

"I—"

He swallowed, leaning toward her.

Auri took another step toward him, until all he had to do was reach out. "Please touch me."

He groaned, his eyes dropping to her breasts. He licked his lips.

Her lungs tightened and collapsed into the bottom of her belly. "Nix."

His gaze jumped to hers. "Auri—" His eyes were filled with struggle, the shape of them offering her a petition— "Please." He shook his head even as he leaned toward her. "Please. Don't tempt me."

Then he turned away, crossing to the opposite side of the pool, and if she hadn't been reading Miss Miriam's story, she might have misinterpreted his behavior as displeasure. But she didn't think he felt that way at all. Not anymore. The evidence told her a different story: his chest straining for breath, eyes dropping to her breasts and rising to her mouth. His words: *don't tempt me.*

Nix was as attracted to her, as she was to him, and

for the first time in her life, Auri felt her heart expand,
then take flight.

Nixus

Nix was content with the routine. Content was probably the wrong word. Accepted it, perhaps, was more accurate. He'd accepted the routine he'd established with each key keeper and beyond them. Only, the usual routine had been demolished with this key keeper. He'd had to go rogue, attempting to find his way back to it. He'd accepted ways to keep himself isolated from Auri. Offering the books and the rose garden had filled her time and supplemented his forced isolation. Forced torture was more like it. His allowances of being near her for dinner and escorting her to her room to inquire about her wish—both terrifying him at the prospect of possible changes it would bring but calming him in case she had one—had become the highlight of his current existence. It was getting harder to justify staying away despite what he knew the spell would bring. So when she called for him, he'd been both elated and alarmed.

She'd said she missed him. This grabbed ahold of his cock. Said she was lonely. This grabbed ahold of his heart. Now, she stood across from him, naked in the bath house he'd conjured, asking him to touch her.

She was right.

He was lonely, but he was also desperate.

Stars, he wanted to touch her. He wanted to reach out and put his hands on her. He'd connected with her mind. Now he wanted to connect with her body. But he fisted his hands, Flora's face and the other key keeper's faces, and their hatred toward him haunting his present.

He turned away from her and closed his eyes to correct his balance and perspective. Then he whisked them from the bathhouse, wrapping them both in robes, because he knew he wouldn't be able to handle seeing any part of her naked. Hell, he didn't need to see her naked to want to touch her. He took a deep breath and opened his eyes.

"What's going on?" she asked, looking around her room, clasping the fabric closed at her neck.

"I—"

"You don't want me?"

"Auri…" But he stopped. He couldn't lie. Fuck. "My wants are complicated," he said. Technically an equivocation, but it wasn't untrue. He cleared his throat. "The spell."

She made a noise in her nose and narrowed her eyes. She didn't believe him. "You have thorns. You know that right?"

Thorns? The rose garden. He swallowed. "You mean horns?" The joke didn't make her laugh.

"You're running away."

"I'm protecting you."

"Me? Or you?" she asked.

Fuck.

"I think I'd like a nap before dinner," she said, turning away from him. A dismissal.

He turned to walk through the door.

"Nix?"

He looked over his shoulder at her, afraid of the next truth she might hit him over the head with, but she said, "Thank you for spending time with me."

He bowed his head toward her. "It was my pleasure." Then he stepped from the room into his own, stalked into his bathing room like an angry, stormy night. He stepped into the shower and turned on the water to cleanse his body of the minerals at the bath house. But he couldn't cleanse his thoughts of Auri, of her smile, her throaty laugh, her admission that she missed him, her gorgeous tits, and with a hand wrapped around his cock, he pumped himself to relieve the building pressure of all the built-up desire wanting her. After he came, he was able to draw a deeper breath to clear his mind.

As he dressed for dinner, he pondered his desire for Auri. He'd wondered initially if his loneliness was the only reason he longed to be with her. While it was a possibility, none of the other key keepers made the depth of his loneliness so intense. He hadn't spent his waking moments thinking about them. He hadn't cared to please them. He hadn't waited and wished for them to call to alleviate his longing to free him from his self-imposed confinement. He hadn't ever forgotten he was trapped to a spell because he'd found it fun to laugh with one.

Until now.

He slipped his arms into his white shirt and buttoned it, considering that maybe his longing for Auri was more than just his loneliness. There was the hint of warmth at the center of his chest now when he thought about her, and it made him smile. Learning about her over their time together—it was difficult to keep track—about her hopes and fears, her family, the way she was practical about most things but had a romantic streak, made him want to know it all. He decided that his attraction to Auri wasn't about his loneliness at all. It was her.

And she wanted him.

Fuck. She wanted him.

And there was the spell to remember.

He fastened the cuffs of his shirt with emerald links and took a deep breath before donning the dark jacket.

The magic would adapt to his feelings, and considering she hadn't made any wishes, and given how much time she was taking to make her first wish, she wasn't likely to make the kind of typical wish with which he was familiar. He wouldn't know how to prepare her, how to fix it—not that he could.

With another deep breath, Nix closed his eyes and when he opened them, he was in the dining room to await Auri's arrival to dinner. He stood at the window overlooking the night sky speckled with stars across the universe. The longer the key keeper was there, the more time he'd have to nurture the seed of attraction planted in his heart. That seed couldn't take root, for a myriad of reasons. Pushing her to make her wishes seemed the right choice.

A sound at the doorway drew his attention. He turned, knowing Auri had arrived, but his breath jammed up in his chest when he saw her.

She offered him a tentative smile as she smoothed her hands over the deep green shimmer of her gown, as if she were nervous. But it was Nix who suddenly couldn't swallow.

The bodice hugged her torso, creating a plunging neckline that offered an enticing view of her decolletage. Roses graced each of her shoulders, holding the bodice together. Her arms were bare but for the red ribbon tied to her wrist, while the skirt of the dress skimmed her hips, the excess fabric trailing on the floor behind her.

Her mahogany hair was up, loose curls teasing the

skin of her neck, and it made Nix think of the bathhouse when she'd pulled it up. How different this moment from that one, and yet how enticingly the same.

"You look stunning," he said, his heart twisting in his chest, as if it too were trying to get a glimpse of a goddess. He cleared his throat, and then remembering himself, walked to her chair at the dining table. He used it to provide himself balance, then pulled it out for her.

She turned in a slow circle, her head bent as she regarded the dress in the low light of the dining room. "It is a stunning dress." In the back, the fabric draped from shoulder to shoulder, cascading like an emerald waterfall to the small of her back and leaving her skin bare.

Nix swallowed. "The woman in the dress, I'd say."

She looked up and beamed with pleasure at his compliment. "You are kind."

"That, I am most assuredly not." Nix knew where his thoughts were. He pulled her chair out for her, waited for her to sit before taking his own.

"That is a lie."

"I cannot lie."

"I think, perhaps, Nixus, god of night, you might be a trickster."

"Perhaps that is also a truth." He grinned and raised his glass to her. "To the beautiful woman in a beautiful dress and to not being lonely."

She raised her own. "Here. Here," she said, sipped, and replaced her glass on the table.

The conjured servants dished out their first course, ladling soup into shallow bowls.

"Have you given any thought to your first wish?" he asked, cutting right to the heart of things. Seeing her bright smile, her twinkling eyes, her teasing, her in that dress. Recalling her in the bath asking him to touch her. He needed to speed things along.

His routine was fucked.

"So soon?" She smiled at him. "You usually wait until we're standing outside of my bedroom door." She tasted the soup, and Nix couldn't help but watch her mouth close over the spoon. It made his body tense, so he looked away, skimming his own spoon through the creamy vegetable bisque. "I'm considering. I promise you," she added after she swallowed the bite. "I just haven't settled on it yet. You will be the first to know."

Push her, his head said, but instead he said, "Fair enough."

Silence descended around them but for the clink of their spoons against the dishes, and the awareness that she was as silent as he was. It made him wonder what she was thinking. Was she thinking about what happened in the bath? About him running away? Why hadn't he touched her? Damn. He was a fool. He imagined swiping the dishes from the table, grabbing ahold of her, and setting her on the tabletop to eat her for dinner.

His spoon slipped from his grip, landing in the bowl with a clank. "Sorry," he said, then chastised himself for his fantasizing. He needed to not wonder. His cock wasn't as good at compartmentalizing.

"I was wondering…" she said, breaking the silence and giving him what he wanted, "how come your family hasn't found you? I mean, they are gods." She set her spoon down, and a worry line appeared between her brows. "I think my family is probably worried. I can only imagine how worried yours is, and with the missing night–"

"I would venture to guess that Lucian has fed them a convincing lie." He picked up his wine glass and drank deeply.

"And the missing night?"

"You said it still gets dark, yes?"

"Not completely–"

"He has help, then, to mimic the darkness." It hurt Nix to think that his family hadn't looked for him, but he wasn't exactly surprised, especially if Luc had come up with a convincing story. "It wouldn't be a surprise for a god to disappear for a time, shirk their responsibilities in a fit of willful petulance."

"Are you willfully petulant?"

"Incessantly."

Auri leaned back in her seat as the servants removed their first course and replaced it with the second: a small plate of fresh greens sprinkled with fresh fruit, crunchy nuts, nuggets of soft white cheese, and drizzled with a golden dressing. She moaned when she took a bite, like she always did when she tasted most of the dishes she'd been served in the time he'd known her. Nix loved that she was so vibrant and appreciative about the food, but the sound always hit him right in the groin, tingling with awareness of how she might sound with his head between her legs.

He cleared his throat and his mind of the image. "I know of a god—Felix Sturmrell, god of the song—who disappeared for over a century. As the story goes, he'd been angry with his father for insisting on a specific marriage partner for him, when it was common knowledge that he'd had already fallen in love with the god of artisans, Atwin. They ran away together and hid from Sturm's wrath."

Auri had stopped eating and was watching him with rapt attention. "What happened? Did songs disappear?" She took a sip of her wine.

Nix couldn't help but look at her mouth. He noticed her tongue dart out to lick a leftover droplet, then dragged his gaze back to his plate. "Not that I'm aware. In fact, I think love songs have become even more prevalent, which should appeal to your romantic nature." He looked at her then.

She pressed her lips together and narrowed her eyes in mock indignation, making a noise as she set down her wine glass. "You're teasing me."

"Why would I do such a thing?"

Her eyebrows rose over her eyes.

Nix grinned and continued the story. "I believe Felix and Atwin reemerged, tired of living in hiding, and by that time, Sturm was more amenable to Felix's choice of partner."

"Your family might not even be aware you're stuck here?"

He raised his glass and tipped his head toward her in affirmation.

She heaved a big sigh. "I am sorry about that."

"Why would you be sorry. You didn't do it."

"It's called empathy." She took a sip of her wine. "I empathize with your plight, and since I'm also caught in it, I can sympathize with you too."

The servants returned with the next course: a bit of meaty smoked fowl layered in a decadent cream sauce sprinkled with fresh herbs. The aroma—earthy with a touch of spice—was enticing, but Nix didn't touch his meal. He was too engaged in watching Auri luxuriate over hers.

She leaned forward and allowed the fragrance to entice her. She smiled and hummed. "That smells delicious."

Nix thought she looked delicious and wished he could run his tongue along the seam of her lips to taste her, but he kept that to himself. Instead, he offered her a noise of agreement, looked away, and took another drink of his wine. Though he encouraged himself to keep from looking, he couldn't help watching her wrap her mouth around the bite, and he tensed, thinking about her mouth around his cock.

Her eyes were closed as she moaned. "So good."

He nearly groaned and shifted uncomfortably in his seat. This wasn't going to work. He looked away at his own plate and picked up the wine again but didn't drink from it. He needed something stronger and changed his wine to scotch. "I'm glad you can sympathize, but I wish you didn't have to."

"Do you think you really loved the first key keeper?"

Surprised, his eyes jumped from the glass in his hand to her. "That's what I implied when I told you the tale."

She offered him a nod. "Yes. I did catch that you *thought* you were in love. Words." She grinned at him.

Nix leaned back in his seat and wished his plate away. He wasn't hungry for food anyway, his appetite more in line with the woman pushing him with her questions. "Isn't that enough?"

"I don't believe so," she said.

"What do you believe?"

"That there are phases of love."

"Have you been in love?"

"There you go, changing the subject again." She smiled. "No. I have not been in love, but I have been witness to it."

"Your parents?"

She nodded and leaned toward him, her elbows on the table and her head in her hands. "Now, stop avoiding my question."

Nix leaned forward. "In retrospect, I was in lust. Lucian had been right."

A becoming blush glowed on her cheeks. "Phase one."

"Of what?"

"Of love."

"Something you've picked up from Lady Miriam?" he teased.

She laughed and leaned back. "Yes. But curse to you because Roderick—her true love—has died."

"You believe we can only have one true love?"

She shook her head. "It's doubtful."

"You know the gods believe there is that possibility?"

Her head twisted and tilted. "Really? Fickle gods?"

He chuckled. "Yes. It's called a god-yoke, and the belief is that every immortal carries a piece of a star in their heart. When that star finds its matching piece, the god-yoke forms, linking the two hearts for all eternity."

"Now, that is very romantic," she said and leaned back.

"Even if it's fiction?"

"Even then," she said and took a sip of her wine. "It sounds like an epic poem."

"Maybe you could write it," he suggested and thought about Lady Miriam's story. "You've reached Roderick's demise then?"

She tilted her head. "Thanks for that. I laid in bed sobbing when I read it."

The thought of her crying stabbed his heart with a million needles. "Well, take heart, she's about to meet Mr. Henner." He smiled, knowing exactly what sorts of sordid things she was about to read.

"Why do I have the impression that you are secretly teasing me."

"Oh, I am not teasing you, Auri." No. He was thinking about all the ways Miriam's exploits were about to throw open the door to her world about a woman's pleasure—and he longed to be a part of it.

Nix found himself no longer accepting of his routine, or the torture he'd forced on himself. The longer he was with this woman, the reality of wanting to be near her hit him like a lightning bolt. He wanted her, and he knew, without a shadow of a doubt, he couldn't have her. He shouldn't. He wouldn't be able to forgive himself for the pain the spell would heap on her because of the way he felt. Crossing lines, connecting would complicate it further since he already had feelings. He liked her enough to know he would struggle another hundred years to recover from the hate he'd see in her eyes when she looked at him. But he didn't know how to stop it. He didn't know if he wanted to anymore, but fuck if he wasn't trying.

After dinner, he extended the walk between the living room where they'd sat and talked of their childhoods, and the hallway where Auri had delighted him by regaling him with the tale of her first crush. They laughed together, and he enjoyed the feel of her holding onto him, her arm linked with his. Her skirt brushed his pant leg, and her shoulder intermittently bumped against his. His thoughts drifted to how much he was indulging in his time with her, how free he felt being with her.

And as soon as he realized he'd ignored the fact they were stuck to the spell, not just two people enjoying one another's company, he hurried her door to them.

"Here we are," he said.

Auri released his arm, stepped toward her door, and stopped. Then she turned to face him, looking at his throat, before tilting her chin up to look at his face. "I am loath to go inside."

"Why would that be?" he asked, even though his head had advised him to let it go.

She allowed her gaze to wander his features. "I have had a delightful evening with you, Nixus, and I find I wish it didn't have to end." She took a step closer to him, the air in her chest moving more quickly as she did.

Nix's heart stopped, convulsed, then dropped through his chest toward his feet. He took a step closer to her, his lungs tight, and forced out words even as his mind warred with his body. "I have enjoyed my evening with you as well, Auri Fareview."

"Does it need to? End?" she asked, reaching out, and laying her hand on his arm. It was a light touch. He couldn't technically feel her skin, but heat told a story in his body anyway.

His eyes jumped from her hand to her eyes. "What are you saying, Auri?"

Her gaze slid up from her fingers, up his chest, over his mouth to his eyes, but she didn't reply, and he wondered if she even knew what it was she wanted.

Nix looked at her mouth. He longed to kiss her and stepped closer, so close he could feel her chest graze his with each breath. He reached out, taking a lock of her hair between his fingers, and forced himself to keep his eyes on that piece of hair. To focus on the silky texture contrasted with his skin. He couldn't look at her mouth, because he knew he wouldn't heed the warning bells ringing in his mind. But it didn't keep him from the thought of pressing his mouth to hers. Of pressing her up against that door and exploring all the soft places he wanted to touch. He wondered if the magic he felt pulsing inside his body was more than his imagination.

Except he knew what was to come after she made her first wish. He knew how she would feel about him soon enough, and complicating things would prove more harmful in the long run. So he leaned forward, pressed his nose against her hair, and instead of kissing her lips like he wanted to, he kissed her cheek. He didn't draw away immediately, lingering, waiting, hoping.

Auri held both of his arms, a hand on each, as if using him for balance, but she didn't turn her face toward him. He knew it was for the best.

Her breath hitched. Her scent sweet of roses and something earthy, tempted him to press his mouth against her neck next.

With resolve to do the right thing, Nix stepped back, dipped his head, and wished her a good night with a smile. Then he effervesced away to his own room to find relief and seek contentment once again.

Auri

uri leaned against the closed door with a frustrated sigh and dropped her chin to her chest. For a god, Nix was being rather chivalrous. She pressed a hand to her face, where Nix's lips had touched her skin, then ran her hand to her own mouth, pressing her lips with her fingertips, imagining his kiss.

She leaned her head back against the door and wondered where her bravery from earlier had gone? What had happened to the bold woman who'd stood in the bath baring herself go? She could have grabbed ahold of that courage and kissed him herself, but a part of her, the part that watched him back away, turn and leave after she'd tried, was determined to rule.

She pushed away from the door with a sigh, prepared to let it go, but after donning her night shift and slipping between the cool sheets, she wasn't tired. She was keyed up and antsy, like she needed something but couldn't name it. So she read.

Lady Miriam's exploits delved beyond romantic love to visceral physicality with a new character, Mr. Henner. Just like Nix had mentioned, which made Auri smile, knowing he'd read it. Mr. Henner's purpose in the story seemed to empower Lady Miriam to understand her own pleasure.

Soon it wasn't just Auri's cheeks that were warm as she read—all of her was, including the tender place between her legs. She squeezed her thighs together to relieve the ache there due to imagining the heroine's explicit exploits:

> *Mr. Henner stood at the end of the chaise, his eyes watching me, and said, 'Show me, Miriam. I want to see you. All of you."*
>
> *I spread my thighs for him. My robe dropped open to reveal what was hidden underneath.*
>
> *"Touch yourself for me," Mr. Henner directed.*
>
> *With my hand, I explored the folds of my flower, a soft caress that worked the heat deeper into my core and allowed me to liquify. With a single finger, I sought the tender seed of my pleasure. When I'd found it, using my other fingers, I spread the folds of my petals to expose*

Auri slammed the book with a frustrated smack, doused the light, and sunk into the luxurious sheets. She shivered, though not because the fire was banked and dark, but because she felt the unfulfilled desire raging inside of her. She closed her eyes and imagined Nix, his smile, his laughter, what had become his teasing, his mouth, the feel of his breath against her cheek as he'd lingered.

When she opened her eyes, and she stared at the fabric of the canopy, needing to not think of Nix, of his mouth, of the way the feel of his light caress lingered like a delicious burn—but she couldn't stop.

Images of Lady Miriam, her hand between her legs while Mr. Henner watched, persisted in Auri's thoughts. While her body heated enticingly, imagining Mr. Henner's kiss between her own thighs, it was Nix's face she pictured. Auri pressed her knees together and rolled onto her stomach to alleviate the pressure. It didn't matter if she shut her eyes or opened them, her curiosity to find that pleasure was triggered, and her body was aflame.

She rolled back to her back and sat up in her bed gazing out at the heavy darkness, the shadows of the bedroom hidden in the thick body of night, the light of the fire now nothing more than embers. Like Mr. Henner, she imagined Nix there, watching, and whispered, "Nix?"

Of course, there wasn't an answer. She was diving into a fantasy imagining Nix with her, imagining him there to teach her about her own pleasure, imagining him offering her the bravery to try what was running through her mind.

Touch yourself for me, Mr. Henner told Lady Miriam, but Auri imagined Nix's voice.

She closed her eyes and thought of Nix's smiling face, his dark gaze, then ran her fingertips across the scooped neck of her nightdress, teasing her own skin, dipping below the collar until she touched her own breast, tested the curve and the tingle wrought by exploring her own nipple. She recalled Nix's body in the bath, the ridges and planes, the dusting of hair that disappeared beneath the dark water and considered the contrast to her own pliable form. Her full breast, the nipple hardening under her own touch. Touching it felt good, sparking hot sensations that darted through her.

She'd never done this before. Sharing a room with her sisters and the laws if caught had made it impossible. She'd been curious, of course, but afraid. Guilty. Ashamed. But Lady Miriam wasn't afraid.

There is nothing to fear here. Nix's voice in her head gave her bravery.

In her imagination, Nix had joined her in her room after dinner. They kissed, and she helped him remove his jacket, his shirt. He helped her, pushing her dress up, kissing her, their lips and teeth and tongues exploring one another. With her other hand, she smoothed the fabric of the nightdress to the hem that had ridden up to her knees and pulled it up to her waist, imagining it was Nix's touch.

Auri let her fear go, drawing her fingertips over her stomach and pressing her hand between her thighs to alleviate the pressure that had been building there. It just wasn't enough.

She imagined Nix, standing at the end of the bed like Mr. Henner, watching her. "I want to see all of you," he said.

Auri spread her thighs—just like Lady Miriam—and slid her hand over her sex, exploring herself, picturing Nix, his smile, and the way his tongue would wet his bottom lip as he watched her. Her skin heated imagining him being there as she ran her fingers through the down of her hair and tested the silky smoothness of the folds. Auri rocked her head to the side, drawing in a shallow breath. She couldn't seem to grab ahold of a deeper one.

The sensations her fingers made were heady and addictive. She was wet and sought the source, finding her opening and exploring it with her fingertips. With Lady Miriam's words as a guide, Auri touched herself, opening her legs wider. Wanting. Needing more, but she wasn't sure what it was. She searched, imagining Nix's mouth on her, like Mr. Henner, and found the nub her body instinctively knew was where she needed relief, and working it with her finger, until she was writhing and moaning under her own ministrations. Then suddenly, heat, like the golden stardust bursting behind her eyes, sped along her limbs to the ends of her, and she arched, biting her lip to keep from crying out with both pain and pleasure.

It can be both, Nix had said of kissing.

The release dissipated the ache, but as she caught her breath, she felt acutely alone. While her own touch hadn't been unsatisfying, imagining Nix with her left her wanting more, wanting him. She could lie to herself and say that her desire was born of her never having been with a man, but she recognized that as a lie. She'd been attracted to him the moment she saw him in the meadow, drawn to him and his darkness. That had only deepened the more she got to know him.

Of course, I am, she thought with a smile. *He's a god.* The god of night and darkness.

You only need to call my name and I'll be there, he'd said.

She sat up with the realization, her heart beating a hectic rhythm that made her breath catch. Grasping the sheet to cover her nakedness, she stared into the darkness of her room. "Nix?" She whispered his name, both afraid he was there and afraid he wasn't.

Then the darkness moved, drawing together from the pervasive blackness around her, pulling and forming until Nix stood at the end of the bed, hands in his pockets. His dark eyes gleamed, sparkling like stars. "I want to see you touch yourself again."

Auri's already racing heart lurched with anticipation. "Again?"

He reached out and put a hand on the post of the bed as though to steady himself. "Please, Auri." His voice was hoarse, rough, and deep. It sounded broken and needy, as though she were the god, and he was the mortal. Rather than shame, she felt powerful, so she dropped the sheet, and let it pool around her waist.

She could feel his gaze like a caress as she watched him drink her in with his eyes.

"Take off your shift."

Her heart found its rhythm, racing ahead of her. With shaky limbs, she lifted the flimsy garment over her head and dropped it, then turned her head to look at him again.

"Stars," he breathed. "You are beautiful." His grip tightened on the bedpost, the wood creaking. His chest rose and fell with shallow breaths. "Please, Auri. Touch yourself for me."

The sound of her name, the way he sounded pained, spurred her forward. She ran her hands over the curve of her breasts, skimmed her sensitive nipples with her fingertips.

"Lift them," he said.

She did.

He groaned and pressed his temple to the wooden post but didn't take his eyes from her. "I want to see you make yourself come again."

"Again?" Though she repeated the question, but she already knew he'd been there. He'd seen.

"Auri. You called for me." He took a ragged breath. "Stars, why did you call for me?"

She searched her feelings and thoughts and saw the truth. "I wanted you." She pulled the sheet away from her body, and like Lady Miriam, mustered the bold woman she knew she could be, spreading her legs for Nix. "I wanted this, with you." She slid her hand from her breast, over her stomach, down to the apex of her thighs where she was still sensitive, softer even, wetter, and just a touch made her moan and jolt.

"Does it feel good?" Nix asked.

She nodded. "Yes."

"I want you to feel good."

She closed her eyes and leaned back on one hand, using the other to worship herself. With her feet flat on the bed and her legs spread for him, she tilted her hips toward her hand, sliding through the soft skin and inserting a finger. Her mouth opened, her head falling back as she drew in a sharp breath. She withdrew her finger, slid the wet tip through her folds to her clit, and caressed herself. It was quick, the coming. She knew where to touch, how to do it, and without preamble, found herself climbing toward the precipice again.

"Open your eyes," Nix said.

Auri did, lifting her head to meet his gaze sparkling with a wild light. She mewled as she moved her hips against her own hand, creating glorious friction. As she came, she held his eyes, never looking away, quickening with the sensations as they moved through her.

He licked his lips.

Emboldened, she removed her finger and brought it to her mouth and sucked it.

Nix groaned, his knuckles white as they gripped the post. "You're going to kill me."

"Would you like a taste?" she asked, channeling the boldness of Lady Miriam.

"Yes." But he didn't move.

Auri didn't wait for him, returning to fondle herself, finding satisfaction in making Nix, whose breathing was labored, weak. "I feel lonely," she said.

Nix moved then, crawling across the bed to meet her. "Tell me what you want."

"I want to feel your mouth. Your tongue."

As if it were a dream, his head was between her legs, his mouth and tongue tracing a line up her thigh, until the sensation of his tongue lapping at her wetness made her moan. "Oh–"

"Fuck, Auri. I knew you'd sound like that." He growled the words, and she tilted her hips toward him, needing the swirl of his tongue around her clit. "You taste like honey," he said against her sex.

Auri whimpered, moving against him, needing that release she'd found on her own—but this time, with him. The sensations he was creating built a beautiful constellation behind her eyes, swirling with light.

Nix grasped her hips and tugged her roughly toward him, then held her captive against his mouth, his arms wrapping around her, locking her in place. She grabbed his head, fisted his silky locks of his hair, and arched her back, trying to get closer, seeking the hint of the explosion that was converging.

He let go of her hips, and with his palms on her thighs, spread her legs wider. "Fuck, Auri," he said against her body. He made a sound, a hungry sound, then devoured her.

Being devoured by him made her moan louder. She was unable to control anything happening in her body. The sensations he created with his tongue crested over her, covering her so she was drowning in them. Her first orgasm she'd provided herself was pleasurable, the second empowering, but this was something entirely different, building toward something deeper, more meaningful, threading a connection to Nix with golden light. She seized his arm holding her hips against the bed.

"Oh–" She panted the word, but she wasn't sure of any of her thoughts and dug her nails into the fabric covering his skin.

Light pulsed through her body.

"Come for me," Nix said. The rumbled of his words sent vibrations moving out through her limbs, pulling her taut.

Auri whimpered, searching for the light just at the edge of all sensation, drowning in the dark when suddenly heat and ebullient gold, like Nix's stardust, crashed over her, rushing through her limbs to the very edges of her fingers and toes. She cried out, full of pleasure, his name on her lips, then convulsed as the sensations ebbed like the tide.

Nix kissed up her depleted body.

She opened her eyes.

He hovered over her, weightless, as if he weren't there at all. A dream. He smiled, reaching out to smooth her hair out of her face, his fingertips like butterfly wings. His eyes moved around her features until they met hers. "I liked hearing you scream my name."

She smiled back at him.

Her vision was hazy, and her mind tried to tell her to stay awake. *Remember,* she told herself.

"You should sleep well now," he said, but he was gone as if he'd never been there at all.

With a sigh, Auri closed her eyes, smiled, and dropped into the chasm of a deep sleep.

Nix swirled in a convergence of darkness and shadow from Auri's room into his own. "Fuck. Fuck. Fuck!" he chanted as he coalesced into pacing the dark room. The firelight was a collection of embers in the grate, the room cast in shadow.

A little while ago, however, he'd been watching red-gold flames of that fire flicker, drowning his desire in scotch as he contemplated kissing Auri. He was just wishing he had kissed her when he heard her say his name. Concerned, he'd answered her call. After all, he'd promised she only had to say his name and he'd be there.

When he'd appeared in her dark room, the fire had been little more than coals, the darkness he'd brought with him only adding to the deep shadows. She'd been sitting up in her bed, the white, linen night dress she wore, loose over her shoulder, her unbound hair draping down her back. Her head had been tilted as she'd stared into the darkness, at him, but unseeing.

His body had flared with want, the muscles in his back tightening and moving down his back where the need collected in his groin. With a deep breath to keep himself in control, he'd moved to reveal himself.

But she'd moved, her hand trailing over her shift and edging under the fabric to touch her breast. She'd laid back, and he'd frozen, listening, and realized her saying his name hadn't been a call.

He'd turned to go, but then she'd gasped with pleasure, and when he'd looked back, she'd lifted the night dress, her hand between her legs. His breath had caught in his lungs as his body leaned toward her, even though he hadn't made a move for fear the fantasy he was witnessing would collapse.

Recalling the vision of her pleasuring herself drummed up his desire all over again, and he dumped his body into the chair where he'd been sitting earlier, elbows to his knees. "Fuck."

He hadn't been able to look away from her as he'd stood there, watching her, taking pleasure in her pleasure. He hadn't left. He'd stood there enraptured by the sight she made. And though he knew being a voyeur to her pleasure without her knowledge was vile, and he hated himself for it, he just didn't hate himself enough not to replay it over and over in his mind.

Nix closed his eyes and shoved his hands into his hair, fisting his fingers and pulling so he'd feel the tension. He'd fucked himself. He'd crossed the line. Not only by watching her, but also because he hadn't been strong enough to leave. And then because he hadn't been strong enough to abstain from participating.

Fuck!

Closing his eyes, he pictured Auri in her bed, her hand between her legs, her gorgeous body pulsing as she sought her pleasure. He recalled and memorized every word she'd told him: *I want you. I want this with you. I want to feel your mouth.* Running his tongue over his lips, he could still taste her and wanted to return to her to finish what they'd started. But he couldn't—except the reason why felt so very distant and flimsy in relation to his immediate wants.

But he couldn't.

There was no going back for him now that he'd touched her, tasted her, heard her siren song as she'd climaxed. Now, rather than simply fighting his attraction, he was going to be wrestling with the desire to hear her moan like that again, to taste her again, to make her scream his name.

What the fuck had he done?

When she'd first found the key, he'd wanted her gone. Knowing how the predictable pattern of the wishes and obligations played out, getting her through the endeavor so he could slide back into the routine of his debauchery within the confinement of the spell seemed like the best plan. He just needed the routine to exist here.

But nothing she'd done so far had been predictable, and somewhere between meeting her and tasting her, his desires had shifted.

He didn't want her to make those wishes.

He didn't want to be alone.

Nix flopped back in the chair. "Fuck."

Though he'd wanted to stay in that bed with her, wanted to bury himself inside her, he'd instead compelled her to sleep. Still thinking of the spell, he'd thought he could protect her by making her think it had been a dream. But her words from earlier slapped him. Hard. *You have thorns. Why are you running away?* And he knew as he sat there in the chair, thinking about why he'd gone through with the compulsion, he hadn't been trying to protect her. He'd done it to protect himself. From her possible anger. From her possible regret at having been with him. From her possible hatred. From the pain of being alone.

He could blame the spell all he wanted. And while that was still an issue they'd have to face when she made those wishes, it wasn't what was keeping him from Auri any longer.

"Fuck," he mumbled.

What had he done?

Nix stood and paced.

He should apologize.

He turned and walked the length of the room in the other direction.

His original objection to allow his desire for Auri—rooted in his fear of the spell—had been obliterated. He'd fucked that argument into bits. His desire for her was as clear as the stars at night, and having crossed the line, there wasn't a way to hide their shine.

Nix took a deep breath, the first he'd taken in days. Admitting he wanted Auri made him feel freer, somehow.

He wanted Auri, and he knew she wanted him.

Nix stopped mid stride at that realization and stood up straight.

She'd invited him into her bed, asked him to actively participate.

She'd wanted him there.

She'd offered him her pleasure and provided him with his own. Freely.

His heart jumped up into his throat and thrummed with an addictive rhythm. He wasn't sure why he was avoiding the enjoyment of this woman who had invited him to her bed.

What was he doing fighting it?

The spell would do what it would do regardless.

He could work to forget it and let her believe it had been a dream. He could go back to torturing himself with isolation until she made her wishes. Except he knew he couldn't go back. He didn't want to. He just knew that after twisting the experience into a lie of omission, he didn't deserve her. He could admit it, apologize. But then again, if she had thought it was a dream, he never needed to tell her. She could believe it had been a fantasy. They could move forward from the moment he'd said goodnight.

He would know in the morning when he forced her to eat breakfast with him. He'd know what she felt when he saw her. He'd know what do to, then.

But for now, Nix laid down in bed, his hands behind his head as he stared up at the ceiling, his heart thumping a tremulous beat. A tentative smile found a place on his features as he pondered what might lie ahead.

Auri

When Auri opened her eyes the next morning, the room was still dark. She was naked in her bed, the sheet wrapped around her. She kicked at it to free herself, trying to clear her hazy thoughts filled with residual dream fog where the lines of what was real and what was fantasy crossed. She remembered touching herself, learning her body as Lady Miriam had, giving herself pleasure, followed by the vibrant release. Then there'd been Nix, but moving through the events in her mind were so aligned with Lady Miriam's story, Auri was sure she'd dreamed it. She glanced at the book on her nightstand and wondered what other erotic experiences were described between the pages. If they left her dreaming like that, she wanted to keep reading.

She finished extricating herself from the sheets and crossed to the bathing room. She loved this space and its luxury. *Perks*, she thought as she twisted the faucet to fill the bath. The memory made her smile. She was looking forward to seeing Nix.

She slipped into the water and basked in the magnificence of a hot bath, enjoying the slippery feel of her clean body, now awake with sexuality. Seeking and finding pleasure once again, she replayed the vivid fantasy of Nix, only this time in the bathhouse, amidst the flickering candlelight, in the steamy decadence of the warm water.

After her bath, she donned a gray pair of trousers with a white linen shirt. Unwilling to spend more time on her hair than necessary, she twisted it into a messy bun, secured it, and rushed from her chambers as her stomach rumbled with hunger.

When she walked into the dining room for breakfast, she wasn't surprised it was empty—Nix hadn't been joining her for breakfast—but she was surprised to find it devoid of food. Confused, she stepped out the door and back in, but it remained the same. A servant, however, appeared and bowed before her.

"I was looking for–"

The manservant maintained his posture, eyes to the

floor. "Breakfast has been served in the yellow room."

"I don't know where that is."

The servant straightened. "I can show you, my lady."

"Is that where Nix eats?" she asked as she followed him.

"He is there."

Her heart stilled, then thumped wildly in her chest, her cheeks heating with the knowledge she was about to face the object of her fantasy. When the servant stopped before a white door and reached for the doorknob, Auri took a deep breath to compose herself, needing the added boost of confidence to behave as if nothing were different. She could meet his gaze. She could. But then she imagined his head between her legs, and her skin blazed hot all over.

The door opened.

The problem wasn't the dream, she decided. She might have created a fantasy and played it out alone, but the truth was that if he had been standing in her chamber the night before, she would have welcomed him into the bed. She would have done more than what her fantasies had conjured.

Understanding what occurred between men and women to create progeny was nothing to her new awareness. Before, she hadn't really understood how restraint related to sexual relations. But she was beginning to. If she felt this intense pleasure just by touching herself while fantasizing about Nix, she could certainly understand how sharing that experience would potentially be even more gratifying.

The servant stood aside for her to enter the room. She stepped through the doorway, her eyes on the servant instead of Nix, giving her a little more time to prepare herself. "Thank you, uh–"

"Greene." He offered her a quick smile and a slight dip of his head.

"Mr. Greene." She offered him a smile before turning to face the man who'd inspired her fantasies.

The room was smaller than the formal dining room, smaller than many of the rooms where she'd spent time in the maze. Though the ceilings were high, the space was cozy and intimate, with two windows draped in yellow brocade, and walls painted white with yellow accents. A small fireplace and inset shelves housing trinkets and baubles adorned the other walls. A table sat in the center of the room covered with an array of fruits, bread, butter, and a coffee service. And in one of the seats was Nix.

Despite her discomfiture about their imagined intimacy, her eyes lingered on him. The sight of him nourished her. He held a book in one hand, a cup of coffee in the other, legs crossed. He was the picture of ease and comfort in his light shirt, buttons open, and dark pants, the anomaly in what would be an otherwise warm room. He wasn't cold, however, and his eyes, watching her, made her feel hot all over and chilled at the same time, as if she had a fever and needed something to cure it.

"Good morning." He smiled at her and took a sip

from his cup.

"This is a surprise," she said. "Why the change this morning?"

He grinned as he swallowed his sip. "Whatever do you mean?"

"You haven't ever broken your fast with me."

He set his cup in the saucer, the slide of the porcelain loud. "Yesterday was illuminating. I found I wanted to explore a bit more."

"In what way?"

He smiled again at her and nodded at the door. "Do you like him?"

"Who?"

His gaze went to the door. "Greene?"

She glanced at the door, then turned back to Nix. "He seemed nice enough." She forced her feet across the expanse of blue rug between them.

"That wasn't the kind of *like* I was referencing. Perhaps some kissing lessons with Greene?" He smirked.

She blushed. "Oh. I–" she stammered for a word to finish her thought– "I don't know him."

"Do you know me?"

She cleared her throat. "Not well," she admitted and stopped, holding the back of the chair for support. "I do think I know you a bit more than Mr. Greene. We've spent more time in one another's company. I just met Mr. Greene."

"Does the length of time you know someone preclude you from feeling attraction?"

"What kind of attraction?"

"Sexual."

Her blush deepened.

He smiled—noticed her blush—his eyes roving across her face, and his smile widened so she could see his dimple.

She blinked, then gritted her teeth, irritated with him for some reason. He was being strange and weirdly charming which put her on edge. "I'm not sure I understand your meaning." She sat.

"For the sake of exploring, take Greene for a moment." He closed the book and slid it onto the table next to his cup.

She glanced over her shoulder at the closed door, thankful Greene wasn't standing there any longer, then picked up a napkin to lay over her lap.

"Do you feel attracted enough to him, to say, allow him liberties–"

When Auri looked up at him, Nix was studying her as if he were feasting on her discomfort.

"–with your person," he finished.

"Like kissing?" she asked.

"Among other things."

Her cheeks burned, the fantasy on display in her mind, and she had the uncomfortable feeling he could see right into her private thoughts. She recalled those kinds of liberties she imagined. Of liberties she would consider even now in the dim light of Nix's day.

He was baiting her, however, though she wasn't exactly sure why, so she lifted her chin and engaged with his little game. "Greene is handsome enough to allow liberties, but–"

Nix leaned forward, elbow on the table. "Oh really?" he interrupted. He raised a brow. "What kind of liberties?"

"But," she said, ignoring him, "I think that knowing someone, perhaps, would make the liberties allowed more enjoyable." She glanced at Nix's mouth, wishing it were on her for real, feeling bolder playing this game—whatever it was. It was interesting. So she refused to back down from his teasing.

His eyes dropped to her mouth.

Her breath broke apart in her chest, and she found she couldn't keep looking at him and breathe at the same time. She looked away, focusing on the food on the table. "What has gotten into you this morning?" she asked, pouring a cup of coffee to do something with her hands.

When he didn't respond, she decided a straightforward approach was best. "To address your rather forward question, I should think," she said, "given I haven't experienced much of anything, I should like to test out all sorts of activities." She glanced at him over the rim of her cup.

Both of his eyebrows shot up over his dark eyes, now twinkling with light. He leaned back in his chair, humming a response as he crossed his arms over his chest, then tilted his head as he regarded her. "You know you only have to say the word, and I can conjure you anything you desire to test out. It could even be a wish if you wanted it."

She set her cup down with a slosh, her hand shaking as she contemplated all manner of things—though not with Greene, but with Nix. "You are being–"

"Being what?"

"Odd."

He smirked. "Odd." He snuffed a closed-mouth laugh. "It must be because I didn't sleep very well. But I trust you did?"

Her skin heated, and she reminded herself she'd been dreaming as she reoriented the napkin on her lap. "I did. Thank you. And I had a lovely bath this morning."

He seemed to want to say something but then didn't. Instead, he just nodded, then picked up his cup and sipped, before replacing it again. "Do you have a wish today, my lady?"

Right. The wishes.

"Not yet." She drew a slice of warm bread from the pile and placed it on her plate.

"There is nothing you want?"

She buttered the bread and watched the butter melt, thinking of his mouth on her. It was a selfish desire and not enough for one of her wishes. "There are things I want, but I haven't thought much about how I might wish for them. I can think about wishes for my sisters and brother, for my parents."

He leaned back in his chair. "But those aren't the kinds of wishes you are allowed to make."

She nodded, looking away from his intense gaze, and picked up the honey pot from the table. Using the wand, she twisted it in the nectar, scooped it from the jar, then hovered it over her plate where it dripped onto the warm slice of bread.

Nix cleared his throat, adjusted in his seat, and leaned forward. "You like honey, then?"

"Love it." She returned the wand to the jar, set it back down, and licked her sticky fingers.

He made a faint groaning sound, then hurriedly cleared his throat as if trying to disguise it, and Auri's eyes jumped from her toast to his face. His eyes—dark now—were on her mouth.

He swallowed, moved his eyes up to meet her gaze, and said, "I had some rather delicious honey recently. Last night, specifically."

Everything moving in Auri froze, including her breath—except her eyes, which slid away from his to the slice of bread glazed with honey. He'd said that in her dream: *you taste like honey.*

Her eyes jumped back to his.

He leaned forward, his elbows on the table.

Her heart swelled inside her chest, pushing everything else out of the way, and her stomach dipped. Had it been real?

His tongue darted out to lick his bottom lip. "It was so fucking sweet," he continued. "I dreamt about savoring it again." His eyes dipped to her mouth.

Her mouth opened, then shut as her mind tried to realign what she'd assumed was a dream. The truth was in his gaze, in the teasing of his words, in the manner of his presence, in the fact he was at breakfast with her. And though it was a ridiculous question, she asked it anyway. "It wasn't a dream?" The breathiness of her voice sounded unsure, but she wasn't.

Bright light flared beyond the windows, turning the dawn into day for just a moment.

Nix stood. "Not now. Fuck."

"What is it?"

"My brother." He glanced around as though to find a hiding place, but then held out his hand, "Come here. Stand behind me."

She realized the hiding place wasn't for him, it was for her. She took his hand, and he pulled her from her chair.

"I'm going to shield you in my shadow. Don't leave it, or–" Nix drew her around him, and Auri obeyed, stepping behind Nix and his broad frame. He reached around to pull her closer, his touch burning through her shirt.

"Or what?" she asked, pressing her hands against his shoulder blades.

But he didn't answer, because the door to the morning room flew open just as his night wrapped her in its dark embrace. She rose onto her tiptoes and peeked over his shoulder.

Just inside the doorway stood another breathtakingly beautiful man. So this was Lucian, god of light and day. He looked like a version of Nix—they were twins, after all—only the antithesis of each other.

Whereas Nix was the embodiment of night, Lucian was the embodiment of day. He wore light, in the brightness of his clothing, in the sunlight of his golden hair, in the glowing aura that swirled around him, but he tempered it as he stepped into the room.

He glanced around the space. "This is a lovely room. I love what you've done with it. It reminds you of me, I'd guess."

"What do you want?" Nix asked.

"Is that a way to greet your brother?" Luc's eyes, laced with golden threads, glanced at the table, then at Nix. He looked around the room as if searching. "Have I disturbed something?"

"You are always a disturbance."

"Oh, come now, Nix. We are brothers."

"No. We are adversaries."

Luc made a tsking sound with his mouth. "No familial bonds then?"

"You could release me," Nix said, "and prove your brotherly devotion. Perhaps I would only make you suffer for a millennium."

Luc sat in the chair Auri had occupied and chuckled. He studied her plate and shifted, facing Nix, crossing his legs and leaning with the arrogance of someone with no care in the world. His eyes flashed to Nix, flared with gold. "Where is your guest?"

"Why would I tell you?"

"Hidden somewhere in your labyrinth, I'd guess," he said and glanced about the room. "Here?"

"Again, you presume I would tell you."

"A new key keeper."

"As you well know. That is the only time you selectively visit."

"Oh, come now. Not the only time," Luc said, and fingered Auri's toasted bread. "This looks delicious." Luc picked up the bread and took a bite. There was something about the action that angered her. "Male or female?"

"Does it matter?"

Luc finished the bite and dabbed his mouth with a napkin. "I suppose not. You've failed equally with both."

Auri wanted to reach out to hit Luc for his arrogance and for eating her toast.

"So why are you here?"

"To lay eyes on the new key keeper, of course. To see what my brother has caught–"

"And try to claim them for yourself?"

Luc's eyes flashed with annoyance. "I don't need to take what my brother has, and I didn't want that idiotic woman." He shuddered.

"Then why trap me?"

Anger moved through Luc, his light flaring for a moment, but then he smiled, and the light receded. "You can bait me all you'd like, little brother. You know why."

"Four minutes, Luc. That's all."

"Four minutes still makes me older." Luc smacked his thick thigh. "Why don't you sit? Break bread with me?"

Auri realized Nix would have to sit on her if she remained where she was. Hoping she was still shrouded, she started to step to his side, but Nix turned as if to look for his seat, caught her eye, and forced her into the seat with a look. Then he sat, and somehow, as if it were as natural as breathing, she passed through him until she was on his lap. She adjusted, but he grabbed her hips to stop her.

Now, she was face-to-face with Luc, but he couldn't see her, as if she were a transparent spirit. Nix had camouflaged her somehow, and Luc focused his gaze on his brother's face.

The god of light took another bite of her toast, and she pressed her teeth together, wishing she could snatch it out of his hand. Her body tensed to slap it away, but as if anticipating her, Nix wrapped his darkness around her and pulled her tighter against him.

"Do you have any coffee?" Luc asked.

A cup and carafe appeared before Luc. "Pour it yourself," Nix said, his breath warm against her cheek, mellowing her in his arms.

Auri felt the rumble of his words reverberate through her back and travel through her body, igniting her nerve endings with heat. Though she'd passed through him, as if he were no more substantial than a shadow, now all she could feel was his corporeal form connected with hers. And she liked it. The unforgiving sinew of his thighs against hers. The unyielding wall of his chest against her back. The strong band of his darkness crossed beneath her breasts. She felt her nipples harden, and she settled deeper into his lap. His darkness tightened around her, and she relaxed, laying back against him, her head on his shoulder.

"So, tell me about the new key keeper."

"You seem to think you're owed something," Nix said. "Let me remind you, you are a guest here." He turned his head slightly so that his mouth grazed her temple. "And I don't wish you to be here." The band of darkness around her ribs eased, replaced with one of his arms, his fingertips teasing the fabric of her shirt.

Her heartbeat and the air in her lungs moved faster. She was sure she could feel Nix's matching rhythm though her back, reverberating like an answering echo inside her body.

"Just give me a hint." The glee with which Luc said it was laced with something else. Fear? Anxiety? Auri wondered if the possibility of Nix being freed from his prison was a point of concern. Nix's vengeance would wreak havoc for his brother. Maybe he had more to gain by Nix remaining imprisoned.

"No."

Luc's eyes moved over Nix's face before returning to his tiny cup where he sipped the dark liquid inside. "A woman then."

"What makes you think so?"

"You only hide women."

Auri thought it humorous that she was sitting across from the god of light, hiding in the shroud of Nix's shadow by sitting on his lap.

Nix hummed. She felt the sound and it warmed

her. She thought about the night before, Nix's mouth and hands working his magic, and adjusted so her hips pressed deeper against Nix, seeking relief for what was building inside of her.

"I wonder why," Nix said, though his words sounded pained. His hands went to her waist, stopping her movement, and his mouth dropped closer to her ear, his breath fluttering against her skin.

Oblivious, Luc took another bite of her toast. "She hates you already? That's why she isn't here."

She thought about examining Luc's comment, but all she could think of was Nix and the feel of his body. He lifted one hand from her waist, skimming her torso, up, up until his hand teased the side of her breast. The movement of his fingertips against the linen of her shirt brushed her sensitive nipple with delicious friction.

She longed to lean into his touch, twist just a bit, but his other hand slid down her thigh over the fabric of her trousers to her knee, and the feel of—oh—his hardness pressed against her backside. Auri's breath moved with excitement through her body, quick and anxious.

She turned her head to look at Nix but couldn't see his face, just the sharp edge of his jaw hidden underneath the neat shadow of scruff.

"You really should let it go about that first girl. What was her name? She was a vapid creature. She would have bored you."

"You really should let me go." Nix's hand framed

her jaw while his other hand worked its way from her knee up her thigh with slow, deliberate movements.

Her breath caught, and she felt both decadent and debauched, wondering what Luc was witnessing, then realized it was what Nix created for him to see: Nix sitting still in a chair—alone. That was exciting and heady.

"You know I have tried. I'm doing all I can."

"All?"

Luc sighed. "Has this not had its advantages in some ways? A place without the interference of anyone else? A place to conjure worlds and dreams all willy nilly. A realm of anything you desire. To control everything."

"I am not free, Luc." Nix continued to caress Auri's thigh, moving higher. She breathed in sharply, longing for him to touch her like last night, needing it. The hand on her face covered her mouth. She grasped the outside of his thighs, squeezing him, and squirmed to intensify his touch, needing relief.

"Are any of us?"

Nix's caressing hand stilled. "What's that supposed to mean?"

Luc waved a hand. "Nothing." The god of light stood and walked to the door. "Since you're being so secretive with this one, I'll be off." He stopped and turned back. "Oh, one more thing. This is the last time."

"What do you mean?"

"This key keeper. If this one doesn't take the

sacrifice, there won't be another." At this, Luc somehow exuded regret.

"You can end this at any time," Nix reminded him.

At that, Luc's remorseful countenance brightened. "Well, let's hope it doesn't come to that." Then in a flash of light, he was gone, and complete darkness descended around them.

Without her sight, Auri had to rely on her other senses, which were overloaded with information. The way his breath caught in a quick syncopated rhythm, matching hers, his breath a fire against her skin. Splayed across Nix's lap, she could hear the way the fabric of her trousers created resistance against his. She could feel the way her nipple brushed against the fabric of her shirt when she moved. The sensitivity of his hand against her leg. The sensations were heating her from the inside out.

"Yes," Nix said and leaned his head down into her neck, his lips and tongue drifting like a whisper across her skin.

"Yes what?" She breathed the words, lost to their meaning, and reached up to tangle her hands in his hair, to hold onto something concrete or risk drifting into the darkness filled with sensuality.

"It was real."

Last night.

Real.

The dream had been real.

She withdrew her hand from his hair and tensed, her skin now aflame with other emotions conflicting with the desire coursing through her body that had been informing her she wanted more, more of his touch, more of his mouth, more of him.

Except now, there was also annoyance. Humiliation. "It was real," she repeated, and her cheeks blazed.

She jumped from his lap as if he were on fire. The memories of his touch, his mouth, and the pleasure of the night flashed through her mind. She pressed a hand to her lips and wrapped a hand around her stomach to keep all the betrayal contained.

"Auri?" Nix said behind her.

The dark gentled until Auri could see the room in the blue morning light once again. But she couldn't turn to look at him. It had been hard enough when she'd thought it was her dream alone, her fantasy of him, but knowing he'd stood there, watched her without her knowledge, and then tried to take the truth away by hiding it in a dream made her want to scream.

"What is it?"

She twirled and faced him, her hand still over her mouth, her chest now heaving with fury.

His brows came together between his eyes with a mixture of concern and consternation.

"You lied. You have spent all this time–" she groaned– "I don't even know how long–" She stopped and focused on what she was feeling. Anger. "You've spent all this time telling me you can't lie but you did! You lied."

Nixus

Nix searched her face, which was furious at the moment—gray eyes flashing, her lips pouting with her frown, her body rigid—and struggled to douse the desire for her. "I didn't lie. I'm telling you now."

She glared at him, her eyes turning icy. "Is that what you're telling yourself? You tricked me."

"Which technically isn't a lie."

"So that makes you a saint?" She turned away from him and moved across the room, increasing the distance.

"No. I'm a god." It hurt to think she didn't feel safe

with him, and his physical longing waned, clearing his mind. "Why are you really angry? Because I was there last night?"

"No! Because you made me think I'd dreamed it."

He opened his mouth to argue, but then stopped. She wasn't angry about what happened. His body flared and surged with lust. "That was to protect you. I didn't lie."

"To protect me? Or yourself?"

He wanted to argue but couldn't. She was right. "Both. I didn't know how you'd feel about it." Nix huffed an angry sigh and turned away from her toward the window, which shifted from the countryside into the black of nothing. The room dimmed around them so the only light was that of the fire.

"I bared myself to you in the pool. I asked for you to touch me. You can't claim you didn't know how I felt."

Nix swallowed. The visions of both swirled through his mind and into his bloodstream like a mind-altering concoction.

He folded his arms over his chest. "You called me," he deflected.

She was silent.

Nix didn't turn to look at her. He didn't want to see her anger. He deserved it, and that was really why he'd hid in the guise of a dream. He also knew he should just admit it, but his pride seemed to be the louder force. Besides, he knew she was as invested in what was physical between them as he was. He could feel it in her body, hear it in her sighs, sense it in her touch.

"You could have left." Her words were quietly spoken.

He turned and narrowed his eyes. "Yes. I could have, but I didn't." He stalked across the room toward her, wanting her, wanting to touch her, to press his body to hers, to bury himself inside her. He was so bound up with want for her.

She backed up until she was pressed against the wall.

A painting went askew, but Nix was too focused on her to stop. He leaned forward, a hand on either side of her. "I didn't. I didn't want to."

He licked his lips, anticipating what hers would taste like.

She watched his tongue and bit her own bottom lip.

"Why are you really angry?" he asked. "Because I concealed it or because you enjoyed it?"

"I don't like feeling like it wasn't my choice." She turned her face away from his gaze, disconnecting from him.

That gutted him. He stepped back.

"You made me think it wasn't," she added.

"I asked you."

"And then hid it in a lie of omission. You don't get to choose for me."

"I thought if you thought it was a dream, you wouldn't regret it."

"Why did you assume I'd regret it?" She pushed away from the wall and stepped closer to him, filling the space with the scent of roses.

"The spell."

"Why?"

"The key keepers always hate me."

"I'm not the others."

His awareness for her rushed toward his groin, and he tensed.

"I'm stuck here, but I should be able to face the shame of any choices I make on my own terms. At least then I know I made them."

"Stuck? Don't tell me about being stuck," he snapped, and his eyes dropped to her mouth, then returned to hers.

Her chest heaved with anger, but her eyes bolted between his lip and his eyes.

His mouth dried out, and he swallowed.

Her lips parted.

He wanted to claim her mouth with his. He wanted his hands all over her again. But he didn't move. Instead, he just stared at her, his brain suddenly hanging up on something she'd said. "Shame? Why would you feel ashamed by what happened?"

"Isn't that why you hid it?"

Shocked, he took a step back, then recovered and stepped back toward her. "No."

"You thought I would be embarrassed about how I behaved."

He shook his head. "No. I made you think you

were dreaming so you wouldn't regret—"

"If not my behavior, then what?"

"Being with me."

"Why would you think—"

"And to conceal that I hadn't walked away." He stopped, shoved a hand through his hair with a sigh, then turned away from her, walking back to the table to sit. "That's my shame, Auri, not yours."

Her mouth dropped open, then closed with whatever she'd been about to say.

He rubbed his hands over his face and sighed. "I am sorry for that." He glanced at her. "Forgive me?"

She sat. "What exactly are you sorry about?" She rearranged her setting as if erasing Luc from the space, then grabbed another slice of bread.

Nix watched her scrape butter over the bread. "For concealing that I'd been there."

She set the knife down. "And?"

"And?"

Her eyes rose to meet his. "You can't say you're sorry, Nix, and not know what it is you are apologizing for."

"I'm a god, Auri. I don't usually apologize."

"Practice then." She offered him a short smile, and he felt as if maybe she were the god bestowing favor.

He watched her add honey to the bread and looked away. He'd finally lost his mind. "For taking away your choice."

She took a deep breath and sat back, her eyes scanning his face. Then she looked away and nodded.

"I forgive you." She sat forward and poured herself another cup of coffee. "Thank you."

"So easily?"

"What did you expect?"

"I don't know. Gods like to make those who have wronged them pay." He offered a thin smile.

"Is that what you plan to do to Lucian?"

His mood darkened further. "Luc will pay if I ever get out of here." His brother's words resurfaced: *This is the last time.*

Her expression dimmed, then grew serious. "What did Luc mean?" she asked, as if reading his thoughts.

"It would seem there's an end to the spell."

"Did you know that?" She picked up her toast.

He shook his head.

"And if this whole final test thing doesn't work?" She set her toast down again.

"I don't know."

Her eyes jumped from her plate to his face. "What do you mean you don't know? How can you not know?"

"I didn't cast this spell, Auri. Poe and Luc did." He thought back to Luc, earlier. "Even my brother seemed surprised."

"Could you be stuck here for eternity?"

"Perhaps."

"Could you cease to exist?" Her gray eyes grew, and Nix might have thought she was afraid for him.

"Maybe."

"How do we find out?"

"I should probably speak to Poe."

"How do we do that?" Auri asked.

Nix noted she used the word *we*. It wiggled its way into that warmth near his heart that seemed to be expanding, but it also made him tense with awareness. With an end one way or another in sight, he had to think about how to move forward strategically. "I'll summon her."

"And she just shows up?"

"Like Luc, she is able to cross somehow. And yes, she'll show up because she's compelled to. I'm a greater god."

Needing to move, he stood. Looking at her and thinking clearly didn't seem to work in tandem, so he stood and stared out the window at what he'd changed back to the countryside of Elcadia. He needed to keep his perspective in check. He couldn't lose himself in the pleasure and the golden glow in the center of his chest. She was the last key keeper, and that changed things. These were the last three wishes and the last three consequences. If he wanted out, he needed her to choose to end the spell, to choose whatever sacrifice she faced to save him. Only having failed with the first six, he wasn't sure how.

Nix pressed his fingertips to the warmth in his chest, afraid. He needed to sever their connection but was beginning to wonder if maybe it was too late.

"And then what?"

He wished he had an answer for her. "I don't know. I've been given six opportunities to figure it out, and still haven't." He wasn't sure about anything. The attraction. His physical need. The pinch of his heart in his chest. Whether to push her on her wishes or wait. To work to sever their connection or to nurture it. And none of his usual reasons resonated.

Here the spell was set to end, taking him with it somehow, and he was powerless to change the outcome.

"What can I do? A wish?" she asked.

His heart fluttered, and he looked over his shoulder at her. A key keeper had never once considered to use one of their wishes for him. They'd tried to figure out how to use it for themselves in relation to escaping the spell, but not for him. "That kind of wish won't work."

She nodded. "Right."

The urge to gather her in his arms, to kiss her, to find relief in the physical connection they shared made him open his hands and stretch his fingers and palms before fisting them again. He imagined dragging her into his lap and kissing her to ignore the demons of unease chasing him.

Maybe he needed to conjure her another partner and keep himself free from this entanglement.

He thought about the way she'd smiled at the conjuring of Greene earlier, the horrible way it had made him jealous. The way he'd wanted to stake claim and remind her what had occurred between them the night before. And Greene wasn't even real. Maybe that would help him cut any emotional connection to her.

He was afraid. The belief that this spell was for

eternity had offered a sense of comfort. Now, knowing there was an end offered him a double-edged sword. He could throw caution to the wind and just exist, because one way or another it was over. On the other hand, he needed to be cautious to make it out of this spell, whatever it took.

He turned back to the window and stared out at the conjured countryside.

He just didn't know what it took. What he did know: as soon as she started making her wishes, she would hate him.

"If I can't make a wish, what can we do today to help you?"

"We?" He tilted his head and smiled, noticing how she put them together in this predicament again. The fluttering inside his body went still at her offer. Another offer to do something for him, be there for him over her own wants. He couldn't recall ever feeling like he'd been in a partnership with a key keeper before. It had always felt adversarial, and maybe that was still to come. It added to the dangerous glow of hope.

"Perhaps we can find some answers about the binding of spells in the library while we wait for Poe."

She smiled, her eyes alight with joy, which Nix found strange considering she'd just been angry with him. He wasn't used to anger dissipating so quickly, but he didn't question it. He just accepted her forgiveness, then fretted because he had. He should be pushing her way. He should be presenting the god she would come to hate to make it that much easier.

But stars help him, he didn't want to.

When she finished her toast, she took another sip of her coffee and set it down. "I don't regret it," she said, drawing Nix away from the window. He returned to his seat across from her.

"Excuse me?"

"Last night." Her eyes connected with his, and she swallowed, moving her utensils and reordering things on the table as she said, "I couldn't regret you."

Unable to hold her tentative gaze, he looked down at the coffee in his cup, now cold. As much as her admission pumped his heart to full, he knew that when she faced that first consequence, whatever it would be, she would regret everything about him. Though if this was going to be his end, at least he would have had a few happy days spent with this woman who smiled and laughed and made him feel bliss so hot in the center of his chest he was sure it would send him up in smoke.

Two days, a half a dozen tomes, and two mind-blowing dreams about fucking Auri later, Nix knew he needed to do something drastic. This woman was under his skin, and he couldn't exorcize her from his thoughts or his senses. He felt like he'd been given a potion, and he was bewitched by her, the need to be near her, the desire to touch her. It was like she was moving through his bloodstream, taking over his autonomy. He could have blamed the spell, but he'd never felt this way about the other key keepers, even Flora. The others had opened the spell, made their wishes, and departed. There hadn't been time to dwell, ponder, and feel things. This wasn't the spell. It was him, and he needed to find a way to control it.

Bent over the table in the library with several new books they hadn't yet examined scattered over the tabletop, Nix tried to concentrate but couldn't keep his eyes on the book. Every few seconds, they were drawn to Auri an arm's reach away. Her hair was up again today, ribbons of her mahogany hair curling against her bent neck, and as she read, she twisted a strand around her finger, the red ribbon sparkling on her wrist.

He imagined grabbing ahold of her hand, flipping it palm up, and bringing the underside of her wrist to his lips. Then he'd work his mouth up her arm, drawing her into his lap so he could have easier access to her neck, her jaw, her lips. She'd moan, and he'd lift her onto the table, run his hand down the center of her shirt between her breasts, opening buttons as he did. Then—

"It says here that spells are created by witches and wizards, but it's a demon who gives them power." Auri's voice snapped him from his imagination.

Fuck.

She looked up at him, and her skin indicated how much she appreciated looking at him, a blush staining her cheeks.

His attraction for her was going to kill him. Not literally, of course, but he couldn't stop noticing everything about her, and it made his heart stall in his chest with anticipation of her every move, look, sound, thought.

"Did you know that?"

He scowled at the book lying in front of him, annoyed with himself. "I didn't."

She slid the book and herself closer and pointed at the passage.

The fragrance of roses and a hint of something sweeter came with her. He both inhaled deeply and fisted his hands to keep from grabbing her, to keep from burying his nose against her neck. Glanced at the passage she pointed at, he stood and put some distance between them, crossing the library to the hearth.

"Are you alright?"

More astute than he was giving her credit for.

"I am well. Worried." Which was true, if a bit misleading about his current thoughts.

"Maybe if you knew where the power of the spell came from, maybe it could be removed."

It was a worthy idea, and something he could ask Poe when she arrived. Two days since he'd summoned her. She usually presented herself around the fourth spell day.

He stood at the hearth, staring at the flames undulating inside. "That's what the blood sacrifice is for."

"What's that?"

"The blood oath is the origin of the spell, and the blood sacrifice is the end of it. In this case, the blood oath is more complicated than just drops of blood. According to Luc, he tried that, but it didn't work."

"What does that mean?"

"That the spell is a lot more powerful than Luc and Poe knew when they cast it."

When Auri hummed, he glanced over his shoulder at her, his body responding to the sound.

She wasn't looking at him, bent over the book. "So maybe a very powerful demon?" She continued reading.

"Maybe." He looked back at the fire.

He had to fix this, because staying the course wasn't going to work. She was taking her time with her wishes—and resisting the attraction to her wasn't going to be an option. He was already too far gone. Knowing she would be open to him was wreaking havoc on his willpower.

He sighed and watched the glowing coals slip through the giant metal grate.

The end was coming.

Did he want an end? Yes. But he was conflicted as well. With the other key keepers, that had always been his end game: release from the spell. Only then, there hadn't been the weight of knowing that it was truly an end. Instead, eternity stretched inside this spell. But if the spell was ending, what did that mean for him if he wasn't released by the key keeper.

Obviously, he hadn't a clue how to get a key keeper to not look at him as the villain. He'd tried different techniques. Flora notwithstanding, but subsequent key keepers had become a ground for his experimentation. Friendship with the second, being a confidante with the third. After three failures in a row, he'd then paid attention to the fourth's choices and astutely studied the spell's response hoping to learn. And failed over and over. It always came down to the final sacrifice, after the key keeper thought him vile and vindictive. Their choice was never in his favor. He couldn't control that.

But what if he could?

If he could figure out a way to lessen the impact of the spell's obligations so that she might still choose him.

He just wasn't sure how.

The fire crackled in the silence like thunder, and Nix heard Auri turn a page. He glanced over his shoulder at her, and heat flared in his chest, confused by this response. Was he attracted to her? Absolutely. But he'd been attracted to Flora. He'd thought he'd loved Flora, but he'd never felt the heat at the center of his chest, or the possession of his mind stealing his ability to think clearly, the unceasing need to be with her. It was maddening.

The lingering question in his mind about the intensity of his connection to Auri was that it was inexplicable. Gods were capricious by nature, and he didn't think he was any different, but there were rare instances of gods making connections that lasted for eternity. Had that been the god-yoke?

He turned his back to the fire so that he could study her. She made a beautiful picture, sitting at the table concentrating on the book. He'd never believed in the god-yoke and didn't think it was possible with her either. She was a mortal, which precluded her from the legend—if the legend could be believed.

Pressing his fingers to his warm chest again, he glanced inadvertently once more at the red ribbon around her wrist, then started back to the table, working through how to approach her in a way that might save them both.

He had to do something.

He figured he had three choices. He could do nothing, which felt like a path toward his uncertain demise.

He could avoid her, face her hurt and anger, which was impending anyway. But his avoidance hadn't worked, since he couldn't seem to sever what was happening inside of him. Maybe he could sever her attraction to him, which was always an option to keep them from strengthening any bonds that had been started. Of course, it could still lead to her not choosing him, but Auri was logical and rational. Maybe it could work.

Another idea was to learn more about her. This appealed to him. He already wanted to know everything. Only this intense study needed to be done quickly before she started wishing. After all the time they'd been together, he'd learned a lot which reinforced his belief that she wasn't going to make the typical wishes. If he could understand more about what contributed to her thought process, then maybe he could get ahead of the spell's obligation by helping her refine her wishes. But this would require some manipulation on his part, which made him feel uneasy knowing how she'd felt about him compelling her to sleep to influence her.

Nix returned to the table and his seat. Auri looked up as he sat and offered him a pleasant smile. He glanced at the book and reread the same passage he'd attempted to read, retaining none of it. His mind was considering exactly what he needed to discover about her, as if committing to that option. "Auri?"

She hummed in acknowledgment, her eyes on the page as she turned it and continued reading.

The sound conjured all sorts of elicit thoughts, and Nix shook his head of them. *Focus.* "May I ask you a question?"

"Yes." She straightened, looking up from the book to meet his gaze.

He bit the inside of his bottom lip, suddenly unsure about this plan. He didn't really want to manipulate her or her wishes. His heart constricted with an ache with which he wasn't familiar, but he knew what was coming, and she didn't.

He looked down at the book and turned the unread page. "Would you want to wish for, say, a love match?"

He could anticipate that the obligation to such a wish would be a lifetime tied to someone she abhorred, which would be his role, of course. He swallowed and pretended to study the book rather than look at her, hating himself because he didn't want her to make that wish. A more expedient tool would be to manipulate her dreams again, dive into her unconscious thoughts to learn about her, and attempt to plant suggestions. It wasn't ideal, but he could use it.

"Nix?"

The sound of his name on her tongue like a question made him look up and meet her gaze. He fortified his best god look of impassivity and waited for her.

"Are you—" She paused, her gaze flicking up to the ceiling as she thought. "Words," she said, more to herself than to him, and he knew she was considering how she phrased her question. Her eyes fell back down to his. "You aren't acting like yourself. Why are you equivocating?"

Fuck.

He pondered her words, her question, and looked for a way through it. "I am concerned about the spell." Truth. "And you have a wish to make." Truth. "Having gotten to know you and your circumstances, I thought perhaps it was your lack of experiences keeping you from making your first wish." Truth. "I thought maybe I could help you." Truth.

Her eyes narrowed. "I feel like you're leaving a lot out of those statements."

Truth.

He shrugged. "I cannot control your perceptions, Auri."

"What are you talking about?"

He'd annoyed her. He could see it in the downturn of her mouth, and the set of her jaw, in the way her eyebrows drew together. And he realized that was one of his options that could help him achieve the other. Pick a fight. He engaged in it. "Look, you're here for one reason: the wishes and hopefully to end the spell. I'm just trying to get you going."

She looked down at the book, and rather than being angry—which he assumed he'd see—she looked hurt. He didn't like that at all and wanted to reach for her.

She closed the book with a thud. "Okay." She stood but wouldn't look at him. "I'll go try and figure out what I want my first wish to be, since you're in such a rush." Then she looked at him. "But it will be my wish, Nixus. Not yours."

Turning, she walked from the room, and he wished he could go after her. But he didn't. Instead, he changed the room into his private study where he planned to drink himself into a stupor while pondering how to manipulate this woman and her wishes. Pressing his fingers to his aching heart, he worried that perhaps there was more happening to him than he understood. He didn't know how to fix that.

uri tried to keep track of the days, but it was difficult in the perpetual darkness. It was either twilight or deep night. Since their argument and his equivocation in the library, Nix had made himself scarce, making it even more difficult. While he was avoiding her again, she'd done the same. He'd annoyed her with his meddling, so isolating herself from that annoyance seemed the better option. Except she missed him, which annoyed her further. Plus, she was no closer to her first wish, and she'd fled from him with the promise to decide.

Left to her own devices, she'd spent time exploring the manor. She'd gone back to the garden, looked for the butterflies. Somehow, in Nix's maze, she was always able to find her way back to the familiar places.

There were more servants now, and she befriended them, chatting up varied versions of Greene and a maid named Jada, though chatting was generous. None of the conjurings had much of a personality. There were those in the dining room when she arrived to eat her meals. No Nix. Those who cleaned the spaces. No Nix. Those who stood at attention at the tops of stairways or opened doors that she wanted to enter. No Nix. Nixus was obviously conjuring people to make her not feel so alone. Only it made her feel even more so. The only one she wanted to see was him.

She returned to the library, where she was alone and grateful not to have a bowing or bobbing servant in her path. Laying on the chaise near the fire, she was reading Lady Miriam exploits, which had indeed provided an education thus far. Besides the passages exploring oral and hand pleasure, the lovely Lady Miriam had found release with both men and women, with multiple partners in a variety of ways which she described as "a shop of just desserts."

Each explanation by Miriam made Auri's heart race, the ache between her thighs more pronounced. It made her think about Nix. Now that she was more aware of her own sexuality, however, she'd looked at Greene a bit longer the day before. The way his eyes were shaped like Nix's. Or the way the bow of his mouth had sharp peaks, and it made her think about running her thumb over Nix's lips. Being curious about the many variations of Greene had her considering what she'd done with Nix. And noticing the beauty of Jada and her variations had Auri wondering what being with a woman would be like. Her thoughts made her wonder about the Kaloma law. She didn't have anyone to consult on the matter, however, besides Lady Miriam's wisdom, who wrote:

> *But whose right is it to my body? To my pleasure? To whom do I owe the feelings wholly mine and wrought about by consensual pleasures when no one else's heart and body is at risk?*

Auri closed the book, drew it close to her heart, and watched the fire gyrate inside the giant hearth. Who did the Marriage Law truly benefit? Certainly, the suitors had more to gain from a marriage than Tarley, Brinna, or herself. While they might be protected by the man's status, at what cost to her own person? Did Tarley or Brinna know her mind? Know their bodies, as Auri was learning now? And how might that understanding impact Brinna's choice if she had one? Would Tarley suggest marrying herself to Cobble if she did?

Auri didn't think so.

Did any of them deserve being selected as a fourth wife? Nothing more than objects to collect? A part of a man's sexual collection. No woman that she had heard of ever married multiple husbands, and she knew something like that in Kaloma would constitute heresy. It made her think of Mrs. Flimm being thrown to the bottom of the river, accused of witchcraft because her husband had died.

The rambling of her thoughts made her sad.

She imagined her parents. While she didn't want to think too long about them in that sense, she knew they were a love match. They had five children, which exemplified their longing for one another in an intimate nature. She blushed, realizing she now understood what those secret kisses had been when they thought no one was watching, or the touches meant only for one another. And they lived in a very small cottage. It was impossible not to hear things.

Then she thought about Mattias. Did he understand his body and his wants? Perhaps he had more power to choose a wife, but without means, it would be difficult. It didn't exempt him from following the marriage laws.

What about Jessamine? Maybe she was lucky to escape the marketplace as the lone unmarriageable of the family, but was being without a partner what she truly wanted for herself?

Auri yawned, the heat of the fire and its dance inside the fireplace relaxing her.

Maybe that was what her first wish would be—change the Marriage Law somehow. It would follow the rules of the wishes, since it would directly benefit her, but it could also benefit those she loved.

Her eyelids grew heavy, and she yawned and closed her eyes.

Yes. That was what she'd do. But she had to find the proper…

Wording…

As she had the thought, thinking about words, the letters in her mind fell into the darkness of sleep.

When Auri looked up, and she was standing in the Sevens marriage marketplace, behind the barrier where she usually stood with her sisters. Only she was alone. She leaned over the balustrade to find the marketplace was empty. Perplexed, she looked down at herself. She was wearing a shimmering green gown with golden accents. Suddenly the dress shifted around her, tightening to skim her shape until it was only panels of green fabric wrapped around her body held closed by a golden cord.

When she looked back up, three men stood before her: Crossbie, who was ogling her with his disconcerting eyes, a stranger with blond hair and a pleasant smile but a nondescript face, and Nixus, who quirked one of his brows and offered her a smirk.

"What is this?" Auri demanded.

"We're here for the pairing." Crossbie sneered and licked his lips as he reached over the space and grabbed ahold of her wrist.

"No," she snapped and snatched her arm out of his grip.

Crossbie disappeared in an explosion of golden magic dust.

She took a relieved breath and looked at the next man.

The stranger bowed. "I'm looking for someone." He smiled, and Auri wondered if she'd ever seen him before but couldn't place him.

She shook her head, confused. "I don't know you."

The stranger smiled and took her hand in his. The touch was dry and incorporeal somehow, as if he wasn't even there. He lifted her hand to his mouth. "That's alright. I'll make you part of my collection." He kissed the back of her hand, his lips only a hint rather than an actual touch. When his eyes fell to the ribbon tied to her wrist, he paused. His thumb ran over the ribbon, though she couldn't feel it. "Interesting," he said, and his eyes jumped back to her face.

Auri pulled her hand out of his grasp. "I won't be part of a collection. No."

The stranger continued to smile, but it didn't reach his eyes, giving him a feral look. He didn't effervesce, but turned and walked away, fading from view as he did.

She turned her head to look for Nixus, but he was gone, and in his place was Greene. "Where is Nix?"

"My Lord has gone, but he insisted that I offer you pleasure."

"No. I don't want you," she said.

Greene collapsed into golden light until all that was left was fluttering golden granules of magic that drifted to the floor.

Men appeared to offer her their companionship,

their wealth, their time, to give her pleasure. Each time she declined; they would disappear. And though she waited for his reappearance, Nix didn't return.

Irritated with the repetitive nature of the scenario, feeling trapped by the circumstances of the marketplace, and angry that Nix abandoned her, Auri pushed the gate open and stepped out into the corridor, where another version of Greene awaited her decision.

The aisle stretched out in both directions like Nix's maze, an infinite marketplace. She decided on a direction and walked, passing empty booths, until she came to one where a shadow coalesced inside, capturing her attention. Auri stopped and stood in the aisle as if she were the suitor. The shadow became Jada, who stepped forward, smiling at her. "My lady."

"What are you doing?"

"I'm on display. Do you like what you see?" She began to unbutton her bodice.

Auri shook her head, her skin heating with a blush. "You are beautiful, but–" She shook her head. "No."

Jada stopped, smiled, and evaporated into gold dust that fell to the floor inside the booth, floated toward Auri, and disappeared at her feet.

Auri spun in a circle. "What is this?" She rushed up the corridor of the marketplace looking for a way out, only it stretched on forever with variations of Greene and replicas of Crossbie blocking her path. She rushed through the throng of bodies, but there wasn't an exit.

She stopped and shouted, "I want out," and shut

her eyes. When she opened them, she was in the hallway of the manor.

"Nix?" she called, hoping he would appear.

He didn't.

Her heart bolted forward, pounding faster in her chest, heating her through, though she wasn't sure why. "Nix?" she called and started down the hallway, but he still didn't appear. Instead, the doors melted into the wall, smoothing out into a reddish colored wallpaper swirling with golden paisley and intermittent sconces wavering with flames to light the way. It was a long, doorless corridor.

"Nix?" she called, louder this time. She grasped the fabric skimming her legs and hoisted it up so she could run. Her heart was beating with fear, now.

She looked over her shoulder, and a myriad of people appeared behind her. Faces she recognized like Crossbie and Greene, but others she didn't, and the thrumming in her body was fear. She ran. A dark part of her understood why they were chasing after her and what would happen if they caught her. Her beating heart told her to be afraid.

"Nix! Nix!" she cried as she ran.

He didn't appear.

"You promised!" she screamed.

Her heart felt as if it might burst.

A single door appeared. It was brown and tall with a golden doorknob. When she tried to open it, the door rattled but wouldn't open. Locked.

The key. The key.

She looked for pockets, but there weren't any in the strange dress she wore.

"No. No," she moaned as she patted the fabric.

A glance down the hallway told her the throng was almost to her. "I need the key!" she cried and felt it's weight in her hand as if it had been there all along.

She shoved it into the keyhole, turned it, and pushed through the door, slammed it closed just as the hoard banged against the other side. With her head in her hands, she leaned against the closed door and cried, her body trembling with fear.

"Auri?"

She looked up at Nix. Though he was blurry through her tears, he was there, standing in front of her, his eyes wide with surprise.

"You promised!" she cried and launched at him, her fists connecting with his chest.

He grabbed hold of her hands. "I didn't know that would... how?"

She threw her arms around his neck. "You left me."

"You don't need me."

"I wanted you."

"But I'm trying to protect you," he said, wrapping his arms around her. "I'm sorry."

"It isn't your choice," she said. And then louder, "It isn't your choice!" until she was screaming it at him, tears streaming down her face as she pushed against his chest.

Nix grasped her wrists. "Auri."

She froze at the sound of her name on his tongue. She'd seen Crossbie, Greene, and many others who'd offered themselves to her. But Nix was the only one she wanted. With every fiber that made her, she grabbed ahold of his cheeks and said, "Yes," then pressed her mouth to his.

With a noise that reminded Auri of when she tasted something delicious, Nix's hands grasped her face, and he kissed her back, hungry and powerful before pulling away, his chest rising and falling rapidly.

"Auri?"

Her eyes flew open.

She was still lying on the chaise lounge, Lady Miriam's book beside her, the fire still warm in the fireplace. She turned her head. Nix was sitting at the end of the lounge, near her feet.

"You called me." His eyes examined her, but he didn't touch her.

"I was dreaming."

"What was it about? Your voice sounded terrified."

She sat up and turned so she didn't have to look at him. She didn't want him to know she was hurt that he'd left her alone. Hurt enough to dream about it. She closed her eyes and tried to work through what she could remember of the dream, spinning on the fact she'd chosen him. Being hurt by Nix's absence seemed a ridiculous thing, really. She was just the key keeper, a wish maker, who, for all intents and purposes, was there to break the spell to free him, so she kept it to herself.

"It wasn't anything. Where have you been?"

"Doing things."

"Like?"

"God things. Causing drama and chaos." He waved a hand.

"But you're confined here."

"I am."

Then, because she couldn't keep herself from saying it, she said, "You left me alone."

Nix stood and ran a hand through his hair with a sigh, putting more distance between them. "I felt it was the right thing to do. I tried–"

"Tried what?"

"To stay away. I find myself–" he paused, looking for the right words– "distracted when I'm around you."

She stood and faced him. "Distracted? What is that supposed to mean?" She was annoyed. Annoyed by his absence. Annoyed by the dream that had shaken her so much she could still feel it in the deep places of her body. Annoyed by the circumstances. "So, I'm just a plaything subject to your whims?"

Nix whirled around to look at her, frustration riding his brow. "No!"

"Then what is it? What do you mean?"

He moved quickly, his darkness swirling around them like smoke. It pulled her in, obscuring them together in it as the library dissipated, becoming nothing more than a suggestion, their dark cocoon more prevalent. She could smell the spice of him, like cloves and smoke, and the pine of Whitling Woods.

He reached up and wrapped a curl of her hair around his finger. "That isn't what I mean."

"Then why? Why don't you want to be around me?"

"What I want won't work. I know what's coming," he said and leaned forward, his lips brushing her temple. "I just find myself so distracted by you. I can't think straight. So I stay away."

Her heart was now a drum beat in her ears, pushing her pulse for a new reason. She couldn't see his face and looked at the hollow of his throat, the way the muscles moved there as he tilted his head. The heat of him seeped into her. She grabbed ahold of his shoulders to steady herself.

"The real truth, Auri, or the easier version?"

"The real one. Always."

"I want to fuck you every time I'm in the same room with you. No. That's a lie. All the time, even when I'm not." His hand cupped the back of her head, and he pressed his lips against her temple. "I see your lips and imagine them around my cock. I see you in those fucking trousers and remember the taste of you on my tongue. I want to fuck you until we both can't walk straight, and then I want to do it again. I haven't felt this insatiable—ever—and I'm a fucking god, for fuck's sake. It's a gods-damned distraction that won't end this nightmare."

His admission made her burn, the words running over her skin as if they were his hands. She trembled with the thrill of his coarse language and sighed at the memory of his mouth pleasuring her. She understood being drawn into the desire. She wanted him too, but his last words bit at her like a rabid animal. *End this nightmare.* Nightmare. If she were being rational, she might interpret it to mean his ordeal, but she wasn't.

She straightened and disengaged from his darkness, moving away from him. The library reappeared, and she had a feeling he'd let her go. "Fine," she said and turned away from him.

"Auri?" His voice sounded hesitant, maybe surprised by her severing the moment between them.

But she was insecure and emotional. "I will remove the nightmare from your vicinity. Maybe you can conjure me a companion." But even as she said it, she knew there wasn't anyone else, no one she wanted. She'd only said *yes* to him. "I won't bother you anymore by just being in the same space." She whirled back to face him.

"You want someone else?" He said it quietly, but his gaze was hard as he took a step toward her.

She took a step away. "Maybe. I don't know." She lifted her chin, wanting to hurt him back but knowing that was probably impossible. He was a god. "Yes! Yes, I do."

"I won't do it." He started toward her.

Auri backed up across the expanse of rug toward the bookcase. "You said you would."

"Well, I won't anymore," he replied and stalked after her.

Auri turned and ran in between the bookcases, and then wondered why she was running. So she stopped and turned to face him. When she saw his face, the raw hunger, the dark look that she knew would devour her in more ways than one, she understood her flight but didn't want to flee. She wanted to run toward him.

"What if it's my wish?" she pressed, him even as she backed up against a bookshelf.

Nix hemmed her in, his hands on either side of her head, and his strong body pressed against her. "Because I tried that already. You didn't want any of them." He dropped his head forward to fit it against the skin of her neck, where he kissed, then sucked, then nipped. "You only said 'yes' to me."

"What?" She breathed the word because finding air to fill her lungs was suddenly difficult. His mouth devoured. And as holding herself up was also suddenly difficult, she reached to grab ahold of him, her hands grasping his taut back.

He lifted his head, his eyes dark and swirling with golden light, licking his lips as if to continue tasting her even if he wasn't kissing her neck anymore. "You think I wasn't there? In your vision? Who do you think conjured it? Except for those first two. The ones from your mind. Who were they?" He pressed his hips against her, holding her in place, and grasped her face between his hands. His eyes skimmed her features. "Who were they?"

"You conjured it?"

"Yes," he admitted, and his gaze dropped to her

mouth. "You filled in most of the details. I know you're probably angry."

Truth.

Auri suppressed the exploding desire threatening to overtake her, annoyed now, and pushed him away, stepping around him. "How could you? You said you were sorry for doing that. Did that apology mean nothing to you?"

"Auri. Look at me." She heard him move closer to her, but she didn't turn around, and he didn't touch her. "I know what you're facing when you begin to make your wishes. I was trying to help. It wasn't because I was trying to hurt you. I gave you choices. It just didn't go the way I thought."

"How does manipulating me help me?"

"I thought if I could get ahead of the spell and what's happening between us, then the consequences wouldn't be so painful."

She whirled on him. "What's happening between us, Nix?" She was devastated by his duplicity.

"You want me, Auri." He pressed his hands to his chest. "Me. And I want you. The spell is going to make me your villain, and I'm going to crush you. And I've tried to stay away, but I can't stop wanting you." He turned and made a frustrated noise, pushing a hand through his hair. Then his hands went to his hips, his head tipping forward as he said, "Everything I did in that vision, you broke, and I can't figure out how you did that." He turned toward her. "You did that, and you shouldn't have been able to. You found me, pulled me in. You conjured the right door when I tried to remain hidden. You opened it."

She heard the truth. Heard what he was saying, though she didn't understand how she could have controlled his conjuring, but it felt insignificant when compared to his manipulation. "You tricked me," she said. "Again."

"I was trying to help. And I never removed your choices, Auri, which was what I apologized for. Why are you really angry with me?"

She opened her mouth to tell him why she was angry, but the words fell away. She didn't really know anymore. Yes, he'd conjured the vision. Yes, he'd presented her with choices. Yes, he'd been heavy handed about it, but had he really hurt her? Had he done anything to break her trust? Other than do it without telling her? No.

He stepped toward her again, but this time she held her ground. He stopped with barely a space between them. "Why are you really angry with me?" he repeated. He reached up and smoothed a lock of her hair from her cheek, tucking it behind her ear.

The move was distracting and encouraged her desire to lean into his touch, but she bristled and said, "I'll go, so you don't have to face this nightmare," because she didn't have an answer to his question. Then she turned and stalked across the library. Away from him.

He called her name, but she didn't stop.

After her fight with Nix, she'd moved between her room, the garden, and the library. She hadn't wanted to eat with him, hadn't wanted to look at him, unsure how to make her misery work. She was miserable without him and angry at him for manipulating her. She wanted to see him, talk to him, hear him, and avoid him at the same time.

She was in her favorite room, the library, when she heard the violence of a thunderstorm, the swirling winds of a tornado, the explosions of an ax hitting solid wood, the sound of a thousand voices rising in distress. Complete chaos. And then it was silent.

Auri opened the door to the library and peeked out into the hall.

Nix appeared. "Poe's arrived. Stay here," he ordered.

Seeing him pressed a button in her chest, a warmth illuminating the darkness she carried there. She wanted to extinguish it with her anger but seeing him made the glow more vibrant. It didn't mean her anger was gone, simply less acute. She said, "You don't get to order me about. And I won't stay."

His gaze narrowed, and he grunted with irritation. "I don't want Poe to see you."

"Why is that?"

"Because I don't know how she and Luc will use you against me."

"And how might they do that?"

"Each and every key keeper has been swayed not to help me in the end."

"Or maybe it was just you, manipulating them."

Angry, his darkness swirled like a storm around them both. He pressed his jaw together, so it protruded under his skin. "I said I was sorry, Auri."

"I know. And it doesn't change that I'm going into that room. So I can go with you, or by myself. You choose. That is a true choice."

He crossed his arms over his chest and stared at her, as if he might be able to make her submit to his will that way.

She didn't, crossing her arms over her chest.

"Fine," he said. "With me. But I'll obscure you."

She acquiesced with a nod.

Poe sat in the living room, looking like the goddess she was. Her bright white hair was sleek and straight to her shoulders. Her icy blue outfit clung to every curve she possessed. "You summoned me?" she asked when Nix walked into the room, Auri obscured by his shadows.

"I did."

Poe stood up from the loveseat. "To what do I owe the honor of your summons?"

"I want to know more about the spell."

"You know it all."

"I obviously don't. No one told me that there were

only seven key keepers."

"Oh. Right. That." She waved a hand.

A dark tendril lashed out and grabbed Poe's wrist though Nix hadn't moved. "You didn't think to tell me that after you tricked me?"

"How did you find out?"

"Luc."

"We didn't know," she said, fighting against his bond and unable to break it. "I promise."

"And you think I should trust your word?"

"We didn't know until the sixth, Nix. I promise on a blood oath."

"Haven't you used enough blood oaths?"

"I promise. We'd hoped the last key keeper would work, and when he didn't, we went back to the spell to see if there was a way to ensure the next one would. That's when we discovered the limit. That the next one was the last."

"Wait. To help?" His eyes narrowed, and the darkness spread throughout the room. "You want me to believe you and Luc were trying to help me with the key keepers instead of manipulating them?"

"It's true. It doesn't help us if you remain in here, Nix."

"Tell me what happens? If the seventh fails?"

"I'm not sure."

"How can you not be sure? You helped cast the fucking spell, Poe!"

"We don't know!"

"What the fuck?" He released her and sighed, then

walked across the room, Auri following in the wake of his shadow.

Poe rubbed her wrist. "How many times do I have to tell you I'm sorry?"

"Forever."

"This hadn't even been Luc's plan, you know. He'd just wanted to protect you from that stupid girl. We both thought this was temporary, and we were too stupid to research the spell."

"If it's a blood spell. His blood should break me out."

"We tried."

"I know."

"I think the only way to break it is for Luc to die."

"A willing sacrifice. Like the spell, the key keepers." Nix's hands went into his hair, and he twirled around, unseeing. "Words matter," he said more to himself, then spun back to Poe. "Why didn't he tell me?"

"Probably because he's ashamed and stupidly trying to save face, keep up his hero act as god of light. The longer we fail to figure out a way to break the spell—because believe me we've looked—we're stuck faking the night and lying about where you are. We tried to lure the right key keepers, looking for the perfect one, but now–"

"Lure them?"

"How do you think we've made it through six key keepers? Every time one of them fails, the location of the key changes. We're left to attempt to find it again, using powers and magic to figure out where it went. When we find it, one of us lures a key keeper. He decided on the new one because he said mine keep failing, and he knows you better anyway." Poe stopped speaking and looked around. "Where is she?"

"Luc already knew who she was?" Nix glanced at Auri.

Poe nodded. "He helped her find it."

Auri thought of the dollops of golden light leading her through the forest.

"Who's the demon behind the spell?" Nix asked.

Poe tensed, leaning back and tilting her head. "What? What are you talking about?"

"Every spell is powered by a demon. Look it up. We need to find the origin of this one."

"Shit." Poe's chin dipped to her chest. "Yes. Okay." She looked up. "I'll talk to Luc right away."

"Tell me the end of the spell," Nix said.

"Grant me the power," she said. "I'll summon the book."

"Granted," he replied.

Poe snapped her fingers, and a large book appeared, old and worn. It was hideous in contrast to Poe's soft, feminine hands. Dark green leather, aged and cracked with time and use. The title read *The Book of Discord* made of what looked to be bones. Auri shivered to look upon it.

"It reads, 'End the spell. One to start. Seven to complete. No magic to restart. Open doors, realities transcend. Freedom and Power. A Feast to End.'" Poe sank down to the chair, and the book burned away, bright gold between her palms. "Nix, I'm so sorry."

"I don't want to hear it. Leave me," he said and swiped his hand. She collapsed into the stardust and was gone.

"Nix," Auri said.

He looked at her, his darkness receding into him. "Lifetimes," he said, his eyes rimmed red. "For what?" He swung his arms, and everything to his left was picked up and tossed across the room, smashing against the wall. Auri jumped.

Nix stalked from the room, and when the door slammed behind him, the room rearranged back into its normal presentation, everything in its place and put together as if nothing had happened at all.

She didn't follow him, not that she knew where he'd disappear to. He wouldn't let her find him if he didn't want her to. Instead, she turned about the room and wondered if she looked hard enough, the chairs, the rugs, the fireplace, the windows framing the black of nothing would disappear and cast her into an enchanted darkness. She walked across the room and stood at one of those windows where nothing existed beyond.

She didn't know how to fix the spell. What she did know, however, was she had the power to end it. She had the power to save Nix. But that meant she needed to start making wishes. Each wish would get her closer to returning to her family, back to her life, and Nix back to his realm. While she might be angry at Nix for manipulating her, making her wishes was the only way forward, and she finally knew exactly what her first wish would be.

"I know what I want my first wish to be," Auri told Nix after dinner, sometime later. She wasn't sure on the timing of things anymore and had begun just existing in the moment as the spell seemed to dictate.

Nix was sitting in his usual chair in front of the giant fireplace, watching the fire with one of those amber drinks hanging precariously in his grip. He lifted the glass to his lips and took a sip. After he'd swallowed it, he nodded. "Okay."

Their rift obviously still loomed large between them like the wall of snow that had hemmed her into the lonely meadow. At dinner he'd been a quiet, brooding god offering her hums, harrumphs, nods, or silence. She wasn't sure how to breach the rift, though every part of her missed the ease with which they'd once existed at the onset of this circumstance. There was an ache in her heart when they were apart, but since their fight and Poe's visit, she knew making a wish seemed the best way to move forward. She knew she didn't want either of them to exist in the stagnancy of this enchantment, knowing she could help to change it. That would be like choosing to remain stuck in the horrible purgatory of the marriage market. So, she'd worked through the words to settle on a wish she thought would serve her hopes.

"I thought you might be happy that I'd settled on something, given how often you've asked about it."

His eyes flashed to her, then away. This was how things had become between them: tense and terse. Though she couldn't be sure, it seemed only days ago he'd admitted to wanting to have sex with her whenever they were in a room together, and now this was his response. The indifference stung, but Auri didn't take the time to examine why.

Instead, she sighed and sat across from him in the chair she'd come to think of as hers.

"What is it?"

She wasn't sure if he was commenting on the sigh or the wish, so she decided it was the wish. Besides, she didn't want to comment on her sigh. "I have thought a lot about this wish and the wording because you said it matters."

"It does." His gaze was lost somewhere in the liquid of the drink, the look on his face dark like everything about him. From the dark clothing to his dark eyes to his dark hair and now the somber carriage of his mouth in conjunction to the loss of the camaraderie between them, his brooding was exactly how she might have once imagined the god of night and darkness.

Auri smoothed the front of her dress. "At first, it may seem like it doesn't directly benefit me, but I assure you it does."

He looked up at that with a frown. "That doesn't sound promising."

"It fits within the parameters."

"Alright." His gaze returned to the fire.

"I've told you about the marriage laws and how I have to go to the marketplace to be discovered by a prospective husband." Auri plucked at a loose thread in the pocket of her dress, then reached into the pocket to grab the key.

Nix straightened in his chair, taking a sip of his drink, then looking at her over the rim of the glass.

She held up the key; the firelight flickered against the shining metal. Then she put it back into her pocket and looked at Nix, who was watching her. "I've been thinking about how unfair it is. The whole system is geared to favor a man. The man chooses a wife, and though there's a provision that a woman must accept the man's offer, a woman without means—like my sisters and me—are stuck. A man can even marry multiple women, and a woman has no say in that. My sisters and I faced that, well–" she paused and gripped her hands together– "the last one–" She stopped, not really wanting to think about Crossbie and what had happened, what could have happened, now understanding more clearly what occurred between men and women and what Crossbie's intentions had been. She shuddered.

"What about the last one?"

Her gaze danced to Nix to find him studying her, his elbows on his knees, his drink forgotten in his hand with his attention fully on her.

She swallowed, abhorring the need to relive it, but felt it was only fair to explain so he understood. Needing to move, she stood and paced around the room as she told him about her experience at the marriage marketplace before finding the key. When she got to Crossbie grabbing her, replaying what he'd said, Nix stood up and walked to the fireplace, his back to her.

"One of those men. He was in the conjuring?" Nix asked.

"Yes. Crossbie. The first man."

Nix's eyes caught her and held. "He put his hands on you."

She shuddered, recalling it, but didn't respond to what he'd said unsure if it was a statement or a question. "So, you see," Auri concluded, "our prospects are grim and gaunt. A woman has no rights over her–" Auri stopped rambling, her bravery seeming to break apart in her throat.

"Over what?" Nix asked. He looked over his shoulder at her, dark emotions riding his brow.

She swallowed to clear her throat, reassembled her bravery, and said, "Over her own body. Before coming here, before meeting you, before reading *The Romance of Lady Miriam,* which I would never have had access to read before coming here, I knew very little. I would have been imprisoned or put to death for trying to learn."

Nix returned to his chair, where he sat and leaned forward, his elbows on his knees once again, one of his hands loosely holding the drink between them.

"Women have no choices." She paused and took a deep breath. "I have no choice."

He sat back as if she'd pushed him with her words, and she wasn't sure if it was because of their fight or something else, but he looked down at his drink, and damn her if she didn't notice the thickness of his lashes fanned out over his cheeks. When he looked up, he asked, "What is the wish?"

She recited the words in her head, the ones she'd decided on after determining the right way to word the wish for what she truly wanted. "I wish for women of my homeland, which includes me, to have the freedom to choose what they want for their bodies in all ways."

He stood and walked a few steps away from her. Knowing him, he was trying to find the loopholes in her wording before granting the wish, and she knew he would help her. That is all he'd ever done. Then he sighed. "Auri… the consequence–" He looked pained. "Are you sure about this? Please be very sure."

"I'm sure."

"Your wish doesn't exactly change the Marriage Law," he added.

She stopped near where Nix stood at the hearth. "I tried to come up with a wish that the law be changed, but it doesn't change the fundamental problem."

"Which is?"

"Women having rights over their person, to choose their life. It comes down to controlling their own bodies. If a woman can control that, she could choose not to marry, right? She could choose who to marry? If she wanted to have children—or not. She could choose to–"

"–to what?" His dark gaze landed on her.

"Who she wants to have sexual relations with and when." She forced herself not to look at Nix; she realized as she said it that she wanted to have sexual relations with him, and she was sure it would be written on her face. When she did finally chance a glance at him, he was staring at the fire.

"I can't guarantee that the Marriage Law will be impacted by the wish. What happens if the law is changed to control women in some other way?"

Her own earlier realization hit her then. Nix had only ever tried to help her, protect her. Maybe he'd orchestrated the dream, but he'd also been honest. He may have manipulated the situation, but he hadn't taken away her choices inside of it. He had presented her with fair options—the fear had only come because of her own insertions in the conjuring. Perhaps he had been underhanded, which she didn't condone, but Nix had never once been malicious.

"I understand that, and I still think that having a say over one's own body would be a start."

She watched him as he pondered, his broad back moving with each of his breaths. She wished she had the bravery to move closer, to reach out and place her palm along his shoulder blade, to take some of his strength, to find security in that connection.

But she didn't.

Eventually, he sighed and asked, "Is this your final wording?" He looked over his shoulder at her. "Remember, it isn't just the wish, Auri. There's the price for it, and this one will be very high. I can imagine what it could be. When a key keeper has wished for health, they have spent the obligation sick and broken. You understand?"

"Right, the obligation." Her heart pounded in her chest considering it, but this wish felt right in the very center of her being, so she nodded. "Yes. This is the final wording for my wish."

He looked at her, then back at the fire. He was silent for an extended duration, as if he didn't want to grant the wish, then closed his eyes. "Granted." He looked into his glass as if he could find the answer he was looking for in the liquid, then took a sip.

"That's it?"

He turned away from the fire and walked back

across the room to the drink decanters, not that he'd ever needed one. She recognized that he was moving because he needed something to do with his energy. He filled his cup. "Did you expect something else?"

"How do I know what happened?" She returned to her chair.

"You won't until you leave the spell."

"My wish could have made things worse?" Her hand flew up to her mouth as her breath came in a gasp, imagining the worst for her sisters.

"Auri—"

There was a loud, dull sound, then Nix was in front of her, taking a hold of her arms to draw her out of the chair and into his embrace. It was the first time he'd touched her since stalking her in the library and wrapping them in his cocoon of darkness. His hands on her back, the front of him pressed against hers, burned her skin through her dress.

"I can't see a problem with your wording other than what I pointed out."

Auri nodded. "I know."

"You do?"

She lifted her head, leaned back, and met his gaze. "I do." She tried to fill those two words with everything she knew to be true, hoping he would comprehend all of what she'd come to understand about him over their time together. She'd only known his kindness. She'd known his respect, his generosity, and his passion.

He searched her face, reading the way she looked

at him. His gaze dropped to her mouth, his arms tightening around her, and she thought perhaps he would break open the wall between them by finally kissing her. But then he stepped back, dropping his hands back to his sides.

"Are you ready for the price of your wish?" he asked, turning away. He retrieved his drink and downed it in one go.

"What is it?"

"The rules of the consequence are always tied to your wish." His eyes moved to hers, and the look in them begged her to understand.

"I know. The spell."

He nodded, looked at his drink, and watched it refill. "The joy of the wish is usually obliterated by the price of the obligation to pay for it."

"Okay," she said, repeating her wish in her head. The freedom to choose. Her eyes collided with his.

"The price for your wish, Auri," he said, "is the loss of the freewill over your body in all ways."

She stepped back and bumped against the chair, her knees buckling as she sat with a thump. The very thing she feared was being exacted, but she'd had a sense that would be the case. And though she'd chosen to walk this path, it didn't lessen the fear she carried to achieve it.

He sat down in the chair across from her. "Prior obligations haven't lasted more than a day and night, though I can't promise it won't feel like a lifetime. It's the spell. If I had the power to take it away, I would," he said, and the sound of his voice made her think he was trying to beg her to believe him.

She nodded, but tears filled the breach and threatened to flood. Somehow, she managed to say, "When will this obligation occur?"

"For the others, within that first day of making the wish and it being granted."

She swallowed and nodded her understanding again, unable to say anything, afraid the tears would fall. She didn't want them to. She wanted to be brave, or at least appear to be. Nix had lived in this reality for a lifetime, trapped by no choice of his own, his freedom tied to the spell. The least she could do was face it with bravery.

"Auri." He reached for her as if he knew.

She moved away from him, reminding herself that the price was temporary, but her wish wasn't. She couldn't look at him and shook her head, turning to leave the room before he could say anything else. Before he might offer her comfort, because she knew she'd lose control of her emotions if he did.

As she hurried through the maze to her quarters, she was beginning to understand why he'd been so adamant about protecting her from the spell, about what was to come. When he'd asked: *why would anyone want to choose to make a sacrifice for the villain in their experiences?*

She was about to experience everything she was fighting against—with Nix as her villain.

Nix watched Auri go, tears shining in her silver eyes, and suppressed the urge to go after her. He wanted to wrap her up in his arms and apologize profusely for being the bringer of her impending misery. But he didn't. He looked at the glass of whiskey and wished he could disappear inside of it rather than hurt her.

But he knew the spell would ensure he would.

That realization shredded the golden spark around his heart into filigree, then opened fissures he wanted to fill with her but couldn't.

He'd dropped his guard in the library after the conjuring he'd manipulated, unable to forgo the shock of what she'd been able to do. When she'd taken it over—changed the circumstances so that he was at her will instead of the other way around—he knew there was more to Auri than just a peasant girl wearing a spelled ribbon on her wrist.

Caught off-guard, curious, and fighting the attraction he felt for her, he'd succumbed to his own wants and admitted his thoughts to her. He wanted her in a primal way as if she were the very threads that made him. The heat in his heart expanded every time he was with her, and as much as he tried to rid himself of it, he couldn't.

She hadn't shunned him for his admission.

Rather, her anger was rooted in her perception of what it meant to be free. Now, though, the spell was going to rip any semblance of choice she might have thought she had here.

The story of the farmer putting his hands on her, attempting to take her against her will, made him want to obliterate the man. Beyond the confines of the spell, he would. He would visit the bastard and eviscerate him with his darkness, but here Nix was useless. He was an impotent puppet, beholden to the spell that had him trapped.

He shattered the glass in his hand. The shards rained onto the floor, a bright sound as they landed on the hearth. The liquid drained around his hand until what was once broken was but a suggestion, a new glass in his hand, filled with liquid, undisturbed.

He was the bringer of her terror, of her pain, of what she was wishing away. She'd already been hurt in her life, and here he was going to perpetuate hurt on her again. How could he follow her and offer her comfort when he would become her jailer? She'd made a wish he couldn't predict, but he could imagine it.

Layered in the pain of realizing his own powerlessness was the acknowledgement that she was something altogether different. Different in her approach to wishes. Different in her approach to life. Different in her approach to him. Somehow different in her abilities within the rules of this spell. Nix had to acknowledge that these differences bolstered hope inside him. Hope that maybe the outcome could be different too. Because of her.

He was hesitant however, wary of allowing the hope. He would still take the position of villain, no matter her wish. Though her wish might be unlike anything any key keeper had wished for, the obligation of the loss of her choice was exactly what she fought. And at his hand. The thought brought apprehension to his already dark heart.

With a shout, Nix threw the glass into the fireplace, where it shattered, the fire flaming bright, then settling back into its usual rhythm. A new glass appeared in his hand, full, and he drank it down.

It was the nature of this horrible spell, where he could manipulate it as if there were no consequences to the pleasures it could provide them as inhabitants. It was an awful irony that he couldn't lie, but that was all the spell did was lie. He could conjure dreams that lied to the senses, but he couldn't affect what fucking mattered. He was powerless to it, to stop it, to control it. And what good was he if he couldn't protect her?

When Auri woke the next morning, she didn't remember her wish. Not at first. She stretched, enjoying the feel of the sheets against her skin and wondering where Nix was. If he'd come to breakfast. She thought about her family, missing them. It was then she remembered the wish she'd made.

As she blinked open her eyes, she recognized her eyes were swollen from crying the night before. She pressed a hand to her chest recognizing the way her lungs tightened with fear and considered hiding in her bed for the duration. But then she pictured Tarley. She recalled her sister facing those horrible men, shaking out her skirt and addressing them like a queen. Auri knew that was how she should face what was coming. Brave, like her sister.

So she got up.

She bathed and dressed, donning the most scandalous dress she could find in the wardrobe instead of her favorite trousers. It was a dark green dress with strategic strips of fabric covering necessary places and cutouts that showed off skin to tease and tantalize but didn't allow for undergarments. The neckline plunged low, nearly to her belly button, so that the roundness of her breasts was on display. The fabric was threaded with golden accents. A fitting dress for an awful circumstance, though somehow empowering. She would lose her free will at some point that day, but in this dress, she felt like she was spitting a curse in the spell's direction.

When she walked into the yellow room, Nix looked up at her and shot out of his chair. It flopped backward with a thud. His eyes skimmed her, his mouth open, eyes wide, taking in the way she'd pulled her hair up, the coal that lined her eyes, the display of her flesh.

"Why are you dressed like that?" he asked, his voice catching on the words. He had to clear his throat to get them all out.

"I initially thought I should dress scandalously as a comment on what was coming, but after I put on the dress, I felt—empowered." She ran her hands down the front of her torso.

Nix cleared his throat again and turned away, righting the chair that had fallen.

"I miss your trousers," he said, "but you look–"

"Don't say beautiful. I know I do." She sat in a flurry of rustling fabric. "I am beautiful and feel beautiful no matter what I wear. Thank you. Just don't say it. Not today."

He nodded, sat, and smiled into his glass of water before he sipped, which made her annoyed. "I was going to say 'different.'"

"Is that funny?"

He shook his head.

"It would seem that is a falsehood."

His eyes slid up to hers, amused. "I haven't seen you this way." He waved his hand.

"Trussed up like a girl being delivered to the king's harem?"

He choked. "No. With this dramatic flair." He snorted a laugh.

She made a noise and rolled her eyes. "So how does this work? Do you torture me with the obligation?"

His smile faded. "Or something like that."

"The suspense of waiting is making me antagonistic."

"I hadn't noticed."

She didn't want to acknowledge that he was talking to her again, flirting with her even, and she didn't want to acknowledge that she liked it. Even in her current mood. "Nix, you have always been generous and gracious. Will you please prepare me for what is to come?"

"Your wish was—"

She repeated the words of her wish. "Yes. I know. I made it."

He nodded. "Right. The key points are the freedom of choice, bodies, and all ways."

"So, I lose my freewill over my body in all ways."

He nodded.

"And the obligation could have me slap myself if it wanted."

He offered her a wan smile. "Possibly."

She mocked him with a fake laugh. "Please, Nix." She stood, her hands clenched together in front of her, and paced the room. "It's not knowing that's terrifying me."

He sighed. "I can't exactly tell you. It isn't because I don't want to. I just don't know. The spell will compel me, and neither of us can avoid it." He swallowed thickly, as if hoping by silencing the words they wouldn't come to pass. But then he added, "I know what's in my head, and that is what I'm afraid of."

"Will you hurt me?"

His eyes flicked to hers and his eyebrows drew together. "That isn't in my head, Auri."

She went still, her heart constricting at the sound of his voice, and turned toward him, the silk of the fabric twisting around her legs to show off the skin of her thighs. Her heart unlocked and raced at the way he was looking at her. "What is in your head?"

He wet his lips, then closed his eyes. "You know."

She heard him in her head: *I want to fuck you every time I'm with you.* "That hasn't changed?" she asked quietly. "I thought–"

"You thought wrong." He stood and moved past her to the doorway.

Auri turned and followed him. "Nix, please don't leave. I don't want to be alone."

He stopped with his hand on the door. "Why would you think that had changed?"

"Because of our fight. Because of the spell and what Poe said. Because now you barely look at me." Her heart twisted in her chest with longing.

"My desires are no different, Auri. It's worse, stronger even, and I'm terrified that–" he paused and took a deep breath– "terrified that I'll steal the right for you to choose. That I'll be no better than that horrifying man—Crossbie."

He started to open the door.

"So don't." Auri's heart raced, and her mind moved through all the reasons why what she was about to say was a bad one, but she couldn't think of any. She wanted Nix. She swallowed. She wanted the choice. At some point, it would be taken from her. "Don't be like him."

He pushed the door closed, laid his hand against it, and leaned into it. "You don't understand–"

"I do." She steeled her spine and channeled her sister's power. "You won't be able to control the obligation. You're as much under its power as I am. I understand that. But we aren't right now. At this moment."

His turned his head to regard her. "What are you saying?"

"The choice is mine now, right?"

He nodded, straightened, and turned his body to face her. Studying him, her mouth dried out, and heat pooled low in her belly. He was simply dressed in gray trousers and a white shirt open at the collar. She saw him swallow, his eyes skimming her again, skimming the dress that left very little to the imagination. His eyes darkened further, and his jaw sharpened under the neat scruff of his dark, trimmed facial hair. She wanted to reach out and run her palms over it, skim her thumbs over his mouth.

"Right now," she said. "It would be my choice, yes?"

His breathing was erratic—like hers—but he didn't move. He fisted his hands. "Is that what you want?"

Her heart pounded in her ears, the rise and fall of her chest matching his, and she nodded. "Yes."

He closed the distance between them, his hands framing her face. "You're sure? Because Auri—"

She nodded, interrupting what he'd been about to say by pressing her mouth to his.

He groaned, and the kiss exploded with sensation as he joined her. It was lips, angles, and then tongues and teeth. It was ferocious and full of movement. His hands grabbed hold of her hips and pulled her tighter against him.

He drew back, pressed his forehead to hers. "You're sure?" he asked.

"Yes. Nix. I want you. I choose you. This." She looked up at him.

He smiled, a smile that reached his eyes and made them explode like the cosmos with color against the velvet black of his irises. A smile she hadn't ever seen before. And suddenly, they weren't in the breakfast room anymore. Instead, they were in his chambers, the lights low, the fire heating the room to the perfect temperature.

With one hand cradling the back of her head and the other wrapped around her, he kissed her. She liked this kiss. Nix's lips, his tongue, his hands roaming and claiming her body, his body pressed against hers. Her hands found the hair at the nape of his neck, as she tilted her head for closer access to him. She wanted to feel him. She ran her hands down the slope of his shoulders, gripped the muscle of his back.

He broke away as if it pained him, breathing heavily. "I don't want to go to fast. I want to savor you." His eyes skimmed her form, his hands touching, learning. She leaned into his hands as he pinched the fabric near her collarbone. "Oh, this dress, Auri. You look like a goddess in this dress. Holy fuck. When you walked into the breakfast room."

She blushed, pleased. "Is it time to take it off?"

He shook his head. "No. Is there anything under it?"

"Not much," she admitted, her blush deepening. "It shows too much. Like here." She pointed to her bare hip.

"I want to fuck you in it. May I?"

"I knew it was a powerful dress," she murmured as his fingertips skimmed the skin between her breasts.

With a fingertip, he pushed her backward. "The woman in it, I think." He walked her backward toward that giant bed. She remembered staring at it the first day she'd been drawn into the spell. It was as if it had been a portent of what would happen between them.

"I've been thinking about this," he said.

"You have?"

"Fuck, yes."

"Me too," she admitted.

"What do you think about?" he asked, stepping closer, pressing his lips to her bare shoulder.

"About that first time. Your mouth."

Nix groaned. "Yes," he growled, grasped her face, and captured her mouth with his.

It was a punishing kiss that felt like paradise. She couldn't get close enough, reveling in the feel of his tongue, of his hands, of the way stars were growing inside her. Nix's mouth drifted over the skin of her jaw to her neck, inspiring sounds that came from her throat that she couldn't contain. He lifted her, the split panels of the dress making it easy to wrap her legs around his waist. His hands gripped her thighs, holding her up. With her hands in his hair, Auri drew his mouth back to hers and sought his tongue again, wanting the promise of that suggestive dance.

He climbed onto the bed with her, then laid her down and followed her, his thigh pressed high between her legs. His weight was wanted and welcomed. Auri tilted her hips against his leg, delighted at the friction, and she moaned.

"I love that sound you make." He looked at her and swallowed. "Stars, Auri. You are magnificent." He pulled a leg up so her knee was bent, the fabric panels draping around her like silky water. Nix ran a hand over her exposed knee and down her thigh, then over her hip and up to the gap of the dress that exposed the swell of her breasts. He drew the fabric back, freeing her for his gaze to feast upon before his hands savored. Auri delighted in the feel of his palms kneading her. He dipped his head and tasted, swirling his tongue over her nipple, and she gasped.

Nix grinned against her skin and drew the peak into his mouth and pressed down with his teeth, a gentle sensation that made Auri arch her back into him, holding his head against her, and lifting her hips to meet his body.

He returned to her mouth. "You like the pain, my goddess?" he asked, maneuvering so that both of her legs were free. He sunk between them, settling in between her hips, his erection pressed against her.

"Yes," she breathed, moving under him, undulating against him.

"Auri. Fuck. That's good." His head fell forward, his silky hair covering his face. She grasped his head, moved the hair from his face so she could see him, and tilted his head so her eyes connected to his. Lifting her hips, she pressed against him, the hardness of him creating an addictive friction between her legs. She moaned.

"Auri."

She loved the sound of her name in his mouth.

He moved, then, leaving her behind, savoring her skin as he trailed his lips, tongue, and teeth lower.

She gave a cry of disappointment.

"You'll like where I'm going next better." He laughed, a low rumble in his chest, then pressed his lips to her inner thigh. "I remember that first time, Auri." Kiss. Lick. "The memory of you has been on my tongue since." Kiss. Nip. He moved achingly slow, but anticipation built inside of her until he was at the joint between her leg and her sex, his tongue and breath were hot. When he moved the panels of the dress and discovered she wasn't wearing any undergarments, he stalled and looked up at her. "That's fucking hot, Auri. You're so wet. Is that for me?"

She nodded, unable to draw a full breath. All her feeling rushed through her chest like a rising tide, and when he inserted a finger inside her, withdrew and lifted the finger to his mouth to taste, she panted, feeling like the tide threatening to overwhelm her.

"Just like I remembered," he said and dipped his head between her legs, lapping his tongue over her. He spread her open with his fingers and found ways to worship her with his mouth, teasing, gentle, soft, and lingering like the first kiss of a lover. He swirled and sucked and savored, until Auri's sounds grew breathy and persistent. She grabbed his head, reveling in the feel of his silky black hair against her palms, moaning and moving as if she'd tasted something delicious. What he was doing with his mouth was incredible.

"Auri, look at me."

She lifted her head. When she met his gaze, her heart expanded with vibrant heat.

His dark eyes swirled, but instead of the gemstone colors they were a cosmos of stars threaded with gold, glowing. He was hungry, and she could see it. She shivered.

"I want to see you come." He closed his mouth over her clit, his tongue swirling, flattening, licking, all while keeping his cosmos eyes on her.

She couldn't look away, mesmerized by the sight of his feasting, at the way he relished her. She wanted him to know how he affected her. Her lips parted as she expelled a pent-up breath, then she moaned as his tongue continued to delight while his finger found her entrance, pushing in. She mewled, moving her hips against him, all the while watching him watch her.

He pushed her knees open wider. "This is my heaven," he said and continued.

Auri's head fell back, her eyes closing.

"Auri."

She lifted her head, forced herself to keep her eyes open, on him. The sensations he was making through her body enveloped her like the whiteout of a snowstorm. She couldn't see straight, couldn't think, existed only in the blizzard as the pulsing of his tongue and fingers made her hot. She clawed at the sheets, at him. "I can't," she said.

"Can't what?"

"Can't—Nix," she cried.

"Let go, Auri."

The sensations were amplified, everything in her body tightening, expanding, until she felt as if she might explode with that white heat. She cried out, her hips bucking against Nix as she came.

Nix kissed up her exposed belly. "You, Auri, are my night."

She grasped at his shirt, pulling it over his head. He tossed it and returned to her, so they were both stretched out together.

"I knew you would be this perfect," he said, and drew a nipple into his mouth while his other hand kneaded the opposite breast. Then he switched, giving each equal attention. "I wanted to do this in the pool."

"I want to feel you, Nix." She reached down and tugged at his pants. "I want these off."

"Your wish is my command," he said, and they were gone.

"But I want to see you," she said. "All of you."

"As you wish." He crawled away, then stood before her, naked and vulnerable.

Her eyes drank him in, and she hadn't known how thirsty she was until the sight of his body quenched her. She took a breath. His body was chiseled and defined.

His chest, carved and wide. His waist, tapered. His hips, sharp. Her eyes dipped to his sex, erect. "You are beautiful," she said on an exhale. "Very godly." She smiled at him, her eyes meeting his.

He grinned back and gripped the base of his cock in his hand. "I'll show you godly."

"I want to touch you," she told him and sat up.

He made a deep noise in the back of his throat. "I won't last that way," he admitted. "I'm already too excited to be with you."

"I thought you were a god."

"I am, but that doesn't mean I don't come, and I want to come with you."

"What about a baby?" she asked, knowing that was the sole purpose for this endeavor in Kaloma.

Nix nodded and opened one of his hands. Inside lay two capsules. "These are what we use to prevent pregnancy."

"What are they?"

"A concoction of herbs and magic?" He smiled.

She took one.

He took the other.

She reached for his hips. "I've thought about you inside me since that day in the breakfast room."

"When you were on my lap?"

She nodded. "You moved me, then," she told him, rubbing her hands down her own chest. "I feel it here." She pressed her fingertips against her heart.

He made a deep sound in the back of his throat, returned to her on the bed, and kissed her, settling between her thighs. Reaching between them, he took himself in hand and worked the tip up her slit. "The first time," he said brokenly through uneven breaths, "it might cause you discomfort. Do you still want this, Auri?"

"Yes. I'm not afraid," she told him, holding onto his strong arms. It was the truth.

He grabbed hold of her hip with one hand and guided his sex to her opening with the other.

She knew she was ready. "Fuck me, Nix."

"Auri." The way he said her name sounded reverent. He pushed himself gently inside her with gentle pressure, groaning with it. Her body stretched around him. It was a divine friction, slow, steady, controlled.

Auri drew in a shaky breath, wanting more, wanting all of him. She reached for his hips, lifted her own, and pulled him forward until he was buried inside her, and she arched into him, crying out. *Pleasure in pain,* she thought.

He drew a breath, still. "Auri? Are you okay?"

"Yes," she breathed. "I wanted all of you. More," she directed him. "More."

He lifted one of her legs, draping it over his hip, and moved in and out of her. Their joining was perfect. The give and take. The partnership. All the ways he'd presented her with her own power. All the ways she'd learned to love herself. She was completely in control of the moment.

She lifted both legs, framing his hips, the dress

pooling around her waist, and he pushed in and withdrew, the muscles of his arms straining to maintain control.

The pressure built again. "It feels good," she panted. "You feel good."

"Touch yourself," he said through his teeth. "I want to make sure I feel you come again around my cock."

Auri reached between them and found her clit, while Nix fucked her. Not only was the feel of him filling her, propelling her toward a high peak, but her ministrations added to this climb they were taking together. And, suddenly, like standing at the mountain top and looking up into the night sky, she jumped and flew into the stars, splitting open, crying out with her climax and becoming stardust.

Except she wasn't alone.

"Oh gods," Nix murmured through his teeth, and cried her name. "I'm coming." He grunted and broke open with her.

In the space between the beginning and the end, Auri took ahold of Nix, wrapping him in her arms, and found completeness there. Still joined. Breathing. Alive. Her emotions rushed forward, and she blinked back tears, holding onto them for the beauty of what it felt like to choose. For herself.

Nix rolled to his side, drawing her with him, still joined. His fingers trailed across her skin, a repetitive cadence, back and forth, that made her feel seen.

"That was—" she started, looking for the right

word, trailing her own fingertips across his skin and fighting the tears. She hadn't known it would be so beautiful, being with Nix. Maybe she'd suspected, but she hadn't known her heart would feel so gloriously warm.

"What?"

She gave him a teary smile. She knew it would never have been this way with one of the men she'd met in the marriage market. Her wish, she hoped, would change that forever.

For this, she was willing to pay the price. Everyone should know this kind of pleasure. "It was perfect. You are perfect."

Raising his head, Nix met her gaze, searched her eyes, and said, "That was everything." He bent toward her and kissed the crook of her neck. "You are everything." Then, against her skin, he said, "Please don't forget, Auri. Please." His arms encircled her, holding her tighter.

Nodding, she pressed her lips against his skin and whispered, "I won't."

Nixus

There'd been a thought in the back of his mind when he'd first thought about his attraction to Auri, that if they had sex, the inexplicable connection would pass. It would reveal that he'd instigated the intense feelings, making them bigger than they were because he was lonely.

But now that they had joined, Nix didn't feel less for Auri. He felt that glow in his chest all the more strongly. It was expanding. Deepening. The more he thought about it, the more he couldn't get the idea of the god-yoke from his mind. It didn't make sense, but it was beginning to make more now that he knew Auri was more than she appeared. As much as he wanted to discredit the idea as a myth, his mind wouldn't let him. If it was, in fact, the god-yoke, that would mean Auri was meant for him, and he for her. That it had always been Auri, written in the cosmos of the stars and ether. Everything, including being stuck in this stupid spell, had been leading to this. And somehow across space and time, they'd found one another.

It felt like a terrible joke due to the impending doom of what was about to happen.

Perhaps the god-yoke would help him fight the compulsion of the spell, but he knew next to nothing about it. How it would impact either of them. If it was even real.

Auri was nervously chatting as they laid in bed, her naked leg draped over his.

He was anxious too, but every time he thought about it, he chased it away by fucking her again. And again. They'd remained in bed most of the day, talking, laughing, and fucking.

"Now that we've had sex," she said, pulling his hip toward her with her leg, "what more could you possibly want?"

"You'd be surprised." He pressed his hands against her lower back. His cock was waking up again, and he tilted his hips to press against her core.

"Again?"

"Yes. Again?"

"Yes," she said, kissing him.

He grasped her hips. "And again," he said and pushed into her with a groan. "Fuck, Auri. Again," he breathed. His head dipped to her shoulder, and he nipped at her skin with his teeth.

She mewled and took it, her sound pushing him faster, deeper. Every touch, every sound, every look. He loved the way she lost herself with him.

He rolled her onto her back and lifted her legs, draping them over his arms. "Fast?" he asked.

"Yes. Harder." She reached down between them to add to her pleasure, and his.

He rode her until they were both gasping with each thrust. And when she came, she cried out to fill the room with her orgasm, her body tightening around his, leading him over the edge with her.

After, Nix maneuvered himself between her thighs until he was laying with his head on her belly, feeling the impending march of time. He wished he could stop it, stay right here in this perfect moment.

"I can't imagine what more there is," she said. "This is bliss." Her fingers were in his hair, and he liked it.

But Nix lifted his head, his chin on her stomach, then hoisted himself onto his back so they were side by side. He looked up at the ceiling, then turned his head and looked at her, offering her a wan smile before turning back to stare at the ceiling. "That's what I'm afraid of," he admitted. "My fantasies can run dark, and though I've had the opportunity to experience a plethora of sexual debauchery, I haven't with you."

"You're afraid of me being a part of your fantasies?"

"Not that you'll be a part of my fantasies, but that the spell will conjure something you don't want to do but will have to because of the obligation. I don't want that, Auri. I want you to want things with me. I'm afraid by the end of the twenty-four hours, you will hate me. You will see a side to me that you won't like."

She didn't say anything, but then what was there to say?

Time moved forward. A countdown to the impending first obligation.

He left her with a promise to get them food.

As he waited for Auri to arrive in the dining room, anxiety swirled inside him, worse than he'd ever experienced in all his time tied to the spell. He rubbed his palms over his face. "Please don't hurt her," he said to no one in particular, as if there were an entity manipulating the spell. It was useless to try and mask his connection to her. "It isn't her you want. And you've always had me." He dropped his chin to his chest. He knew it was foolish. There was no grand wizard behind the darkness, it was a spell.

He looked up at the window, black with nothing because that's how he felt, though it pulsed with shadow and layers of darkness. He tried to imagine what could happen but couldn't settle himself enough to think through it, to plan. It couldn't be planned for.

Auri walked into the dining room, and Nix turned to look. The warmth in his chest expanded again, taking up more room and encompassing his heart. She looked like herself again, dressed in her trousers and shirt, her plaited hair neatly draped over her shoulder. She smiled when she saw him and came to stand with him at the window.

She took his hand in hers, threading their fingers together.

Nix leaned forward and pressed his nose into the space between her shoulder and neck, inhaling her.

"I don't think I can eat," she admitted.

He straightened and looked over his shoulder at the spread, then back at her. "Me either."

The room disappeared, and he sat with her in his lap in front of the fireplace in the living room. He handed her a snifter of whiskey. "This might help settle your nerves, but it will hit like a wall on an empty stomach." He smiled, but he could feel the lie in the smile. He wasn't feeling happy. He was feeling afraid.

Auri took a sip, grimaced, then handed the glass back to him. Her hand found his cheek, and she worked her fingers through his hair. The feel of her touch did more to calm his racing heart than the whiskey. He closed his eyes, allowing himself just to feel this for the moment, because he wasn't sure what the following day or beyond would bring.

The first obligation had always changed everything.

"I want you to know," she said. "I've thought a lot about this, and my choice, no matter what happens next, is to believe the best in you."

Nix opened his eyes and lifted them to meet her

gaze. His throat closed over words he wished he could say but couldn't formulate regardless. Instead of words, he showed her by wrapping his arms around her, by drawing her closer and fitting his head between her neck and her shoulder once again. In the last several hours, it had become a place of refuge. He pressed a kiss to her neck, then reached up and tilted her head toward him so he could kiss her. He imbued his kiss with everything he felt so that she would remember it, hoping it would be enough.

Auri kissed him back.

Nix pressed his forehead to hers. "Please be the truth."

Then, as if right on time, shadow and darkness enveloped them both.

Through the haze of the glitter of gold dust settling onto the floor, Auri knew the obligation had begun. She was in a new room she'd never seen despite all her exploring. A small cage wrapped around her, the sheen of the brass bars sparkling in the flickering candlelight. She was alone, wearing a shirt of opaque fabric that reached the top of her thighs, her legs bare.

She looked out beyond the bars of her enclosure and found Nix. He sat in a large black chair, the back of which stretched out beyond him with intricate dark swirls like a throne. He wore a gauzy white shirt, loose and unbuttoned, his long legs stretched out in dark pants like he always wore.

A profusion of candles glowed and flickered, casting the room in their glow. Beyond Nix was a bed with the ivory and gold linens mussed as if they'd already been used. And beyond that, Auri could see the dull matte of metal bars against a wall of blackness so thick nothing could penetrate it. She was inside a cage within Nix's cage.

Her heart constricted with trepidation, and all of Nix's earlier fears added to its beat inside of her chest.

"Nix?" Auri called wrapping her hands around the bars to look through them at him.

He turned his head, and for a moment, his eyes flashed. He opened his mouth, but the light in his eyes shuttered, making his irises a dull black, trapping the Nix she knew inside. Nix was the spell. The spell was Nix. The entity that looked like Nix raised a hand, and the lock on her cage door clicked as it released. The door swung open with a creak.

"Out," he said and beckoned her with a flick of his wrist.

Her heart fluttering with fear, she didn't move from inside the cage and tried to open her mouth to speak, but she couldn't. Her mouth remained shut, her words trapped inside of her, and just like Nix locked inside the spell, Auri realized she was imprisoned inside her own body.

Loss of freewill over your body in all ways.

The spell's order— "out"—compelled her to move.

Auri's brain scrambled, attempting to piece together what a loss of power over her will, her body could mean. What did she have control over? Her eyes snapped to Nix as she stood, her body moving because the spell willed it. Sex. Yes. But what else? Her ability to speak and express herself. Her ability to move, to decide.

"Sit here," Nix said, indicating his lap with a nod of his head, his voice devoid of his usual affect.

Compelled, Auri sat on Nix's lap, though she didn't think it much of a hardship. Despite knowing neither of them was in control of what would happen, and the anxiety pulsing through her at the prospect, Auri reminded herself she trusted Nix. She knew this wasn't him, just as it wasn't her. And as afraid as she was, she reminded herself it was temporary, that she was strong even if she was afraid. That she could pay this price if it meant she and her siblings would be free.

Nix's arm wrapped around her waist and drew her back against his chest. "Relax."

Her body responded, wilting against him.

"Drink."

A glass of red wine appeared in her hand, so she drank. The bitterness of the grapes bit her tongue, but she drank it because she had to.

Nix leaned forward, his mouth near her ear. "Watch," he said. "There."

She shifted her gaze to the bed across from where she was draped over Nix's lap to a tableau of bodies entwined: beautiful forms writhing, moaning, touching, licking, kissing. Auri tried to turn her head, to look away, but she couldn't. She couldn't close her eyes, forced to observe what was happening in front of her. Whereas her heart was racing earlier with fear, now it knotted up with a forbidden beat, intrigued by the movement, the sounds, the pleasures given and received.

Miss Miriam's book had described something like she was seeing. Auri had chosen to read about Miss Miriam with a man and a woman, their three bodies giving and deriving pleasure with each other all at the same time. It had made her warm and fluttery as she read. Now she didn't have a choice but to watch a similar display. Several of the beings cried out as they came, a cacophonous symphony of ecstasy.

She thought about her choices of what she consumed. What she ate and drank. What she chose to read or allowed herself to see.

Auri's breath was moving more swiftly through her body, her body responding physically. One of Nix's hands squeezed her thigh, and she could feel the length of him hard under her.

"Open your legs," he whispered, his lips caressing the lobe of her ear as he ordered it.

She complied.

Nix took her earlobe in between his teeth and bit down gently, teasing her skin with his mouth. She gasped. He created a trail with his tongue from her ear down the length of her neck to the tender, sensitive flesh where her neck met her shoulder. She moaned and thought about tilting her head but couldn't. Nix, however used his fingertips to take her face and move her head to allow him more access while his other hand slipped along the skin of her leg to the apex between her thighs to tease her there.

The sound beyond them receded and the spectacle of bodies disappeared, gold dust drifting across the expanse of the bed to the floor as if they'd never been there. Now it was just her and Nix in the chair, her body responding to his touch. The feel of his fingers touching her, the racing of her heart, the moan that drifted from her chest through her mouth out into the expanse beyond her, as she was unable to control her response to him even within the obligation of the spell.

Nix bit down on the flesh of her shoulder.

She cried out with both pain and pleasure.

He continued to manipulate the bead of her sex and then inserted a finger, and another, until he was fucking her with his hand as he bit down on her shoulder. She was helpless to the physical onslaught and all the sensations awash in her body, until she was on the verge of an orgasm. But before her climax, blackness descended around them, and everything stopped, becoming nothing.

Her eyes opened once again to the inside of the cage. The linen shirt. The same version of Nix sitting on the chair. The flickering candles. The messed bed. It was as if what had just occurred had never happened.

The lock clicked open, and the cage door creaked open.

"Out," Nix ordered.

Her body complied, and just like before she stopped before him. He lounged in the same large chair, his long legs spread wide, his chin resting in one of his hands, the elbow propped up on the armrest as if he were a king sitting in judgement. Instead of telling her to sit, however, this time he said, "I want you naked. Strip."

Her body moved. Her hands went to the top button of her shirt, and she unbuttoned the first button, then the next.

One of Nix's fingers moved across his mouth as he watched. She wondered if he were trapped like she was. If his mind was moving in contrast to his body, or if he was just gone. *Nix?* she thought, wishing he could read her mind. *Are you there?*

Soon her shirt was open, the white fabric falling open to reveal a slice of her body from neck down. She started to shrug out of the shirt, but Nix's voice stopped her.

"Leave it."

She stopped.

And she waited, moments ticking by. She watched Nix, and from her vantage, he looked strained, as though there was a battle going on inside of him, and he was at war with whatever the spell was initiating. She wished she could speak to him, but she was locked inside of her own thoughts. So she waited, at the will of the spell.

"I want to watch you receive pleasure," Nix said,

but the sound arrived like the blade of an ax hitting a tree.

Two men materialized from the darkness and walked through the bars of their outer cage. Gold dust flowed around them as they did. They were beautiful, completely naked, and large. Dark hair, dark eyes. They walked toward her, eyes devoid of life, and though she wanted to shrink away from them, she couldn't.

"Pleasure her," Nix ordered the two men. "Look at me, key keeper," he told her.

Her mind receded even as her eyes fixated on Nix. *This is the spell. This is the spell*, she reminded herself.

The men framed her, one on each side, and she felt tiny between their large bodies. The first one slid a hand under her shirt, grasping her breast. The second one slid a hand up her thigh and stopped when he met the resistance between her legs. He slid his fingers through the crease of her folds until he found her center, and she was unable to control her physical response, gasping as the first man, kneading her flesh, leaned forward and slid his tongue across her jaw.

"No kissing," Nix ordered.

The first man straightened.

And just like before, Auri was brought to the peak of pleasure, darkness descending just before she came.

She opened her eyes once again inside of the smaller cage. Same clothing in its original state. The same version of Nix sitting on the chair as if nothing had happened. The flickering candles. The messed bed.

The lock clicked opened. The cage door creaked.

"Out," Nix ordered once again.

Like before, Auri was compelled to respond to the whims of trapped Nix. Over and over. Same situations were replayed. Old situations reinvented with new parameters. Altogether new situations. Again and again.

"Out."

"Eat."

"Drink."

"Watch."

"Touch."

Always at the moment of physical release, darkness would descend, and Auri's eyes would open once again inside the bars of her small cage, only to do it all over again. The click of the lock opening. The creak of the cage door.

"Out."

Auri complied and stood in front of Nix yet again. And she waited. Waited for Nix to order her into a new situation where she was at someone else's will. She was tired, defeated, and broken. She'd thought she knew the true terror surrounding the loss of her free will, the injustice of not being able to decide her own life, but now, playing out the reality of it in the horror of this obligation—her understanding was visceral.

She was no longer afraid. She was demoralized.

Nix sprawled in his chair like an unfeeling, uncaring god. And even as she tried to remind herself that he was as trapped as she was, it didn't change the anger she felt, the frustration, the hurt weaving its way through her. Tears filled her eyes and spilled down her cheeks, and she wasn't sure this was something the simulation willed but realized her emotions, her feelings, weren't something to be controlled. They had nothing to do with her free will. And though she couldn't seem to express the sound of her despondency, the tears flowed.

Still, she waited, standing before Nix, awaiting an order.

Tears blurred his image.

She waited until the power of the tears waned, depleted.

For the first time, Nix stood, removing himself from the chair. The movement seemed to pain him, his face and muscles straining as he did, and sweat glistened on his skin. He was in opposition to the will of the entity that held him. "Auri," she heard him say, the harsh sound of her name a thread wrapped in struggle, and though she couldn't move, she could watch him.

With her thoughts, she strained toward him. *Nix!*

He straightened as if given added strength, and like the time he'd hidden her from Luc, or the time in the library, his shadows coalesced at his chest, only this time, they were threaded with golden light, like stars, like the shine in his eyes she'd noticed as long as she'd known him. The shadows and golden light expanded, and he took a step through it toward her. Then another, until she was wrapped up in the aura of his power, the golden threads twirling around her limbs like sparkling energy, unlocking her body and her tongue. When she looked down at her own body, threads of golden light reached from her to him, threading through him. Their own cocoon inside the spell.

"Nix?" She reached and grasped his face. "What's happening?"

His arms wrapped around her, pulling her against him. "I'm sorry," he said. "I don't know how long I can hold this. The spell is fighting it."

"How?" Her hands moved across his form, taking reassurance in his strength, in this Nix, the real one.

He took her face between his hands. "The god-yoke. I think. It must be. Remember when you changed the conjuring? You found me. I wonder if you could do that here? The threads between us–"

And as soon as he said it, the spell tore him away, lifted him up and away, then everything went black.

Auri opened her eyes. She was inside her cage once again. Everything was the same—except Nix's fighting the spell, finding a way to her, asking her if she could change what was happening. It replayed like a loop in her mind.

The lock clicked open, followed by the creak of the cage door.

"Out," Nix ordered. Once again.

She stopped in front of him, the spell in control. Once again.

But she didn't cry this time. Instead, she wrapped her thoughts up in the golden threads Nix had fought to give her, the ones that seemed to emanate from her, and internally lifted her chin.

He fought. So could she. But she wasn't sure how. She hadn't known that she had changed his conjuring, so she didn't know how to do it. She'd just wanted him. Only him.

Fight it as she may, the obligation continued. Auri existed in it, powerless to it, Nix powerless to stop the spell from using his mind to conjure ways to control her body, bringing her to the brink of pleasure only to halt it at just before release. It was a complete loss of autonomy.

The longer the spell went on, the more Auri's mind drifted away, cracking and separating to protect herself. She spun away from the obligation by focusing on something beyond it, picturing the golden threads connecting her with Nix, understood she had become inexplicably threaded with him beyond the spell.

These feelings expanding in her chest, like the tears she hadn't been able to control earlier, told her a new story. She couldn't snip the emotional threads that seemed to grow from her heart, reaching out like those same golden threads Nix had freed her with for a moment. She couldn't stop the racing of her heart when Nix was near. She couldn't stop the desire to please him no matter the cost. She couldn't stop the hopeful light in her core that began to fantasize that there was a future, even if she knew it to be a lie.

Nix was a god. She was a peasant who happened to find the key. She couldn't stop the fear that blossomed at the realization that the end of wherever this journey was taking her, her heart would be broken.

Understanding that her heart was at stake was more frightening to her than anything that had occurred thus far, even this obligation. She knew that of everything, her heart sliding toward Nix hadn't been a choice she could make. It was inevitable. Falling toward love with him meant she was well and truly powerless.

The Key Keeper's 2nd Wish . . .

ix's eyes opened to the ceiling above his bed. He was in his room, still dressed as if he'd stumbled into bed drunk. Had he? He worked back through the haze of memories, trying to put the pieces together. When his mind reconnected to Auri's first wish, to spending the day in bed with her, then to the payment of the first obligation, he sat up with a start, then stumbled from the bed, mindless in his panic.

Auri.

Where was she?

The obligation flooded his mind. The cages. The

physicality. The cold detachment of his body even as his mind fought. His subconscious's conjurings. The fucking as the spell brought them together over and over only to collapse into darkness. Designed torture. He'd known it would be brutal, but he hadn't known.

She would hate him.

He needed to find her, apologize.

In a hurry, he snapped himself through bathing and dressing with a thought, though a quick scan at his reflection indicated he was haphazard in the chaos of his own mind. His dark hair was damp and curling around his ears, his beard a little too unkept, his shirt buttons misaligned and stuck to his still damp skin. "Fuck," he whispered and tried to put himself back together. Except he didn't really care. He cared about finding Auri, forgetting he could use his mind to find her, moving instead.

He stepped through the door of his chambers directly into the dining room. It was empty. He turned and stepped through the door into the yellow room. No Auri. He turned and walked over the threshold into the living room. No Auri. He checked some of her favorite spaces: the rose garden, the jungle filled with butterflies, and finally the library. She wasn't anywhere.

His breath tightened in his chest, making it difficult to breathe, and he felt sick with it. Rationally, he knew she couldn't be gone—the spell wouldn't release her until all the wishes had been made—but emotionally his thoughts were a jumbled mess. He crossed the threshold out of the library to her bedroom door.

Rather than step directly into her chambers—he worried about crossing the threshold without her invitation, especially now—he stood outside of it, his hand pressed against the door.

"Auri?" he asked to the closed door.

Silence.

The fear closed his throat.

In the whole of his existence, inside and outside of the spell, he couldn't ever remember feeling fear like this. The fear trapped up in the center of his being wasn't about him as much as it was about her, this woman he'd discovered made him feel a different kind of way, even if he couldn't quite identify the specifics of how. It was the suggestion of an essence rubbing at his sharp edges and sanding them down

He'd known even before the obligation had played out, even before she'd made her first wish, that this would be the consequence: her hatred. Then, he knew she would hate him because they all did. His struggle then had been wrapped up in needing her to still face that final sacrifice choosing him. After that obligation, he wouldn't blame her for her abhorrence.

But nothing could have prepared him for what she would face. The torture of losing her ability to choose for herself, and then being brought to the brink over and over, only to have it denied over and over. Absolute loss of control.

"Auri? Are you in there?" he asked again and leaned his forehead against the wood.

When Auri had stood there crying, her soul and

spirit in her eyes, he hadn't been able to contain the rage. Somehow, for the first time in all the years he'd been trapped, he'd been able to fight the spell. It had hurt, exacting a toll on his powers and draining them like wax melting as a candle burned, but his power alone hadn't ever affected the spell. The connection reciprocated by her—the threads coming from her to him—tethered them somehow, boosting his power with it. He hadn't known what to make of it in the moment, just tapped into it and called them both forth, sheltering them for a moment in a cocoon, even though it had been just to touch her, to offer her comfort.

Reciprocated.

He'd felt it.

Nix knew that he and Auri had chemistry. The sex had proven that one hundred times over, then one hundred times added to that. They seemed to enjoy one another, too—laughing together, talking, and sharing truths. He knew joy in his body when he was near her—an effervescence of warmth and a desire to please her—but as he'd connected to Auri in that spell, he'd understood, she had feelings too. Like his.

Was it the god-yoke?

He suddenly understood why he was afraid. It was the presence of hope.

And it was frightening.

He couldn't wait for an invitation and moved through the door like smoke. He needed to see if she was there. He needed to know she was okay.

Auri was still asleep, still in her clothes like he had been, curled up on her side on her bed. Her face was serene and beautiful.

He breathed a sigh of relief.

Relieved that she looked peaceful.

Relieved that she was still there. A part of him had been terrified she wasn't, even knowing it was impossible for her not to be.

Relieved that she wasn't conscious enough yet to express her hate.

He moved to her bedside and whispered in her ear, "I'm so sorry." Pressed his lips to her temple, he smoothed her hair on her head, drawing in a breath as he did to fill his lungs and memory with the now of her peace. Then he covered her with a blanket and made sure the heat from the fire was a temperature to keep her comfortable.

He removed himself from the room, reappearing in the library and looking around as if the room were brand new. He'd been in it hundreds of times, but he felt different. He pressed his fingers against the burning in his heart, wondering if perhaps he should break his fast first to ease it. Then realized it wasn't hunger, but a need for... Auri. He wanted Auri.

He snapped his fingers, and several books flew across the room to land on the table in a neat pile. He had some things to research.

One was how to break the damned spell. Though he'd researched what he could after Flora had left him behind, before the second key keeper had arrived, he wondered if maybe he'd find something new. He didn't want Auri having to pay any more obligations if he could help it. He also didn't want her facing that final sacrifice at the end if there was a way to change it. If he went through it all again, maybe he could find something new to change it. He didn't have a lot of hope in finding anything, but it was worth another look.

The second thing he needed to research was the reality of the god-yoke. He needed to find the actual legend, unsure if it existed beyond spoken lore or was documented somewhere. Maybe he could discover the tether connecting him to Auri and what it meant.

He tipped the book currently in his hand and looked at the cover. *The Art of Courtship*. He might never have had to woo a woman before, but he wasn't opposed to learning about the grand gesture for this woman who may or may not have been a romantic. He wasn't exactly sure why, but rather than consider the why, he smiled, thinking that perhaps for the first time in his life—before the spell even—he'd never felt this kind of happiness, and it was something he wanted to hang onto.

uri was in the library curled up on the chaise near the fireplace. She'd tried reading but had been unable to concentrate on the words, so she'd taken to staring at the fire and fiddling with the ribbon on her wrist.

The obligation had left remnants of memories playing games with her mind, and while it was disturbing, that wasn't the foremost thing haunting her thoughts. Rather, it was her realization that her true feelings were mixed up with Nix.

Since the obligation, he'd apologized and done his utmost to be compassionate and accommodating. He'd given her space. She understood, appreciated it even. It allowed her to wrestle with her own struggles about what her feelings meant, about how to reconcile her wants with her needs. She'd taken to avoiding him too, though for reasons she was sure she couldn't share with him. Understanding it was hazy and distant, as if she were walking toward it, and it just got further away. She didn't know how to approach this with rational grace anymore.

And while the space was appreciated, she missed him—and hated that she did.

When he appeared in the library, she felt him, a gentle movement of the air in the room, but she didn't see him. Her heart tightened with both elation and trepidation—the latter for fear he would see her heart in her eyes. He moved about the labyrinth like an apparition, so she never knew when he might arrive or depart.

"Auri."

Her heart flexed in her chest, then melted when she looked up to acknowledge that she knew he was there. Her breath caught in the bottom of her lungs as it always did when he was near. He stood across the room, still giving her space, wearing his characteristic clothing: navy trousers and an ivory shirt open at his throat to contrast with his golden skin. No jacket or tie.

His sleeves were rolled, revealing his beautiful hands and forearms, and she thought about his hands on her, wanting to feel that again, but unsure how to separate the physical from the emotional. His dark locks were unruly and boyish, while the scruff of his face was consistently days-old—long enough to be soft, short enough to remind her how perfect his features were. She wasn't sure he shaved or if it stayed that way because he willed it.

Her mouth dried out thinking about being with him intimately again, the hunger and thirst she felt in his presence always flirting with her wants and needs. She glanced at the column and cording of his neck, wishing she could press her lips there, but the reality of after sat in her heart, keeping her from it.

He offered her a smile. "I've come to…" His thought drifted away. He sighed and said, "Do you need anything?"

Besides him?

She shook her head. "I'm content," she answered, hoping if she said it enough it would be true, then looked down at her book to keep from bursting into tears.

She heard him cross the room to her, knowing he could have done it without the warning of his footsteps and didn't. He was at her shoulder. "You've finished Lady Miriam then?" he asked.

She closed the book and looked at the cover, at the embossed gold letters that she couldn't seem to read because of his proximity.

"Yes." She set the book in the space between where she sat and where he stood, then glanced at him. Could the heart of a god be touched?

"A romance?" he asked.

She looked at it again, not even sure what she'd pulled from the shelf. It took her a beat too long to come up with an answer. "No." She stood to put distance between them, walking toward the fire. "I don't have my next wish." She looked at him for a moment over her shoulder. "In case you were here to ask."

His brow compressed with an emotion that made her chest ache. "That wasn't why–" He paused.

She knew she was supposed to be deciding her next wish. But the thought of another wish and obligation made her anxious.

"What is it, Auri?" He put his hands into his pockets and looked down at the floor near her feet.

She turned and walked slowly to one of the bookshelves, pretending to peruse the books there so she didn't have to look at him. "What's what?"

He was silent, so she looked over her shoulder, but he was gone. She sighed, turned back to the shelf, and stopped short. He was standing in front of her, blocking her path. He reached out and tucked a loose strand of her hair behind her ear.

"You're avoiding me."

She couldn't deny it. He would know. He always knew. "I have things on my mind."

"I'm sorry."

"You've already said that," she said and pulled away from him. "It isn't necessary to say it again. You have my understanding. I told you that."

"I feel like I do."

"You don't."

He searched her face, then said, "You hide it well." Resignation marred his beautiful features.

"What?"

"How much you loathe me. Most key keepers can't contain it. You do."

"I don't loathe you. I promised."

"Ah," he said. "But see, I wouldn't hold you to it. What happened—"

She reached out to touch him but stopped. She wanted to reassure him but had a feeling that if she touched him, she wouldn't stop. It would lead to her burying herself in his embrace, crying, confessing, and trying to find a way to imagine this could be something more than it was.

He stopped speaking, studying her hand.

She fisted it and forced it back to her side. "I mean what I said. I don't blame you."

He took a deep breath. "Then what is it? I know there is something amiss."

She met his gaze and struggled to hold it. He could compel her to tell, and though he might have weeks ago, he now seemed to understand her desire for agency and respected it. That didn't mean, however, that he wouldn't. He was a god, with a god's sense of entitlement.

"I'd rather not talk about it," she said anyway, even if he might probe. "Any luck on the spell?"

His eyes searched her face, so she passed him, maintaining her pretense of perusing the shelf.

"No." He followed a step behind.

"Maybe you need the whole spell," she offered. "It never works to read only part of a story. There's always more to it."

"I'll summon Poe again and ask for the whole text."

"You could also let me help," she offered.

"Auri." He took hold of her arm to keep her from walking and drew her back to face him. "I want–" He swallowed and seemed insecure suddenly, letting her go as his eyes darted away from her to the space between them.

She tilted her head and waited.

He sighed. "I'd like to do something for you." His gaze climbed the expanse between them and settled securely on her eyes.

"It isn't necessary," she said. "As far as being captive to a spell goes–" she waved her hand about– "this isn't all that bad." She gave him a smile and turned away, starting down the aisle again. "Perks."

"I would like to take you somewhere," he blurted. "Well, I mean. A conjuring. A perk."

She turned back, her heart opening and melting into her belly. "What?"

"I don't like this space between us, Auri. I don't like your reticence with me. Reticence that started after the obligation, because this space wasn't there before."

He paused, and she wondered if it was so she would remember their coupling. That was unforgettable. She started to deny it.

"And–" he held up a hand to silence her– "I know you say it isn't because of that, but the distance is there. You feel it too."

She didn't deny it.

"I don't know how to fix it. But I want to. I think the proper mortal response is to do something nice."

She backed up against the bookshelf. "Mortal response?" How could her heart ever find purchase when he was doing things like this? It continued to slide down the incline toward him.

Nix stepped closer. "Auri."

"Yes?" She breathed the word, her breath coming in short gasps with his mouth and his body in such proximity, her heart tied up in knots wanting him.

"Don't shut me out. I don't like it." He took another step closer, and the smell of spice and pine and a hint of black pepper rushed in to assail her. He stepped even closer, the front of his body aligned with hers, but he didn't touch her. Auri grasped onto the shelf behind her to keep from reaching for him, to keep from grabbing his face and kissing him, to keep from jumping at him like some deranged, sex-starved woman. To keep herself from telling him her trivial mortal feelings.

He leaned his head forward and whispered. "I can't promise to honor your wishes if you shut me out."

"Is that a threat?" she asked and shivered. Damn her stupid body for responding to it, because she knew she'd enjoy whatever punishment he would make her pay.

"Does it need to be?"

She shook her head, knowing she had to do something before she said something stupid. When the warmth of his breath teased her neck and danced along her collarbone, she nodded, giving into his request and putting her heart further at risk. "Fine. Yes. Okay. What do you want?"

Having gotten his way, he stepped back and smiled. It was a bright smile that made the gemstone flecks in his eyes gleam. "Meet me…. in the living room. Before dinner." His grin made him sparkle despite being the god of night and darkness.

She nodded, her heart cheering in her chest. She pressed a hand over her traitorous response, the heat there pronounced and spreading toward her fingers.

His eyes dropped to her hand, jumped up to her lips, then to her eyes. He smirked with knowing, though she wasn't sure what it was he knew. Then he was gone in a swirl of shadow, as if he'd never been there at all.

Having decided on her second wish shortly after Nix left her in the library, she walked to the living room of the manor knowing she would have to share it with him. Her feelings, regardless of what they were, all led to needing to help him get beyond the confines of the spell. When she arrived in the living room, he was waiting for her.

He smiled, but seemed strangely edgy, as he adjusted his clothing: white shirt and gray trousers. Her gaze caught on his bare feet, their perfect proportions showcasing his godly perfection.

"Ready?" he asked.

"You're not wearing any shoes."

"We don't need them."

"What do you have planned?"

He crossed the room. "You'll see. There's this place I like to go. I want to take you there to eat dinner."

She nodded. "Without shoes?"

"Ready?" he repeated and grinned.

"I'm not sure."

The living room fell away from the ceiling to the floor. What remained was a place Auri had no words for, like no place she'd ever seen in the whole of her life.

As she turned where she stood, her feet got caught in the course ground. She looked down at it, at the imprint of her feet being swallowed by grains of land.

"We're outside." She took a deep breath, looked up at him, and then back down at the shifting earth.

"Sort of. It's my memory. It's sand," he said. "I'll take your shoes."

Now his bare feet made sense.

Her shoes disappeared from her feet, and the sand swallowed them. It was warm and stretched for an infinity beyond Nix. When she looked over her shoulder, the sand stretched in the other direction, disappearing around a thicket of trees that reached toward the sky. She smiled at the sight of trees again, but these trees weren't like any she'd ever seen. They had thin trunks, bent with leaves like outstretched hands, fingers wide and waving in a warm, gentle breeze. Sentries standing guard.

She closed her eyes, enjoying the feel of the breeze, even if Nix had only conjured it. When she opened her eyes, he was watching her.

He smiled. "Do you like it?" His eyebrows shifted over his dark eyes with the question, making her wonder again if he was nervous and why that might be so.

She looked away, her skin heating at his perusal. She knew he was waiting for her to take it all in.

Opposite the trees was an expanse of water that stretched as far as her eyes could see. It pulsed, moving toward her, folding over, then rushing up along the sand toward them before drawing back and repeating the process. As it did, it made a sound like a summer rainstorm, but also like the cadence of her beating heart.

The visual of their bodies locked in motion surfaced in her mind. A similar cadence, the ebb and flow, the in and out rhythm as Nix had entered her. The sound of her breath as she'd gasped and released with the glorious movement of their bodies. She shook her head slightly to clear the unbidden thought, grateful for both the blue twilight to hide her blush and the breeze to cool her.

To disguise her thoughts, she asked, "Is that the sea?"

"Do you like it?" he repeated.

She heard the hope in his voice. "You've conjured me the sea? How could I not?" She was astonished. "It's beautiful. A little frightening." She could imagine being taken by the power of that water. It made her think of Nix, of being pulled into the power of him and swallowed whole.

He offered her his arm. "I'm sorry there is no sun. Luc would have needed to be invited and empowered, and truthfully, I don't want my brother anywhere near our outing." He led her down the beach. "The ocean at twilight will have to do," he said. "I hope you don't mind."

She threaded her arm through his and allowed herself the enjoyment of his warmth. She'd earned this indulgence of just being with him.

Up ahead was the faint glow of a light. "Is that where we're going?" she asked.

"Yes." He smiled, puffing up a little bit at his effort, though for someone who could fill a wine goblet or change a room with a thought, she didn't think it had required much. She didn't point that out, however, content to enjoy him any way that she could.

"This is a place you enjoy?"

"Yes."

"What is it that draws you here?" she asked, looking down at the sand to watch her feet sink, struggling with it, and realizing what a nuisance it was to walk.

He tugged her closer to the water, but she resisted. "It's okay, Auri. I promise," he said. "I won't let anything happen to you."

She capitulated, allowing him his way, trusting that was true.

"It's easier to walk where the sand is wet," he explained.

He was right, but she warily glanced behind him, watching the water, afraid it might reach up and drag her in.

"I come here because I can," Nix told her a moment later.

"That is a horrible answer."

He smiled and looked over his shoulder. "What do you keep looking at?"

"The water."

"It's beautiful."

"It's terrifying. It won't grab me, right? There isn't a god of water waiting to reach out and drag me under?"

"Not here, Auri." He shook his head with a grin and a quiet laugh. "I've conjured it. There's nothing here that will hurt you."

"Forgive me for doubting. I touched a key, and now I'm here." She'd meant to be funny, but it wasn't. It sounded bitter. She knew he was thinking of the obligation. She did and regretted that she'd tried to be flippant, because his smile faded.

"If anyone were to drag you away, they'd have to contend with me." His protectiveness stayed any further response she might have had, and they continued forward.

"To answer your question more satisfactorily," Nix said, bumping her shoulder with his, "I come here because it makes me feel small."

She turned her head to look at him, surprised by this. "Whyever for?"

"I have been imprisoned for so long. My life before was short as far as gods go, and since that time so drawn out and…" His words faded a moment. She wondered what he'd been about to say. Then he continued, "When I come here, I watch the water, the way it hits the shore and the sand, the way the land shifts and changes under the pressure of the sea, and it makes me feel infinitely smaller, as if just for a moment, I am a man walking the seashore of a normal life watching the changes wrought by something more powerful and infinite. No spell. No magic."

"But you *are* a god."

"Yes." He looked at her, and the ocean stopped, frozen in space and time, the vastness and violence of it falling silent behind him. "I am a god, and how little it has wrought me but heartache, betrayal, and loneliness. And still, despite that, I'm powerless, truly, in this spell." The sea moved again, the sound resuming around them once more. "Sometimes I wonder if I had only been a man–"

He started walking again.

Auri, her arm linked with his, offered him a companionable squeeze. "I would never have known you."

"And would that be such a regret?" He looked down at their feet as they walked. "You are stuck with me. Imprisoned as the key keeper as you pointed out." He stopped and released her, then picked up a stone and threw it into the tumultuous water.

Faced with her feelings, she knew if she spoke, she might reveal the truth to him, but it seemed infinitely better than him thinking she regretted touching that key and calling him forth. It was a risk to share how she really felt, and while she hadn't been a risk-taker outside of Nix's realm, here she hadn't been able not to be. She'd left the library realizing she had no idea how much more time they had together and considered how she might want to use what remained.

"Please don't think I spoke so because I have regrets."

He turned to face her and tilted his head, waiting.

She tried to find the right words. Words mattered, but in the moment all she had were feelings.

And suddenly she understood what he meant. In the expanse of this place, she did feel smaller, just a woman with a man she knew she loved.

Loved.

Oh stars. Loved.

And now, she understood; the realization that had seemed so hazy and far away earlier was now right in front of her. Her heart wasn't at risk of falling in love. She already had.

Her chest constricted with her realization, her heart tightening, then flooding with heat so it relaxed and expanded. The heat spilled through her body, raced across her skin, out to her fingertips. She had the sensation of a slight tightening and pinch at her wrists, and then the heat rushed away, moving back to her heart.

She looked down at the sand, biting the inside of her cheek to get her emotions under control. When she reached the end of three wishes made and three obligations met, then faced a sacrifice to break the spell, she would still be mortal, and he would still be a god. She would be alone. But she could also see that perhaps she would be content knowing she'd found this happiness once.

She swallowed, threaded her arm with his once more, and turned to continue walking toward the light ahead.

"Auri?"

"I was thinking about all that I have experienced since meeting you."

He sighed.

"No. Hear me out before you get all broody like the god of night and darkness." She offered him a smile.

He grinned down at the sand.

"On the day I went out to collect twigs and herbs, the day I found the key, I had been happy to be in the woods. So much better than being at the marketplace. I was happy for the reprieve."

She stopped talking for a moment to catch her breath, her heart racing. She glanced at Nix, walking beside her, his head bent as he listened. He turned his head to focus on her, his expression somber.

"As I walked through the woods, I wondered how I might be able to escape the law. Considering my family's lack of resources, there wasn't much hope of it."

Nix stopped walking but didn't look at her.

Auri continued, turning to face him as she walked backwards, increasing the distance between them. "I thought about running away but being in the middle of winter made it impossible. It was a hopeless business, you see. My prospects would have been as a second or third or fourth wife, or, if I was very lucky indeed, the first wife to a farmer." She recalled Crossbie and shuddered. "Or a lowerlord. But, as fortune would have it–"

"You found the key." Nix walked toward her.

"I found the key." She stopped walking. "Before meeting you, I thought I'd found a treasure to save my family, but then you arrived and righted my understanding. Even amidst the turmoil of being thrust into an adventure I could never have foreseen I might have been saved. You see? The first wish—if it worked—perhaps, even stayed me from a loveless–" The word caught in her throat, so she took a deep breath and tried again. "A loveless marriage, or as a wife to add to some man's collection."

"Auri," he started.

But she ignored him, turning and continuing toward the light ahead. "So, no, I don't regret picking up the key and calling you forth. I don't regret that you are here, or that I'm standing in this place with you. I don't regret the night of obligation if it means my siblings and I have been freed."

He caught up to her, catching her by the elbow and turning her to face him. "But?"

She searched his gaze, the glittering in his eyes bright in the blue light. "I regret that you are still here, trapped." She allowed herself the gift of touching him, and reached out to smooth his unruly, breeze-tousled hair out of his face. "But I don't regret a thing, Nix."

He captured her hand with his and drew it to his mouth, where he placed a kiss against her palm. She thought he might press his next kiss to her lips, that he wanted to, but he didn't. Instead, he drew her forward by her hand in his, leading her toward the light. When they arrived, she saw there was a table set for two on a raised platform.

Auri stepped up onto the platform, releasing Nix's hand to take a small tour of the space. Food and drink appeared, ready for them. "When I leave, there will never be a man able to live up to this." She looked over her shoulder at Nix.

He was watching her, his mouth set in frown, his hands shoved into his pockets.

"What is it?" she asked.

He shook his head, dropped his arms to his sides, and walked across the platform to draw the seat out for her. "I have nothing to say about your after, Auri."

She sat. "We will both have an after." She reached for the bubbly, golden drink and raised her glass. "Let's sip to breaking the spell."

Nix lifted his glass and took a sip.

The fizz startled her, but it tasted lovely.

"I think I have come up with my second wish," she announced, picking up a strawberry. "You gave me the idea today in the library."

"Me?" His gaze followed the strawberry to her mouth.

"Yes," she said and took a bite.

Nix's eyes watched her mouth, then slipped up to meet her gaze. His tongue licked his lips.

Auri looked back at her plate. "I was thinking that if we could solve the riddle, it would help me in the end."

"No," he said, picking up his glass and drinking deeply from it.

"Don't you want to hear the rest?"

"No." He set the glass down with finality.

She set down the stem of the fruit on her plate and leveled an irritated glance at him. "Nix."

"Auri." He shook his head and picked up his fork. "It won't work. It isn't a wish I have the power to grant within the confines of the spell. No matter what you say, it benefits me, not you."

"But–"

"Auri." He set down the fork and looked at her. "Do you think none of the key keepers has ever tried to wish the spell ended in some way to end their torment? To no avail." He leaned back. "Thank you. Truly. Thank you for wanting to make that wish, but it won't work."

She wanted to argue, but he was instrumental in the proposition of wish making and obligation fulfillment, so she nodded. That didn't mean, however, that she wasn't going to find a way to help him. She was going to free Nix from the spell if it was the last thing she could do. That was what it meant to love someone, she decided. She'd seen it every day in the example set by her parents.

She would find a way. Even if it was the last thing she would ever do.

Nixus

"Why are you still keeping her a secret?" Luc asked Nix. "This is the longest one has ever remained."

Poe was lounging on a couch in the living room rather silent as Luc baited Nix, which wasn't very different from their usual interactions.

Nix, obscuring Auri when they'd appeared in the living room after the goddess of chaos arrived, hadn't realized that Luc would be with her. At the sight of his brother, Nix had pulled up short at the doorway. The painful truth of it was that he loved Luc, and that was what hurt the most about this whole thing. His favorite brother's betrayal.

Luc had turned with a bright smile. "Brother! I've come to help."

He'd been grating Nix's last nerve since.

Nix, now bent over a table where the spell book lay open, told Luc, "Mind your business or leave." He'd been reading it and rereading it looking for the loopholes, the clues in the language.

Words mattered.

Luc chuckled. "Little brother, I think you like this one. Usually, you hide them for a week and lose interest, or they rush through their wishes, and it's over before it begins. How long has it been, Poe?"

"Here or on the outside?" she asked, studying her sharp nails painted a vermillion to match her suit.

"What does that mean?" Auri asked.

Nix glanced at her and gave a slight shake of his head. His power could obscure her from sight but not sound.

"Oh. So, she *is* here!" Luc smiled, standing up to wander the room. "I have heard her siren song." He opened his palm, and a bead of light formed at its center. "I'll just offer a bit of light to see by."

"That won't work here, Luc," Nix said. "My conjuring, remember? I decide what you get to see."

Luc snapped his palm shut, dousing the light. "Well, you might not let me see her, but I can speak with her." He started around the room, poking at the space as he did. "What that means, key keeper, is that time doesn't function the same here as it does outside of the enchantment."

"Luc." Nix wasn't sure why he was worried about her knowing this. It wasn't like it would make a difference, though if he looked closely enough, he'd see it was because he was afraid of making her more miserable than the spell's power already did.

After their excursion to the ocean, there'd been yet another shift between them. Auri wasn't actively avoiding him, but there was something she wasn't saying. She'd always been forthcoming with her opinions and now seemed to be holding them back. Add to that the mystery of their connection. The rush he felt in her presence. The heat. The desire. The longing. The pain when he wasn't with her.

This was more than infatuation; the visceral response he felt just being in her proximity was maddening, and yet he wanted more of it, of her. He hadn't discovered any concrete evidence about the god-yoke, but he didn't want to bring it up with Luc or Poe, even though they'd have access to more knowledge.

When Auri had shared her experience beyond the spell and what she'd endured, the strength of his response had been to eliminate all mortal men, which he knew was ridiculous. He'd wanted to tell her he would protect her from all of that, but he had no power to make any promises to this woman. Thinking about an after for her, beyond him, felt like someone had taken his veins and yanked them from inside his body out through his fingers and toes. An after without her made him ache with horrible emptiness while igniting a rage strong enough to bring down mountains.

"By my calculations," Luc said out loud to the vast space of the room, "you've been in this realm for the equivalent of seven days in your realm, which is roughly two months here." Luc continued his tour about the room. He peeked behind a curtain. "Key keeper, key keeper, what color is your hair?"

"Shut up, Luc," Nix said, straightening. "You already know, remember. Didn't you lure her?"

Luc dropped the curtain, looked over his shoulder at Nix, then glanced at Poe. He looked put out that she'd revealed this fact. "She was wearing a hat."

Nix ignored him and continued with the work at hand. "Who made the oath?" He looked up at Luc across the room.

Luc smiled a feral smile. "Wouldn't you like to know. I'll tell you for a price."

"Poe, who made the oath?"

"Don't, Poe," Luc said.

"Boys. Boys. You know both of you are trying to compel me right now. I know I am a lesser god, but you working against one another negates the compulsion."

"Stop hiding me," Auri told Nix.

Luc's eyes brightened.

He looked at her and shook his head. Another of his fears at work. Revealing her to Luc and Poe made him feel weak, somehow. Hiding her meant she was his alone, in some way. His.

The god-yoke?

He'd discovered, according to god lore that in the beginning of things, the haphazard mating of gods made for tumultuous chaos in the universe. Orah, goddess of all things, in her infinite wisdom, removed the breath of life from all the gods. Then she embedded a sleeping star and its mate within them before returning their breath. When the star within them found its mate, the power would expand to encompass them both, tying them together. It was a story, but could the hunger and heat wrapping chains around his heart be explained by it? It made him feel possessive and upended around her.

He glanced at Auri. His power had tethered to her, and though he didn't know if it was the god-yoke and that she couldn't feel it because of her mortality—at least he hadn't found anything to suggest otherwise— he knew she cared.

She put a hand on his arm. "If it will get you the answers you need, then just do it."

"Yes," Luc said with a toothy smile. "Just do it, brother."

Nix honored her choice, as he always would, and dropped the glamour.

"Well, hello, there," Luc said, walking across the room toward her. "Aren't you a pretty thing?"

Nix stepped between them.

Poe turned in the loveseat and leaned over the back of it, giving Auri a thorough stare. "What is your name, key keeper?"

"Aurielle."

The goddess of chaos made a humming noise, disinterested, then turned and sat back, her bored expression resuming as she fiddled with her nails.

Luc, on the other hand, acted far more interested, which annoyed Nix. His brother's gaze moved across Auri as if he were going to create her likeness in paint or redress her after undressing her first. It made Nix want to shapeshift into a three-headed dog, bare his fangs, and rip his brother to shreds.

He shoved the annoyance down into the deep recesses of his belly. "Who made the oath?"

"I did," Luc said. "But it's a useless path." He studied Auri. "Dark hair then, Aurielle. And gray eyes. Ample–"

"Luc," Nix said, his teeth pressed together. "If you so much as say another word, I will fucking cut you in half, and you can put yourself back together outside."

Luc laughed. "But the blood, brother."

"Maybe it will break the spell." Nix gave Luc a pointed stare. "Let's try it."

Luc held up his hands. "Okay. It hasn't come to that yet."

"Why is it useless?" Auri asked.

"Because Poe and I tried a reverse spell using the oath. It's blood-binding."

"Which means the sacrifice is binding," Poe said from the couch.

"Do you think those last lines have anything to do with breaking it?" Auri asked, leaning over the spell book, reading. Nix watched her use the tip of her finger to trace the words as she read them.

"No."

"Because you can't solve it?" Nix asked Luc.

"No. Because it isn't about breaking it. It's about the seven. It's useless to take that path. There are only three ways this ends. With her," Luc nodded at Auri, "with you stuck–"

"That's what the words reveal, genius, if this doesn't work. I might be obliterated by failure. What the fuck does 'feast' here mean. See?"

"Well, it won't come to that," Luc said, and for the first time in a long while, Nix saw his brother grow serious. "The third way is by my sacrifice." He looked at Poe, who was watching Luc with a look Nix couldn't identify. Sadness? Concern? "I–" he started, then stopped, but Nix understood where his brother had been headed with his thought.

They might have been two halves of a whole at odds with one another, but Nix understood Luc's thinking. Luc was planning on being the final sacrifice to the spell, the fulfilled blood sacrifice if the seventh key keeper failed. Redemption for his mistake.

But Luc didn't say it, instead smiling at Auri. "I have a good feeling about this one, brother."

Then Luc was gone, Poe and the book of spells with him.

"He's going to end it if I don't." Auri turned away from where Lucian had disappeared, walked to a window on the other side of the room, and watched as the view faded from a countryside vista to black with Nix's mood. She glanced over her shoulder at him.

He ran a hand back and forth through his hair and made a frustrated noise as he crossed to stand beside her. "If he hadn't fucking started it, he wouldn't have to."

Auri turned to him but didn't move. "I need to talk to you about the second wish."

Nix took a deep breath. "Okay. Not a repeat of the

other night, right?" He faced her, his arms crossed, his hair a riot on his head. He looked undone, and she thought about grabbing his hair, yanking on it, and dragging his mouth to hers.

She didn't.

"No. I just don't have any wishes." Which wasn't exactly true. She wanted his love, but that wasn't something to be wished for. It wasn't something to compel. It was something to be given freely.

"How can you not have wishes?"

"There is nothing I want." It was a lie, but the spell didn't deny her the ability like it did him. She crossed the room and sat down in the chair near the fireplace.

Nix remained at the window but turned to face her. "Nothing? No riches? Everyone always wishes for riches."

She shook her head and crossed one leg over the other, leaning back in the chair. "Look at what you provide."

"But when you leave?" He frowned, then moved across the room and took the seat across from her. "What about then?"

The thought of leaving him made her heart ache, and she was sure it would be written on her face, so she looked at the fire in the hearth instead of at him, suddenly feeling angry at the fact. It was a cruel twist of fate she'd fallen in love with someone she couldn't have.

She could admit that riches would change things considerably for her and her family, but she wondered at the cost.

She sighed. "My family may not have wealth, but we are wealthy." Saying it aloud, she knew it was the truth. Her parents loved one another and them. Her siblings loved her, and she loved them. They had what they needed.

Then she recalled something Luc had said about the time and frowned. "Do you think my family is worried about me? That I'm causing them pain by being gone?"

Nix sat back. "In all your talk of them, you exude love. I should think they are broken-hearted."

"I don't like that," she said.

She considered wishing it away, but again, what would it cost? Their memories of her? Hers of them? She could wish time to stop while she was with Nix, but what would the price be? That she would lose all time and her memories with him later? She wasn't willing to pay that price, so she didn't say more about it.

"Do you want for nothing?"

She looked at him and opened her mouth to say she didn't, but the lie wouldn't come forth, so she closed it.

"There is something you want," he said and smiled.

She slid her palms down her thighs, irritated he was pushing her. "It is not a wish."

"Of course it is. Everything can be wished for."

"Not everything." She stood and walked out of the room—only to walk right back into the same room.

Nix now stood in front of his chair.

"You can't walk away, Auri. Remember what I said about shutting me out. I don't like it. It makes me feel petulant and unruly."

"You're being overbearing, and I'm not talking about it with you."

"I insist."

"I choose not to."

He swiped a hand over his face, then pushed it through his hair to the back of his neck. "Auri."

"Leave it alone, Nix. I mean it."

"I can help you." He straightened, his arms coming out to his sides. "With the wording."

"Why? Are you in such a rush for me to finish the wishes?"

He opened his mouth, then closed it. Then, after a beat, he shook his head. "No. I'm not."

"Then?"

"The longer you're in here, the longer your family is without you. The spell—I've messed with your life enough as it is, Auri. The sooner this is over, the sooner you can get on with living."

"So that's what you want? Me to get on with it?" She was annoyed. Annoyed at the circumstance. Annoyed at her feelings. Annoyed at knowing this was a path to nowhere. Annoyed at herself for picking a fight with him. She wanted to scream.

She gritted her teeth, made a frustrated sound, then glared at him before turning on her heel and walking from the room.

Only to walk right back into it again.

This time, Nix was waiting for her near the door. She raised her arms and made a frustrated sound.

"Talk to me," he said.

"Let me go to my rooms."

He crossed his arms over his chest. "Not until you tell me."

"What do you want me to say?"

"What do you want that you won't wish for?"

"I won't tell you, and do you want to know why?"

"Why?"

"Because I don't have to! It's mine." She leaned toward him, pressing her fisted hand to her heart. "And making it won't change anything. It won't help me or you. It isn't something that can be wished for. Stop asking!" She turned away from him and stomped from the room.

This time, as she passed through the door, she walked into her bed chambers, but Nix was already there, waiting near the windows dark behind his back.

"I brought you to your rooms like you asked. Now, tell me."

She shook her head and tears filled her eyes.

Nix started across the room toward her, and Auri evaded him, putting a chair between them. He stopped and smiled, but it wasn't a friendly smile. It made her feel like prey. Her core heated and melted, flooding the place between her thighs.

"I like to play chase, Auri. I always win, though. And if I catch you, there will be a lot of things involving your body parts and my mouth."

It was a promise, and as much as she wished her body wouldn't react, it did. And as much as she wished she could spurn him, she couldn't. Instead, she smiled even as tears spilled down her cheeks.

"I can't tell you," she whispered and met his gaze.

Nix reached out a hand, and suddenly she was in his arms as if there'd never been any distance between them. His hands framed her face. "Auri. Please. Your silence kills me."

She pulled his hands away from her face with her own wrapped around his wrists. "My silence?" A question. "My silence." A statement. She scoffed.

He looked surprised.

She glared at him. "My silence is my protection."

He narrowed his eyes. "What are you talking about? Protection from what?"

"You!"

He looked surprised and pressed his own hand to chest. "Me?" Then he looked crestfallen, as if perhaps he deserved what she was giving him, which made her angrier. He thought he deserved her anger. Because of the spell. He didn't deserve it.

She'd thought she was just angry, but really, she was just… sad. But she was committed to this fight and suddenly understood her sister, Tarley. Tarley's strength had never been about being strong. It had been about the walls she erected to keep everyone out. It was exactly what Auri was trying to do to Nix.

She stalked past him, which left her cornered

between him and her bed. She whirled on him anyway. "Yes, you, lord god of the night and darkness." Now she was the petulant and unruly one. Gods, she wanted him.

His arms went out to his sides. "What have I done now?"

"Nothing."

His hands went to his waist. "I took you to the ocean. Was that nothing?"

She rolled her eyes and made a noise with her mouth. Then she swiped at her remaining tears and crossed her arms. "What would you like for that?"

"The truth about what is fucking bothering you, Auri!" he yelled. "I don't know what else to do to reach you."

"Reach me? I'm here!" She held out her arms.

"You've built a bridge, crossed it to the other side, and burned it down between us." He paused. "I don't blame you. I don't. The spell—"

"This isn't about the damned spell!"

His eyes widened, his brows arching high. "What is it about?"

But she pressed her lips together, crossed her arms over her chest, and glared at him.

"Tell me, Auri."

"Would you compel me too?" She released her hands to her hips.

He grabbed his hair with both hands. "I've thought about it. I have." He let go of his hair, his eyes burning into hers. "But I know it would make you angry."

"I want the choice now too, but you won't listen."

"Because–"

"Because what?" she yelled, her arms out to her sides. She pointed at him and took a step forward. "I tell you this isn't something I can wish for, and you push and push." She took another step toward him. "What do you want from me?"

He took a step toward her. "The truth! What can't you fucking wish for?" he yelled.

"Your love!" she screamed at him, now close enough she could just reach out and touch him.

He froze and blinked.

Her chest heaved.

The tears spilled from her eyes, obscuring him, and she dropped her face into her hands.

"What did you say?" he asked, his voice now quiet and even. His warm hands wrapped gently around her wrists, and he drew her hands away from her face. "Look at me, Auri. What did you say?"

"I can't wish for your love," she whispered, her eyes still downcast. "I won't do it. I don't want it that way. And what good would it do anyway?" A broken sob rushed through her chest.

"Are you saying that you love me?"

She took a deep breath, raised her eyes to his, and nodded. "Yes, Nix. I love you. And I–" But she didn't finish her thought, because Nix framed her face with his hands and pressed his lips to hers, silencing whatever she'd been about to say.

Nixus

She loved him.

He claimed her with his mouth, and she clung to him.

He had once told her he was everything, but he knew it wasn't true. She was everything. Her kiss was everything. Her touch was everything. Her smile. Her laugh. Her life. Those words. She had somehow become his everything, and whether that was being god-yoked or something else, he needed it, now. Needed her.

He kissed her with the ferocious need inside of him. Kissed her so that it would show her what she was, what she'd become. Her kiss matched his, and it quenched a thirst deep inside him, watered a seed that had been planted and shriveled inside the pain of this spell.

But then she disengaged, leaving him stranded.

He took a step toward her.

But she held up her hand and stopped him. "No," she said.

He fisted his hands at his sides.

Her tears renewed in her eyes, glowing like liquid silver. "I know what my wish will be."

Nix shook his head. "Auri." He knew what she was about to do, and he wouldn't accept it.

The tears spilled over and down her cheeks. "I wish–" Her voice broke.

"Words matter," he told her.

She folded her arms around her as if to hold herself together. "I wish–" But she stopped, her eyes darting about as if to find the words. Then she looked up and swallowed as more tears fell. "I wish–"

Nix stepped toward her. "Auri, wait. Please. The consequence would be what you'd be wishing to avoid."

She shook her head and looked at him, her eyes shining with more tears. "I wish my heart didn't hurt. I wish I hadn't fallen in love with you. I wish–" But her voice broke, and she bent forward, crying.

Nix gathered her in his arms. "I can grant none of those wishes," he told her, and realized that wasn't truthful, so he said, "No. I won't grant any of them.

The price for them is too high."

"But–"

"Try again." He leaned forward and kissed her cheek, kissing away her tears, then kissed the opposite side, holding her face between his hands and using his thumbs to wipe away new tears.

"I wish–" But the words died as he leaned forward to kiss the corner of her mouth.

He added another kiss to the opposite side. "Try again, Auri," he murmured against her lips, then kissed her again. Wrapping an arm around her back, he drew her closer and slid a hand in her hair, tipping her head so he could press a kiss to her neck, just below her jaw. "I want your wishes, but not those."

He pressed his lips to the skin there, following the tears that had escaped his attention and kissing the trail down her neck to the hollow of her collarbone. "I want your love. I want your body. I want the stars you create in mine."

She clung to him; her hands wrapped around his arms. "I wish to feel like this forever."

Her words added warmth to the golden glow alive inside his chest. "Yes. Another?"

"I wish to stay here. With you."

That made his chest flare with heat, and he groaned with pleasure. "Yes. Another?" He nosed the collar of her shirt aside to expose her skin and swirled his tongue to taste her. Then, because he knew she liked it, he used his teeth, exerting just enough pressure for her to tilt her head further and mewl with want, her fingers digging into his arms.

She shoved her hands into his hair and held the back of his head as his lips continued their trek across her skin. "I wish you could be mine."

"I already am. And you are mine," he said and finally returned to her lips, kissing her with a force she matched. He grabbed her hips and held her against him, his forehead against hers, hands in her hair. "I am yours." His erection pressed against her belly, exposing him to the vulnerability of her power over him.

She grabbed the back of his head with one hand and pulled him back to her mouth, kissing him like she owned him, and with the other reached between them to rub his length. His mouth relaxed against hers as she stroked him, and he sucked in a breath.

"I wish for this to be inside me," she said.

"Yes," he said, the word harsher than he intended, but kissed her harder.

He wished their clothes gone, so they were, becoming piles at their feet.

Nix reached down and lifted her. She wrapped her legs around his waist, the head of his cock pressed against her silken, wet warmth, and he turned and sat on the bed, Auri in his lap with her legs wrapped around him.

He ran his hands over her hair, down her neck, over her shoulders, then leaned back slightly so he could see her face. "Say it." He needed to hear her say it again, wanted to feel the pulse of light inside his chest at those words.

Her silvery eyes mapped his features as if to memorize them and store them away. "I love you."

The words burst like a flash fire inside him, and he moaned with pleasure at the feeling they ignited. He burned. He lifted her from his lap, palming his length, and she adjusted her body to accommodate him, her knees framing his hips. When he was right where he wanted to be, Nix guided her down onto him, and she released her weight, stretching around him, until he was buried inside of her.

She gasped at the filling.

Nix pressed his lips against her throat. "Auri. You're mine." When she tried to move, he squeezed her hips to stop her. "Wait. Let me feel you," he said, breathing heavily, and pressed his forehead to hers again. "Let me stay here. Let me worship you."

Auri held onto his shoulders, offering more to him, swaying in his lap. "Yes," she sighed. "More."

He found her mouth again, the light moving through him, pulsing with power, and with his hands squeezing her hips, he helped her find a rhythm, riding him, the gentility of her against the severity of him.

"Oh, Auri."

Boldly, she moved, lifting herself from his lap only to glide over him again. Feeling the slick slide of her over his length, and he sucked in a breath at the delicious friction.

"More," she said. "More."

"Yes." Nix flipped her over onto her back, and tugged her to the edge of the bed, where he stood and pushed himself into her again and again. "Fuck, Auri." He pulled out of her because he didn't want it to end. Not yet.

"No," she cried.

"Yes." He kneeled before her and took her in his mouth. "Come for me," he ordered. He worked his tongue around in slow swirls, savoring the way she tasted, the movement of her hips, as she climbed toward her orgasm. Holding her hips, he kept her exactly where he wanted her, his mouth firmly attached to what he knew she liked.

"There," she panted. "There."

He relished the taste of her, and as his golden glow built with hers at the center of his being, she tasted even sweeter.

"Nix." Auri panted his name as if he alone were what she needed to breathe. "Oh. Nix."

That glow spread, and he could feel it inside of him, and knew, suddenly it wasn't his. It was hers. Her fire, her pleasure speaking directly to his. It was hot heat, and it spread outward until she was bucking against him, her hands fisting in his hair. He hummed his want, all the feelings building in him against her, feeding that fire.

"I'm coming," she moaned, full and heady, mixing with his need.

When she tightened up with her orgasm, he couldn't contain himself anymore, grabbing her hips and impaling himself all the way inside her. He groaned with pleasure as she cried out with bliss at their joining.

"Fuck," he bit out. He pushed into her, withdrawing only to repeat it again and again, groaning, feeling her spasm around him, squeezing, her orgasm alive within him and heightening every nerve in his body with intense sensation.

Wanting to know if he'd imagined it, he rubbed her with his thumb. "Come for me again, Auri. I want you to fucking come again."

And she did. Again. Crying out with her orgasm, quick and loud. The sweet pain of it made her body clench around him. The glow he felt with her orgasm lit up like lightning; he was sure he was exploding, brightening the room as the light broke out of him.

"I'm coming, Auri," he bit out, and with a loud grunt and a final thrust, his chest broke open as he poured everything of himself into her. All his hopes, all his needs, his desires, and vulnerabilities. He shared them and sighed with the release. Content. Perfect.

Falling forward, he caught his weight with his hands on either side of her. Auri reached up and pulled him all the way down, taking his weight. When he'd caught his breath, he slid them both over the top of her bed and then laid with her, depleted, but smiling. Basking in the warm glow of their joining, he reached for her, and she turned into him, her arms around him as he drew her closer.

She loved him.

He curled around her, and even if he'd wanted to stay away, he couldn't, and fell into sleep still smiling.

Nix's breathing evened out, growing deeper.

Auri turned her head to look at him—asleep, still smiling—and the size of her heart tripled in her chest. This was love. And something more she couldn't name. Each time they coupled, something happened between them that was beyond the physical, and this time, as she'd found release and Nix had found his, she'd seen it: a bright, golden glow, like the threads from the obligation. It had wrapped around them both, but not like arms, more like veins, pulsing around and through them, connecting them with an external lifeforce.

Magic.

She extricated herself from Nix's embrace so he could continue sleeping, climbed from the bed, and padded into the bathing room. After she started the bath, she climbed into the water filling the basin, needing the solitude to make some decisions about what was before her. Being with Nix made it difficult to think clearly.

She smiled thinking about him. About his words. His touch. His smile. She loved him, and now he knew. Perhaps the magic between them was love here in the spell, but he hadn't said he loved her. He made her know she was wanted. It was clear her enjoyed her and her company. She knew he wanted her and said she was his, but she wasn't sure how love worked for a god. It made her think about the obligation, about the golden threads when he'd said something about a god-yoke. Maybe it was that? Whatever that was.

She smiled and pulled the bubbles on the surface of the water toward her as the tub continued to fill.

What she'd told him was true: she didn't want to leave him. But staying here in the timeless realm wasn't possible. Not for her or for Nix. He wanted his freedom, and she understood that desire. The question was: what did she want now, for herself?

The spell had saved her from standing in the marketplace waiting for a man to claim her has a wife, or so she hoped when this was over. That had been what she wanted, but since making that wish, her want had shifted to Nix and the feelings he awakened in her. She wanted his freedom, and she wanted to be able to face her after without him with bravery.

The door to the bathing room slammed open.

Auri started.

Nix stalked in still naked. He was glorious—beautiful and brutal. Ridges and planes that forced her eyes to his groin, where he was endowed like the god he was. Her body heated from head to toe, thinking about wanting him again. His darkness followed him, a storm on his face, but when he saw her, the storm receded, and the darkness eased.

"You were gone."

"Did you need to do that?" She nodded at the door. "I know you can just think your way into any room."

"It was more dramatic that way." He looked at the door, then back at her. "I woke up and you weren't there."

Auri sank deeper into the bubble bath. "Not gone. Just here. Where am I going to go?"

He stepped into the tub, settling across from her, the bubbles exploding around them as he did. "Gone from the bed. Gone from my side."

"I'm not always going to be by your side, Nix."

He rubbed his hands over his face, his skin shiny with the water, then over his hair, bubbles catching on the strands. "I know that," he finally said. "But that doesn't mean I like it."

She smiled and moved through the water, closing the distance between them. Her legs caressed his when she got close enough to swipe the bubbles out of his damp hair. "I figured out my wish," she said.

He smirked. "You made some really good ones earlier. Is it going to be like one of those?"

She smiled. "Will this be my last wish then?"

He frowned. "No. Still the second." He grabbed her hips and pulled her onto his lap.

She liked the feel of his strong thighs and his length between her legs, his wide hands on her hips, the water moving about her making her feel even more sensual. "It really felt like a few of those wishes were granted." She smiled, moving her fingers through his hair.

He tilted his head toward her hand and pressed a thumb into the valley of her collarbone. "That wasn't the spell, that was my hospitality."

"Ah." She smiled and pushed against his chest, moving away from him. "Your hospitality. I see. Did you show the other key keepers such hospitality?" She still faced him as she moved backward through the water.

His lips curled up with a partial smile. "Is that jealousy I detect?" His hand closed around her ankle under the water.

"Loads of it. I'm green with it," she said, and twisted out of his hand, turning to return to her seat. But he was already on the other side of the tub, waiting there, smiling like the cat who caught the mouse.

She screeched with a laugh and twisted away, but not before he captured her waist with his hands and pulled her against him. She slid against his taut form, her back to his chest, the hair on his torso and his legs offering friction that excited her.

He laughed and banded his arms around her middle, trapping her against him to nuzzle her neck with this mouth. "I like you in green. Very becoming," he said against her skin, one of his hands covering her stomach and drifting lower. "It makes me think about you in that green dress and all the things we did while you were wearing it."

"Before you do anything to distract me—"

His fingers began to tease her. "You read my mind. Why didn't you tell me you had this power?"

She sighed, then hummed, enjoying the feel of his ministrations. "Really, Nix. My wish."

"Yes. Go ahead." His fingers continued their tantalizing dance against her flesh.

She pressed her hips against him and sighed. "I can't concentrate when you do that."

"I don't want you to concentrate. I want you very, very distracted."

"Nix."

"What is your wish?"

She moaned when his finger swirled around the seed of her sex. "To be brave. When I leave here. To stay brave."

His hand stilled, but he didn't remove it. Instead, he just held her and pressed his mouth against the skin of her shoulder. "You are brave."

She shook her head. "I wanted to run away."

"For good reason," he said. "That has nothing to do with bravery, Auri. That was about survival."

She turned in his arms. "But I was afraid. Of the marketplace. Of marriage. Of losing my autonomy."

"Of course you were, but I have only ever seen you brave, here."

"Because you told me I have nothing to fear."

"You don't." He lifted a hand from the water and pressed it to her cheek.

"But out there—if the marriage laws exist, even if the first wish was granted—I still feel afraid."

"What do you need this bravery to face?"

She looked at his throat and watched him swallow, then looked up to meet his gaze. "Being without you."

He pulled her against him in a hug, his chin resting on top of her head. "I wish the spell didn't exist," he muttered, then said, "I would find you."

She smiled and listened to his heart beating in his chest. "Let's break the spell, then."

He sighed. "I'm beginning to think it isn't possible." He paused. "So, to prepare for the fact you will soon be beyond my realm and my reach, I will grant your wish, but you must phrase it for me. Don't forget the obligation, Auri. If the wish is about bravery, then it will involve fear."

She nodded against his chest and moved through the cooling water to put some distance between them. "The words matter," she said and turned away, drifting through the bubbles as if the right words would magically appear. She lifted a thumb to her mouth and chewed on the corner of the nail, contemplating, but realized she couldn't overthink it. There would always be a loophole. If she agonized about the obligation to make the wish, she would never make them. While each wish got her closer to saying goodbye to Nix, it also was one wish closer to freeing him. It made her floating heart constrict and sink.

"Auri? Did you take off your ribbon?"

She looked at Nix. "What ribbon?"

He nodded at her, his eyes dropping to the hand near her mouth. "On your wrist."

She looked. "Oh." She twirled in the water, eyes on the surface, hands swishing the bubbles around to clear the surface. "Oh no." She looked up at Nix. "I didn't."

"Maybe it unraveled?"

"How? I've had it since I was a baby." She continued looking through the water.

Nix helped her look in the water. "Maybe it's somewhere in the manor," he said when they couldn't find it.

"She told us to never remove them." Losing her mother's gift felt like she'd lost something essential. She rubbed at her wrist, disappointed

Nix hummed as if pondering that. "Did she say why?"

Auri shook her head, tears filling her eyes.

Nix noticed and met her in the middle of the bath. He grasped her face and made her meet his eyes. "We'll keep looking." He offered her a smile. "We'll retrace our steps."

She nodded.

"Your wish then?"

She appreciated his effort to help her take her mind from the loss. "Bravery. I wish to carry the bravery I've found with you, Nix, into my future beyond being the key keeper," she finally said.

She studied his face as he rolled the words around in his brain, looking for a possible problem, but then he nodded.

"Granted." He looked down at the water. "The price for your wish, Auri, is you will be faced with your greatest fear in the present as the key keeper."

Her heart picked up a pace of anxiety, her belly swirling with it. She pressed a hand to her stomach and took a breath, but she looked at Nix and offered him a tentative smile. "I figured as much."

Nix wrapped his arms around her and pulled her into a hug. "I'm sorry."

The bathroom melted away, revealing the darkened interior of the bathhouse. Torches and candles flickered with golden light, illuminating the mosaic tile work around them. Steam from the pools rose like fragrant spirits.

"I don't know how to prepare you for that wish."

"Please, don't." She reached up, framed his face with her hands, and pulled him down to her, pressing her mouth to his. He wrapped his hands around her wrists, and his fingers replaced the ribbon, filling the gap in her heart. She smiled against his lips, then pulled away to look at him. "I've told you my parents are a love match, yes?"

He nodded. "I'm not surprised.

She tilted her head to measure him as he spoke. "Why?"

His dark gaze grazed her face, and he reached out to grab her hand. "Because you are who you are. Amazing. Kind. Compassionate." When he noticed her brows bunch between her eyes, he asked, "That surprises you?"

Auri nodded.

"Of all the key keepers before you, none of them ever made wishes like yours. They all asked for material riches even when faced with the obligation of everything being stripped away from them. A few asked for access to vices. They asked for happiness. One demanded the death of someone who had harmed them."

"You remember all of the wishes."

He smiled. "There is a lot of time to ponder." He pulled her closer. "No one ever asked for something like freedom over their person. No one asked to keep something they'd found here—like bravery." He skimmed his fingers along her jaw. "And not one of them ever said they loved me. So, I'm not surprised your parents love one another, because they have taught you how to love. Your heart is the most beautiful thing about you."

She wasn't sure how to respond, her heart overflowing in her chest. "They aren't perfect, mind you."

"Is anyone?"

"Not even gods?" she teased.

"Especially gods." He smiled.

"I have seen them fight, rare as it is, but I learned something from them."

"What is that?"

"After they have said, 'I am sorry,' it is done. Forgotten. Please don't fret about the obligation."

"As you wish," he said and tipped her chin up, then leaned down and kissed her. "Now," he said against her lips, "about those other kinds of wishes."

"**I** think I found something," Nix told her the following day. They were both in the library and had spent very little time away from one another since she'd acknowledged her feelings for him. Though he hadn't said the same, she felt his adoration. He made sure of that.

She glanced at him, smiling with her own adoration. He was across the room, sitting at a table, scribbling away on parchment as he worked through each word of the spell.

He frowned. "But wait." He paused, straightening in his seat. "The words…" He looked up at her, his unruly hair obscuring part of his face. "Then–"

Auri, who was lying on the chaise with her legs wrapped in a blanket and a book in her lap, sat up. "What is it?" she repeated and felt as if maybe she'd sat up too quickly, dizzy with the movement.

He didn't answer her, his head bent over the text.

"Nix?" she asked, and fear hit her in the chest like an arrow hitting the bullseye of a target straight and true. She'd spent much of the day before—after their foray in the baths—worried about the obligation, deciding that it lurked around each corner of the labyrinth. Then she'd decided she was wasting her time; it would happen regardless, and she couldn't spend her time worrying about it when measured against the joy of just being with Nix. But she was afraid that whatever he was about to say was her greatest fear. That there was no hope. That no matter the outcome of her wishes, that no matter what she did, Nix would never be free, and she would always be without him.

Her vision flickered; Nix tilted in her line of sight as though a headache was about to ram a hot poker into her brain. She blinked.

He stood. "What is it? Auri?"

But the edges of her vision crumpled and burned like paper. She threw the blanket from her legs and stood. "Something's wrong."

Nix was immediately next to her, his hands checking her. "Tell me."

A shadow coalesced between Nix and the fireplace,

crawling from the edge of her vision, a shadow looming and collecting the dark toward it.

But that wasn't right, Auri thought, because Nix controlled the dark. When the darkness finished collecting, it stood. It was a creature with a large maw, sharp teeth, and dozens of red, seeping eyes.

She screamed, grabbing a hold of Nix and pulling him away from it.

"I am the End," it said in an unnatural voice like rock scraping over more rocks. "You, Nixus Uraiahs, god of the night and darkness, have failed. Your failure to obtain a willing sacrifice has wrought the feast. I will become the lord of the night and darkness henceforth as decreed by the spell."

"No!" Auri screamed and pushed Nix out of the way. "I'm willing!" But the monster hit her as if she were no more than an insect needling its shadowy skin.

She flew across the room, crashing against one of the bookcases and crumpling into a heap on the floor. As she tried to catch her breath, stretching to see if anything was broken, she heard Nix yell her name. At the horrible fear in his voice, she struggled to her feet, grasping onto a shelf for help. Nix was facing her, starting across the room just as the creature grabbed hold of him.

As the monster's claws sand into Nix's flesh, he yelled, arching into the pain. The creature stuffed Nix into its distended mouth, its teeth crunching down and crushing Nix's bones. He cried out in agony, and his darkness exploded outward. The creature released its hold, and Nix fell from its mouth, the darkness consumed by the creature.

"Nix," she screamed and rushed across the expanse of floor that seemed to stretch, keeping her from him.

Nix struggled to his feet to face the monster, bent at the waist, holding his wounds and fighting for breath. "You aren't welcome here," he said and drew the dark toward him. What little shadow Nix could muster he threw at the creature like sharp spears of night. The dark spears pierced the creature's skin, but instead of harming it, the creature's body swallowed the shadow.

The monster laughed a repulsive laugh. "I am the End," it repeated. "You, Nixus Uraiahs, god of the night and darkness, have failed. Your failure to obtain a willing sacrifice has wrought the feast. I will become the lord of the night and darkness henceforth as decreed by the spell."

It reached out a clawed hand and picked up Nix again, whose darkness had retreated from him, changing masters.

Auri screamed, rushing forward; the creature's horrible eyes found her.

"Key keeper," the monster said, "You are done."

Something flashed, hot, bright, and broken, as if tiny shards of glass had exploded, knocking Auri back. And everything went black.

When Auri opened her eyes, the gray sky of day above her was pierced by the black points of winter treetops. Snow was falling gently like wisps of lace and melting like cold kisses on her skin.

"No. No. No!" She sat up, looked around and realized she was in the middle of the meadow where she'd first met Nix. The Whitling Woods.

But there was no manor, no library, no Nix.

Here, there was no wall of snow, no golden light. The sled sat across the glen, and she was dressed as she had been the day she'd found the key.

"No!" she screamed and scrambled through the loam on her hands and knees, searching. "I still have one more wish," she cried. "I wish to save Nix." She checked her pockets—empty—stood and spun. "Take me back."

But there was no answer except for the echo of her own words flung back at her, and the flight of a murder of crows in the distance cawing at her disturbance. No one to grant her wish. She was alone in the meadow without the key, and the realm where she'd found love and happiness gone.

She collapsed, rolled into a ball, and sobbed.

She felt Luc before she saw him. His warmth and light permeated the cold. She knew she should have been cold—it was the middle of winter and snow was collecting around her—but somehow, she wasn't. Then, she was lifted from the ground and carried from the meadow.

"I can't leave him," she cried. "I have to end the spell."

"He's gone. I failed," Luc said.

The woods floated around her as Luc carried her through them.

"There was a monster," she said. "The spell—it took his power. You unleashed a monster. You killed him," she cried and fought against Luc's hold, lashing out with her hands, arms, feet and legs. "You killed him!"

Luc set her down. "Stop! Aurielle, stop!"

But she didn't. She reached out and slapped the god of light.

He flared with anger and removed the warmth from her.

She shivered immediately.

"Stop." Luc took a deep breath. "Let me help."

She turned and started through the forest back to the glen, but she was turned around and didn't know which way to go. She whipped back around to face Luc. "Take me back," she ordered.

"I can't." His chin dropped to his chest, and he reached out with his light and wrapped her in the warmth again. "He isn't there. The realm is gone. I can't find it."

Auri crumpled into a heap, sick with the understanding that she'd failed, that Nix was gone, that her life stretched ahead of her without him.

Luc crouched in front of her.

When she looked up at the golden god, she saw his face broken with emotion like hers.

"Let me take you home, and return you to your family," he said. "Nix would want that."

She didn't answer him, but she didn't fight him either.

The cozy cottage seemed even smaller. It stood small among the giant evergreens, surrounded by its protective hedge. The mullioned windows cross-hatched with metal glowed faintly with the light from within. A puff of smoke hung above the rock chimney. When she and Luc entered, her family was frozen in a quaint tableau. Her mother stood in the kitchen bent over the stove, adding more wood. Jessamine was sitting in front of the fireplace, her sewing in her lap, but her eyes on the still fire rather than the sewing in her hands. Her father wasn't in the room, nor were Mattias, Brinna, or Tarley.

"We stopped time," Luc explained. "The moment you entered Nix's realm."

"How?"

"Eressa, goddess of time," he said. "You were the longest key keeper. I thought–"

"Thought what?"

"You could break the spell, but I was ready to–" His throat seemed to close on the word. He tipped his head back and turned away from her. "It's my fault."

"Yes. It is," she said.

He sniffed. "I would take it back, you know. The moment I did it. The moment Nix disappeared. I knew something had gone wrong when my blood didn't change it. I'd just meant to teach him a lesson, nothing more." Tears like diamonds collected in Luc's eyes, and he blazed with light, burning them away.

He looked around the tiny cottage before his eyes returned to Auri. "They will think you are only returning from collecting." He pointed at the pockets of her patchwork skirt. "There is a gift in your pockets. Nix would want that," Luc said and sniffed again. He took a last look around, turned his head to look at Auri, and nodded. And then he was gone.

Her family burst forth, Brinna and Tarley moving through the doorway, their father and Mattias behind them.

"I don't want to go back," Tarley announced, pulling the scarf from her head.

"Your mother and I decided you wouldn't. Not after yesterday," Father said, stomping his boots on the wooden floor.

"Outside!" Her mother yelled from the kitchen. "You're always making more work for me."

Her father grinned, wandered toward her, and caught their mother by the waist to pull her back flush against his chest. "You love my dirt," he said gruffly against her cheek.

She smacked him playfully, then yelled at Mattias, who'd gone straight to the kitchen for a treat, to get his "grubby hands out of supper."

Auri flinched at the affection.

Brinna sat near Jessamine. "If we don't go, we could all be arrested. Then it wouldn't matter anyway. The outcome would be worse." She turned in her seat to look at their parents.

"Worse than those blokes at the marketplace

yesterday?" Mattias asked.

Brinna's hand pressed against her mouth and her eyes filled with tears.

"A birthing house would be better? Or a lord's harem? Prison? Death?" Jessamine asked, sewing again and poking the embroidery in her hoop with more force.

Mattias frowned.

Auri's heart stopped up with anguish. Her legs grew weak, so she reached out and grabbed a hold of the back of a chair to steady herself. Everything had been a waste. Her wishes were useless. Nix was gone, and now she would still have to face the Marriage Law, maybe even life with someone like Crossbie.

"I'm going to offer myself to Cobble," Tarley announced.

"No!" they all yelled at the same time.

"He's a nice man," Tarley said.

"You wouldn't be making the decision because it's what you want," Auri said. "It would be because you're afraid."

"What do you suggest, sister? I run away. Is that better?" Tarley asked, her voice bitter. "Aren't you afraid?"

"Yes," she said. Completely and utterly afraid. She wished she had a way to fix it, that her wish had worked. But it didn't, and she had nothing.

"How was collecting today, Auri?" her father asked.

She watched him walk across the room and sit in

the rocking chair near Jessamine.

There's a gift.

She reached into her pockets. Her hands closed over two bags that fit into each palm. She pulled them out.

"What's that?" Mattias asked.

She swallowed. "I found them today."

Her brother darted through the room, grabbed one, and darted away probably hoping she would chase after him. She didn't. She didn't have it in her. Didn't know if she ever would again.

He pulled it open. "Holy night."

She flinched, thinking of the prayer meant for Nix. "We're rich."

"Stop," Brinna said. "You're always teasing. What is it?"

"Truthfully!" Mattias said and dumped the clinking material into his hand. Inside were gold coins and gems blazing bright, reminding her of both Nix and Luc.

She dropped the other unopened bag on the table. "I need to lay down," she said. "I feel a headache coming on. I think I got too cold today." She backed from the room and her family's glee, then buried herself in the bed she shared with her sister to cry until she fell asleep.

"Auri?"

The sweet voice drew Auri from a horrible dream. She opened her eyes. The bright light shining through the frost on the window made her squint, it was so intense. Her head hurt from a sleep too deep.

"Mother said it was time for you to get your bones out of bed, even if you've earned the right to sleep in."

Auri rolled to her back. "I had the strangest dream," she said, squinting at Brinna sitting on the bed near her. Brinna's auburn hair was plaited into a braid pulled over her shoulder. It was a hairstyle she hadn't worn in a long time, not since starting at the marketplace.

"What was it?" Brinna asked.

"I don't know where to begin."

"Oh. One of those. Twists and turns. Was there a man?" she asked in a conspiratorial whisper, her hazel eyes laced with flecks of silver, sparkling with mirth. "Or maybe a woman? Did you kiss?" She wiggled her eyebrows. "I love those dreams."

"You do?" Auri asked. She'd never heard her sister talk so.

"Yes. I especially like when–" She stopped and blushed. "Never mind. Answer the question. Was there kissing?"

Auri smiled. "Yes." But her smile faded. "There was a man. I met him in a magical meadow."

"Where you found the treasure yesterday!"

Auri leaned up onto her elbows. "The treasure?"

"Yes! You had such a shock. You went to bed right

after bringing it home. It's worth a fortune!" Brinna exclaimed. "You didn't even feel us come to bed. You were so gone. I want to hear all about how you found it."

She stood and smoothed her patchwork skirt, then busied herself with gathering Auri's clothing. "But come! Father bought meat from Farmer Boilyn for luncheon, and he said come spring they're going to build an extension onto the cottage."

She flitted about the room dreamily. "It's a miracle. You and I won't have to share this room with Tarley and Jessamine for long. And Mattias is going to be able to attend second studies now," she chattered, jumping from topic to topic as her thoughts carried her. "And we're going to plan a trip to the marriage market in Fulstrom! Think of it! You saved us, Auri."

Brinna stopped at the side of the bed, sounding so much more like she had when they were younger. "No Buteress or Gromley or that nasty man, Crossbie for us."

"There's still the Marriage Law then?"

Brinna stood and reached over to feel Auri's forehead. "Did you catch a fever in the cold? What's wrong with you?"

She offered Brinna a placating smile. "It must have been that strange dream."

"Sure enough. Come eat. I'm sure that will help you."

When her sister flounced out of the room—Auri hadn't seen Brinna flounce anywhere for so long—

Auri flopped back onto her back and stared at the wooden beams of the ceiling. Tears smarted her eyes. Nix was gone, and yet, while her wish hadn't been answered, there was a sense of hope. For them at least.

But she didn't feel the same hope.

A tear rolled from the corner of her eye, and the other, leaving trails of tears on her temples. "I just wish to go back," she whispered, wrapping her arms around herself and squeezing her eyes shut, hopeful that her wish would be heard and granted. When she opened them, it was to the roughhewn beams of the ceiling in her attic room.

She couldn't stop the tears and lost herself in them. She didn't want to go to Fulstrom to find a love match. She didn't want to marry anyone. She'd already fallen in love, and her heart was now eviscerated. She just wanted to find Nix, but he was gone forever. When her tears subsided, though her throat was closed around her grief, she took as deep of a breath as she could and got up. She made the bed and dressed for the day, knowing this heartache wasn't something she could share with her family.

Now, she would have to face the rest of her life.

The day passed.

Then another.

Followed by many more, all the same. All stretched out into lengths of moments where she relived the joy of being with Nix, then the awful remembrance she was without him. Forever. Her pain felt exponential, compounding each day into something larger and more despondent, the ache threatening to suck her into its darkness.

Her mother noticed. "Auri? You are not yourself."

"I will be well," she told her and pressed a finger to her heart where the ache lingered and stretched around the cavity of her chest.

And her mother watched her, as a mother does, with knowing in her gaze. Her eyes dropped to her hand. "Where is your ribbon?"

Auri looked at her wrist, checked the other side, though she knew it wasn't there, and looked up at her mother. "I don't know–"

"You weren't to take it off."

"I didn't. It just–" she rubbed her wrist– "wasn't there."

"How?"

But how could Auri explain when its disappearance was a mystery to her as well?

Her mother sighed. "I will need you to remain behind to do the chores when we travel to Fulstrom with your sisters."

"Yes, mother."

Her family left a few days later, and she remained at the cottage to milk the cow and feed the animals, content to be left behind. She did the foraging and continued with the chore of making tinctures and ointments for her mother's booth at the marketplace. All the while she thought of Nix, missing him, wishing she could return and find a way to end the spell. Though she wasn't supposed to leave the cottage for the woods, she did, trying to find her way back to the meadow. When her family returned nearly three weeks later, Tarley had found a match as had Brinna, with marriages to follow.

Time passed.

As the days stretched on endlessly, Auri found comfort in the woods, as if it made her somehow closer to Nix. After the marriages of both Tarley and Brinna, her sisters were now safe from collection as Auri's drew nearer. The cottage was emptier, with only Jessamine and her remaining with their parents. Mattias had left for New Taras to study at second school. Auri would have to find a match in the coming season, but not today.

The forest called. She spent most of her time in the woods, continuing her search for the meadow. Besides, her mother wouldn't allow her beyond the confines of the woods. She wouldn't even allow her to the marketplace.

"Not until it is absolutely necessary," Scarlett had said. "Then we'll go to Fulstrom."

The trees were less severe now that summer was upon them, the pine of the evergreen and the flutter of deciduous leaves between them, but her heart felt cold and empty. She collected kindling and searched for summer herbs and berries as she went, wishing circumstances were different.

The breaking of a twig startled her, birds announcing there was a disturbance in the forest.

Auri straightened and turned in a circle, looking for

what had caused it. A hungry bear awake from its winter hibernation? Something else? She swallowed, fear alighting in her like a bright flame. She didn't see anything, though, and with the rope of the wagon clenched in her fist, and a hatchet in the other, turned it around to go home. She pulled the wagon along the path, her heart beating in her throat, though she wasn't sure why. Her instincts were talking to her, she decided, and that meant there was something dangerous, but she felt foolish.

The wagon lurched, yanking her back toward it. She pulled it but saw it was caught on something. She pulled it again, and it was stuck. After a glance around, Auri set the hatchet in the wagon bed and bent down to inspect the wheel to clear it of a bundle of roots in the spokes making it impossible to turn.

"Great," she mumbled and started clearing it away.

Suddenly something yanked her by her hair. With a cry, she reached for her braid and was jerked from her feet. Whatever had her, tossed her. She landed hard against the earth; her breath knocked from her lungs. A sharp rock stabbed her hip, but she couldn't catch her breath to cry out at the pain and rolled to her side.

"You fucking cunt," a voice said between her and the wagon. "You think you're too good for me."

A hand pressed to her aching head, Auri turned to find Crossbie, his arms at his sides, a fire-breathing monster. She scrambled backward on her hands and feet away from him. "Leave me alone," she yelled.

"They came for me, and I ran into the woods

where I've been hiding. Ran me off my land, took it, all because you wouldn't marry me."

"I can't help you," she said, scrambling back until she got stuck between him and a tree. She tried to get to her feet.

He took several menacing steps toward her and hauled her the rest of the way, but pushed her against a tree, holding her there. "I'm getting my land back. And you are going to help me do it."

She shook her head. "What am I to do?"

He slammed her up against the tree again.

Auri's breath came in a gasp, the back of her head smacking the trunk, and the bark biting into her scalp.

"Yes. I'm going to put my seed in your fucking cunt. Then they have to give me back my land."

She shook her head again, panicked. "No. No. It won't work that way. You're already wanted for arrest. It won't matter," she said. "They'll kill us both for... for... not being married. They got the land already. And you don't want me. You don't love me."

"What does this have to do with love, girl?" His lip curled up with distaste. "Nothing."

Auri drew up her knee as hard as she could and smashed it into Crossbie's groin.

He shouted, dropping his hold on her as his hands cupped his sex, then he fell to his knees, bent forward, face in the dirt as he sputtered.

Auri didn't wait. She ran, looking for the landmarks to take her home, wishing she had trousers now instead of the stupid skirt tripping her up. She caught on brush, the fabric tearing as she yanked it out of the branches grasp.

"You fucking cunt! I'm going to make you pay." Crossbie yelled from somewhere behind her.

She could hear his heavy footfalls in the detritus, and ran, afraid to look behind her to see how close he was.

"After I rut you, bitch, I'm going to get my land back," he yelled, closer now. "And when I do, I'm going to fucking make you wish you'd died instead."

Think. Think. Think, she coaxed herself, but she couldn't. The fear was too large. It was everything, overtaking all of her. Her thoughts, her muscles, her feet. She wasn't going to get away. There was no hope, she realized. There never had been, but for some reason she still ran, terror a coat wrapping her in its horrible hug.

And suddenly, Crossbie was there. He'd caught up to her, his horrible gasping as he chased her echoing like the hot breath of a monster.

"No," she yelled.

But he tackled her, and she fell forward screaming. "No! No!" She kicked, struggling against his weight holding her down, her stomach against the earth. His hot, horrible breath huffed against her cheek.

"Stop fighting you bitch," he said, grasping at her skirt.

"Never!" She flailed. "Nix!" she screamed, throwing her head back. Then everything went black.

His head in his hands, Nix sat at Auri's bedside, the room cast in complete darkness but for the flickering candle on the table next to him and the coals in the fireplace grate to keep the room warm. Though describing it as a room was generous. It contained only the essence of what it had once been, the labyrinth having collapsed around them as Nix's mind disintegrated with loss.

Auri's body was stretched out, enshrouded in the bedding he'd tucked her into, devoid of her life. It wasn't that she wasn't alive, but that she was just gone, her spirit having abandoned her. So he waited for her to awaken.

And waited. And waited. Time stretched around him inside the spell, and he lost track, his mind devolving.

At first, he'd replayed what had happened over and over. She had stood near the fireplace in the library, declared something was wrong, and collapsed. He'd clung to the belief that if he just relived it again and again, he'd find the answer to the riddle. Where was Auri?

But his mind had continued to fall apart, so he'd taken to talking to her so she could hear him to find her way back. He'd climbed into the bed with her, gathered her limp body in his arms, and begged her to return. He'd kissed her in hopes that it would revive her. In fits of rage, he'd ripped mirrors from the walls and overturned tables, then smashed them to bits, insisting she return immediately. He'd summoned his father and mother to no avail—no one answered. Then he'd dropped into the pit of grief accepting that she was gone, and he was alone—again.

Finally, he'd committed to waiting near her, even if it meant he succumbed to the spell's end as nothing more than a husk of himself. Without Auri, there was nothing left for him.

Time stretched around him as if he were an immovable boulder in the rushing of the river of time.

He was diminishing, his spirit having receded with hers. The pain in his chest became the only way he knew he was still alive. He recounted all his time with her, from her arrival to the moment she was taken, and remembered that this had been what he was afraid of, how much it would hurt to hope. The powerlessness of seeing her this way, of having been loved and now facing an eternity of knowing what that felt like and being stripped of it, of being lost inside the spell alone—again—hit him like a knife to his heart.

His greatest fear.

He struggled to breath around the panic but realized simultaneously it was the obligation.

His greatest fear was being without Auri.

They were in the obligation. It wasn't permanent.

The realization brought him a small sense of relief. But like all the obligations, it lasted a lifetime, stretching the time into an infinity. The horror might be temporary, but the terrors it enacted made his relief tremulous. Who knew what she would return to him like? Would she hate him like all the others, her love stripped by whatever she'd experienced?

He continued waiting, just as bereft without her as before. His spirit faded, only now he was aware of it.

When Auri gasped and rose in her bed screaming his name, Nix lurched from his bedside vigil.

"Auri. Auri. I'm here," he said, his hands seeking to reassure her.

She flailed at the bedding, freeing herself, then swung at him, hitting his arms and kicking out to keep him away. "Get off me," she screamed and backed up across the bed until her back was pressed against the wall, her eyes unseeing.

He stepped back, thinking the worst was coming true. Her hate was alive. "Auri. It's me," he said anyway, hoping for a different outcome.

Then she blinked.

"It's me," he said again, and tentatively climbed onto the bed with her, despite the doubt that she might not be the same Auri. He shoved the doubt aside to be strong for her.

"Nix?" She turned her head toward him.

He brightened the fire, conjuring light on either side of her bed to illuminating the room. "It's me."

"I was so afraid," she cried, dropping her head onto her knees and wrapping her arms around herself.

"I'm here," he said and gathered her in his arms, settling in next to her. He stroked her hair and pressed a kiss to her temple, and when her arms came around him and held on, he took a relieved breath.

She cried, holding him as if he were the life raft in the raging torrent around them. He held her tighter. "I'm here. Oh stars. I'm here." He repeated it over and over, trying not to feel relief that she was there, but damn him, he did.

They sat that way for a time—Nix holding her and Auri clinging to him—deriving comfort from the connection. As though drawing in the magic housed within their bones that they each had deprived the other of by being separated.

The god-yoke? Nix didn't know.

"It was so real," she eventually said, bringing him

out of his thoughts like a lighthouse guiding him home.

He offered her a reassuring hug.

"Was it the obligation?"

He hummed his affirmation. "What happened?"

She shuddered and took several quick breaths, as if trying to reassure herself she could. "I don't know what was real and what wasn't."

Nix swiped a hand over her hair grateful to touch her, to hear her voice. "What do you remember?"

"Were we in the library?"

"Yes."

"I remember feeling strange, and when I told you, you were at my side. That's when it happened."

Nix recognized the partial similarity of her experience with his—her standing—but she'd collapsed immediately after. He'd only made it to her side to catch her lifeless body before it hit the floor. "What happened?" he asked, to keep her talking.

She turned her head into his chest and grabbed hold of his shirt. "A monster. It was terrible."

"A monster?" He leaned away from her, loath to allow even that separation having lived what they'd lived through, but needing to see her face, to see that his Auri was still there.

Her eyes flicked from his throat to his eyes.

Her silver eyes were shiny with fresh tears, and she lowered her gaze to her fingers playing with one of the buttons of his shirt. "It was so real."

"Tell me."

She described it in detail, including the creature's

words, which made Nix sit up and draw away from her so he could see her face. "Have I ever told you my last name?" he asked.

"I don't remember."

But he was sure he hadn't. "And it called itself 'The End' like in the spell?"

"Yes."

"And it would feast?"

"Right. On your power."

Words matter.

Nix's mind traveled over her story, considering now, trying to slide the pieces about what he knew of Luc's and Poe's spell, what he'd learned, the words, the embodiment Auri experienced with what he knew of magic, but he couldn't quite piece it together. "Was that all?"

She shook her head and described the rest to him. The Marriage Law still in place, the awful stretch of time, her mother noticing her missing ribbon, and the horrible encounter with Crossbie just before she'd returned. "I thought—" But she dropped her face into her hands and burst into a bout of new tears. "I was so afraid," she sobbed.

"I'm so sorry," Nix said, over and over.

When her crying subsided, she seemed to reorient to reality, touching him as if reassuring herself he was there. "I thought I'd lost you," she said. "It hurt, like a part of my body had been torn from me, and I was bleeding, but no one else could see it. I could just feel myself draining away."

Nix's heart stalled at her words, comparing his own experience with hers and the identical feeling of having faded away to nothing without her.

God-yoke or not, he knew this was more.

He loved this woman.

But he didn't say the words. Couldn't. He didn't know how he could say he loved her when his entire experience was dependent on her sacrifice. Loving her changed everything. He'd thought all he'd ever wanted was to be free of this spell, and it was true, he did, but not at the cost of her. He would never ask for her sacrifice.

He pulled her closer, ready to face an eternity—whatever it might be—having loved her, but then letting her go, even if it meant he would never be free. At least she would be.

The Key Keeper's 3rd Wish . . .

Nixus

"I need to know everything there is to know about the spell," Nix said without preamble to Luc and Poe when he walked into the living room with Auri. He'd summoned them after the end of the obligation, knowing that he would do anything to keep Auri from having to face another one. He may have decided to refuse her sacrifice if she bestowed it—and knowing her, she would—which meant Nix had to be proactive about how to get her out before it came to that. To find out if it was even a possibility.

Auri squeezed his hand.

Luc, sitting in Auri's usual seat with his legs crossed, noticed their joined hands, but his face remained passive, to his credit. "Hello brother. It's so nice to see you, too," Luc said, plucking something from his white pant leg, then wiping away at nothing since they were as impeccable as usual. "This room could use more light. It's dreary."

Wall sconces, table lamps, and the flare of candles offered added light in the muted shade of the room.

Poe, who stood near the hearth, turned, the fire glowing low and flickering golden-orange light against the sparkles in her pink dress.

"It isn't nice to see you," Nix said, leading Auri across the room to the loveseat. "This isn't a social call. Tell me about the casting of the spell. Again."

"My I conjure the book?" Poe asked Nix.

"Granted."

Luc held out a hand, and the spell book appeared in it. "What do you need to know?"

"I think I've missed something. I want specifics. Who? What? When? Where? The details. Start at the beginning."

Luc exchanged a glance with Poe. The god of light stood, then set the book on the table and slid his hands into the pockets of his trousers before meandering to the hearth at the opposite end from Poe.

Poe crossed her arms.

"The whole affair is a disaster from the word 'go.'"

Luc said. "Not my best form."

"No shit, Luc," Nix snapped.

"I've done many a dastardly thing, as we all have, but you must know, Nixus, trapping you here for an eternity wasn't my plan."

"Stop with the preamble. I know. Tell me. All of it. Stop acting for once and just be honest."

Four glasses of amber liquid appeared on the table in front of them.

Luc grabbed one and lifted it to Nix. "Thank you."

Poe took one.

Nix handed one to Auri and took a sip of the one he kept.

"Thank you," she said and offered him a private smile. His body responded, needing her, but he'd been upended by his realization that he loved her, struggling to understand what that meant in this space. They hadn't been without one another since the second obligation had ended, even sleeping in the same quarters wrapped up with one another, but in the moments when kissing could cross a line, Nix had pulled away, feeling guilt. A new feeling for him entirely.

He offered her an answering smile, knowing he needed to talk to her. Admitting how he felt was probably the right course of action, but it would have to wait. He cleared his throat. "So?"

Luc studied Nix, then his eyes drifted to Auri. "This is your doing, I think." He offered her a short smile and looked back at Nix. "The whole endeavor was meant as a lesson. I'll give you that woman was a vision. When you said you wanted to pair with her, I wanted to save you from the mistake you were making by showing you her lack of loyalty and character."

Nix rolled his eyes. "Got that part. We don't have to replay it." He took a swig of his drink.

"But it does have a bearing on the details." Luc took a sip, and after a beat asked, "Does the thought of her still make you angry with me?"

"No. You trapping me here makes me angry with you."

"Look. I just wanted to prove to you that her loyalty wasn't as fixed as you thought and that's why I went to Poe, because of her particular expertise."

"You chose the spell?" Nix asked her.

She nodded. "After Luc told me what he intended, the trap to reveal her true character, I recalled a story shared with me about a sprite tied to an object, then released with a sacrifice. The story was much more romantic of course, and I think I even embellished it for you when I talked you into that shed."

Nix raised his glass. "Yes. Well done, Poe."

She had the decency to look abashed.

Auri reached over and laid a hand on his shoulder, offering him comfort. The small act pierced his heart, both inflating it with unabashed joy and deflating it with grief. He wanted this woman and understood it wasn't in his story. How could it be? The spell would punish her for a third wish, then ask her to sacrifice for him? What if the sacrifice required her life? Or even giving up her wishes. What would have it all been for then, for her to have to return to a world where she could be forced to marry the likes of someone like Crossbie? His story had always been to end here, and he'd been gifted, knowing love with the final key keeper. He couldn't ask more from her.

"When Poe told me the story," Luc continued, "it seemed like the perfect way to demonstrate the maiden's true intentions—the wishes and the sacrifice—and for you to understand she was using you. I'd suspected she wouldn't follow through in the end, but I thought I could break the blood oath with the blood sacrifice." He looked at Poe. "Poorly done on our parts."

"Did you know?" Nix asked Poe.

"That it wasn't a simple blood pledge?" She shook her head and stared into her glass. "I thought the sacrifice would be something harmless like pricking one's finger. Not a full-fledged life for a life." She glanced at Luc.

"Who gave you the spell?" Nix asked.

"I don't know," Poe admitted.

"Wait. I thought someone told you the spell," Auri said.

"Well, mortal," Poe said with derision.

"Check your tone, Poe," Nix warned her.

Luc chuckled.

Poe cast a murderous glare at Auri. "I said I was told a story by a water nymph. Her name was Maiades. We were—" Poe stopped and smirked into her drink before taking a drink. "Well, I don't kiss and tell, but the spell book–" she nodded at the book on the table in front of them– "was on my table sometime after that, and you both know how much I love gifts." She raised a glass in mock celebration. "I added it to my collection and didn't think much of it until Luc came asking for my help to teach you a lesson. That was when I remembered Maiades's story and my new book of spells."

Luc stared at her, and by the look on his face, this was the first he'd heard it. "You didn't think it odd that a spell book just happened to show up on your table?"

She snorted. "I have many playthings, and my playthings like to give me gifts. So, no."

Luc turned to Nix. "Did you figure out the last lines?"

"I thought so, but then–" He stopped and looked at Auri. "Will you tell them about the obligation?"

"Did my brother just ask?" Luc smirked into his drink.

"Luc," Nix warned him.

Auri sat on the loveseat next to him and recounted what she'd experienced. The monster and its oath, the meadow, Luc, time, and her return. By the time she'd finished her retelling, Luc was sitting, elbows to his knees with his head in his hands. Poe had turned away, her back rigid and her eyes on the fire.

Nix had lifetimes to develop his hatred for Luc and Poe. At one time he'd thought all he wanted was to get out of the spell and end them, but now, observing them and hearing their story with a clearer head, the hatred had tempered. Sure, they'd messed up and deserved to face consequences for it, but he wasn't sure that had Luc been making a mistake. Nix might have tried something similar to save his brother. That, ultimately, was what Luc had been trying to accomplish—in a horribly misguided way.

Nix glanced at Auri, next to him, took her hand in his as she finished her story, and understood his new perspective was because of her. Someone who so selflessly made wishes, endured obligations, and had still learned to love him despite it.

When she finished, Luc raised his head, his face pinched with pain. "The spell created that?"

Nix pointed at the book on the table. "The last line reads, 'A Feast to End.' At first, I thought maybe it meant the spell would eat itself upon an end and me with it, but after Auri's story—I think the spell was design to ensnare any being with power to usurp it."

"And because of my stupidity, it's you." Luc stood again and laced his hands over the back of his head. "Fuck!"

"Wait." Auri looked at Nix. "Wasn't it just a vision?" She glanced around the room, panic in her voice.

Poe turned and looked at her. "Yes, sweetheart. It was a vision, but it was also prophetic. The monster's oath, Nixus's name, Luc's appearance. It's all the embodiment of the spell. What happens when the seventh try fails? Nix's powers are taken by whatever the creature embodies it—maybe the demon whose power it draws from—and is gone." She snapped her fingers. "Banished to whatever hell the spell has created for him."

"Who says the seventh try has to fail?" Auri asked. She turned to Nix, and he felt the love in her heart in his own, the warmth that spread through his body as he did. "I have every intention of freeing you."

And that was the crux of it. She would sacrifice herself, and Nix didn't want her to. There wasn't any way out of the spell. No way around it. Only through. No way to avoid a third wish or a third obligation. Auri would have to endure it one more time.

Maybe he could talk her into making a wish he knew wouldn't be as painful. He might have to engage a bit of manipulation to make her forgo the final sacrifice, but he refused to accept his freedom with the loss of hers.

He sighed, stood, and set his glass down. "I do," he said and walked from the room.

uri turned on Luc and Poe the moment Nix walked from the room. She was angry and frustrated, not only at the circumstances, but at them for doing this to Nix in the first place. "Is there nothing else we can do?"

Poe's blue eyes flashed at Auri with barely veiled condescension, and she set down her drink. "I have some ideas which begin with a water nymph named Maiades." Then in a swirl of light and sound, she was gone.

Luc was still watching Auri when she turned to him. "I need to ask you for a favor," he said. He bent his head as if he were acquiescing to her will, which

Auri knew wasn't more than a manipulation on Lucian's part. A game he played. "And I will owe you."

"I don't want anything from you," she snapped and smacked her glass on the table, then stood and folded her arms over her chest, furious now. "I'm not playing your games." She wanted to rant about what he'd done to Nix, to her. Except her next thought reminded her if he hadn't, she never would have known Nix. Her ire cooled significantly, making her more amenable to listening.

"You understand that a god owing you something is highly favorable for you."

She scoffed, annoyed at him again. "And you think that is why I would listen?" She huffed a frustrated noise at him and started out of the room after Nix.

"Aurielle," Luc said, stopping her with his tone. In her limited interactions with him, the obligation notwithstanding since that conjuring hadn't been him, he'd only ever been amused or arrogant. This sound, however, brought her back to the brokenness of the meadow during the obligation.

Though she didn't turn to look at him, she stopped and waited.

"Your vision—"

Auri turned to look at him then. He set down his glass next to Poe's and shoved his hands in his pockets. He didn't look like the calm-and-collected god of day and light he always tried to be. This was Nix's brother, worried and concerned, regretful.

"—it had it right. It was me that lured you into the

meadow. The spell knew. It knew things I'd done that even you didn't—like working with Eressa to stop time—which means the spell Poe and I cast wasn't just our spell. There's something or someone else behind it."

She folded her arms. "So?"

"I need you to make sure you don't make the next wish. Not until we can ferret that out. Maybe then, we can get Nix–"

"Out? Tell me is this for you? Or him?"

"I'm begging you." He ran a hand over his perfect hair and grasped the back of his neck, the most undone she'd ever seen him. "I need to make this right. No matter what. He's my brother." His voice caught, and he swallowed whatever emotion closed his throat, then put his hands back in his pockets, composing himself.

She wondered how often the spell was aware of Luc's sadness about what he'd done to his brother. If a spell could be aware.

He cleared his throat. "He… there's something he sees in you. He's different."

"Why does that matter?"

His amber eyes met hers, his brows shifting with confusion. "We're young gods. And I know I was wrong to do this to him, but he was so adamant about that woman."

"I'm not sure why this is important–"

Luc sighed. "Look. When you're young, when the god powers have gone through the Conveying, we get arrogant and full of our own immortality. That was the

Nix that entered this spell."

"I'm not sure you're past it yet."

He offered a humorless laugh. "He wasn't like this with her. You…" His eyes searched her as if trying to solve the mystery. "Well, whatever it is that's changed him, he's only ever wanted out, and for him to know he has that opportunity and refuse it from you means something."

Auri wasn't exactly sure what to make of what Luc was saying. "Why are you telling me this?"

"He's going to try and get you to make those wishes. He's going to tell you to make a wish so that you can be free of it before the end—whatever that entails. I'm just asking you not to allow him to rush you into the next wish, please."

"You think so little of me that I would make that wish knowing he doesn't want me to make the sacrifice?" She leveled him with an angry stare. "You know nothing." Then she turned and left the room

Her heart raced as she stepped through the door to face her own room. But she didn't want her own room, she wanted to see Nix, so she turned and started down the hallway. But every door was hers.

She made a frustrated noise and considered calling his name, then wondered if he needed space.

Since the obligation, he'd been emotionally attentive but physically distant, as if he were afraid he might break her somehow. Only the obligation proved to her without a doubt how important he was to her. She'd been afraid to offer him her heart and face the loneliness of life beyond the spell without him, but now she understood she was strong enough to do so. Only now, she couldn't stand the idea of him not existing when she could have saved him. She needed him alive and free. Then and only then alone could she face a future without him.

When the doors continued to be hers, she finally walked through one, shut it behind her, and leaned against it with a sigh, willing to be respectful of Nix's need for space.

It wasn't but a breath later that Nix appeared, leaning on the door next to her. "What took you so long?" he asked, looking down at his hands.

"I was looking for you," she said.

"I led you here. Repeatedly."

"Oh. I didn't think you–" She shook her head and looked down at the swirls in the green rug. "I thought you wanted some space." She tilted her head up to look at his face, then turned, leaning on a shoulder to face him.

"I don't know how much time we have left, Auri." He reached out and skimmed her cheek with his fingertip. "I'm not wasting a moment of it. I've spent a thousand lifetimes in this box—alone—and I finally found the version of this life I like with someone I care about."

She reached out, covering his heart with a hand. "I love you."

Nix covered her hand with his, the other cupping the side of her head. "When you were gone, all I could think about was wanting you back. Time stopped. I could see you, feel you, but you were just empty. Gone. And I was alone, again." He took a deep breath. "Auri–" He paused, looking down at their hands. "Stars, I'm terrible at this."

"At what?"

"Expressing my feelings."

She smiled. "I thought gods were good at everything."

"Great at mucking things up. Excellent at experiences that deal in self-centered choices, selfish desires, arrogant hubris, and fucking—due to all the practice." He grinned, but it faded. "Terrible at being real. Awful with matters of the heart."

"So treat it like fucking and practice."

He offered her a tilted grin, and the butterflies inside of her alighted in a flurry of fluttering.

She took a step toward him. "I'm listening."

He rubbed a thumb over her bottom lip, watching with dark eyes, then met hers. "My heart did this little twisty thing in my chest when I looked at you in the glade–" he demonstrated with his fingers– "and that twisty thing is like a tornado now, big, unwieldy–"

"–destructive," she joked.

He dipped his chin. "Let me finish."

She pretended to lock her lips but struggled to subdue her smile.

Nix ran a hand down her arm and grabbed ahold of her hand. "Every time I'm with you, I feel the expanse of that storm, the lighting, the thunder. I love that electricity. When the last obligation took you, those hours felt like an infinity of loneliness. I didn't have you to talk to and laugh with. I wasn't thinking about the electric storm, I was thinking about my companion. I wanted her."

Auri sobered, recognizing herself in those words, and took a step closer to him. The linen of her shirt grazed his, and she noticed his pulse thrumming. She reached out and curled a hand around the back of his neck. "I'm making that sacrifice."

He shook his head. "I've spent a lifetime being selfish," he said, his dark eyes dropping to her mouth, then back to her eyes. "Luc was right about the first key keeper. I realized quickly that what I'd thought was love wasn't. It was a seed dropped on dry ground that never would have grown. I don't know that I have ever truly loved anyone besides myself. Until you. I don't want anything to happen to you."

Auri searched the words looking for the pretense, but it wasn't there, because he couldn't lie. His words left nothing out, didn't create divots on which to trip, or sharp little corners around which to hide. His feelings were there, clear and articulate.

She lifted their combined hands, pressed them to her heart. "For so little practice, Nix, that was rather perfect." She opened his hand and pressed his palm to her racing heart. "Feel that?"

He nodded and took her face in his hands. "I love you, Auri." He leaned forward and pressed his lips to hers. Then he drew back, just a touch so that he could look at her. "And because of that, I'm not willing to let you sacrifice yourself for me."

She met his gaze, then pressed a finger to his lips. "Except, I love you, and I'm not willing to lose you to this spell. Not if I have the power to fix it. It isn't your choice to make. It's mine."

He groaned, extricated himself from her embrace, and flopped on the settee, his body splayed out.

Auri suppressed a smile at him, ignoring for a moment what they were talking about. "Is this the *arrogant hubris?*" she asked, waving her hand about, "Or the *self-centered petulance?*"

"I knew you would bring up the choice thing."

"Of course I'm bringing it up."

He lifted his head to look at her, then threw an arm over his eyes, dropping his head back to the cushion. "I shouldn't have said anything. I should have just manipulated you. Compelled you. I still might, Auri."

"Don't Auri me." She knelt between his legs on the settee and sat back on her heels but laid her palms on his thighs. "And if you do, I will punish you."

He moved the arm cast over his face, lifted his head and dropped his gaze to her hands on his legs. His eyes jumped to her face once more, and he arched an eyebrow with amusement. "Oh? Do tell." He smirked.

It had been too long since they'd been together. Since before the obligation, which itself had been a lifetime. She wanted him. She wanted his mouth, his hands, his cock. She swallowed. "Is there a rush? A ticking clock on the last wish?" She ran her hands up his thighs.

He sat up, grabbed her hands, and hauled her up, and before she could draw another breath, he'd flipped her to her back. "My, my, seductress. How the tables have turned." He smiled and ran a finger down the collar of her shirt to the first button, which he pushed open. "You're suggesting we just exist here–" another button popped open– "in this treasure box full of fantasies for the duration?" Another button. He pulled a panel of the shirt aside, exposing her breast, and ran the tip of his finger around her areola to her nipple so it peaked with sensation.

That ever-persistent, ever-present ache for him throbbed between her legs. She sighed, enjoying his attentions. "Is there a time limit on the wishes?" She reached up and touched his chin, running a fingertip down his neck slowly.

He made a noise indicative of his hunger but frowned. "I don't know. Luc spoke truthfully about the others. They went through the wishes so quickly. You're the first who's ever taken time to ponder her options." He bent his head and took her nipple in his mouth, then looked up at her and grinned, holding her nipple between his teeth. "Let's assume there isn't." His lips closed. His tongue swirled.

She gasped and ran a hand through his hair, loving the silk of it in her palm and the swirl of his tongue on her skin. Sighing, she reveled in the pleasurable jolts his mouth was creating, arcing through her body to grab the base of her spine. "I think it's important to determine if there's an expiration date before we decide to play in the treasure box for the duration. We don't want to get caught with our pants down."

"I wouldn't mind you catching me with my pants down," he said, his hand slipping between the other side of the shirt panel to give the other breast attention.

"Nix."

"What?" he asked, his mouth full of her breast. He looked up at her without moving his mouth away, his lashes thick and dark, his eyes laced with bright golden light. "This is more enjoyable than thinking about sacrifices, wishes, blood oaths, and being destroyed. I could stay here forever with you." He bent his head to continue his play.

"Oh," she said. "I want you. Please." She breathed the words.

Nix's lips left her breasts and trailed down her stomach. Auri widened her legs to accommodate him, curling one around him, and took a deep breath, drawing in life as he brought her forward, making her feel vibrant with it. "What about the time?"

He leaned up and pulled at the fastening of her trousers with his teeth. Then suddenly they were gone, leaving her in only her lacey undergarment. He must have conjured them off.

"Oh." Auri mewled the word as his tongue traced the edges of the fabric covering her. "Nix?"

"I'm busy."

"Nix."

He stopped nibbling and licking and met her gaze. "What about it?"

"I'm not immortal. And time passes more quickly in here."

He sighed, pressing his forehead against her belly. Then with another sigh, he kissed up her body until his face even with hers, his welcome weight pressing her back into the sofa. She shifted her hips against his erection.

His dark eyes took in her features, then he sighed a second time and sat all the way up. "I forget."

"What?"

He sat on the edge of the loveseat, his elbows to his knees. "That you are mortal. You are a goddess to me. My goddess." He turned his head to look at her.

"It would seem we both have an expiration date here." She sat up and scooted closer to him, threading her legs around him, and resting her chin on his shoulder.

"I think you should make the third wish and move on."

"There he is."

"Who?"

"My broody god."

He grinned, though he clearly didn't want to.

"I'm making the sacrifice."

He opened his mouth to argue, but Auri stopped him with her hand. "So, let's just wait and see what Luc and Poe find out about the spell's power. Then–"

He pulled her into his lap, settling her perfectly so

their pleasure points were aligned. "Then what?" he asked, but he leaned back and looked at where he was pressed against her, then reached between them and rubbed his thumb over the fabric covering her sensitive clit.

She sighed. "We can decide then."

"We," he said, still fondling her, but he leaned forward to press his mouth against hers. "I fucking love it when you say *we*."

"Can *we* fuck, please?" she said into his mouth as he kissed her and rocked her hips against his hand. "I want you in me."

Nix growled as he stood, still holding her, and walked her to the bed. Then he proceeded to show her how much he loved her.

A flash of light warned them that Lucian was incoming. Auri looked up from the table where she sat with Nix and watched Luc hurry into the library. Definitely not the calm, cool, and collected god of light she was used to seeing. His golden hair was unruly, when usually it was styled and tidy. He looked more like Nix now than ever. He wore his mixture of neutral, light-toned clothing, but his jacket was missing, his shirt unbuttoned without a tie, and his sleeves were rolled to his elbows. His face exuded stress, tension riding his brow.

"I fucked it, brother. I seriously fucked it."

No preamble. No witty hellos to throw Nix off,

just truth.

"Yes, Luc. You did."

Luc ran a hand through his hair, and it stood up in a haphazard mess. Auri suppressed a smile. She liked seeing Luc this way. This unguarded god of light seemed so much more authentic.

"I don't know why I didn't see it."

Nix just waited for his brother to get to it.

"Poe."

"What about her?"

"She's gone, and I've tried to summon her, but she's done something to keep from having to answer. Try and summon her."

"Okay, but tell me first. Besides, it takes her days in here to answer me." Nix closed the book in front of him and settled back against his seat, giving his brother all his attention.

Luc turned away, then turned back as though unclear how to settle himself. "I don't think she's going to answer at all. It was her all along. She knew what spell she was using. I just trusted her."

"The goddess of chaos."

Luc looked at him, his countenance frazzled, then sank into a chair at the table, his elbows on the top, his head in his hands. "How could I have trusted her?"

"How do you know?" Auri asked.

"It was your story," he said, turning his head in his hands to look at her. "I appeared in the obligation spell, and I kept wondering how did the spell know? It defies everything we know about magic. Magic doesn't have consciousness. It is a tool." He stood again and paced. "It is power and movement and energy, but the spell knew I had pushed Auri to the glade. It knew I had used my power to help her find the key. It knew I had Eressa help me stop time." He pressed his fingertips into his eyes, rubbed them, and sat again, elbows to tabletop and head in his hands.

He took a deep breath. "I couldn't stop thinking about it after I left here. Why would a spell behave differently than any kind of magic I've ever seen? How would it know my movement, my choices?" He sat back, leaning against the chair, and took another deep breath. "I realized the spell wouldn't, but someone did, and only two of us knew. The answer was obvious. Poe was the only one who knew."

"What does that mean?" Auri asked.

"She cast the spell." Luc's eyes jumped from Auri to Nix and back again, as if the answer were obvious. "Whoever powers the spell–"

"The demon?"

"She's been colluding with *the* demon?" Auri felt the shock on her face like a wide-eyed mask she'd seen zealots wear at the spring ceremony in Fulstrom.

Luc nodded. "I think so. Or told someone who is. Poe would have been the only one able to share those particulars. That's how they ended up in the spell's conjuring."

Auri looked at Nix to gauge his reaction. He didn't seem surprised, but he was troubled, his look so much like Luc's just then. "Are there rules for lesser gods crossing greater ones?" Auri asked.

"Not rules exactly. Gods have long memories." Nix stood and walked across the room to the fireplace, where he stood watching the fire. Thinking. He turned. "What's she trying to do, then?"

"Usurp a greater god's power," Luc said.

"Why mine?"

"Perhaps, Mr. Hubris," Auri offered, "it isn't about you."

"She's right," Luc said. "It could have been any god. Anyone with power." He stood again, then sat again, unable to keep himself still. "She was just waiting for the opportunity, and I gave it to her. Fuck!" He stood and paced to one of the windows, then stopped abruptly. "Fuck. Fuck. Fuck," he murmured, this time as if something had just occurred to him.

"What is it?" Nix asked.

Luc turned and leaned against the window as if all his energy had been depleted. He didn't look at Nix, however, just sort of spoke into the room. "What's better than usurping a greater's power?" he asked. "Fuck. Brilliant, really."

"What the fuck are you blathering on about?"

Luc looked up then. "The blood sacrifice. She knew that was my plan." He froze. "Oh my–fuck. It wasn't my spell. We used my blood, but I didn't cast it. That's why my blood won't work–ever. Shit. She did. Poe cast it and used my blood for the oath. But she cast it. When I told her I would provide the blood sacrifice. She jumped in to help me find the key keepers. I thought she'd been trying to help."

"She chose all of them?"

Luc turned and looked at Auri. "All of them but you and the first one."

"Should I give you a round of applause?" she asked.

"Of course not. I'm just pointing out that she chose key keepers she was sure would fail to get us to this point. With Nix gone and me gone, she was going to make sure the key keepers failed—"

Nix walked back across the room, returning to the table, reopening the book. "She didn't think the key keeper would even consider the sacrifice." He looked at Auri.

"I will," Auri said.

"Right, which has Poe reeling. She can't mess with you in here and she needs the spell to fail for the rest of it to work. For the End to occur to keep whatever bargain she made with whichever demon powers the spell."

"You can't make the final wish," Luc said.

"She can't stay here forever, Luc. The time. She's mortal. I can't change that until we're out."

"And the moment you make that last wish, everything goes to shit."

Auri frowned. "Do you have another idea?"

"I'm happy you asked, Auri. I know it isn't the best of options," Luc started, "but I think it's time to go to Lexa for help."

"You mean you haven't asked for help?"

"No Nix. I haven't. Who from? Mother and Father? Fuck no! I was trying to fix it on my own first. Even going to Lexa means I'm fucked. They'll probably strip me of my power and banish me." Luc offered the hint of a smile. "But look. I'm redeeming myself, right?"

"Get Auri out in one piece. Get me out in one piece, and stay alive yourself, then I will decide," Nix said.

"Will you still seek vengeance?" Luc asked.

"Yes," Nix said and was silent. Then he said, "If what you said about Poe is true, I don't see her not answering my summons."

"Why's that?" Auri asked.

"She'll be curious. She'll want to know what I want, what I've figured out. She'll want to know how close she is to succeeding. Plus, she thinks I will keep you from offering the final sacrifice."

"We could set a trap," Auri suggested. "Use her blood to break the spell?"

Luc snapped his fingers in agreement and pointed at Auri. "How long does it usually take Poe to respond?"

"Three days. Sometimes four."

"I can work with that," Luc said. He turned away from them, started walking to the door, then turned back around. "I'll be back with Lexa. I'll need some time to butter her up. You better prepare her." He pointed at Auri, and then he was gone.

Auri looked at Nix. "What just happened?"

"Hope, I think."

A while later as Auri was bent over the table reading texts about demons with Nix, she looked up from the book to him. "What did Luc mean, to prepare me?"

He looked up from the book and smiled at her. "You're going to meet our older sister. She loathes mortals. Well, perhaps there is a fine line between loathe and love. You'll see."

Auri stood up. "Great."

Nix straightened, stepped between Auri and the table, and leaned against the tabletop, then pulled her in between his legs. "You have nothing to fear, remember." He smoothed her hair with his hands.

"Well, that doesn't settle me by any means."

The room shifted around them, the stretch of green land with a swath of a river cutting the crops, fields of grapes moving past them until the tall spires of cathedrals and the columns of buildings took their places.

"What is this?"

"Elcadia. My home," he said.

When the landscape stopped moving, they were in a city, standing at the base of a set of wide stairs leading up to a massive building that looked carved out of white marble with grey veins. It was difficult to see the top, but the columns gave it a wealthy, austere appearance. "Alabastrine." He straightened, took her hand, and led her up the marble steps.

She tugged on his hand, stopping their progress. "I

can't. I look–"

"Beautiful," he said. "Don't worry. They are projections I create, remember. Real for you, but not for them. But if it makes you feel better," he glanced at her.

Auri looked down to find she was in the green dress—the one she'd donned the day of the first obligation—the panels crossed to cover her breasts, then wrapped around her torso until they draped between her legs, leaving her legs exposed to her hips. She looked up at him. "Really?"

"Fuck, yes. I love that dress on you." He grinned and licked his lips as if remembering the taste of her. "It makes me think all kinds of thoughts."

He drew her up the steps, through oversized columns, and through an oversized door. Everything was massive and bright. Luc would fit right in. Nix, not so much. Their footsteps tapped in the wide corridor, and Nix stopped at an open door. Inside were three beautiful women smiling and laughing, heads bent together.

"That's Ifrit, Ora, and Ennis, goddesses of girls."

Their heads were bent together as if they were sharing secrets, reminding Auri of her and her sisters.

"That's how I remember them," Nix said.

She glanced at him. Though he'd said it matter-of-factly, sadness crept through her at all he'd missed. Squeezing his hand, they continued walking, and he showed her several more gods and goddesses, all full or half siblings.

"Your parents didn't love one another?"

"Why would you think that?"

"They had so many children with others."

He made a humming sound and seemed to reflect on her thoughts. "I think they love each other. Eternity is a long time, and their fights have been epic. They've fought wars, created rifts in space and time, messed up the seasons. They might have had other lovers, but they've returned to one another over and over."

"Oh."

"You don't approve?"

She shook her head. "It isn't that." She imagined Nix with another woman and felt her heart flush with red-hot heat. "I couldn't share if I had an eternity with you. War would be the only option."

"Are you saying you'd be jealous?" He grinned at her as they continued through the corridor.

"Yes. Exceedingly."

"I would like to see that." He pushed her toward a wall until her back was flush against the cold marble, then reached down and ran a hand up her thigh. "Fiery you is incredibly sexy."

A strange woman peeked out from behind Nix, and her hands moved over his shoulders until she turned his head to capture his mouth with a kiss.

Auri raised her eyebrows in warning. "Nix."

The woman disintegrated, and Nix grinned at her like a devil.

"Hurt me isn't sexy. It's just hurt. Do you want to see me with other men?"

He frowned. "I have. Remember. The obligation."

"Or–" her voice stopped up, her throat thickening with sadness, but she finished the thought– "when this is over and I return to my realm, and I find someone new?" She waved her hand about.

Nix stepped back, giving her room, then shook his head and shoved his hands into the pockets of his black trousers. "I don't. I don't want to think about it at all. I don't want to think about being without you. I don't want to think about you with another man, one who you choose as your partner. The one you bear children with." His chin dipped to his chest.

"Maybe it works for your parents, but I know that kind of arrangement could never work for me." She threaded her arm through his needing to change the course of their conversation. These were things she couldn't think about. Their being together was far-fetched and unrealistic. What they were, she understood, was temporary. A beautiful by-product of the enchantment. A treasure she'd carry with her forever, but she was a mortal, and he was a god. Nothing changed that. "Come on. Let's not go there. Not yet." She squeezed his arm with hers. "You're taking me to meet Lexa."

He looked at her and nodded. "This way."

They continued through the space until they found a dark corridor and followed it. This was a space where it looked like Nix belonged, and Auri thought perhaps this was where he had once lived. It reminded her of the manor of his maze: dark stone, muted light, high walls.

Eventually, they came to a stairwell that descended into the recesses of a wall, twisting out of sight. They started down the staircase twirling down and down and down into the dark. Wall sconces sputtered to keep the stairs illuminated, and the air grew colder and more still, as if she could feel it on her skin like a gossamer caress. When they reached the bottom and stepped into a hallway, Auri's heart was thin with nervousness.

"There's nothing to fear," he said, as if reading her mind, and reached for her hand, threading their fingers together.

The hallway stretched out into darkness.

"Goddess of the underworld, you said?"

"Yes. Well, of death."

He eventually stopped in front of an unassuming wooden door, arched at the top with a large doorknob and a keyhole gaping at its center.

"Do you have the key?" she whispered.

"Why are you whispering?" Nix whispered back.

"I don't know."

He chuckled. "I don't need the key. It's a conjuring, remember?"

"So, we've never needed a key?"

He grinned his answer, and the door disappeared. Beyond it was an expanse of blackness, but for a faint light flickering orange and red. A fire.

"Come in, brother."

Nix stepped through the doorway, drawing Auri by the hand with him. "Lexa. I brought someone to meet you."

"You know I don't like surprises."

"Yes. I know, but this is a good one." Nix looked at Auri and smiled.

The flame was doused, putting them into complete darkness.

"Lexa, you know that won't work on me." Nix pulled the darkness away like a blanket, wrapping it up into his arms until it was no more.

At the heart of the room was a giant red dragon with shining scales that looked like sparkling fire, curled into a ball. Her head was up, tilted, and her yellow eyes with slitted pupils studied Nix. Then her eyes went to Auri and narrowed menacingly, the pupils widening to an unnerving black. Her nostrils flared.

"You brought me a mortal to eat? I'm grateful, brother. It must mean you want something."

"No. This is Auri. And she won't be for eating."

"But mortals are my favorite snack."

"Lexa. Can you please change so that we can have a proper conversation?"

"Only for you, baby brother." The dragon's edges softened, shifted, and red smoke swirled around her as she shrank, until a stunning woman stood before them. She was tall, lithe, and colored much like Nix with bronze skin and dark hair. Her red dress, a variation of the dragon's scales, draped around her form and moved with her as she crossed the space. She walked around Auri, studying her. "If she isn't for eating to fill my belly, may I eat her in other ways to satiate my pleasure? She is lovely, Nix."

"No. She's mine."

"My loss," she said. "But perhaps, your mortal would like the pleasure of my tongue, and you would lose her to me."

"Lexa," Nix warned. "I've only come to introduce you."

Lexa made a huffing noise through her nose. "She must mean something to you, then. Fine. Greetings, mortal."

"Hello."

Lexa looked at Nix. "Are we done? I have things to collect for my treasure and souls to collect for my realm." She shifted back into her dragon form and stalked into the darkness.

The scene fell away, and Nix and Auri were once again in the manor maze's library, in the same position at the table as before.

"That's Lexa? I can see why Luc might need to 'butter her up'."

Nix laughed.

"How can she help?"

"The goddess of the underworld? She's seen most everything and has collected a plethora of souls who speak when coerced. If anyone knows how to get to Poe, it will be her."

"And in the meantime?" Auri asked.

Nix grinned, the devil back on his face as he grasped her hips, pulling her against him. "Would you like to play a game?" The room changed, with a table and cards at the center, then fell away. "Maybe you'd like to take a bath?" The bath house appeared, then fell away back into the library. "Or maybe you'd like something completely new? They are all my favorites."

His lips found her neck, and he drew her skin between his teeth and sucked. "I find I need you. Can you feel that?" He rocked his hips against hers.

At the feel of his hardness, she drew in a breath, her lower half tightening in anticipation. "Your appetite astounds me."

"And yours meets it. Let's play."

"Yes. Let's. Take me to the first obligation."

He drew back. "What?"

She looked at him and offered a coy smile. "Just you and me. No cages. I want you to tie me up."

His eyebrows arched over his dark eyes, swirling with a cosmos of color. "But that doesn't give you a choice."

"Oh, but it does, sweet Nix." She leaned forward and teased the corner of his mouth with her tongue. "It's my choice to let you."

Nix turned his head and claimed her lips as the library dropped away into darkness.

Luc and Lexa arrived later the following day to a flurry of light and flame. Nix had stretched the living room to accommodate Lexa, sure she would come with Luc but unsure if she'd show up as a dragon. She didn't.

"Where are you, Nixus?" she said upon arriving. She wore an outfit not much different than the one Nix had imagined for her in his conjuring, an equally beautiful crimson. Rather than a dress, it was a silky pant suit that skimmed the goddess's alluring shape. The manner of dress was different than anything Auri knew, but she could see why anyone—man or woman—would be taken with Lexa.

"Lexa," he said, releasing Auri's hand to go to his sister, the room shrinking around them.

"I thought you were on holiday. Father is ready to tether you to a rock and let the buzzards have at your body since you've ignored his summons. He wants the night to return."

"I've been a bit tied up." He hugged her, and she allowed it but didn't hug him back.

"Obviously." Her hands came out to her sides, alluding to their surroundings.

Nix stepped back, slipping his hands into his pockets. "Why does he think I haven't answered his summons?"

She shrugged. "Longer time has been spent taking in the sights, sounds, and flavors of the cosmos by brooding gods, and you, brother, always have been a brooder."

Auri snickered.

Lexa turned and narrowed her unnerving yellow gaze on Auri, sweeping her from head to toe before returning her attention to Luc. "Had I known–" She glanced at Nix and placed a hand on his cheek, a nurturing gesture, but for just a moment, then looked at Luc again. "I swear to you, Lucian. I'm going to flame the skin right off you when this is over. See if you can lure women with no skin."

"It will heal," he said.

"Until I burn it off again. That will be your prison in my underworld."

"It's a good thing I don't die then."

"Wait until Father gets ahold of you when he finds out what you've done. He might give you to me to imprison."

"Joy. Will that be before or after he strips me of my powers?"

"You'd deserve it." Nix moved to Auri's side, and Lexa turned to watch him.

Lexa's eyes narrowed once again, and her upper lip curled upward with distaste. "Luc told me you were taken with a mortal, little brother."

"Little brother," Nix scoffed under his breath.

"I find mortals are only good for eating or fucking." She looked at Nix. "The fucking must be good, or you've just been stuck in here too long. Maybe I should sample her and decide for myself." Lexa approached Auri and walked a tight circle around her, cutting between Auri and Nix and drawing in a deep breath. "But she smells like you." Lexa wrinkled her nose. "And something else." She sauntered away.

"Lexa. Mind your manners."

"I'm the goddess of death and the underworld. I don't have manners. Give me a drink."

A drink appeared in her hand.

Lexa took a sip as she walked about the space, studying objects. "Why do you like this stuff? Give me something sweeter." Her glass changed, a tall flute of a bubbly drink. "Yes. Better. It reminds me of a tasty cunt." She took a long, deep drink and hummed her appreciation. "Delicious."

"Well. On that note," Luc said with his eyebrows high, looking away toward Nix. "Let's discuss a plan."

"He told you about Poe, then?"

Lexa nodded. "I'm not one to disparage other gods of any rank, but Poe is a twat. She deserves my wrath for dabbling with the demon Mangle."

"You found where she got the spell?" Nix asked, looking from one to the other.

Lexa sniffed. "If Lucian had come to me sooner instead of spreading lies about where you were, I could have told him where the spell was from. Idiot." Lexa sat in one of the chairs, lounging more like an emperor of the space than a guest.

"What is the lie he's been telling?" Nix asked.

"Brooding. Heartbroken. Off world." Lexa snorted again.

"How have you gotten past no night?" Nix asked Luc.

"The sun still sets, and Drisstol uses a deep cloud cover."

"That isn't night," Auri said. "Who is Drisstol?"

"God of storms."

Lexa cleared her throat. "Can we get back to the matter at hand so that we can have night once again?" She stared at each of them and said, "Mangle, a lesser demon from Asphiksan, has been maneuvering a millennium to acquire powers that would allow it into the realm of mortals. The last I saw it, I subdued it in my lowest cast, chained in the Lake of Defecate for dabbling with nymphs and slaughtering the lot of them."

"Maiades," Nix and Luc said at the same time.

"Poe was telling the truth about the nymph, but not about the book of spells," Luc said. "Mangle gave the book to Maiades and in pleading for her life, promised to deliver it to the goddess. I think Poe had been looking for it all along."

"Of course she was, you dolt," Lexa told Luc. "Poe has been trying to acquire additional powers since her conception. She drained her mother as a fetus, for stars' sake. Impressive, really. She's the goddess of chaos. It is her lot in life to incite change, discord, and drama." She rolled her eyes, muttered something under her breath, and took another sip of her drink.

"So how do we break the spell?" Auri asked.

Lexa looked up, surprised. "Is she speaking to me?"

"Mortals don't speak to you?" Luc asked.

"No. They are either screaming as I eat them or screaming as I eat them."

Nix scrunched his eyes shut.

Auri laughed, amazed at how good he'd presented her in his projection.

"They laugh?" Lexa tilted her head regarding Auri.

"You've never spoken with a mortal," Auri asked, amused.

"Rarely. They are too scared." Lexa stood. "You're speaking with me. Now. I find it–"

Nix drew Auri against him.

Lexa waved a hand at Nix. "No need to protect

her, Nixus. I can control myself. I find her intriguing."
She examined Auri again. "Tell me, mortal, is it my
brother you like, his power, or just his cock?"

Luc choked on his drink.

Nix looked like he was going to throttle his sister.

Auri looked from Nix's storm cloud face to Lexa.
She smiled. "I'm Auri, and I find myself satisfied with
all of him."

Lexa studied her an extra beat, then threw back her
head and laughed. "Spirited." Smiling, she took
another sip of her drink and stared at Auri over the rim
of her glass.

"You can change the direction of your thoughts,
Lexa. She's mine," Nix said. "The spell?"

She heaved a sigh. "Fine. Poe must break it, since
she's the caster."

"And I don't know if her blood will be enough,"
Luc said. "She said it would take a life sacrifice."

"Idiot."

"Stop calling me that. I didn't know. And Poe
won't," Luc said. "The only one with any power in here
is Nix, and he'll only be able to expel her."

"That's not true," Auri said.

The three gods looked at her with varying degrees
of curiosity.

"I'm the key keeper. I still have a final wish, the
final obligation, and the sacrifice choice before the
spell expires, right? What if I used it to grant them
powers in this realm?"

Nix shook his head. "Not a benefit to you."

"Oh. But it is." She turned and looked at Nix, ignoring Luc and Lexa, who were watching them. "You are a benefit to me. And if we don't stop Poe, I will lose you." Her heart stalled with a moment of fear at the thought.

Nix's eyes searched hers.

"Oh. That's what I smelled," Lexa said, loud enough that they all could hear. She made a gagging sound. "The fucking god-yoke. What the hell, Nixus?"

"What? That's real?" Luc asked, his head snapping back and forth between Nix and Lexa.

Nix didn't respond, but his eyebrows arched over his eyes. He glanced at Auri, his eyes mapping her features, then back at his siblings. "So, it is real?"

"Of course it's real." Lexa shuddered. "It just doesn't happen very often. Once or twice every millennia. What a horrible atrocity."

"Why?" Auri asked.

Lexa's mouth pursed with distaste. "Who would want to be linked to another like that where there's so much variety? Awful business."

Auri glanced at Nix and felt her face heat. She wasn't sure what the god-yoke meant but didn't think the idea of being linked to him was so bad. The look on his face, however, wasn't an expression that made her feel secure.

"How is that possible?" Luc asked. "To a mortal?"

Lexa drained her glass and studied Auri as it refilled. "You sure you're mortal?"

"Yes," Auri replied. She wasn't exactly sure why

the idea of the god-yoke was bothersome to Nix, but it didn't matter if he wasn't able to be free of the spell. "We should focus," she said, moving so she could catch his gaze with hers. "What if I asked for power to compel Poe?"

"The words matter," he said.

"But what if the spell completes and takes you with it, Nix?" Luc said. "I'm not sure we could risk making this final wish."

"Because you don't want to sacrifice yourself?" Auri asked.

"His sacrifice won't work. Not if Poe cast the spell," Lexa said.

"We will have to make the wish," Nix said. "Auri can't stay here." He turned and looked at his siblings. "The spell is explicit in three things: the wish, the obligation, and the sacrifice. The first six experienced it in exactly that order. The final lines don't express that the seventh will change the pattern, only that the completed seventh will create the end."

"The monster," Auri said.

"I am a monster," Lexa said. "I defy whatever the spell creates to face me."

"But to do it here—Auri is right—you will need your powers." Nix turned to look at Auri again. "It could work, but the wording must be just right."

"And Poe has to show up."

Nix looked at Luc, "She will. She's too close to the end."

"I agree," Lexa said and looked over the rim of her

glass at Auri again as she sipped the bubbly. "Let's see what this mortal can do."

That night, while lying in bed, Lexa ensconced in her own quarters and Luc's promising to return, Auri and Nix refined the wish. They looped back around and over the words, considering how it might have an impact beyond the wish. Auri was lying on her side facing Nix, with her knee resting against his thigh. He was on his back looking up at the ceiling, his hands tucked behind his head, the sheet loose around his waist. She loved looking at him. Loved that he allowed her to see him this way, undone. She recalled their play a few nights prior, her hands tied to the bed frame, Nix pleasuring her from behind, and her blood heated her body, feeding the fire between her legs.

"It's the obligation that bothers me," he said and turned his head to look at her.

She kept her hands tucked up under her cheek instead of touching him like she wanted to. She imagined dragging her fingertip across the plane of his chest to circle his nipple, then running it lower over the ridges of his abdomen. Down... She blinked, reminding herself this conversation was too important. "Why?" she asked.

"If you're wishing for power, that means you will pay with power, and what if Poe arrives while in the midst of the obligation?"

"She doesn't know what we're planning. If she does arrive, you can stall her."

"Only if I'm not involved. But if the obligation

were like the first one, or others that I've been compelled to act out. This wish creates another unknown, and I feel like I need to know to keep you safe."

"The spell will have its way with the obligation, Nix. You know that. It won't matter what we do."

"What if, in the midst of the obligation, she arrives and disappears before we get her to break the spell."

"She will resist. Are you willing to kill her to break it? Even if it might not work?"

Nix sighed. "We're fucked." He looked back at the ceiling.

"Luc and Lexa will stall her." She pondered his concern. "We have another day?"

"Give or take. It could be anytime. I summoned her two days ago."

"We don't know you'll be actively involved in the obligation. You weren't with the last one."

"No. I just had to face my own fear." He turned his head again to look at her.

Auri watched the worry work his features, and he grabbed his shoulder to knead the muscle there. "If I make the wish now, then maybe we'll get lucky, and the obligation will be paid before she arrives."

"I don't know."

"I don't think we have a choice."

He rolled toward her. "I'm fucking insecure and overthinking, and I don't do this, Auri." He grasped her face between his hands. "I don't want to watch you slip away and—" He stopped; his eyes cast down.

She noticed the thickness of his dark lashes and leaned forward to kiss them. "If we do nothing, Nix, that's exactly what's going to happen. I will be stuck on the outside, you'll be gone. Poe and that demon will have collected your powers to unleash beyond the spell, and I will have done nothing to stop it."

He drew her into his arms and entwined his legs with hers, his fingers drawing swirls over the skin of her back. Heat raced from their origin to her core. "It's weird that I hate that we're here, but I'm so grateful, too. Do you think if I hadn't been stuck to the key, that I would have ever met you?"

"I don't know. Did you do much roaming in the woods looking for peasant women?" She smiled against his skin.

He laughed, a low rumble in his chest that reverberated through hers and spoke to her heartbeat. "No. Not so much."

"You would have offered your immortality to the first key keeper."

He blanched at that. "Luc was right."

"In a very twisted and untenable way, he was." She closed her eyes and enjoyed the sensation of his hands, but his worried look earlier flitted through her mind. "What is the god-yoke?"

His caress stopped.

"You mentioned it before. During the first obligation."

He signed and drew away from her, enough so that he could see her eyes. "I wasn't sure if it was real or just a story."

"There's always a layer of truth in stories, wouldn't you say?"

His lips curled for a brief moment with a smile, but it slid away just as quickly. "It's a tethering between two gods—people, I guess—because they carry matching stars."

"How can that be?"

"I don't know."

"Maybe it's the magic of the spell?" Auri asked, trying to understand, rationalize.

"Maybe, but there were six key keepers before you, and I didn't tether to any of them because of the spell."

Auri searched his face and could see he was worried. "Does it bother you? The idea of being tethered to me?"

Creases formed between his eyebrows, and he leaned forward, pressing his forehead to hers. "No. Absolutely not."

His conviction made her heart feel safer. "Then why are you worried?"

He was silent for an extra beat that told her he was thinking about what to say.

"Just say it."

"I don't know enough about it. You heard Lexa— it rarely happens. So, I don't know what it means, really. And it doesn't make logical sense."

"Because I'm a mortal."

"Because you're a mortal. Unless–"

"Unless?"

"Your parents?"

She shook her head. "They're just ordinary folk." But the thought niggled her mind with a curious doubt.

"Let's worry about one thing at a time," he said, lifting his lips to her forehead and pressing a kiss there.

But she heard—or maybe felt—his worry, because there was something he wasn't saying. She wanted to push him on it but also felt as though it wasn't the time. They had to worry about the spell and Poe and how to make a wish that would help them get through what was coming. She needed Nix safe and free. Whatever the god-yoke was and would entail could wait.

"Right," she said. "Let me make this wish."

He nodded. "Okay."

"Here goes–"

"Auri, wait." He pressed her back against the bed and shifted so he was between her legs, then leaned up onto his elbows, hemming in her upper body as he touched her hair, her cheeks, her lips.

She looked up at his beautiful face, at his dark eyes, and fell in love with him all over again.

His full lips formed a kissable pout as he considered what he was going to say. "I need you to know that whatever happens, I'm so grateful to have had this time with you." He leaned down and kissed her, slow and filled with emotion, then drew back and added, "I love you. And just… in case something happens. I need you to kn–"

She reached up and pressed her finger to his lips. "First, let's plan for the best. Second, though this isn't what I would have expected of my journey, I'm so grateful." She paused, her throat closing around the words, but she forced them out. "I don't know how to face an after."

"Let's get through this," he said, "then we can think about after."

She nodded, running her fingers through his hair around his face, then grabbed the back of his neck and pulled him down to meet her lips. She put all the feelings she could into that kiss, every emotion she felt for him that had bloomed inside of her. His body responded, coming to life between her legs. She tilted her hips to encourage him, running her hands down the length of his back before fitting into the curve there as she angled her head for a deeper kiss.

Nix adjusted, reaching between their bodies and guiding himself into her, agonizingly slow as he joined them, his breath ragged and moving the hair near her ear.

Auri moaned, wrapping her legs around the back of his thighs, pulling him deeper into her. She relished his pleasure-filled groan as if he'd been without her for a lifetime and had finally quenched his thirst.

"Auri," he said against her mouth, unmoving, as if all he needed was to connect. He pressed his forehead to hers. "Auri," he repeated.

She pressed her hands against Nix's cheeks. "I love you," she said. "I love you."

"Auri," he said again, as if her name were the only thing keeping him alive.

Then, with Nix deep inside her, Auri made her final wish, the words they'd decided upon together. "As the key keeper, I wish to be granted the capacity to modify the outcome of the spell holding Nixus Uraiahs and me, Aurielle Fareview, hostage."

Nix altered his body, a slight movement that drew his breath and hers. He propelled his hips forward, pushing against her pelvis. She moaned, grasping onto his body for support as he began to unmoor her.

"Granted," he answered. "The price for your wish, Auri–" His breath caught as she grabbed his hips, then the taut flesh of his ass, now moving with more urgency to hold him against her. The effort of attempting to hold himself back produced beads of sweat that worked its way through his dark hair, the curls caught against his face. "The price for your wish," he repeated as Auri pressed her feet against the mattress and tilted her hips toward him, wanting more, wanting all. He groaned. "The price for your wish," he said a third time, "is the loss of capacity about your particular circumstances within the spell."

She slid her hands up to press them against the small of his back. "Is that's all?" She offered a smile, then arched her back with a gasp as he grabbed her leg and forced it over one of his hips, pushing into her with more urgency. "Nix," she panted, over and over.

He grabbed her other leg, pressed it up against her chest, and pushed into her again and again, until they were both wild with mutual need. Their bodies climbed the precipice together before jumping into the oblivion, but when they did, Auri thought she saw the room erupt with golden light around them.

Nixus

ix opened his eyes, a warm feeling of contentment lighting the otherwise dark room. Which, in the haze of sleep, seemed strange, given he was the god of dark and night trapped in a spell. A warm body was pressed against his side. He turned his head and smiled, rolling to draw Auri into his embrace. He loved sleeping with her, waking up next to her. He loved everything about her. Though he didn't understand how it was possible they'd found one another, he wasn't going to throw this joy away either because it seemed too good to be true.

She nestled against him, her naked backside rubbing against his cock, now wide awake and hardening as he smiled, pondering if he should wake her up with it. Pressing his lips to her shoulder, he slid the hand he'd fitted around her waist onto her belly.

His mind shuddered and slipped, like sliding in mud and getting stuck in it, knee-deep. He blinked to right the tilting, but when his vision refocused, it was as if he were looking at the world through a tiny keyhole, locked inside of a box.

Fuck. Fuck. No! Nix tensed. *Not now,* he thought even as his hand slid down to cup Auri between her legs when he would have pulled away. He tried to fight the movement but couldn't. The obligation had begun, and he had no idea what the fuck it was or what to expect. *Fuck!*

Auri stirred against his fingers and moaned, a soft sound that made his dick harder.

He felt when she came awake. Her body tensed against him for as long as it took to take a breath. She tilted her head to look down at his hand moving between her legs and screeched. Flailing about, she caught him in the shin, and though the pain was distant, he grunted involuntarily.

She struggled from the bed until she was standing on the other side of it, a pillow held against her naked body, anger blazing from her eyes. "Who the fuck are you?" she screamed.

"Who the fuck are you?" spell Nix echoed.

No! Auri. no! I'm here, Nix thought but couldn't say it.

She looked around the room, her eyes frantic, her chest heaving. "I don't know where I am."

"Here," spell Nix replied. He smirked at her.

"Where are my clothes?"

Spell Nix flicked his hand and clothes—not hers—appeared on the bed.

"How did I get… How did you do that?" She took in the clothes, the bed, the rumpled sheets, spell Nix naked and kneeling on it. "Did we?" she asked.

Spell Nix smirked. "What do you think?" He grabbed the base of his hard cock. "I'm a god. I can do anything I want."

Nix cringed and waited for Auri to throw something at his head. But nothing happened. Instead, she tilted her head and watched spell Nix fondle himself for her as a kind of invitation. The Auri he'd come to know would have said something sarcastic and stomped away while blushing furiously. But this was spell Auri.

Nix moved through the language of the wish in his mind. Capacity, or wisdom, with respect to the spell. Which meant what for an obligation?

He watched Auri watching spell Nix tug on his dick, but instead of revulsion, she appeared tentative but curious.

"Are we going to get caught?" spell Auri asked, reaching for the shirt laid out on the bed, her hand stopping before touching it.

"By whom?" spell Nix asked and slid his hand up cock to its tip. "And why would it matter? I'm a god."

"I don't understand. How is that possible?" Auri clutched the pillow against her body with one hand and drew the shirt against her with the other, but her eyes tracked his movements.

Spell Nix's hand wrapped around the shaft of his penis, moving, drawing his hand up to the tip, sliding his thumb over the head, wetting it before moving back down.

"Will the enforcers come?" She whispered the words as if any such person was lurking in the shadows of the room, her eyes locked on his movement. "I don't want to go to a birthing house," she said and swallowed, then straightened, her eyes jumping to his. "Or to jail."

"They won't," spell Nix said. "But I will quickly unless you join me."

His innuendo flew over her head. "I don't know you."

"I'm Nix."

He's not! Nix thought and willed Auri to know it.

"I don't think–" She paused as if trying to get her bearings on herself, on the situation, and couldn't. Shaking her head, her hair fluttering around her shoulders, she still gripped the pillow covering herself. "I'm Auri, and I don't remember how I got here. With you."

"Does that matter?" spell Nix asked.

"Because you're a god?"

"Exactly. And as you can see, we've already gotten to know one another. Rather well. Obviously…" He looked around the room.

She blinked, slowly, as if caught in a tangle inside her mind and trying to remove the knots.

Nix's heart twisted watching her try to think it through, but there was nothing behind her dull gray eyes, and he knew that Auri was probably inside herself, screaming, fighting. Just imagining Auri fighting made Nix want to fight, but the sensation of his hand working his cock was making thinking more difficult.

"I guess not," she said and took a step closer, relaxing her hold on her pillow and the shirt. "Where am I?"

"In my house."

"In Kaloma? Did we get married?"

"Sure. If that's the way you want it." Spell Nix stopped tugging on his cock and waited. Inside, Nix breathed. *Think. Think.* But stringing together coherent thoughts in competition with spell Nix was making it difficult.

"Am I your first wife?"

"Yeah, okay. Sure."

Her eyes flicked over the top of the bed, to his face, to his stalled hand on his dick. "Why did you stop?"

"Why are you watching?"

"I've never seen… that."

"You like it?"

"I don't know. Am I supposed to?"

Spell Nix's hand slid up and down his dick again. "Come over here. I'll show you how I like it."

She shook her head. "I'm confused." She took a step away.

Spell Nix moved toward her, walking on his knees across the mattress, until he was standing on the same side of the bed. "I promise, you'll like it."

Auri hadn't held her ground, backing up until her back was pressed against the wall. Nix hated that she was afraid but reminded himself this was spell Auri, and this was spell Nix. Everything that was happening was the spell working to make him into the villain he was supposed to be. He thrashed around in his mind looking for a solution but couldn't find one. Spell Nix was palming his cock like the reckoning was impending and coming was the only way to survive.

He wished he could stop, and closed his eyes to think, but things were happening too quickly.

"I will?" Auri asked.

"You already did," spell Nix said, his eyes drawing up and down her body, naked behind the pillow. "Why are you naked if we didn't?"

"Why don't I remember?" she asked. She squeezed her eyes shut and rubbed her forehead with her hands, and the pillow slipped, revealing one of her breasts. "Why don't I remember?" Her volume was shifting, climbing in tone.

Spell Nix's eyes fell to her nipple. "We're married? In Kaloma, right?"

She settled suddenly. "Married. If we are naked," she reasoned, "it must be so." She opened her eyes, her gaze on him, moving around his form.

"So why are you hiding from me? If I'm your husband?" spell Nix asked, manipulating her. He reached out a hand.

Fuck! Nix fought against the twisted nature of the spell working against him. A pervasive fear worked through him that everything he and Auri had been through was about to be torn apart.

Auri glanced at his hand, then dropped the pillow and the shirt. Her complexion was pale, fear on her face, but she didn't question it, didn't question the circumstances. She just accepted them as if she was unable to think for herself at all.

"Are you denying me? Your husband?" spell Nix asked.

Nix's heart tripped as he struggled inside his own body.

Auri blinked, hesitated, as if she too were fighting the impulse, but stepped forward with her hand outstretched anyway. "A silent woman is a wise woman," she recited, as if coached to say it.

"Good girl," spell Nix said and led Auri back to the bed. "Since you aren't sure if you like to watch, I'm going to teach you how to use your mouth, like a good wife."

"Okay," spell Auri said, her voice devoid of the Auri Nix knew.

"Get on your knees."

She complied.

"I enjoy you like this," spell Nix said. "Docile. Subservient. It's addicting. Open your mouth."

Auri complied.

Not this way, Nix thought, wishing he could look away. He wished he could find a way outside of his own skin, to put a stop to this. He wished he could talk to Auri, but he wasn't a wish maker. He was the villain. The sensations raged through him, physically making it difficult to string his thoughts together. He was fucking Auri's mouth and—

The god-yoke.

The thought hit him in the middle of the chest as spell Auri pleasured spell Nix.

Nix struggled to keep his mind right, the pleasure center of his brain wringing out his thoughts and pulverizing them into dust. When his body released, and he came into spell Auri's mouth, his physical body grunted and jerked, until he fell back onto the bed, ignoring Auri on her knees before him.

She didn't move.

Spell Nix and trapped Nix lay on the mattress, trying to catch their breath.

The god-yoke. Nix grabbed onto the thought when his brain began functioning again.

"Come here," spell Nix ordered.

Auri stood.

"I want to fuck you, too. From behind, like a dog. So, when I'm ready again, that's what we'll do."

Spell Auri nodded and sat down on the bed, still and stiff as if she was nothing more than the receptacle for spell Nix's pleasure.

"Then we'll eat. Would you like to do anything?" Spell Nix folded his hands together under his head and stared at the fabric of the bed's canopy above him.

She didn't turn to look at him. Staring straight ahead, she said, "A silent woman is a wise woman."

Internally, Nix tried to recall how he'd broken through the first obligation, remembering Auri standing before him in tears. He'd tapped into his heart. The emotions. He tried again, as spell Nix tried to put them to sleep. Nix fought the lull. *No. No. No,* he chanted, looking for the warm threads he knew were there. He'd seen them, and as if the magic had its own mind, they came forth like a burst of light behind his eyes.

Golden threads, like tributaries of a river, sprang from him, out from his being like an aura. And not only from him, but from Auri, reaching for him. They connected.

Nix sat up, grabbed ahold of Auri, and drew them both into his dark cocoon, lit inside by whatever golden light they had between them.

"Nix?" Auri's voice made him tighten his grip with relief. Her arms wrapped around his shoulders. "I kept thinking about how I'd found you in the conjuring you made."

"Yes. Yes!" Nix held her tighter, concentrating. "I thought about that first obligation. I don't know if we can hold this, Auri." He remembered the spell fighting back and could even now feel the tug of it, though it was weaker than he remembered.

Auri leaned back, grasping the sides of his face, to make him meet her gaze. "We can hold it."

"We didn't last time."

"Because we weren't then what we are now," she said and pressed her lips to his.

Nix kissed her. Slid his tongue between her lips to meet hers, finding solace in the comfort she offered. Finding faith in the connection that sheltered them for the moment, however long it would last. Her faith in what they were bolstered his, gave him hope they could fight the obligation.

He broke the kiss. "I'm not letting you go," he whispered and wrapped his body tighter around her, hopeful that though the power beyond their cocoon that might try to pry them apart, together they could overcome it.

The return of her mind and body was a gradual thing. From the moment she woke at the onset of the obligation, the fear of finding a stranger's hand between her legs to the acquiescence of everything about her to someone she assumed was her husband, willingly, was an awful payment for wisdom. She'd felt the fracture immediately, a splitting between what was a lie and what she consciously knew was the truth.

She'd fought, knowing Nix was fighting too behind those dead eyes, and found slips through the blackness of the spell's control, grasping onto her own desire. *Nix. Nix. Nix.* A beacon calling forth her heart. When she found the warmth, she'd held onto it. *Nix. Nix. Nix*, she'd thought, knowing he would come when she called. And he had, even as she'd reached for him.

Even now, as the darkness around them eased, Nix's tight cocoon relaxed. With her arms wrapped around Nix, her mind concentrating on him and him alone, she wasn't sure how long the obligation lasted, but she knew she could feel its power wane as a tremor moved through her body and then subsided.

"Nix?" she asked, still wrapped around him.

"I'm here," he said, his voice comforting in her ear.

"Is it over?"

He pulled back and met her gaze. "I'm hesitant to move." He offered her a smile.

"We need to check," she said. "If it's over–"

His eyes widened with realization, and he released the darkness, allowing muted shadows to stretch out around them, opening the labyrinth once more to the twilight.

"Fuck." Nix moved, rolling from the bed where they'd insulated themselves from the obligation.

Auri's muscles protested the movement, but she got up, naked as she rose, and dressed by the time she stood because Nix willed it.

"We did it?" Nix asked, turning in a circle as if to correct his equilibrium.

She looked around at the room, at her hands as if they contained power, at him. "I think we did."

He rushed and picked her up. "I have never had more hope that I do at this moment." He kissed her like their world was coming down around them, and in a way it was.

She drew away and said, "The final sacrifice."

"Luc. Lexa. Poe." Nix said their names like orders. Frantic. "The final sacrifice is coming. I don't know what happened to Poe. What if she's come and gone?" He wasn't talking to her. Just fretting. He held out a hand, and she knew the second she took it, they would be when everything would change once more.

"Wait."

"We can't–"

"Nix."

He stopped, his fear freezing on his features.

Auri walked to him, took his hands, and pulled them up to her heart. "This–" She took a deep breath. "Remember." Reaching up, she pressed a palm to the side of his face. The fear eased, making way for something vibrant and beautiful. "No matter what happens, I love you." She rose onto her tiptoes and kissed him.

When Auri pulled away and opened her eyes, they were in the living room. Luc and Lexa sat in the chairs where she and Nix usually sat, while Poe stood near the fireplace, a drink in hand. She took a sip, watching Nix and Auri step away from one another.

"There you are," Luc said, his voice as collected as usual, even under the circumstances. "We wondered where you got off to. I made us all drinks. To celebrate."

"It would seem they've already been celebrating," Lexa said.

"I was just telling Poe that we tried to solicit Lexa's help to break the spell, to no avail."

"I could have told you that if you'd asked," Poe said.

"Except you didn't answer my summons," Luc said, a caustic edge to his voice.

Poe took a sip, her gaze sliding to Lexa.

"But you're here now," Luc said, all smiles and light. "Let's not mire our celebration in squabbles." He lifted his glass and drank. Poe and Lexa followed suit.

"Celebrate what?" Auri asked.

"Your last wish, my dear, and the hopeful freedom of my brother, or my impending demise," Luc said as if he were discussing a day trip to share a picnic. "It's your choice, now, isn't it?"

Nix cleared his throat, seeming to compose himself, and started across the room. "We're sorry to keep you waiting."

Auri wasn't as calm as she followed him, unsure what to expect now that final wish had been granted and final obligation paid. How would the final sacrifice present itself? She should have asked Nix since he'd experienced them before. She found her eyes darting about the room at the corners and the shadows.

Nix handed her a drink and looked inside his own glass, somber. Then he said, "Just in case, I–" He looked up and leveled his gaze on Luc. "If it doesn't work–"

"What doesn't work?" Poe said.

"If Auri doesn't choose the final sacrifice," Luc said, "and you have to kill me." He took a drink.

"That's morose, brother," Lexa said. "I would welcome you to the underworld, however."

"That's good to know," Poe said. She took another sip.

"I have told–" Nix stopped and looked at her, then offered a devastating smile– "suggested to Auri that she refuse the sacrifice if it means her life."

"But what about your powers?" Poe asked.

"Thank you for the reminder, Poe. Lexa, will you see that Father chooses a replacement for the night?"

Lexa nodded at Nix. "They'll have to see to a reaping to retrieve them from the underworld, but I will tell him, if that happens." Her gaze jumped to Auri. "Mortal—I highly suggest you take the sacrifice. You might not like my underworld."

"Lexa," Nix warned. "Luc. Whatever happens–"

Luc stood. "No. Now. Let's have more hope than that."

Poe snorted.

"Do you find something funny, Poe?" Nix asked.

She shook her head but smiled. "No. No." She blinked. "Not funny. It's just–" She reached out and put a hand on the hearth. "I don't feel..." Her eyes looked from the drink and flew up to Luc's face, and then she fell to the floor before she could whisk herself away.

Auri turned to Nix. "You gave her a potion?"

Nix hurried across the room. "Luc did. We needed to make sure we had options in case the obligation—" He didn't finish the thought.

She understood. In case she and Nix were stuck.

"It worked." Luc moved to Poe's side and moved her away from the fire.

"I hate the subterfuge." Lexa held a coil of bright golden rope in her hands.

"We have to tie her up. Is that the proper binding?"

Lexa twirled the rope. "Do you think I am ever without proper bindings, Nix."

"Just help me."

"The concoction worked." Luc moved away from Poe so Nix and Lexa could bind her, watching over their shoulders.

"Obviously it worked, Luc," Lexa said, handing an end of the rope to Nix.

"Excuse me for doubting mortal potions," Luc snapped. "How long will it last?"

"She's a goddess. Probably not very long," Nix said and took the gold cording Lexa offered, then threaded it around Poe's hands.

"What happens next?" Auri asked, wringing her own hands with worry. "Nix?" She could feel her panic rising, knowing that at any moment the spell would begin the final sacrifice, which could kick her out of the spell, away from Nix forever. She didn't know what to expect. "How long do we have?"

Nix looked up at Auri and seemed to read her anxiety. "It's okay." He nodded to her, then helped

Lexa and Luc maneuver Poe against the front of the chair near where she'd fallen. "If the pattern holds, the spell will present you with a final choice, as soon as the obligation wears off." He stood, wiping his hands on his trousers, as if to wipe the filth of Poe's actions off his hands.

"What if it's like my vision instead? Can we just get a bit of Poe's blood and end it before that?"

Luc pointed at Auri, snapped, and resumed pointing. "Yes. That."

"We'll do it after Auri is freed," Nix said.

"But what about you?" Panic rose in her chest, making it difficult to breathe.

"Don't forget the wish," Nix told her, moving across the room to stand in front of her. "You made the wish, and the wish was granted. You've already paid the wish price. It's yours. You wished for the capacity, to have the wisdom to defeat the spell, remember?" He grabbed her arms and squeezed them gently as if to imbue her with his confidence. "No matter what, Auri, this is your choice. You know how I feel about you. No matter what you choose. No matter what happens." He placed his hands on either side of her face. "I choose hope."

She nodded and took a deep breath. If he could choose hope, she could choose courage.

Poe moaned.

They all turned to look at the goddess of chaos as she raised her head, blinking back to consciousness. She muttered something incoherent.

At creak behind them, Auri spun, her heart slamming against her chest, afraid of coming face to face with the monster of her vision again. A large door lay wide open in the middle of the room, revealing the meadow beyond, the meadow where she'd first met Nix.

Auri could see the melting snowbank, the trees, the newly sprouted growth. It was changed from the day she'd found the key, warmer and more welcoming. A voice—several voices—could be heard beyond, calling for her: "Auri!" Though she couldn't see them, she knew the voices were those of her family.

She reached into her pocket, where she knew the key was settled inside, and withdrew it.

"Nix?" Luc asked. "Fuck. Where did he go?"

Auri whirled around.

Luc and Lexa turned with her.

Poe struggled against her binding.

Beyond them, another wooden door appeared facing the first, this one closed and smaller. The top was arched, and in its center a doorknob with a keyhole framed in black metalwork. She'd seen a door like it before. Where? Where had it been?

"Nix?" she called, but he didn't appear. Her heart tightened in her chest. Even though she wanted to deny it, she knew the final test had begun. Nix had gone to wherever her final sacrifice would be.

"Let me out!" Poe screeched.

"Shut it, traitor," Lexa said. "Where's Nix?"

"I don't know. Why would I know?" Poe

screamed. "What is the meaning of this?"

"We know everything. Mangle. Maiades. The spell. You set it up," Luc said. "Since my blood won't work, you're going to supply us with yours to break the spell."

Poe shook her head and fought against the enchanted binding. "No. Luc, I didn't know. You know I didn't. We did it together. It won't work."

"Where is Nix?" Lexa asked again.

The chorus of Auri's family grew louder through the door. "Auri!"

"Luc. Listen to me. Listen," Poe begged, sitting forward, her arms bound tight against her body, the golden cord glowing. "This wasn't supposed to happen. You know. You were there. You asked for the spell."

"Nix!" Even as Auri screamed for him, she knew in the core of what made her that he wasn't there. She pressed a hand to the ache that ripped through her heart, and the room shuddered with her cry, as if the realm quaked around them.

"What was that?" Poe asked. "What's wrong with the mortal?"

"I'm thinking her wish may be kicking in," Lexa said.

"What did she wish for?" Poe's eyes were wide with panic. "What did you wish for?"

"Where does that door go?" Auri asked. "I've seen it before, but I can't remember where."

"Auri!" Her father's voice called beyond the open door.

But Auri was staring at the closed one, and she knew where she'd seen it. "Lexa? Is that the door to your realm? The one at Alabastrine?"

"I suppose it's an adequate replica. Why? Have you been?" Lexa's teeth gleamed when she smiled.

"Nix took me there."

"How? He can't leave here," she asked.

"As a conjuring; he made it."

"Auri!" Brinna's voice called.

Auri looked over her shoulder at the open door, understanding what this was. It was a test. She had to choose between the safety with her family and freedom from the key, or whatever lay beyond the closed door. To find Nix and free him.

"Auri!" her mother and Jessamine's voices chorused. "Auri!"

She looked down at the key in her hands. She could walk through the open door into the love of her family. It would be simple. She'd made the wish to give herself freedom to choose her life. She would be free from the key, from the chaotic realm of monsters and magic. She looked up at Lexa and Luc and Poe.

But if Poe's blood didn't break the spell, she would be leaving Nix to a fate he didn't deserve. An ending.

Six key keepers had come before her. All six had chosen themselves, their desires, maybe what was safer. Perhaps Nix didn't deserve such a sacrifice. Maybe he was ruthless and angry, intense and underhanded. But he also had shown her compassion and joy and had helped her find herself and her voice.

Love. He'd given her a choice. She had picked up the key in the glade—no one had made her. She'd called to him, albeit unwittingly, bringing forth his spirit. Perhaps the loss of her freedom to the key had brought forth the consequence of falling in love with Nix. But it required her to be the one to free him, even if it meant leaving behind her family.

"Auri!" her father and mother called.

She looked back at the door.

She knew her parents' love for her, her siblings, and one another. She'd wondered about it many times since being drawn into Nix's realm. She used to wonder how they could find happiness even in the day-to-day drudgery of their poverty. They smiled, they played, and they laughed. They worked side by side. They offered one another secret touches, kisses, and held each other while one cried. Their love required sacrifice, to be sure, but was it truly a sacrifice when they had the love of one another?

In all their lessons, she suddenly understood what true sacrifice meant. It wasn't about losing yourself or your wants. It wasn't about being brave or clinging to hope. It was about being what the other needed when they needed it. The joy, the courage, the hope, the love. Honoring one another. Calling one another home.

"Auri!" her brother called from beyond the door.

"Auri!" Tarley's voice called her home.

Except they weren't her home anymore.

Nix was.

"I love you," she said to the family looking for her

on the other side of the open door. Then she turned away, making her choice.

"Let's end this." She walked across the room to the closed doorway, knowing what was behind it would help her free Nix—wherever he was. It also meant the spell would coalesce to the end.

"Um. Auri," Luc said.

She glanced over her shoulder to see both him and Lexa watching her with varied expressions of surprise.

"Did you know you're glowing? You've got a little–" he pointed and waggled his fingers– "trail of gold dust."

Unsure what they meant or why it mattered, she ignored their expressions. "Are you ready?" she asked them, wanting to hold onto the bravery to open the closed door, terrified of what lay beyond.

"No!" Poe screeched. "Don't open it! What did you wish? What did you wish?"

"Lexa Uraiahs and Luc Uraiahs," she said as she inserted the key into the keyhole, "I grant you your powers in this realm." Then she turned the key.

The darkness through the door was oppressive, more so than any she'd experience thus far in the spell. Auri stepped through anyway, and in the pervasive darkness, she realized Luc was right. A soft, golden glow emanated from her body, illuminating her immediate vicinity as during the obligation.

Lexa and Luc carted a bound Poe with them. She was whimpering about something, but Auri ignored her.

"Nix?" she called.

He didn't answer. She wasn't sure if she expected him too.

"If it's a replica of the underworld," Lexa said, "and if the spell is empowered by Mangle, maybe that is where Nix will be?"

"What. No!" Poe fought her restraints. "Let me go. My blood won't work!"

"Why won't your blood work?" Luc asked. "It should. You said it was a blood oath spell. The reason mine didn't work was because it wasn't my blood that was needed."

Poe shook her head emphatically. "The reason no blood will work is because the spell—or rather the demon fueling it—requires more. I told you the truth. It would take a life. And even if you kill me, Mangle will just absorb my power."

"I'm not killing her," Luc said. "That wasn't part of the plan."

"We can't," Lexa said. "Not if it gives her power to Mangle."

"We won't need to," Auri said, knowing it as clearly as she knew she lived in a cottage in Sevens. She wasn't sure how she knew it, or what specifically she knew, it was more a sense the knowledge was there. *The wish.* "Nix? Where are you?" Auri called into the darkness again.

"Let's see if your wish worked," Luc said and opened his hand. The light flared alive inside of it. "I should be able to break apart the darkness."

But before Luc could, the heavy blanket of darkness withdrew, furling away from them to leave a gray twilight behind.

"Nix!" Auri knew it was him. She'd seen him do it before in his conjuring of Lexa. "We're here!" But her words seemed to drop like rocks in front of her. As the darkness continued to collect, it revealed an expansive space devoid of light and sound.

Unbidden, a thought passed through her mind that she voiced aloud. "That's all he'll be able to do here."

"Why?" Luc asked.

"He's a hostage to the spell."

"But he has power here."

"Only what the spell allows him. I can't change it," Auri said, knowing it like she knew the winters in Sevens were brutal.

"How do you know–" Poe started.

"Shut up," Lexa interrupted.

Luc hurled light to illuminate the dense gray aftermath of this underworld, and at the heart of it stood Nix.

Auri darted forward.

"Wait," Lexa cried, grabbing hold of Auri. Then with a great whoosh of wind, muted sound, and heat, she shifted into her dragon form. "Something feels wrong," Lexa said. Her giant head turned and looked at Poe, who backed up into Luc's unforgiving chest. "The seventh wisher was always going to unlock the outcome of the spell. What is it?"

Poe, with her eyes squeezed shut. "I don't know!"

"Lies." The heat from Lexa's mouth singed Poe's hair, curling the ends.

Poe's eyes flew open. "I was just the recipient!" she

screamed at Lexa. "The seventh awakens the End."

"It's the monster," Auri said, recalling the second obligation. "The End."

"Power is supposed to come to me, but *you*–" Poe seethed, saying 'you' to Auri as if it were a curse. She tugged Luc forward toward in her vehemence, but Luc was stronger.

"Did you really think Mangle would release any to you?" Lexa asked.

"There's an agreement."

Lexa scoffed. "Only idiots make deals with devils."

Auri looked at Nix across the expanse, knowing that it was coming just like in her second obligation, the vision. Her consciousness knew she needed to collect Nix's power, to save it. But she needed to get to him. She didn't think she had time, so she closed her eyes and searched for the golden threads that had tethered them during the conjuring and the obligations. Moving through the spaces of her consciousness, she searched for a flicker of Nix.

Nix? She called through her mind, confident that he had always answered her.

Auri? I'm here.

She started, surprised. That hadn't ever worked before. She wanted to open her eyes to find him and offer him a giant smile but was afraid to break the connection. *I need you to give me your power. The monster is coming for you.*

I don't have it.

You do. The spell can't take it, only chain it, but the monster will take it. Can you give it away? To me? I'm not beholden to the spell like you are. The wish maker has the power.

He was silent for too many beats, working through what she was asking of him. It was a lot, she knew. Maybe too much, but it needed to be done. She knew that. So she said, *I need you to trust me.*

I trust you.

A gasp came from behind her. "What's that," Poe said.

"I don't–" Luc's voice was laced with awe.

Feeling the heat, Auri opened her eyes. Bright, glowing, golden threads surged from one side of the darkness into her. She rose into the expanse, the tether filling her with power.

"I'm not sure that's the wish," Lexa said, the bright light reflected in her dragon's eyes.

Then it was gone, the light, the heat, and Auri was set down, swaying under the weight of whatever she held.

"What was that?" Poe shrieked.

Auri flicked her hand, and a metal clamp wrapped around Poe's head, covering her mouth. "Your mouth isn't useful. Best to keep it closed."

Lexa looked at Auri and grinned with dragon's teeth. "Well, mortal, that's the most god-like thing I've seen today, besides me of course." She swiveled her large head toward the deep black of the space. "We find The End, then."

They started across the expanse, Luc holding up the light, but their target, Nix, receded, never drawing any closer. Then suddenly, the darkness collapsed around them.

"Nix!" Auri screamed. "Luc!"

Luc threw light, and it hit the darkness like a rock, cracking it like ice on a frozen pond. The crack spread like spiderwebs but didn't collapse, creating a wall between them and Nix.

"Is this the spell?" Auri asked.

"Spells don't have a consciousness," Lexa said, moving through the cracked darkness in the direction where Nix had been.

"Then this isn't right," Auri said, accessing the knowledge in her mind she'd wished for. "It seems to be thinking. Could someone control it from the inside?"

"It is possible," Luc said, pushing Poe forward.

"Did you cast the spell with another entity?" Auri asked her.

Poe shook her head.

"I was with her," Luc said. "If there was another entity, I wasn't aware of it."

Words matter, Auri. She wasn't sure if it was Nix's voice or if it was her conjuring the words she'd heard him say so frequently. She turned to Poe and flicked the mouth covering off. "Is it possible that the spell book and the spell were layered with another spell?"

"Fuck you," Poe said.

"She's the only way you're getting out of here," Lexa said. "Your other option is my realm in the afterlife. Your choice."

"I suppose," Poe said reluctantly. "Chaos isn't orderly, so the spell could be manipulated. The additional spell would need to be layered into the original spell."

Auri didn't trust a thing coming out of Poe's mouth, but Nix's words lit up in her mind. "Words matter."

"Excuse me?" Luc asked.

"Nix has always said, 'the words matter.' That's where the adjoining spell would have existed. Layered with the original. That is why you wouldn't have known."

"Listen," Lexa said, stopping and tipping her dragon head. "Do you hear that?"

Auri strained to hear whatever it was that Lexa was listening to, but it wasn't anything she could hear.

Suddenly, the darkness shattered, exploding outward in shards. Auri felt her skin tighten with the cold and then warmth of her blood as it dripped down her cheeks. She wished to draw the darkness away, and it answered her—answered to Nix's power that she held—receding from what lay ahead of them.

"How is that happening?" Poe snapped. "Someone tell me!"

"Mangle," Lexa said and stepped in between what Auri, Luc, and Poe and whatever she'd seen.

Auri peered around the dragon. A great hulking beast stood with a wide head and protruding jaw, teeth the size of arms, and dozens of red beady eyes dripping blood. Its black and green skin was mottled with boils and pustules in various levels of decay, carrying the stench of sickness and death. Wings stretched with dark membrane waved, wafting the stench and heat toward them.

The End.

In its closed jaw was Nix, unconscious.

Auri screamed, shadows exploding from her like a dark firework.

The monster plucked Nix from its mouth, eyeing Auri, then looked at Lexa. "Dragon goddess."

Auri shuddered at the sound of its voice, like rocks scraping over rocks, then rolling with the hulk of an avalanche. It was terrible.

"Here's your kin."

There was the thump of a body hitting the hard ground.

Auri rushed past Lexa between the two giants and collapsed to her knees. "Nix. Nix." His eyes were closed, his body broken, covered in blood. "No. No. No," she chanted, and tears sprang to her eyes.

"Let me out," Poe screeched. "I did what you wanted! We had a deal. Give me my half."

Mangle laughed. "You brought me so much more, goddess. Four gods. A true feast. And–" Its attention fell to Auri once more, holding onto Nix at its clubbed feet. It tilted its head. "What are you? There is power in you," it said. It sniffed. "God power, but something more."

Auri wanted to vomit at the sound of its voice. The horrific timbre scraped over her eardrums and left them raw. She couldn't think but for the horrible sensations it emitted in her body, along with the grief of holding Nix's broken body in her arms. She couldn't tell if he was alive.

"You are in my realm, Mangle," Lexa seethed, a vein of fire shooting from her dragon mouth.

"No, goddess. You are in my spell, where I will collect the power."

Auri drew Nix into her arms, rocking him "No. No. No," she chanted.

Words matter, Auri. Nix's words. Nix's voice. Though he wasn't speaking it aloud, she had the impression he was with her, nonetheless.

"I am in control of this spell, and I will be collecting you all. It's time for my feast."

"No. We had an agreement," Poe cried. "The book for one god and a share of the power."

"But you've brought me four."

"I wasn't a part of the bargain."

"But you are here instead of far, far away, Chaos. I will take it all, then I will burst forth the new lord of all: light, death, night, and chaos." It looked at Auri, then, tilting its engorged head. Luc's light flared. The monster's teeth flashed in the light.

It was enough to distract it.

Lexa leapt and brought forth fire, unleashing it on the demon.

Bent over Nix, Auri felt the heat, and though she screamed she was the sacrifice, the noise was too great to hear her.

Words matter, Auri.

Amidst the melee of the two monsters battling, her mind worked over the words. She'd chosen Nix. She'd opened the door. She'd won, but she hadn't. They were still here. She'd sacrificed her family for Nix, now broken and bleeding in her arms. Why was this happening? She was missing something.

Words matter, Auri.

The giants clashed around her, and Luc appeared to grab onto her and Nix, and dragging them from the battle Lexa waged on the demon, their claws ripping, fire scalding, shrill shrieks resounding.

Once clear, Auri noted the still open door behind them. The space seemed to stretch between her and the door, and just beyond it was the open door to her world—a clean path from where she was sitting, to the meadow where her family was looking for her. And suddenly, she knew Mangle wanted to collect the powers, and it wanted a way out of the underworld.

Words matter.

She knew this monster wasn't Mangle, but an embodiment of the demon. The real Mangle was still in the underworld, waiting to collect upon the completion of the spell to collect the power that would break its chains and allow it to escape.

And the doors were wide open, still.

Which meant, the spell was still wide open, unended.

The spell was order. Nix had said it over and over.

A pattern.

Which meant something still needed to be done to end it.

She may have made a choice to sacrifice her family for Nix, but that hadn't been the final sacrifice. The End was here to feast, and now, she had a choice: herself or Nix?

She hadn't asked to win. She'd asked to change it. She'd asked to fix what Poe and the spell were breaking: order.

She needed to close the door.

Over the course of the spell, she'd wished for freedom, bravery, and wisdom. She had them all now, and she understood what she had to do. She closed her eyes and pressed her forehead to Nix's. "I'm giving it back, now." She looked for their connection, felt for the power he'd given her, and trusting the wish to respond, she willed the power down the tether between them, gifting the power back into Nix's broken body. She could feel the heat swirl around them, feel the warmth, but didn't open her eyes to see.

When the power waned, she opened her eyes. "I love you," she said, pressed a kiss to his lips, and added, "Always."

Auri looked up and saw Lexa swooping in flight, her mouth open as she unleashed fire, hitting the monster, who screamed.

Auri cried out, "Luc—take Nix back through the door."

"What? I can't leave–"

"Trust me," Auri told him, and once Nix was in his

brother's arms, she let him go. "Get Nix out. You too."

Then, she stood and turned to face the creature.

"I am the key keeper," she announced. "I have the power to end this spell."

"And yet, here you are," the creature said dodging Lexa. It held out its awful hands and said, "The key keeper is done." The creature flicked its claws, but unlike the second obligation, she remained firmly fixed to the ground, unaffected by the monster's power.

"Luc. I know what I'm doing," Auri said, straining to speak over a strange wind that swirled around them. "Nix. The doorway."

Luc listened, though Auri couldn't be sure why. Fear or trust, perhaps. Love for his brother. He picked up Nix, slinging him over a shoulder, and in a flash of light, he left them in the dark. Poe screeched. Auri's glow illuminated Mangle's outline.

"Lexa," Auri yelled at the dragon, watching as Mangle's red eyes glowed in the darkness. "You go, too. And take Poe."

"I won't."

"You must. I'm the wish maker, and I know what I must do," she told the dragon. You being here is more dangerous–"

"You need me."

"No. I need you to take your powers from this spell. Yours and Poe's. Luc's and Nix's. Go."

"Afraid you cannot beat me, goddess?" Mangle taunted, as if sensing it was losing something. "I will be free, and I will take you with me by eating your fire."

Lexa's giant head looked at Auri, her eyes glittering in the darkness, and Auri told the dragon alone, "Close and lock the door behind you."

Though Lexa supposedly had such high disdain for mortals, there was something in the dragon's expression that told Auri a different story. In a flurry of sound, light, and heat, Lexa was gone, Poe with her, leaving only Auri with Mangle. Somewhere in the distance behind her, the door creaked, the lock clicked into place, and an echo rushed across the expanse like an earthquake.

Mangle shrieked as the darkness became a monster itself, collapsing. The creature's edges changed, softening, growing slick with the shadows, until its form shifted, shrank, and disappeared, leaving behind the soft gray of a coming dawn. At the heart of that muted light, a human-like creature, neither man nor woman, but pleasant in their countenance as opposed to what they had been, walked toward Auri. They wore a full-length black robe with red whirls, the long sleeves obscuring their arms and hands. Long, slick hair hung about their sharp-featured face.

"You're the demon?" Auri asked.

"I am the spell."

"I thought the spell didn't have consciousness."

"I am the embodiment of the spell, already cast. Key keeper, you chose to stay?" the spell asked.

"I have."

"You have chosen to sacrifice yourself. Not only for only Nixus Uraiahs, god of night and darkness, but for Luc Uraiahs and Poe Demirtitus, deceivers, and even for Lexa Uraiahs, goddess of the underworld, death, and the eater of men.”

“I have. What about Mangle?”

“There were layers, key keeper. The first sacrifice you made—choosing to forgo your family—broke the first layer of the spell, but it opened the second layer.”

“Nix was right,” she said. “And the demon?’”

“Choosing to remain to save Nixus Uraiahs and, by default, the others, broke the secondary spell. The demon hadn’t considered that sort of selfless sacrifice could ever be made, since demons don’t function in selflessness.”

“Is Nixus dead?” Auri’s voice broke on the word.

“He is beyond the spell.”

She didn’t know what that meant. She was hopeful that meant he was alive and free, but she didn’t know. Falling to her knees, she held her head in her hands and burst into tears. “Dead or alive?” she asked. “Please.”

“Key keeper,” the End said.

She looked up to the disconcerting face of the spell’s embodiment. They grasped her arm and helped her stand.

“You cannot stay,” they told her.

“But–”

They shook their head. “We have come to an end. It is finished. The spell is broken.” Then the creature pushed her. Auri fell backward, but instead of slamming against the stone floor, she continued falling through the darkness.

Ever After . . .

One moment Auri was there and the next, Nix stood in the expansive darkness of… nowhere. "Auri," he yelled, but there wasn't an answer, and the acoustics strangely muffled the sound despite the massive space around him. At a twinge in his heart, he pressed his fingers to his chest, as he turned in a circle to get his bearings. It was dark—oppressively so, as if he'd been sucked into Lexa's underworld—only there was nothing.

It was the final sacrifice.

He'd been through six of them, each of them

unique to the key keepers. With Flora—the first time—they'd stood in an open field at springtime, Nix dressed as a groom. She'd been given the choice between her wishes or him.

Or the second time, when the spell had imprisoned Nix in a dungeon with the key keeper. A battle had raged outside the castle walls. He'd been chained, but the wish maker hadn't been. The key keeper was to save himself from where they were being held by slipping through an open passageway. The choice had been to take Nix with him or to leave him behind.

He wondered what Auri was facing, worried for her, and hoped that whatever it was, she would choose herself. He pressed his fingers over his heart again, knowing she wouldn't. For the first time in his existence within the spell, he knew he would be chosen. It was a strange thing to understand that he was loved by her and how deeply he loved her in return. For the first time, he didn't want a key keeper to choose him over her own needs.

He walked in the darkness, though he wasn't sure why he walked. He was alone, and there wasn't anything to walk toward. No bearings, no landmarks, no sounds. Nothing. Is this where he would be for eternity should Auri choose herself and leave him in the spell? Time stretched around him for an infinity, until a sliver of muted light opened in a far-off distance. There were slices of shadow, and he knew in his bones it was Auri, Luc, and Lexa.

"Auri!" he yelled, but the sound collapsed.

He reached out around him and drew the darkness aside, pulling it into him to offer them what light he could, to know he was there since sound couldn't escape the oppression.

And a light flared. Luc. Evidence his power was working within the spell.

Nix smiled.

Auri's wish had worked.

He walked toward them, only he never moved closer, the tiny doorway glowing beyond remaining fixed like a beacon he'd never reach. Their tiny shadows disappeared. Still, he walked, hopeful he could get to them but somehow knowing he couldn't.

His heart heated, and tendrils of golden light grew from his chest, moving beyond him. When he looked up, he saw the golden threads he recognized from the obligations. Auri. He closed his eyes and grasped ahold of them. Connecting. Seeking her presence in the ether of between.

Nix?

His eyes flew open at the sound of her voice in his mind, the bright light around him a welcome warmth in the cold dark. He shivered at the strange sensation, wondering if he'd imagined her talking to him in his head, but answered: *Auri? I'm here.*

And her voice replied: *I need you to give me your power. The monster is coming.*

He was startled. He'd never connected to anyone this way. Never knew it was a possibility. Was it the god-yoke or her wish? He couldn't be sure, but he wasn't going to turn away from the gift of it.

I don't have it, he answered. Wondering why she was asking. She knew he was limited in what he could and couldn't do within the confines of the spell.

But her words supplied the answer to his question: *You do. The spell can't take it, only chain it, but the monster will take it. Can you give it away? To me? I'm not beholden to the spell like you are. The wish maker has the power.*

He paused. Give away his power? It was audacious, but what she'd said made sense—her wish being answered. Only the idea of releasing his power, offering it to a key keeper when he'd only ever been left behind, felt reckless and made his heart race even as the warmth of their connection, the glow that made it reminded him: this was Auri, and she was here.

I need you to trust me, she said.

And he knew, without a doubt, he did. *I trust you.*

And over the tether, Nix released his power, pouring everything he was into it. Maybe he couldn't access it within the confines of the spell, but there didn't seem to be a rule governing what he released. It raced across the tether over space and time until he felt himself depleted. The connection broke, and he stumbled. Empty. The pressure around his heart still thrummed, but everything else was gone.

Auri? he called, testing the tether, but she didn't answer.

He started walking again, then running toward the light, but it never grew any closer.

Then without warning, the light shuddered, the

light collapsing in the distance. The ground shook under his feet, and he had a horrible fear he'd been left powerless in the dark. Alone again. Maybe he'd been a fool. Maybe he'd been duped. His fears drove through him like spikes while before him, a monster materialized. It was black like the darkness, a giant covered in weeping sores and multiple eyes oozing blood. Distended teeth and massive hands with claws as long as arms.

And he knew it was the End.

Auri had seen this creature.

This was why she'd asked for his powers. To protect them from this.

"Nixus Uraiahs," it said with a horrible voice like salt in an open wound, and Nix cringed. "You have failed. The End is here, and I will feast."

Nix's first impulse was to cast out his shadows, but his power was gone. And he recognized this was the spell, the layer that Luc hadn't known about. Auri had taken his power, but it was to keep it from this monster, who would use it to escape this imprisonment in the underworld. Acceptance and gratitude wrapped around him like a protective cloak. "I haven't failed."

The creature laughed, and Nix squeezed his eyes shut and covered his ears, his stomach rolling with the awful sound.

"How will you defeat me?" the monster asked.

"I won't," Nix answered. But Auri would. He knew it as concretely as he knew he'd been trapped all these years.

The creature tilted its head, confused, but then swung its giant arm, hitting Nix.

Nix flew, landing hard against the ground and knocking the breath from his lungs.

"I will collect your powers." The monster stomped to him.

Nix rolled, though his body was slow, and grasped out for something to grab hold of, but the creature picked him up by the ankle.

Nix knew he was going to die, but Auri was safe. His powers were safe. She would survive with Lexa and Luc. They would take his powers so his father could release them for the next Conveying. He smiled, knowing that now, he would be free.

The monster bit, its teeth ripping into him as it bit down.

Nix cried out with the pain of it, and dove into the tether to protect himself.

I love you, Auri. Remember, the words matter, he repeated over and over in his mind, as his body was crushed in the creature's grotesque maw. *Words matter, Auri. I love you. I love you.*

Darkness descended over his mind, and he floated thoughtless until a light appeared, bright behind his eyelids. The golden sensation was warm, cozy, and he rushed toward it. When he opened his eyes, the bright light of day made him squint. This wasn't the realm of the spell, where it was always a variation of his dark. As his eyes focused, he realized he was in a room, the alabaster walls bright, the light coming through open windows, wafting with white gossamer curtains to reveal a blue sky that seemed more like a dream than something real.

"Have I died?" he asked.

Faces crowded around him, and he squinted as the light shifted. He began to recognize singular faces, his gaze jumping from one to another. Saphra, Eitan, Pax, Lior, Lexa, and more. His siblings.

"Because we're all dead, too?" Lexa asked.

He focused on the yellow of her eyes.

"Welcome home," she said with a smile.

He was in Elcadia. Auri had freed him, and the thrum of power pulsing under his skin, around his organs, moving like current, was there. She'd returned it.

"The spell?" he asked.

"Ended." Lexa offered her version of a smile and nodded.

"Where is she?" he asked Lexa and glanced around the room, but it was only several of his brothers and sisters. He turned his head to Lexa for the answer.

The edges of her eyes softened, darkening them to a deep golden color. "She made us leave with you and told us to shut and lock the door. The moment Luc and I made it through the door with you and Poe and locked it, the spell collapsed, and spat us back outside a shed in Elcadia. You've been asleep, recovering at home for several days. The healer kept you sedated while your physical body mended."

His throat closed around his next question. He

couldn't voice it. He reached up and rubbed at his chest, still hot with the god-yoke, and noticed an ache, as if he needed to take a deep breath but couldn't.

Auri? He tried the mind tether, wondering if he'd imagined it. There wasn't an answer.

"Luc was right. She was the one to break it." Lexa added, "And I know I've always said I despise mortals, but it's hard to hate one that saved us." In a rather affectionate gesture for Lexa, she reached and swiped a lock of his hair off his forehead. "One that sacrificed herself for you." She paused, searched his face, then looked away. "Though, I'm not convinced she's mortal."

His siblings all spoke at the same time to one another, their conversations muted, but he wasn't grabbing ahold of them. He was thinking of Auri.

He cleared his throat of emotion. "Is she gone?"

Lexa shrugged and perched on the bed next to him. "The last I saw of her she was still inside the spell. Then it was just over." She paused and took his hand. Another clue she was happy he was safe and was trying to comfort him. "She hasn't passed into the afterlife. It stands to reason, you're out, the spell broken, that maybe she made it out too."

"Poe?"

"She's been imprisoned in a cipher box. Hopefully forever."

His eyes danced through the faces for Luc. He wasn't there. "Where's Luc?"

"Banished," Lior said and grinned at his replica

brothers Pax and Eitan. The triplets.

"Father let him off easy," Saphra observed. She arched a golden brow over an eye.

"Banished? How?"

"He's stuck in Sol and can't come to Elcadia until Father decides how he wants to exact the proper punishment," Lexa said.

"Nixus!"

Nix raised his head slightly at the sound, his siblings moving apart to open a space for him to watch his mother sweep through the doorway and down the stairs toward him.

Aiah, goddess of the seasons, beamed with the light of whatever season it was in Elcadia. Her dark hair threaded with copper was wrapped up in a spiky crown of bare twigs, which meant it was winter. She stopped at his bedside, moving Lexa—the only entity that could—out of the way and sat, smoothing her copper dress as she did. "Son," she said. "I'm so relieved to see you awake."

"Mother."

She embraced him, and Nix welcomed it, relished it even. Thinking he would never see her again, never feel this, made him grateful for it. She was warm and smelled of cinnamon. He'd missed her, even if she meddled.

Aiah leaned back, holding him out at arm's length, and measured his health with her eyes. When whatever she saw seemed to meet her expectations, she gave a quick nod and met his eyes with hers. "I am ashamed we didn't know what was happening. I blame myself for assuming you were sewing your oats in the cosmos."

"You aren't to blame," he said to assure her.

"Luc confessed to what he did." She laid a hand against his cheek. "Your father has banished him to Sol."

"I need him," Nix said.

She stood and sighed, then reached to straighten the white coverlet on Nix's legs. "I know he deserves your vengeance, Nixus. He really does, but I can't have you killing each other. You're both my sons. You're important to the health of the worlds. Besides, the last few years without the night were bad enough. This separation is the best for now. A cooling off period."

"I've had enough of a cooling off period," Nix said, shaking his head. "Years," he said, though he wasn't sure how many outside the spell. Ten? Fifteen? He pushed himself up in the bed so he could sit up. "You misunderstand me, Mother. I don't want to kill him. I need him to help me find Auri."

"You should kill him," Pax said.

"I would," Eitan added. "Or I'd hire someone to do it."

Aiah whirled on her triplets. "Hush. You wouldn't because you'd face the wrath of your father. All talk." She turned back to Nix. Her eyes narrowed, then her nose wrinkled with distaste. "You want to find the mortal?"

"She did save three of your children, and your

niece, who didn't deserve it, by the way," Lexa provided. "Not to mention the worlds by keeping a powerful demon imprisoned."

Aiah made a noncommittal noise through her nose.

Nix glanced around at his siblings. "Can I talk to Mother alone, please?"

With varying degrees of nods, well-wishes, a kiss on the cheek, a rib for being duped by Luc, a squeeze on his shoulder, Nix watched his siblings leave the room, grateful to be with them. Auri had made that happen, and the realization humbled him. It had only been a short while ago, he hadn't any hope he'd ever see them again.

"I'm so blessed to have you home," Aiah said and squeezed his hand. "Night has returned."

"I'm home because of Auri."

"Fine. Yes. You are home because of the mortal."

He studied her, wondering how she was going to respond to the news he was about to share. He didn't know enough about it, but she might.

"What is it?" she asked.

He pressed his free hand over his heart. "I have a yoke, mother."

"A yoke?" She scoffed as if he were joking, but when she saw his face, which he thought was some variation of seriousness, her smile faded. "A god-yoke? How? Was there a god or goddess with you?"

"With Auri."

She stood and walked to the window. "That's impossible." She turned and looked at him. "With a mortal?"

"I'm not sure she is."

"And how would you know this?"

"I don't. Not for sure, but–"

Lexa poked her head back in through a crack in the open doorway, all the faces of his siblings lined in the exposed seam, listening. "I agree with him. I think she's … not mortal."

"Thank you, Lexa," Aiah said from her spot near the window, then walked up the steps, pushed them all out, and shut the door. She turned and looked at Nix. "The yoke is serious business, Nix. Are you sure?"

He nodded. "I don't know anything about it, but it's the only thing that make sense–" He stopped and shook his head.

"Is she still alive?"

"I don't know. But I feel something. Here." He pointed at his chest again. "It aches. Like something is tugging at it. When I close my eyes, I see golden threads stretching toward something unseen."

Aiah closed her eyes and took a deep breath. "The yoke is a binding. It links gods in life, but also in death. And should one of you die, the other will diminish."

"You're saying, perhaps I'm losing my power because she has died?"

She pushed away from the doorway and walked back down the stairwell to him, sat a hip next to him on the bed. "It could be. If the yoke has already been established and you are without your matched star, you both will diminish."

"So if she is alive, she will be hurt?"

"If she is alive, is truly your yoke, then yes, Nix, she will be suffering like you say you are." His mother looked at him with compassionate eyes, their shape changing to exude her motherly affection and empathy. "They say the yoke is the greatest gift among the gods. So rare is the tether, that when it is found, the depth of connection created is the beginning of a new universe." She smiled wanly. "But as is with the balance of all things, the converse is also true. The death of the yoke is the destruction of that same universe."

He pressed his fingers against the center of his chest, feeling the ache acutely.

"If you are tethered and she has died, Nix, you will fade."

He nodded, knowing that if Auri had died for him, he would gladly follow. "Luc is the only one who knows where to look to see if she is alive."

His mother sighed. "Your father isn't going to like this. He set Luc's banishment. And you–" she shook her head– "yoked to a mortal."

"He's had his share of dalliances with mortals. And he's changed punishments to suit his needs"

"Hush. I don't like to think about that. Besides, dalliances are different from yoking."

"Mother."

"First you heal. Then you tell your father, who will hold to the cooling off period between you and your brother, I expect. We don't need a war or something to upend the order of things, do we? Then, we'll summon Luc.”

“I won’t wait that long.” He rubbed his chest again. “I need to find her.”

His mother watched him, her copper eyes tracking his movement. She nodded. “Fine. I’ll talk to him.”

“I mean it, Mother. I will leave.”

She reached out and patted his hand resting on his chest over his heart. She gave him a smile. “Yes. I have no doubt.” She stood. “I’ll be back with food.”

Nix watched her leave. When she opened the door, all his siblings were still outside, no doubt having overheard everything.

He looked up at the layer of soft, white fabric draped about the top of the bed and closed his eyes, trying to drag forward Auri from his memory. He pictured her in the library he’d conjured, sitting in the living room with him, across the table of the yellow room, blushing underneath him as he entered her. The ache of his heart gave him hope that she was alive, and somewhere he could find her, deciding if the connection was completely broken, he would feel emptiness. Then again, maybe the ache had nothing to do with the yoke. Maybe it was the ache to accompany the grief of losing her.

He wished the thought away. She’d saved him. The seventh key keeper, the one he’d doubted, had sacrificed herself for him. He was alive, and he vowed that he would stop at nothing until he knew one way or the other. He would find her, even if it meant tearing the cosmos apart to do so.

Her eyes opened to the broken gray sky leaking threads of blue, and sharp treetops trying to poke holes in the clouds. Auri sat up to the voices of her father and Mattias in the distance, calling her name. She was in a glade, the snow covering the ground around her. She shivered and pulled her coat tighter. Had she fallen asleep? It was alarming to think she had, but her mind and thoughts were disoriented and disjointed, as if she'd slept deeply and dreamed.

She pressed her chest with her fingers, noting a pain there as if a piece of her heart had broken off into her chest cavity and was now tearing apart her insides with its sharp edges. With a gentle massage with her fingertips, she wondered if maybe she'd eaten something that had turned. Her mother would know what to give her to alleviate the discomfort.

"Auri!"

It was time to go.

Auri pressed her hand into the fresh snow to stand, and as she did her hand covered freezing metal. She looked down at the ground, now on her hands and knees, and lifted her hand, revealing a golden key. Her mouth dropped open, and she looked around as if she'd found someone else's treasure, but no one was there. The glade was empty but for a crow cawing from a branch across the meadow.

She'd picked up the key, marveling at its gleam, and testing its weight in her palm, noting the gems set into the bow. Could those be real? It was beautiful.

"Where do you belong?" she asked the inanimate object like a loon and glanced around again. No one there to claim it. No box or doorway in which to use it to open. She wondered where it went.

"Auri!" Her brother's voice drifted, closer now.

The crow argued its discontent at the disturbance and took flight.

"I'm here!" she called out to them and stood, then walked to the sled nestled against a heap of large rocks.

After picking up the pull, she started back through the meadow toward their voices.

When they appeared high stepping through the snow, her father's face was tight with worry. "Good gods, Auri!" he yelled through the trees.

Auri stopped abruptly and looked up at the sky. The sharp points of the trees still pierced the sky, but the leaded color had darkened to a pewter blue. Night was falling.

When her father reached her, he gathered her in his arms, crushing her against his bulk. "I thought something had happened to you. It's getting dark!"

"I think I fell asleep," she said.

"What?" Mattias asked, his face scrunching up with disbelief. "In the woods? Auri, that's dangerous. And now that it looks as if night has returned–"

She nodded in agreement. "I know. I'm sorry. I didn't mean to worry you." She looked up at the sky, her palm pressed against her chest. "I had the strangest dream," she started to say but stopped, the words dropping into a chasm of dark unawareness. A haze lingered, letting her know she'd dreamed, but the dream was gone. The cold metal in her hand reminded her of the key, and she held it up. "But look what I found."

"Holy night!" Mattias exclaimed, grabbing it from her. "Is this real?" He looked it over, flipping it and testing its weight, then handed it to their father.

"Hard to say without more light." Her father held it up, but then handed it back.

Auri, took it, then massaged her fingers against her heart once more. The pressure was constant. "I don't think I'm feeling well. Maybe that's why I fell asleep?"

Her father looked at her hand, then at her face. "Let's get you home. Scarlett will have something to set you to rights." He put an arm around her, and they started through the woods.

Darkness fell quickly, creating thicker shadows under the trees. They walked in a line now, her father, then Auri, followed by Mattias drawing the sled.

"Why do you think the night has returned?" she asked.

"Probably some natural explanation," her father said, his boots crunching in the snow.

Auri followed his footsteps with her own. "But–"

He glanced over his shoulder, and she saw the gleam of his smile in the bluish light. She knew he was getting ready to tell a story—his favorite thing to do. "There's a story they tell that in a fit of jealous rage, the goddess Mynash—over being passed over for a mortal woman—tricked the god of night, Nixus, into a puzzle box and separated him from his powers."

"And that is why the night hasn't fallen for years?" Mattias asked.

Her father chuckled. "It's a story, Mattias. We don't know why the night stopped."

"What about the zealots?" Auri asked.

"They say Nixus was enraged that his faithful have fallen away, so he took the night away to punish them and keep the crops from flourishing. The land never getting cool enough, but that the god of day—Lucian—has offered his favor by keeping the sun temperate."

Auri shivered, though she wasn't sure why other than it being cold. "It doesn't feel temperate now," she said.

"It's never temperate in Sevens," Mattias said.

"All the more reason to get back through the woods in a hurry to the safety of the warm cottage and a hot meal," her father said, turned slightly, and rubbed his belly.

It was a relief to see the bright golden light through the mullioned windows of the cottage come into view. They hurried through the hedge and across the expanse of the space between it and the barn. After putting the sled away with the help of Mattias, Auri carried in the things she'd found on her forage that day.

They walked into the house, and the noises of her sisters and mother along with their father, his hands on their mother's shoulders, made Auri happy, secure, only her smile felt forced. The impression she didn't belong here anymore weighed on her shoulders, and she shook it off. Where else would she be? She pressed her fingers to her heart.

After dinner and the exclamation over the key, which appeared real, Auri sat with her mother, stripped to her chemise, so her mother could examine her chest. There was nothing visibly wrong with it.

"Describe the pain again to me?" her mother asked, her dark red hair cascading around one side of her face as she tilted her head and searched Auri's face. She looked at Auri's fingers pressed against her heart.

"An ache. Like someone took my heart and pulled it apart."

"And it started?"

"After I woke up."

"Did you dream?"

Auri nodded and opened her mouth to tell her mother about it. The memory existed on the fringe of her mind, out of reach, as if there was a veil between her consciousness and the memory. "I can't remember it."

Her mother offered Auri a reassuring squeeze of her arm. "Get dressed then. I'll make you some herbal tea. Maybe it will help."

Auri reached for her shirtwaist.

"Where's your ribbon?"

Auri looked at her wrist where her scarlet ribbon should be. She grasped her wrist and rubbed it as if it would magically reappear, then looked at her mother, standing. "I don't know. I–" She searched her mind for the answer, but it was blank. "It must be in the woods."

Her mother's mouth was set in a grim line. Then she offered Auri a tight smile as her eyes drifted over her features. "You sure you don't remember the dream?"

Auri shook her head.

Her mother nodded and left the room, leaving Auri with the feeling something had changed, only she didn't know what it was.

Auri moved through the woods, content that this—wandering through the woods on a cold day—was where she was. At least for that day.

Over the weeks since she'd discovered the key, things had changed. First, their fortunes. They'd split the key: the gemstones to each of the siblings and the golden key to her parents. Auri, however, wanted the key and traded her emerald for it, hanging it around her neck. The feel of the metal resting against her heart brought her a small relief, easing the ever-present ache that her mother hadn't been able to ease.

Since Auri had awoken in the meadow, she not only had the same pain wrapped around her heart, but she also suffered from awful episodes that drew her into the darkness of her mind, which had made her mother worried. And her mother worried meant more controlling.

As Auri walked through the woods, her sled slicing through the snow behind her, she pondered the changes happening within her family. Mostly her mother. Scarlett Fareview hadn't ever been dictatorial, but since Auri's "Great Nap Escapade," as her father had coined it, she'd gotten annoyingly so, for reasons she claimed had to do with Auri's health. "What if you collapse again? I want you near the cottage where I can get to you." Auri had been put on tincture and remedy making duty, which she hated, because she never got to leave the confines of the cottage or the grounds within the hedge. This had become point of contention between them.

Just that morning, Brinna had asked to go into Sevens to help their mother at marketplace rather than on foraging duty.

"I can go into the woods for her," Auri suggested.

"No," their mother said, spooning porridge into a bowl for Mattias. "Auri stays here and does the mixing," she said, handing the bowl to Mattias and dishing out the next. "Tarley, you can do the foraging today."

"I'm going fishing."

Their mother's gaze jumped between their faces, handing out the next bowl and filling another.

"Mother," Auri said. "We're grown women. We can take care of ourselves. And we're a little old to be ordered about by our mother, don't you think?"

Scarlett's eyes jumped to Jessamine, then down the line until they reached Auri. "I know what is best."

"Scarlett," their father intervened with a quiet tone. It wasn't angry, just a hazy reminder to consider another perspective. Their mother, for all her kindness, compassion, and desire to be helpful, could also be intense and obstinate.

Scarlett looked at Tomas with a pointed gaze. "She doesn't have her ribbon."

Auri tilted her head, then glanced at her wrist. Her eyes jumped to each of her siblings' wrists, their scarlet ribbons still tied there. "What does that matter?"

Scarlett's gaze hit Auri before swinging back to Tomas. Tomas was locked in on Scarlett, who then seemed to wilt.

"It doesn't," Scarlett said and bent over her bowl. "Do what you will," she said, but Auri had the horrible impression her mother was fighting tears and didn't know why.

"If the queen can run a country and have a harem of men and women, I think we can make decisions about where we want to be on any given day," Tarley said, then took a bite of her mush.

"You'd think," Jessamine said. "But gods forbid that a woman be in control of her own life and finances."

"That law needs to be changed," Mattias said. "Maybe after I'm done with second school, I can be in the Royal Assembly and change it."

Auri sensed for just a moment that she'd heard this conversation before, but as soon as the sensation appeared, it floated away as if on a breeze. "I haven't been in the woods in ages," Auri said. "Not since the *Great Nap Escapade*. I'll be careful, Mother. I promise."

"Auri–" her mother started, then looked down at her bowl, shook her head, and took a bite, leaving her thought unfinished.

Auri loved her family, but she'd had the thought a lot lately that she was ready for more space. Her heart skipped thinking about it, tightening in her chest, and she gasped, clasping her hand over her chest. That pinch that hit her so often stole her breath. She stopped to reclaim it.

While she did, she watched a raven drop through the trees and settle on a branch. It watched her with its black beady eyes. She suppressed a shudder and continued through the forest, finding the heavy black birds unnerving. The raven called out. She ignored it and looked up at the gray sky. When the pain eased, she continued forward, the sled slicing through the snow behind her.

She hummed as she went, stopping to stoop when she found some herbs. A flash of sunlight lit the snow ahead, illuminating another herb. She followed it.

Another followed. She continued through the forest that way, enjoying the dances of light which seemed to lead her to the next treasure, and the next of various winter herbs or hearty branches for her fire. She even found some winter carrots following the trail, pulling them from the earth. When she finally stopped to see where she was, she was in a meadow.

The trees.

The boulders.

She turned in a circle.

It was the same one where she'd fallen asleep!

The one where she'd dreamed.

For weeks, it was only at night when she drifted to sleep that the veil thinned to allow her through. Some mornings, the vivid impression of meeting a man in her sleep followed her when she was awake, but they were impressions only. Dark eyes. A reluctant smile. Lips with the perfect bow for an upper lip. Darkness. Happiness. Love. Most of the time, she awoke smiling, but it would fade as the dream slipped away and the pain in her heart returned.

Now she stood in the meadow of the Great Nap Escapade. She'd hoped to find her way back to it, to remember the dream, but her mother's medicinal remedies and her concerns over Auri's health had taken precedence.

A warmth seeded at the center of her heart, easing the pain, then spread through her body, reaching out to the tips of her fingers and toes so that she couldn't even feel the snow. Her heartbeat quickened, and she looked around, wondering if she was imagining night was coming, covering the meadow in twilight though she knew it hadn't even reached midday. She looked up at the sky.

"Auri."

She whirled at the sound of a voice; it was a stranger's voice, but her heart jumped with anticipation as if it recognized the tone and timbre. When she saw the man who'd spoken step from the darkness between the trees, her breath came in quick bursts matching her heartbeat. A stranger.

"Do I know you?" she asked.

The man stopped walking toward her.

"How do you know my name?"

His face—a very handsome face—looked surprised, his brows rising over his dark eyes, but then coming down in confusion. Dressed in dark colors with shadows biting at the heels of his dark boots, she had the thought she should be afraid, but she wasn't. She was… curious. Drawn. She wanted to reach out and touch him to see if he was real.

He took a deep breath, looked down, and swiped at his forehead. "Shit. That isn't something I'd considered–"

Auri tilted her head. "Your voice."

His eyes rose, though his head didn't, not completely, and Auri stepped toward him as if she needed to. Her mind reminded her he was a stranger, and she'd made a promise to her mother to be safe.

But her heart seemed intent on pushing her toward him.

"What about it?" he asked.

"My heart–" she pointed at her chest– "seems to know it."

He smiled, a grin that offered her a shining light along with a deep dimple in his cheek. Though everything about him was dark, he was bright with that smile. The shadows, pets that danced around his feet, disappeared, as if they'd never been there. "Your heart. Yes." He took another step toward her.

Her heart, ignoring her head, pushed her forward, and she took a step closer. "Why would that be? You're a stranger."

"I'm Nix."

"How did you know my name, Nix?"

"We've met before," he said and took another step toward her. "In this very place, not very long ago."

She glanced around the glade. "I don't–"

"There was a key." Another step.

With her heart smacking the inside of her chest with rapid thumps, she pulled the key out from under her jacket and wrapped her hand around it. "I found a key here."

"Yes."

"Is it yours? I'm sorry. I thought–"

He laughed, shook his head, and continued toward her, steady now. "It's your key."

"But–"

And then he was finally standing before her, and she took her first easy breath, which was odd considering he was a stranger, this Nix.

"You don't remember?" he asked.

Auri looked up from the key to his face and searched the depth of his dark eyes flecked with traces of gold, looking for something she recognized. Her heart palpitated, a warm glow heating her at the center of her chest and spreading outward. "Remember what? What am I supposed to remember?"

Nix pressed his hand against his heart and studied her. He seemed to want to tell her something, but hesitated. Then he dropped his hand to his side, seemingly at a loss, unsure and unsteady. He took a deep breath, and Auri had the impression this wasn't how he usually felt about things.

"You said we've met before?"

"May I tell you a story?" he asked.

She nodded.

"It's a bit long. May we sit?" He gestured to the boulders several steps from them.

They sat side by side, not touching. Auri thought it was curious she wished they were and chastised herself because he was a stranger. In the woods!

"It's a magical story. Maybe you won't believe it, but when I finish, you can ask me any question you wish."

Auri nodded. "Okay."

Nix told her of a magic key on which a spell had been placed. A woman came along and discovered the key, unknowing that the moment she touched it, she became a part of the enchantment placed on the key. Inside, she found a trapped god.

Auri squeezed the key in hand as he continued. She liked the feel of his warmth near her so much so, she wanted to lean toward him, but didn't. She liked the sound of his voice as he spoke, and her heart danced in her chest with inexplicable familiarity. She liked the story, which was vaguely familiar, like a dream.

He said the woman was given three wishes and forced to pay three prices for making them, but it was the only way she would be able to leave the enchantment. So, she made three wishes: freedom, bravery, and wisdom. To be free of the enchantment, she was given a final test: she could choose her own path and leave the god trapped, or she could choose the hero's path to free the trapped god.

To finish the story, he asked Auri, "Do you know which she chose?"

Auri thought for a moment, but it wasn't difficult to choose. "She wished for freedom, bravery, and wisdom. I think she chose the hero's path."

"Why do you think so?" Nix asked, looking down at his hands clasped in his lap.

"If you told me she'd wished for things like wealth, long life, or material possessions, I would think the wishes would describe someone who would choose their own path." She turned her head to look at him again.

He smiled, and his eyes moved across her features. "You are correct."

"I liked that story."

"That's the story of how we met." He nodded to the key.

"It reminds me of a dream. I had a dream," she said, then stopped. The dream. His words finally connected: *That's the story of how we met.* Her eyes snapped to his face. "I know you."

"Auri?" Nix reached out and touched her hand.

A spark of electricity ignited a rush of energy from the place his skin touched hers, burning up through her skin straight to her heart and spreading outward like rays of the sun. The light ignited, and images of Nix, of being together, of the spell and the maze, the ocean, the library, his smile, his hands, their kisses, making love, and 'I love you,' hit her like a wave.

She blinked, as if suddenly awake.

It hadn't been a dream.

It was real.

With a jolt, she stood and turned to face him. "What took you so long?"

He stood, and a smile spread across his face. "You remember?"

"Oh my stars, I do. I do. I feel it here." She pressed her hand to her heart. "What took you so long, Nixus?" Then she leapt into his arms, crashing against him, her arms wrapped tightly around his neck. His arms curled around her, holding her to his chest as his face dropped to her neck. She could feel his warmth all over now, and for the first time since waking up, her heart was just right.

"In the spell," she said, "I didn't know what happened to you. Then I was just pushed out. And when I woke up, I didn't remember anything. I thought I'd had a dream," she said, the flow of her thoughts a string that took them from one point to the next. "What took you so long?" she repeated, leaning back to look at his beautiful face.

He laughed, his eyes brightening, now swirling with threads of the same golden light she felt swirling inside of her. "I had some healing to do."

"But I thought you were a god?"

"I also had some vengeance to exact and some revenge to take." He smoothed the fabric of her jacket on her back with his hand. "Then I had to break Luc out of god-jail. Then we waited and waited because we couldn't find you—until today."

She looked up at him and dove into the familiarity of her dream, into the realization that it had all been true. "I thought I'd only dreamed you."

"Auri, you saved me. You saved my brother and sister. You saved your family."

She realized she had. No Marriage Law, though now there were new challenges to face. The emerald had made a difference in their lives. She squeezed the key in her palm. The golden key that had brought her Nix. "I would do it again," she said. "It brought me you."

"It's my turn to save you. I'm the god."

"Such hubris," she smiled. "And arrogance."

Standing chest to chest in the middle of the meadow, she felt shy, suddenly. Tentative. Wanting to touch his face, feel his lips under her thumb, then under her own. Her heart snapped to attention and marched forward, and she pressed her palm to his face. Nix leaned into her touch, his eyes slipping closed as if that had all he needed to remain alive.

"What happened to you?" she asked.

"I woke up at home."

"In Elcadia?"

"You remember?"

"You helped me remember."

Nix released her, and she slid down the front of his body until her feet hit the ground. He pressed a hand over hers as he said her name, his eyes dancing over her features.

"I missed you," she said. "It hurt."

With the hand covering hers, he reached out and slid it over her hair, down her braid, curling his fingers around it. His eyes trailed the movement, then jumped back to hers, her braid still in his hand. "It was real? Yes? I was afraid maybe I'd made it up, and the pain in my chest was from something else. That maybe I was just sick. But you… You really said you loved me?"

Tears filled her eyes, hearing his words, feeling that love like a fire under her skin. She nodded. "Yes."

With the hand holding the braid, he grasped the back of her neck and kissed her, his mouth finishing the story. She grabbed onto his shoulders, steadying herself but also to reassure herself he was there. He was real, this was real and not her imagination. He angled his head, and she hers, seeking depth, more, reorienting, tasting, taking, claiming.

Nix pulled away and pressed his forehead to hers, his hand still wrapped around the back of her neck, keeping her close, the other angled around her back. "Nothing has changed for me, Auri. I could think of nothing else while we were apart, the fear that maybe you hadn't made it out. Lexa said the last she saw, you were facing down the monster, and–" He stopped and took her face in his hands again. "I feared the spell had broken with you inside, that the sacrifice had been you." The last word broke off in his throat, and starlight filled his eyes as a single droplet dripped down his cheek. "I was ready to search the underworld for you."

Auri reached up and swiped at his cheek, collecting the stardust on her thumb. "The spell released me because I had given myself to it, freely, for you. It was my final test."

He kissed her again. Deeper, with a hunger that awakened the parts of her she'd cocooned to protect her heart. He picked her up, but in her skirts, it was hard to get closer.

"I miss your trousers," he muttered in her mouth.

She smiled against his lips.

"Auri. You are mine." He kissed her.

"Yes." She kissed him.

"I am yours." He kissed her again.

"Yes." She kissed him back.

"Come back to Elcadia with me." He kissed her with a tenderness that stole her breath.

She found her breath to say, "I'm a mortal." Then she kissed him in kind, wanting him to feel as warm as she did.

He pulled away, his eyes roving over her face, and he seemed to want to say something but didn't. He waited a beat, then said, "I want you however you will allow me to be in your life. I would like to gift you immortality, but it is your choice. Know that if you refuse me, I will take to following you through the woods just to be near you."

"That sounds rather unhealthy."

He grinned. "I am a god. I do self-centered things

and make selfish choices, remember?"

"I don't think I can just go to Elcadia. Not yet. My family." She paused and grabbed his face as he started to look away. "But… I consent to allow you to court me, Nixus Uraiahs. Until my family knows you—"

"Court you?" His eyes widened.

"I think we need to test out if this is real, or a product of a stressful situation.

"Oh, Auri, believe me, this is real. You have no idea how real this is."

"Then I guess you'll have to prove it to me. On the outside." She turned away from him and started across the meadow toward her sled.

Nix materialized in front of her. "I read a book about courtship." His smile—that predatory one that made her throb—pinned her. "Do you remember when I told you I love to play chase, but I always win."

She smiled. "Yes." She leaned forward and kissed him on the nose. "I'm looking forward to seeing you try."

Not the end. . .

The Wizard

The dank cavern didn't dissuade the cloaked figure standing amidst the flickering candles from completing the spell. He'd spent a thousand lifetimes hiding his true nature and power, in caves, dark rooms below buildings, towers in castles away from prying eyes, and dungeons, which proved to be the right place to incant. Then he hid in plain sight, smiling at the glory that offered him acceptance and praise among the masses in the light of day, providing him riches beyond measure. Little did they know, he could end them with a wish, a word, and the snap of his fingers.

Within the chalk drawing, he chanted the spell and

closed his eyes, and when they opened again, he was seeing through the eyes of the nearest bird while his body remained in the cavern surrounded by stalactites. The whites of his eyes flashed open, the iris and pupil gone. The bird pushed off the branch and flew through the cityscape.

"Find her," he ordered and incanted the rest of the spell.

This spell had been used in realm after realm, world after world, looking for the woman who'd double-crossed him. The daughter of a god and a goddess, who had lost her immortality for love. She'd made him a deal and then disappeared.

For decades he'd cast spells, scried, traveled, employed darklings, and other magical creatures in the hopes of finding her. She would pay the price she'd agreed to for the power he'd added to her own, and yet, she'd eluded him somehow.

The wizard jumped into the next bird over farmland, and the next skimming the swath of a river, and the next as it traveled across the forested terrain of Kaloma. He was looking for the tell-tale gold dust of magic, the aura of its remnants, for surely with as much power as he'd gifted her, there would be evidence. His possessed vision offered him the beauty of the land, but not the sight he wanted. It wasn't the magic he wanted back. He wanted what she'd promised him. He would never stop looking. He would find her and take what was most important to her as his own.

He transferred his sight to a nearby crow. The bird

swooped lower into a northern wood, and though in the cavern, he shivered at the snow. The bird flew to a branch, and perched, watching a young woman pull a sled over the frozen terrain. It wasn't the woman—a stranger—that stopped his heart, but the aura shrouding her.

Magic.

The bird cocked its head, swiveling to watch the girl surrounded in emerald. She paused, looked around as if she sensed him there, watching, then moved on.

He was taken aback by the emerald aura, but looking closer, nestled inside its subdued light, the gold dust was contained. A ward, only it was broken, the gold working its way to the surface. So, he sat and watched from the branch. Watched as she disappeared into a glen. Watched as a man—whose power emanated like an actual star fallen to earth—a god— approached her. The cloaked wizard observed the magical threads of their life forces swirl around one another and her emerald surged to join with the god's starlight, making them difficult to look at.

She was magic.

The watcher wondered if he'd finally found where his power had been taken. It was the first time in all his years of seeking that he had hope that he was finally on the right path. He needed more information, he knew. He needed to know if the thief was here, hiding. So, he sat in the tree and watched, following the emerald girl to a wall in the woods, where she disappeared behind a magical wall, invisible to him once again.

He blinked, leaving the bird, and returned to his tired body. The moment he did, he collapsed inside the chalk lines, the candles burned down to nubs. He wasn't sure how long he'd engaged the spell, but he was hungry.

He smiled. He knew where he needed to go, and he would make her pay.

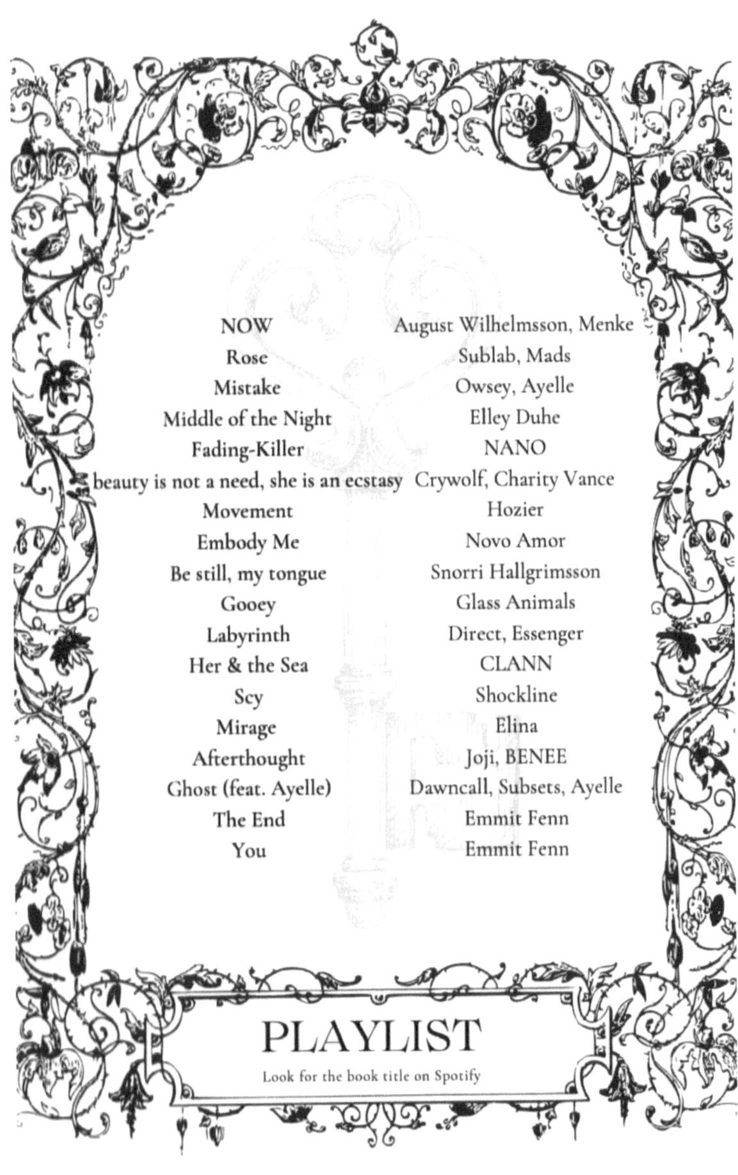

PLAYLIST

Look for the book title on Spotify

In the Shadow of a Hoax

A Fareview Fairytale

Book 2

By Maci Aurora

Tarley

arley, second daughter of Scarlett and Tomas Fareview, wasn't sure if she liked the man sitting across from her youngest sister Aurielle. As Tarley stood at the barrel of ale, waiting for the last of the four tankards to fill, her eyes drifted to Auri, ensconced at a table in a darkened corner of the inn with her suitor. It may have been the middle of the day, but the inn was shrouded in the dark ambiance of too much stone and wood and not enough light. Despite that, Tarley still attempted to assess what was happening between Auri and her suitor in their dark corner. Tarley was protective of her little sister, and she didn't trust easily—especially men.

It had been a little less than an hour ago that Auri had shown up at the back door to the kitchen of The Copper Pot Inn, asking for Tarley to cover for her.

"Auri, Mother is going to kill you." Tarley had lowered her voice so that the words sounded like air escaping from her throat.

"Tarley, please?" Auri had clasped her hands between her breasts, which were nicely displayed in the scooped neckline of her dress, and begged Tarley with her gray eyes. "It's just an outing, which Mother makes impossible."

Tarley had rolled her eyes.

Auri wasn't supposed to be beyond the hedge where they all lived with their parents. Since Auri's *Great Nap Escapade*—falling asleep in the woods and losing her red ribbon, a gift from their mother—she'd been relegated to "around the cottage duties."

"Do you think I want to cross Mother?" Tarley had glanced over her shoulder at the empty kitchen, thinking their mother might materialize. But it had been empty. Even Mrs. Barnwell had been momentarily missing from the room. Tarley had turned back to Auri. "Don't be daft! She'll have me as your second in tincture making, relegated to remaining behind the hedge." Tarley had shuddered. "No thank you."

Auri had stepped through the doorway and straightened her skirts as if Tarley had already said 'yes.' "Mother was called to Denneby and took Jessamine with her. They'll be gone two days at least. And Brinna won't tell. Besides, she and Papa and Mattias are out in the woods today."

Tarley hadn't liked the chicanery, but she also understood. Auri was a grown woman. How could she blame Auri for needing to get out? She did the same—her overnight fishing trips kept her sane. Tarley was sure Auri felt a bit like a prisoner. She would.

"Are you meeting the mysterious stranger you've mentioned?" Tarley had asked, recalling Auri's giddiness a few nights prior. The only question in her mind as Auri had regaled them with minor and evasive tidbits was *How?* How could her sister have met anyone? And in Sevens!

Auri had nodded as a bright smile lit up her face. "Yes!" She'd grabbed Tarley's forearms and shaken her with excitement. "You'll get to meet him. And I'm safe. Nothing bad will happen. I promise."

"Famous last words." Tarley had arched an eyebrow. "How did you meet him again?"

"Oh—" Auri had looked away and fussed with her skirts again. "On a trip to town."

Recognizing her sister's lie, Tarley had narrowed her eyes. "That you never make anymore." Tarley had grabbed at her own wrist, grateful the ribbon was still there.

Her sister had looked—begged Tarley with that look—to acquiesce, which Tarley had done with a nod.

Auri had flown against her, wrapping Tarley in a hug. "Thank you. I will owe you."

"Just so we're clear, I don't trust any man."

"This one, you can." Auri had stepped away and backed out of the kitchen.

"I'll believe it when I see it."

Now, nearly an hour later, Tarley watched the dark-haired man across from her sister smile, lean forward across the table, and touch Auri's cheek. His touch lingered, his thumb so near Auri's mouth. It was such a familiar gesture, Tarley almost felt the need to look away due to the intimacy of it, but she didn't. Worried her sister was being duped by this handsome newcomer to Sevens, Tarley struggled to piece together Auri's timeline. None of it made sense, and that touch suggested they knew one another. Perhaps better than Auri was letting on. Unless she was a bigger fool than Tarley took her for.

Goodness, he was handsome, to be sure. He could probably sway a blind woman without saying a word. Then he would open his mouth and ensnare the deaf woman too. More handsome than a man had the right to be, with that bronze skin dusted with a day-old beard, dark eyes, dark head of unruly curls, and those unconventional dark clothes. It all added to his mystique.

Tarley watched her sister smile, her eyes flickering to the tabletop, then back up to the suitor she'd introduced to Tarley as Nixus Uraiahs. His appearance alone made it difficult to trust he had Auri's interests at heart, but Tarley'd never met a man who had anyone's interests at heart other than his own. This man, Nixus, was named after the old-world mythology's god of night and darkness. Who named their child after an evil god?

To be fair, Tarley only tolerated most men. She loved her father and brother, and she accepted Mr. Cobble, a sweet old man from the marketplace, who adored their mother. Oh—and Horance Forte, the barkeep at The Copper Pot Inn. So far, there hadn't been many instances to like the supposed stronger sex. Most of them had only ever used it to bully, bluster, and burden women, and worse yet, all protected under the law of the Kaloma government.

"Which table, Horance?" Tarley asked Horance as she topped off the last ale.

"That table of four." He nodded from the other end of the counter to the table near the hearth.

A man at the table where she was going yelled, "Where's our drinks?"

Tarley rolled her eyes and said to Horance, "On the way." She turned the spigot off, scooped up the tankards by their handles, and worked her way across the room.

Rather than focus on her aching feet, Tarley looked forward to the fishing trip she was taking. She was leaving after the lunch rush. Five days of being alone in the woods. Heaven.

A strange energy filled with tension worked its way through The Copper Pot just as Tarley moved through the tables. She thought it was because of the impending visit of the Queen of Kaloma, who was to arrive in the village of Sevens any day now. The village was on tenterhooks with anticipation. It was the most exciting thing to ever happen to Sevens in its whole existence, Tarley figured, and the very reason Credence had given her a position in the first place.

Tarley had lived within the confines of Sevens for all of her twenty-six years. While usually a sleepy, inconsequential settlement in the Whitling Woods at the northern edge of the Kaloma Kingdom, the news of the Queen's visit had caused the village to burgeon with new life. And, because it wouldn't just be Kaloma Royals visiting, but a royal contingent from the bordering kingdom of Jast journeying to meet the Queen for whatever it was the royals did, many new faces arrived in the village; all hopefuls seeking to capitalize on the coin the royal visit would incur.

"There ya be," a stranger with terrible teeth slurred as she arrived at the table.

"Four ales," she told the man, set the tankards down on the table, and offered a fake smile to each man there.

At one time, when Tarley and her sisters were younger, they lamented that there was no one their age in the village. But now there were so many strange faces, she wished they'd all go away again. This man and his party were among the newcomers. Most of the new life in Sevens were single men in search of fortune or gainful employment. And most of them were the very men who annoyed, belittled, harassed, harangued, and mistreated women already in short supply.

Sevens was a place that required a certain level of fortitude. It was why it was short of women and families and had mostly been a trading outpost for most of Tarley's life. Winter lingered for nine months of the year, then spring would arrive, and summer would play for a few weeks before it turned cold again. Her own family eked out a living—barely—until Auri had found a key laden with gems in the woods after the *Great Nap Escapade* that enhanced their circumstances. With the wealth they gained from the key, they could have all moved to the capital if they wanted, but her parents insisted on staying in Sevens, in their tiny cottage within the hedge. They loved it there.

Tarley didn't. She loved the woods. She loved being out on her own and independent. She didn't love Sevens of late, either. Now that the Queen had put their small village on the map, and everyone had decided to make a run for their share of coin, it meant putting up with assholes like Mr. Four-Tankards and friends, who were presently making crude jokes meant to taunt her.

She turned her back to the men to collect empty dishes on a nearby table. A meaty hand grabbed a handful of her skirt, including the right cheek of her ass, and squeezed. With a yelp, Tarley swung with the used tankard in her hand, the cup connecting with the face of the offender.

"How dare you!" Tarley snapped. "Keep your filthy hands to yourself."

The man—Four-Tankard's himself—a beefy tradesman who reeked of horse manure and looked stained with dirt, moved from the wooden planks of the floor where he'd fallen to a knee and stood, a hand pressed to the side of his head. "How dare a woman swing on a man." He straightened, bringing him several hands taller than Tarley, his rapidly reddening complexion foretelling his anger.

"But you'd swing on a woman?" she retorted.

"You bitch," he spat, spittle lingering on his lips.

Tarley took a step back. "Among other things," she said, narrowing her eyes and wishing she had more than a tankard as a weapon.

She took another step back and met resistance, colliding with the unforgiving wall of someone else. Afraid Four-Tankards would retaliate if she glanced away, Tarley kept her gaze forward.

Then she realized Four-Tankards was frowning at whoever stood behind her.

"Excuse me?" a deep voice rumbled.

Tarley chanced a quick glance over her shoulder to discover the person behind her was Auri's suitor. He wasn't looking at Tarley, however, his unnerving gaze leveled on the arsehole.

Mr. Uraiahs gently moved past Tarley, placing himself between her and the seething bull of a man who'd dare touch her.

"You should mind your business, stranger," Four-Tankards said, his dirty skin mottled red. "This is between me and the wench."

Mr. Uraiahs turned his head to look at Tarley, his eyebrow quirking up and arching over one of his eyes. "Wench?" Then he turned to Four-Tankards again. "Is that how you speak with women, sir? It's no wonder you would have to manhandle one if that's your tableside manner. One doesn't want to imagine what your bedside manner might entail." He glanced at Tarley and tipped his head. "Please excuse my coarse language, Miss Fareview."

Four-Tankards' face soured even further.

Mr. Uraiahs climbed a few notches in Tarley's esteem.

"It's a wonder he would know his way around a woman at all," Tarley added for good measure, stepping up next to Mr. Uraiahs, willing to fight for herself even if she was greatly at a disadvantage.

Mr. Uraiahs tipped his head back and laughed. It was a loud guffaw of mirth, and though perhaps a bit overdone, it seemed to be committed with an intention to hit its mark. If that was the case, it was an arrow in the bullseye.

"I'm going to show you the way around my fists," Four-Tankards said to Mr. Uraiahs, his voice a low rumble of words ground through his teeth and a clenched jaw.

"Now that–" Mr. Uraiahs said, his tone as cold as granite with the bite of winter– "I would love to accommodate." His mirth was gone, and a menacing look moved over his features that gave even Tarley pause.

"Not in my establishment you don't," Credence Crendell, the proprietress of The Copper Pot, yelled from across the room. She was moving through the doorway past her brother Horance, who'd made his way around the bar. Credence's white hair was an explosion of tight coils that framed her brown face— now frowning. She pointed at the door. "Get out, the lot of you. And anyone getting handsy with my workers isn't welcome here."

Mr. Uraiahs took a step back and with the wave of his hand, gestured that Four-Tankards could lead the way outside.

Four-Tankards stalked past Mr. Uraiahs toward the door.

"Nix," Auri said, blocking Mr. Uraiahs from the path to the door. "Are you sure?"

Nix? Tarley was surprised at the familiarity and wondered if her sister was worried because Mr. Uraiahs was smaller than the dimwit who'd stomped outside. Not significantly shorter, but Four-Tankards had arms the size of small tree trunks. He didn't seem the sort to shy from a fight or a confrontation, which could put Mr. Uraiahs in physical peril.

But Mr. Uraiahs tipped his head to the side, gave Auri an arrogant grin, and arched that dark eyebrow again. "Now, Auri, are you worried for me?"

Auri? Tarley noted something secret passing between her sister and this man. She knew she would have to interrogate Auri sooner rather than later. If their mother found out about clandestine meetings with suitors she hadn't vetted—Tarley shuddered at the thought of Scarlett's wrath. Not to mention Auri's supposed seclusion. Her mother was going to know something was up if a suitor suddenly appeared.

Auri smiled sweetly at him, stepped out of his way, and watched him go, calling, "Maybe don't end him."

"You're not worried he's going to get hurt?" Tarley asked.

Auri glanced at Tarley, her cheeks pinking with a blush, then shook her head. "Not at all."

"This I have to see," Tarley declared and followed the men, stopping in the open doorway.

But by the time she reached the door, along with the rest of the patrons, Four-Tankards was on the ground looking like he'd been through a storm at sea, battered, bruised, his clothing crumpled and torn as blood gushed from his nose and mouth.

Shocked, Tarley looked at Mr. Uraiahs. His hands appeared perfectly fine. Not a bruise or cut marred his skin. Not a shred of his dark clothing was in disarray. He rubbed his hands together as if wiping offensive material from his palms and said, "Perhaps, sir, as you recover from these wounds, you'll take some time to reflect on your treatment of women."

"Who are you?" Four-Tankards sputtered.

"Your worst nightmare."

"I'm going to get you." Four-Tankards spat, the dark soil turning black as it mixed with his blood.

Mr. Uraiahs smiled an unholy smile. "You can certainly try."

Named after the evil god indeed, Tarley thought.

And with that, Mr. Uraiahs turned and walked away, completely unconcerned as he shouldered his way back to The Copper Pot. At the door, he turned to Tarley. "Are you alright, Miss. Fareview?"

She nodded, speechless. He didn't have a mark on him, not a speck of dust, no hair out of place. His skin was as flawless as before. No indication of the violence that had taken place.

Auri appeared and threaded her arm through Mr. Uraiahs's with a bright smile on her face, her adoration shining in her expression.

Light flared in Tarley's vision, weaving golden threads between Auri and her suitor.

Tarley blinked.

That certainly couldn't be right. She shook her head, hoping she wasn't coming down with one of her headaches. After she watched them return to their luncheon, she glanced back at Four-Tankards in the street, now shrugging off his friends' assistance.

It was clear, she decided: not all men were created equal.

Acknowledgements

This book was a surprise! A little like finding a golden key, touching it, and being transported into a labyrinth. I loved the experience of writing it so much. The finished book, however, is because there were beautiful souls along the way to help make it into the treasure it is. So, in honor of them, here are my three wishes:

My first wish is for bravery to the readers who helped me refine the book and my writing tribe for the commiseration. Thank you to Tami and Lavinia, early readers, who offered feedback when the story was still unruly and trying to figure out what it wanted to be. It was a scary endeavor walking into that dark, dense forest. To my amazing Salon group who offer me support and encouragement when I was ready to give up: Mae, Leisa, Maggie, Willow, Kara, Rachel no. 1 and Rachel no. 2, Habby, Robin, Lindsey, Ashley. To my Hawai'i crew: Stephanie, Brandann. Thank you for being voices of reason and sharing your stories with me. And to Jen, and Tara: thank you for listening, sharing your wisdom and support. You all make me brave.

My second wish is for creativity for those who helped me with this finished product. Sara and Kate, thank you for the creativity you offered to make this book what it is. You both are magicians who make what I do come alive for readers. Sara, the beautiful cover, is incredible and absolute perfection. Kate, I am so appreciative that you asked me to be real and face the reality of the project. You helped to make it the best it could be. Thank you.

My final wish is for freedom. To fans of the work who

read, review, and share. You make doing this independent author journey possible. These stories are for you.

Thank you to my family for your continued support. When I said I wanted to write a book with a bit more spice than I'd ever written, you all told me to go for it. You offered me the freedom to follow my heart as a creative, and I am so honored to call you mine. I love you.

As always, thank you to my Lord and Savior Jesus Christ for granting my wishes.

ABOUT THE AUTHOR

Maci Aurora, who also writes as CL Walters, the author of several published books for new adult readers, has been writing stories since she was a child. At eleven, she fell in love with reading Sunfire Historical Romances about girls who made a difference in their lives and still fell in love. Then in high school, a friend introduced her to Lavyrle Spencer and Judith McNaught, and those stories cemented her writing journey to writing stories about love. Maci writes in Hawai'i where she lives with her husband, their children, and their fur-babies. *In the Shadow of a Wish* is her first romantic fantasy novel. To keep up with news, hear about events and be the first to know the good stuff, subscribe to her newsletter at her website www.maciaurora.com and follow her Instagram @maciaurora.